Native New Yorkers, brother and sister team, Tom Johnson and Deborah Ettinger were inspired by the early life of their mother and uncle during the turbulent times of the Great Depression, Spanish Flu Pandemic, Prohibition and WWII. A graduate of Fordham University, Tom is a Bronze Star recipient and veteran of the Vietnam War. Deborah graduated from St Vincent's School of Nursing and Hunter College. After highly successful careers in healthcare, Tom as assistant professor at Long Island University and Deborah as senior vice president of an international health system, they returned to their love of storytelling.

For Mom and Uncle John, who shared a fiercely loyal bond to each other; and to our fiercely loyal and loving spouses, Daryl Johnson and Jeffrey Ettinger.

Deborah Ettinger and Tom Johnson

FIERCELY LOYAL

AUSTIN MACAULEY PUBLISHERS™

LONDON * CAMBRIDGE * NEW YORK * SHARJAH

Ordering Information
Quantity sales: Special discounts are available on quantity purchases by corporations, associations, and others. For details, contact the publisher at the address below.

Publisher's Cataloging-in-Publication data
Ettinger, Deborah and Johnson, Tom
Fiercely Loyal

ISBN 9781685624200 (Paperback)
ISBN 9781685624217 (Hardback)
ISBN 9781685624224 (ePub e-book)

Library of Congress Control Number: 2023909446

www.austinmacauley.com/us

First Published 2023
Austin Macauley Publishers LLC
40 Wall Street 33rd Floor, Suite 3302
New York, NY 10005
USA

mail-usa@austinmacauley.com
+1 (646) 5125767

We gratefully acknowledge our friends Cyndee Woelfle, Bill Reese, Dave Johnson, and Jim Mantle for their early reading, edits and encouragement. And we especially want to thank Daryl Johnson for helping us to figure out how to share documents and putting up with the long hours as Tom and I collaborated, endlessly edited and tortured over every word on FaceTime. And for my Jeff, who always believed in me.

Table of Contents

Ossining, New York
6 July 1949
Colleen

"The Girl from Jones Beach" starring Ronald Reagan and Virginia Mayo
opens today.

In just a few hours, my dear brother Sean will be put in Sing Sing Prison's electric chair to die. Is it too much to expect a stay of execution or clemency? The idea that my brother might die is too much to bear. I am filled with anger, dread, and my miserable hopefulness. Sean is my protector, my strength, my best friend.

Our story is a sad story; I made my way through the miserableness of my youth by escaping into novels. My love for reading about adventure, mystery and espionage stories gave me the respite I needed to avoid the awfulness and dullness of those early years. Now, I can hold my head up high as the owner of a trendy New York restaurant catering to the city's hoity-toity. Sean took another path. His life was decidedly more difficult and punishing. He found within himself the brute strength he needed to help us both survive our early years in a less than charitable orphanage. This strength carried him through the mean streets of Hell's Kitchen and the Westside docks.

Fiercely loyal, he would do anything to protect his family and friends. He learned that a controlled offensive could prove persuasive enough, but he never shied away from overt coercion. Sometimes, a well-aimed fist or gun was all it took. Blessed with a strong dose of common sense, Sean made his way through mobsters, crooked politicians, and coppers on-the-take. Fighting anyone that opposed him provided an irrefutable means to control the ugly of his world.

What he could not control was sensational news stories convicting him in the public eye and an assistant district attorney with political ambitions. He may be guilty just as the ADA of New York says he is, but I know his heart. If he shot that man, it was for good reason; and I'll be damned, he must have deserved to die!

Sean
6 July 1949

They all want me dead. It looks damned good that they will get what they want. All that I wanted to happen is not going to happen. The morning breeze traveling off the Hudson River does nothing to cool me. I'm sweating bullets.

Chapter 1
Orphans

Wilson orders the rest of Atlantic Fleet under Admiral Fletcher and 1ˢᵗ Marine Brigade under Col. John A. Lejeune to Vera Cruz after the Tampico Affair (Sun, 14 April 1914)

Sean

14 April 1914

Staten Island, New York City

As if awakening from a bad dream to a worse consciousness, I am only six and I don't know what's happening. What I do know is that I am at Saint Joseph's Orphanage. I am standing in Mother Superior's office. My own mother is wearing a large hat that has her face in shadow. She is talking about a man who died. Who?

My sister, Colleen, is curiously toddling around. Suddenly, Mother Superior Hilda Perpetua stands, causing the oversized rosary beads hanging from her habit's waist sash to clack together like pistol shots. With a startling quickness, she has Colleen by the arm. She pulls Colleen to a black ladder-back chair.

"Stop that! Go sit in that chair! Now!"

Meekly, Colleen climbs up onto the chair that dwarfs her. As she folds herself up with her little arms wrapped around her knees, she begins rocking back and forth. She cries silently at first. It was not long before the silent crying becomes wracking sobs that shake her little body. At that point, my mother stands and without a word leaves through a door. Going to another door, Mother Superior calls, "Sister Eucharius *und* Sister Corbinian *kommen Sie!*"

With heads bent and hands clasped in front, two nuns seem to float into the office. Sister Eucharius is a tall thin one while Sister Corbinian is short and plump.

"Sister Corbinian, take the girl out of my office and find a crib. Get her out of my office, this infernal sobbing is maddening." Sister Corbinian takes Colleen's hand. Still sobbing, Colleen slides off the chair. Colleen looks at me over her shoulder as the plump nun roughly takes her hand. Then my view of her is blocked by the tall Sister Eucharius. Her eyes are on me. Pale, gaunt, and stern looking, Sister Eucharius is imposing.

Mother Superior's voice turns my head, "Sister Eucharius! You will delouse the boy before he creates a problem. *Schnell!*"

There is a sudden rustle of a nun's habit. As I turn toward the sound, I am slapped hard across my face. Sister Eucharius is shaking her right hand; it is bright red from the slap. My face is on fire with pain. I refuse to cry. In view again, Sister Corbinian is leading Colleen toward the office door. I call out, "Don't cry, Coll, it will be all right. I'll take care of you. I'll be back in just a bit."

Mother Superior pulls out a watch on a black ribbon from under the big white bib of her habit. She merely glances at the watch but her unblinking steel-gray eyes behind her spectacles pin me to the spot. I look straight back. She glances at her watch and back to me again.

"You, you'll take care of her! You can't take care of yourself, you son of a whore!" Turning to Sister Eucharius, she says, "After you delouse him, give him something to do. His hands have the devil in them, but they will not do the devil's work here. Put him on lavatory work." She pauses. "Or, better yet, the kitchen scullery cleaning." She chuckles.

Then Sister Eucharius with her hands in some front pouch of her habit turns to me saying, "Come along, boy. Hurry up! *Mach Schnell!*" I start to call out to Colleen one more time, Eucharius' hand flashes out of her habit's pouch. I am smacked, smacked hard. It sends me to the hard wood floor, ripping my pants leg at the knees. I am stunned. I am grabbed by my shirt collar and hauled to my feet. It is the moment I know that being anywhere close to Eucharius is painful and should be avoided.

With one hand back in the habit's pouch, she inclines her head with its white triangle headdress toward the heavy wooden doors of the room. Still being held by the shirt collar, I need both hands to push it open to a dark

16

corridor. We walk quickly down the corridor only to stop at the top of stairs. It is a well of darkness. Magically, she produces a finger-loop candle while scraping a match with her thumbnail. It sputters, sparks suddenly bursting into flame. She lights the candle then shakes the match out. Looking down, I see that there is some light at the bottom of the black hole of stairs. Holding my collar firmly, Eucharius pulls me down dark stairs. The delousing room awaits. My mouth is dry. The dark air all around is freezing. With each step, the cold air becomes colder. Every breath I take is fast and short. The very air becomes an evil thing. Then, I smell something in the air.

The air around us is infused with two strong odors. Gasoline, thick and as heavy as you would smell with one of those horseless carriages. The other is leather. I know those odors. Separately, they are not unpleasant. I like the smell of leather.

Sister Eucharius propels me through a doorway. A sister in a white smock and elbow-length gloves stands solemnly by a porcelain tub in a stark, chilly black and white-tiled room.

Leaving me standing in the middle of the room, Sister Eucharius walks to a post from which hang several white smocks. She selects one and puts it on. My eyes travel to the other sister in the smock and gloves. She has a brush with stiff bristles in one of their hands and a pink brick in the other.

"Sister, do you have the carbolic soap?" Sister Eucharius asks.

"Yes, Sister," raising the pink brick in her hand, "it's right here."

Sister Eucharius turns to me. "Take off your clothes!" Sister Eucharius orders as she dons long black gloves. The other nun stands silent.

I undress to my underpants. The silent nun scoops up my clothes dumping them into a vat using the brush and a dustpan.

"Everything off, boy, now; we don't have time to waste."

My underpants join the rest of my clothes. I stand shaking with cold fear holding myself with my hands. With two strides, Sister Eucharius has me by the arm and on my toes as she hauls me to the tub. The gasoline smell! Without a word, the two women pick me up and thrust me into the tub. The cold liquid causes me to gasp.

"Close your mouth! Close your eyes and hold your nose."

She pushes me under the liquid. So cold! I close my mouth but not quick enough to avoid a mouthful of gasoline. Like a hundred biting insects, the gasoline bores into my mouth, cheeks, tongue, and even up my nose. I struggle drowning in gasoline. The taste in my mouth is overpowering. My head is held under. Just when I can't hold my breath any longer, I am pulled up by my hair. I spit gasoline out, coughing and retching.

"Don't you vomit *verdammt*!" Sister Eucharius says as I am yanked from the tub to the tile floor. They start scrubbing me with the brushes. They scrub me as hard as they would a stained floor. I beg them to stop. Ignoring my pleas, their brushes scour my skin. When they finally finish, there is more. I am pulled over to a wall where there is a rubber hose attached to a pipe. My eyes are burning, so is my mouth. I breathe through my nose instead of my mouth. That is not much better.

A shock of icy cold-water slams into my chest, making me stagger. I hold my genitals to protect me from that pain. I am sprayed with more water, the force and coldness causing me to gasp. Water is shot into my face, I cannot breathe. One of them rubs the carbolic soap into my arms, legs, and genitals. It is done roughly, hard, fast. With the water still in my face, the brushes start scouring my body, I feel as if I am drowning while being dragged over rough rocks. Finally, water is then directed to my arms and legs.

I swallow air hungrily. The carbolic soaping continues, my hair, face, neck, back and buttocks. I choke. Unrelentingly, it continues with soaping my legs, my chest, my abdomen and my genitals again. Stinging of the soap begins a new sense of pain. The brushing is brisk, hard, and it hurts badly. Then the brushing stops. Water, colder and more forceful than before, knocks me down. I see blood mixed with the water running toward a drain in the floor.

"Get up! Get up!" Another round of soaping begins. I lose track of what is happening. Somewhere, somebody is screaming. The scrubbing stops. The water stops. I don't hear the screaming anymore. I am crying, coughing, and trying to control my breathing. My throat is brick-dry and sore like gagging on nails. I roll around hoping that the cold tiled floor would reduce the pain and the burning sensations. I am shivering. My teeth are chattering violently.

The room is very quiet except for a diminishing dripping nearby. I just lay there. I open my eyes. The nuns aren't there. I am in a pool of cold light, but the rest of the room is impenetrable darkness. I am alone, naked, on my back, lying on the wet cold tile. Above, black, and white spots slowly resolve. No longer spots, I see a ceiling of black and white squares. The ceiling is tiled as the floor is, alternating black ones with white ones. I turn over on my belly. That makes me even colder. I push to my hands and knees on the tile. Using the hose, I pull myself to my feet shaking. My body is striped with broad, raw, and red streaks. Most welts are bleeding, including several on my penis. The skin on my arms looks like a plucked chicken's. I take a step. I slip, fall to my knees.

The door to the tub room opens. Two different nuns enter. They pause, nod toward the back wall. Still on my knees as they enter my pool of light something in the darkness behind them moves. What slowly emerges is Mother Superior. There is a white object cradled in her left arm. As she glides silently closer, I see that the white thing is a cat contrasting starkly against her black habit. With her right hand, she is stroking the cat while looking at me. How long had she been watching? The ceiling lamplight reveals her eyes. Pitiless.

One nun has a towel while the other dumps a pile of clothes on a dry area. That nun turns and leaves. Mother Superior moves slowly still stroking the cat. She walks unhurriedly to the tub room doorway.

"Sister Hildegard, get the boy dressed. He missed dinner. No matter. Take him to the boy's dormitory and find him a bed then come for your meal."

Sister Hildegard nods her compliance. With the cloth of her habit whispering, Mother Superior continues to the door. As she opens the door, she turns again to look at me. I stare back at her defiantly. Then with a rattle of rosary beads against the door, she and the cat leave.

Surprisingly, the nun is not drying me roughly. Sister Hildegard is slow and methodical but gentle. She points at the pile of clothes. I nod that I understand. She reaches over her white neck bib, pressing her hand to her throat, and croaks, "Get dressed." As she withdraws her hand from her neck cowling, I see a black hole in her neck.

Once dressed, she takes my hand, leading me through the door and up the stairs. We come to a landing. She stops and turning to me, again places her hand over her bib. Croaking, "Stay here."

I do not move a muscle, except for shivering. In a minute or so, Sister Hildegard reappears. She hands me a thick piece of warm bread with a piece of sausage and cheese. The cheese smell is very strong.

"Eat," she croaks.

I eat fast. The crust on the bread is hard, warm and tasty. The cheese softens into the bread while the sausage drips fat on my fingers. So busy eating, I did not notice that Sister Hildegard had left. She returns with a white cloth.

Gently, she wipes my mouth and hands, then smiles. *"Gut? Ja?"*

"Ya," I replied.

Sister Hildegard speaks using only her tongue and lips to make words. I listen carefully. I find my eyes drawn to the hole in her throat. She notices my eyes. She puts her finger over the hole in her throat.

"Diphtheria," she says. "*Mein* Papa saved me. I could not breathe. He cut hole for me to live."

It is odd to hear her breathe through that hole. I nod, looking into her eyes.

Taking my hand in hers while holding a finger-loop candle in the other, Sister Hildegard leads me up three flights of unlit stairs. We pass through a hall dimly illuminated by gas lamps to a large door. As she turns the doorknob, there is a sudden rustle of cloth and some squeaking of springs. With the gaslight spilling from the hall into the room, I see beds arranged in rows. Spectral white faces of boys appear. They watch as I am led to a bed with a folded blanket and a thin pillow.

Sister Hildegard points to the bed. I start to climb on the bed, but she pulls me to my knees. She kneels next to me. With her right hand she touches her forehead, stomach, left, and right shoulders before she folds her hands in prayer. I copy her. Only her lips and tongue to make the words, "Our father who art in heaven…"

I repeat after her.

When we finish, she smiles at me, pats me on my still damp hair, saying, "*Sloff schon.* Sleep well."

I am off my knees and onto the bed. Sister Hildegard stands for a moment looking down at me, smiles once more. With that, Sister Hildegard walks to the door closing it gently behind her. The room becomes darker than the inside of a whale's stomach. I hear boys whispering in the darkness.

As I unfold the blanket and lay down, I bring my knees to my chest to get warm. My teeth had stopped chattering, but I am shaking cold, cold, cold to my bones.

There is rustling of sheets and blankets.

"Hey you! Hey new boy! What's your name?" a voice from the dark asks.

"Sean," I said to the voice.

"What kind of fooking name is Sean?" The voice asks.

"It's my name."

I can hear the soft rustle of a blanket.

"That is a sissy name." The voice sounds closer.

"It's an Irish name."

I breathe through my mouth to hear better. My eyes strain to see. The room windows provide very little light. But it is enough to see something moving in the darkness.

"Oh laddies, we have a lace-curtain Paddy here!"

Now, I hear someone moving in the dark. It's a careful sliding of feet.

"Just what we don't need, another fooking Paddy-boy." The voice is closer still.

"I'm no Paddy-boy!"

Silence.

I hear someone moving toward my bed.

Silently, I slip out of bed, bunching the blanket as I do. I roll under the bed. My eyes must have become adjusted to the dark. From under the bed, I see a pair of ghostly white feet softly padding up to my bed.

Whomp! Something hit the blanket above me. From under the bed, I grab a bare ankle and yank hard. The shin hits the metal of the bed.

"Fook!"

Then the rest of the body hits the floor. I am on him fast. I have both knees on his shoulders and hit his face with my elbow.

"Fook, you fooker!"

I bring my elbow back across his face. He grabs my shoulders, but I jab my elbow into his nose hard. He lets go to hold his nose. I rise to my feet and kick him hard in the breadbasket. He doubles up in pain.

Boys are shouting and gathering. There are words of encouragement for someone named "Red".

"Get him, Red!"

"Get up and fight, Red!"

Like a wounded animal, he lunges at my legs. Down we go. We are on the floor, grappling. Again, I try to get my knees on his shoulders to give him a good punch in the kisser. He is quick. As I struggle to pin my knees on him, I only get ineffective punches in. He rolls hard. It throws me off. Now he is on his stomach, trying to get to his hands and knees to rise up. It's my opening.

Like a cat on a rat, I pounce on his back. I pull his hair to get my right arm under his chin just as he rolls again putting me under him. Now, I hang on. My right wrist was under his chin. With my other hand I grasp my wrist and pull, choking him. Thrashing like a fish, he almost knocks the air out of me. Still, I have my arm across his neck and a good grip on my wrist. He tries to elbow me in the gut but because I am skinner than him, he misses. He starts to make gasping sounds. I pull harder on my wrist.

More shouts, "Knock him silly, Red!"

"Red!"

"Cheese, I give. I give," he croaks, barely audibly.

Then a boy cries out, "Someone's coming!"

A scramble and flurry of blankets as boys jump into their beds. Reluctantly, I loosen my grip on him, scuttling away out of reach, fists up and ready. Next to my bed, Red crawls to his feet holding his neck. Noise at the door causes me to jump into bed. Red is stumbling away as the door opens. Light floods the room. Red is frozen by the yellow light from the hall gas lamps. A nun in the doorway is outlined by the jaundice light.

"*Ruhe*! Silence!"

A nun walks slowly, deliberately to the boy in the middle of the room.

"Vat haf you done?" She asks as she grabs Red's ear. She has him up on his toes as she pulls him out into the hall closing the door with a bang. I hear a loud slap.

I beat Red MacGregor. I am half his size, but I beat him. With his fists and his gang, Red rules St. Joe's. His rule is over. Starting tomorrow, every boy and girl at St. Joe's will see the red mark on his neck. While he could not see it, it was plainly visible for over a week. I don't even have a sore knuckle. I have an enemy, but that fight can earn me my own gang. In the coming days, I will have to be on my guard.

The fight warmed me up nicely. A good fight can do that to you.

Colleen

It was at St. Joseph's Orphanage that I found the true meaning of family. My Sean promised me the day we arrived there that he would look after me. Always, always, he kept that promise.

The headmistress Sister Hilda Perpetua, Mother Superior of St. Joseph's Orphanage, laughed out loud at him. "And just what do you think you will be doing to look after your sister? You can't even take care of yourself!"

Sean just glared at her with that dead-eyed stare of his and I saw the black-clad nun actually take a sharply drawn breath. But she remained adamant, and her harsh words echo in my memory still.

"We'll get that devil out of you boy. Don't try that attitude here with me." She almost hissed her next words, "We will give you a bit of work and time to think about how you want to act here, boy."

Turning to her subordinate, Sister Eucharius, she said with a thin-lipped smile, "We'll start this one outright. I think some suitable work for him will be in the boys' lavatories or the scullery. Get him deloused first."

She smiled as Sean was roughly pushed out the door of the office. I heard him call to me, "I'll be back in just a bit, Colleen." I heard a loud smack then silence. I knew even then; he would never cry no matter how much it hurt. He would never give them the satisfaction.

We were separated; for me it was into the girls' dormitory that was more like a jailhouse ward. It was a dark, dreary room of rows upon rows of cheap bare cots each equipped with a pancake pillow and a single thread-bare blanket.

I kept to myself. I had no wish to talk to the other girls. Some of them looked pretty rough and tough. They travelled in packs. Right away, I saw that there were four girls who seemed to be in charge. Mildred, Bertha, Thelma, and their leader Mary Kate were a roving pack of hyenas. They laughed as they forced the smaller, weaker girls to give them their food at mealtimes and on colder nights even took their blankets, leaving them to shiver in the darkness. For some reason, I escaped their focus. It was only later much later that I learned this was Sean's doing.

Evidently, he had beat up Big Red MacGregor on the first night at St. Joseph's and formed his own gang that had some sway in the girls' side. He let it be known that if anyone hurt me in any way, they would suffer for it. Now, mind you, Sean was not a tall boy. But, even at the age of six, he was already tough and strong, and would not back down from a fight. St. Joseph's Orphanage was his brutal training ground. This dangerous side of Sean became the basis of how he lived his life providing him a proven method of operation in Hell's Kitchen and the Westside docks. All this savage experience was gained from this miserable place for orphaned, lost, and abandoned children. It is probably wise to give you a back-story on this orphanage.

The Sisters of St. Joseph ran the place. This particular religious sect was made up of transplants from Germany, having emigrated in 1891 from Bingen, Germany. The Headmistress, Mother Superior Hilda Perpetua, was demonstratively German, Prussian German. Her accent was thick and coarse as her Prussian roots. She seemed to revile anything American and was single-handedly attempting to inculcate Prussian values and deportment on everyone. She demanded absolute silence after 8 pm and during meals. She required every girl to eat with perfect manners, tipping our soup spoon away from us, napkins on your lap, chewing thoroughly, mouth closed, and with the fork neatly placed on the side of the dish and never held in your hand after you took the bite. You would have thought we were consuming a fine meal, while in reality, it was mostly quite awful, scraps really. Until I changed that.

Chapter 2
Dark Days

Bust of Pacificist-Journalist Stead Who Perished on HMS Titanic Unveiled at The Hague (London Times 15 April 1914)

Sean

15 April 1914

It felt as though I had just fallen asleep despite being so cold and balled up under the blanket. Looking up from under the blanket, I could see the white triangle of her headpiece and black dress in the yellow light of the finger-hole oil lamp she held. Sister Corbinian! She yanked the blanket off and pulled me upright then gave me a smart slap across the face. Now, I was awake and angry too. She pulled me to my feet, handing me my shoes and frog-marched me out of the boy's room. At a side door, I was released from her grip as she fumbled in the folds of her habit for something that turned out to be keys. I sat down on the cold floor but only managed to get my left shoe on and tied before Corbinian again lifted me to my feet.

I was still hopping on one foot trying to put on my right shoe as we arrived at the stairs. Corbinian released me, I used the moment to put on my other shoe. The finger-hole oil lamp did little to illuminate the narrow windowless stairwell. It formed a small pool of light at Corbinian's side but precious little light on the staircase. In fact, the contrast made the dark even darker, an almost tangible darkness, a well of darkness.

I finally had the shoe on but trying to tie the laces in the dark I could not manage. I pulled them tight and tucked them into the shoe. Corbinian's dark shape loomed above me. She switched the lamp to her left hand and held the railing with her right.

"*Komm!*"

Down we went with the lamp barely providing enough light to see the next step. I had no handrail just the wall to steady myself. Three or four flights more of narrow, dark stairs then we came to a landing that I mistook as another step. Expecting to step down, I nearly drove my chin to my knees. Corbinian paid no attention to me. With obvious familiarity, Corbinian walked to a wall, found a door that opened to a blinding light accompanied by heat that flooded the stairwell landing.

This must be the door to Hell, I thought.

With quick steps, Corbinian was at my side as I stood befuddled by the sudden, alien, bright light. Corbinian slapped me on the back of my head saying, "*Kommen mit mir*. Come with me."

She strode purposefully through the doorway. Shielding my eyes, I followed.

This was the kitchen and scullery for the orphanage, convent, and rectory of St. Joe's. Noise of pots, utensils, and female voices only confused me. To me, it was a busy blur of continuous movement. There were several women and older girls in dark blues dresses with white smocks moving pots and carrying things back and forth. It was noisy and warm, but voices quieted as Corbinian entered. I saw one woman nudge a girl who was obviously about to speak, jerking her head toward Corbinian who was fortunately looking at me.

Well, maybe unfortunately, because I was slapped again. In half English and half German, Corbinian gave me my instructions. I was to clean the grease traps and the greasy heavy pots. The grease trap had not been worked on for some time. I was given nothing to work with but a pail and my bare hands. The trap stunk, making my eyes water. I gagged. The stench was like an alive thing reaching down my throat. Not looking into it, I reached in to dig out a handful of that God-awful smell and slimy mess that ultimately filled four pails. Each had to be carried out into the cold pre-dawn morning to be dumped into the dustbins. Each time I returned, shivering from the cold. The kitchen was like a steam bath, so I went from sweating to freezing each trip.

Just as I returned from my last grease dump, cold to my bones, Sister Corbinian appeared. What now?

"*Mach schonl! Kessel, beeile dich! Pots Schnel!*" As she pointed at several pots that I could have been comfortably boiled in. I understood her meaning though, not the words she spoke. Clean pots, fast! The first one was not too heavy, but I got my sleeves and knees wet while I was washing it. It was the second pot that nearly brained me! Damn, that thing was heavy! With a crash it hit the floor and bounced off the wall but not before giving me a haymaker to the noggin.

From my vantage point on the floor, things were not looking up for me. I sat up rubbing my head where the pot smacked me. Ouch! I could feel a lump already. While rubbing the lump forming on my forehead, I saw that a tall girl was picking up the pot and lugging it over toward me. Fearfully, I covered my head for the blow that was sure to come.

She squatted down beside me while tucking her skirts behind her knees to keep them off the floor. Then she lifted my chin gently turning my face right and left. She inspected the top and back of my head then my forehead again. She made some sort of clicking sound as she looked at me.

"You'll be getting a fine knot on your noggin, you will. I'll be getting you a cold compress," she said, gathering her long skirt and apron she stood and left me on the floor. Moments later, she pressed a cold cloth against my lump.

"Ouch!"

"Now, don't you go being a wee bairn. 'Tisn't it better?"

"'Tis," I said.

With her assistance, I managed to stand. "Thanks."

"'Tis nothing, laddie. You'll be best staying far away from the stoves, boy. Your perfume smells of gasoline." She paused. "Now, what's your name, boy?"

"I'm Sean, Sean Callaghan."

"My name is Dotty Gale," she said.

"Are you an orphan too?"

"Oh, no, no, not an orphan, exactly…" She trailed off. "I should be getting back to work, I should."

"And I had better clean this pot before that mean sister gives me a thrashing."

"O, laddie, Sister Corbinian 'tisn't the meanest. There are meaner ones than that one."

With that, Dotty turned to rejoin the other women working. She paused for a moment, and said quietly, "'Tis Sister Eucharius. She is a screaming mad banshee and Mother has a stone for a heart and a riding crop that has blood on it. Be very careful around those two, lad, or you'll rue the day you were born."

Dotty quickly walked away to join the women still working at the large black iron stove. Picking up a black pail and a shovel, she opened the stove grate using the hem of her smock. I could see coal burning in the stove as Dotty shoveled in some more. Then she closed the stove grate again using the hem of her smock to protect her hand.

As I watched, I was also thinking about Eucharius and Mother Superior. After my time in the de-lousing room with those two, I needed no reason to doubt what Dotty had said.

Just as I finished cleaning the big greasy pot another appeared but this one had baked on porridge. I found it easy to clean up. When I was done with pot, a large woman brought me a bowl full of the porridge.

"Eat up and get with the rest of the boys."

I watched her as she left me. She walked to a small room offset from the kitchen. The kitchen women were all seated on bench at a wooden table. She took a stool and sat with her back to me. I saw Dotty who glanced at me with a flicker of a smile, then in unison with the other women she made the sign of the cross.

"In the name of the Father, and of the Son and of the Holy Ghost..." they chanted.

"We have German enemies in this country too, and the worst of all of our German enemies, the most treacherous, the most menacing are Pabst, Schlitz, Blatz and Miller." Temperance political statement 1920

THE AMERICAN ISSUE

A Saloonless Nation and a Stainless Flag

WESTERVILLE, OHIO, JANUARY 2, 1919

Volume XXVI   Number 8

U.S. IS VOTED DRY

36th STATE RATIFIES DRY AMENDMENT JAN. 16

Nebraska Noses Out Missouri for Honor of Completing Job of Writing Dry Act Into the Constitution; Wyoming, Wisconsin and Minnesota Right on Their Heels

JANUARY 16, 1919, MOMENTOUS DAY IN WORLD'S HISTORY

Ratification Accomplished in a Little Less Than Thirteen Months with Three States More Than the Required Three-Fourths Resolution Gave Period of Seven Years for the Completion of Task Remaining Ones Expected to Join Their Sister States in This Act, With Possible Exception of New Jersey. United States Takes Initial Step in World-Wide Drive for Prohibition. State and National Leagues Now Give Earnest Attention to Law Enforcement Legislation

TWENTY-THREE STATES APPROVED ACT IN FIRST SIXTEEN DAYS OF 1919; IN 1918, 15; 9 IN CALLED SESSIONS

Chapter 3
Four Years Later: Mikey Arrives

Colleen

Every day I ran to the fence that separated the boys' and the girls' yards during recess which routinely followed mealtime. Often, I would reach 'the spot' in the fence first. Sean had designated this as our place. The other boys seemed to respect this as no one tried to horn in on our fence time. Occasionally, I would see Sean making his way to the fence through a crowd of other boys. I was always amazed at how the sea of boys seemed to part to allow Sean access. I watched him as he approached in his characteristic stride so confident and strong.

"Listen Colleen," he looked at me solemnly, "We are getting out of this place soon. I want you to—"

I interrupted, "Sean, what happened to your eye!"

His left eye was black and blue and partially closed. What I could see of the eyeball was filled with blood.

"This is thanks to Sister Mary *Puss-face* Aloysius *of the bloody hand*. She didn't like my face today during Religion so she decided to reconstruct it." His laugh was more of a snort. Seeing my concern, he continued, "It don't hurt. Just looks bad, I expect."

"You need a doctor," I whined. "I'm going to tell Sister Vianny. She'll help." He reached my arm right through the chain link fence.

"Don't do it, listen Coll I am OK. Don't go blabbing to anyone. These nuns might take away privileges and I want to be able to see you to tell you our plans…" Over Sean's shoulder I saw Sister Aloysius was approaching us from the other side of the boys' yard, I said, "Watch it! Here comes Aloysius now." I pulled my arm away.

"What's going on here you two?" Sister Aloysius didn't wait for an answer. "Colleen move your *arsch* and get back into the classroom, recess is over for you. And you, Sean, look like you've been fighting again. No recess privileges for you for a week. Report to the janitor, I believe he's got a job for you to keep you occupied during recess."

She put both hands on her hips and smirked at us. Her long bony finger pointed directly at me jostling her stiff white bib as she did so. "Move it Colleen or you'll be cleaning the lavatories too!"

As I stepped backward, I stumbled falling and that made Aloysius laugh out loud. "Get up *tapsig* and go!"

Calling me clumsy infuriated me but I brassed it out. I dusted my skirt off without a word.

Later that day, I heard the tough Mary Kate's girls whispering that Aloysius hit Sean with her catechism book so hard that he was knocked off his desk seat. Her book caught him near his left eye and broke the bone in his face. It must have damaged a nerve or a muscle or both because Sean was left with a permanent droop and partially closed eyelid.

Sean
1918

Canadians Sweep the Huns from Vimy Ridge – (Boston Globe, 12 April 1918)

I broke into Sister Puss-face's room on our floor. The room door connected her room with the boys' sleeping room. Mary Puss-face Aloysius was now at some novena or other. Perfect timing, I decide to break in to see what I could find. The room was as starkly white and black as the boy's dormitory. A large hand carved wooden crucifix was over her bed. On the wall was an old daguerreotype of a stern looking woman in a nun's habit. The other wall was a peg row for her woolen black cloak and an oilskin cloak. An armoire stood against the wall at the foot of the bed. It contained a headpiece for her habit and neatly folded black things. I closed the armoire. There was a single wooden chair and a wooden kneeler at the foot of her bed. That is when I saw the other door. Not the door that I used but a second door. The second door interested me. Where did it lead? I put my ear to the door and listened. When I was sure that no one was on the other side. I turned the doorknob and the door opened easily.

I was in a hall that led to a narrow staircase that must go to the fifth floor. As quiet as a mouse, I crossed the hall. As I stepped on the first step of the stairs, it gave out a loud creak. I froze.

Unmoving, I waited for eternity, then as slowly as I could, I took my weight off my foot on the step. There was a slight squeak of the step but it was not as loud. Now with both feet at the bottom, I looked up to the top of the stairs. There was no door. An unseen window threw a shaft of light filled with dust motes.

Under the stairs, I found a door with a wooden turn-lock. Inside were broom, mop, pail, and a few rags on a nail. There was precious little light to see. Feeling along the wall, I did not touch anything except spiderwebs. There was a good amount of space.

I could use this space!

I could hide things, things that Colleen and I will need when we get out of here. My mind flew. Ideas came, went and circled my head like the gossamer of the spider webs. Like the spiderwebs, they stuck on me.

Before I opened the door, I put my ear on it to listen. It was a good thing that I did. At first, I was not sure, then it became obvious that someone was climbing the stairs up to the fourth floor. Heavy steps were accompanied by quicker lighter steps. Labored breathing. I heard the clacking of the rosary beads worn on a nun's habit. Cripes!

"Go on, go on!" I heard Sister Mary Aloysius tell someone. Silently, I pressed my back into the darkness of the closet.

"Yes, Sister," a younger woman's voice said.

Then, there was a clatter of feet running up the stairs over my head. It showered me with dust. It was all I could do not to cough. I listened, barely breathing. I heard a door open with a key. It closed with a click. Puss-face Aloysius was in her room.

Cripes! I was trapped in this broom closet. I was due to be in History class. If I went missing and they found me here, I would get the beating of my life. Puss-face was in her room. I was not sure where the stairs led if I went down. Stop, don't panic. Think. Think. Wait! These must be the stairs that lead to the kitchen. These were the ones that I took to work on the grease traps and pots that first morning at St. Joe's. If I could make it down four flights, then I could

32

make it outside to where the dustbins were. I could circle around to the yard doors then into the History classroom.

Carefully, I opened the door then stepped into the hall. I listened. I looked up the stairs. No one. Good.

I tiptoed past Puss-face's room. I could hear her moving around. At the top of the stairs, I held my breath as I gingerly eased my toe then my foot on the first step. No noise. I held on the banister rail while slowly stepping to the next and the next and the next step. I was doing well.

But at the second landing, I heard a door open and brisk steps approached the stairs. The steps started down from only one floor above. Whoever it was they would see me in a few seconds. I took a chance. Removing my hand from the banister, I took the stairs two at a time.

"Who is there? Who is there?"

It was Corbinian's voice. If she caught me, I would be beaten to the edge of death. I could not let that happen. I did well taking two steps at a time. I was smiling to myself as I reached the last steps above the kitchen and the door to the dustbins. On the last steps, I decided to leap three to the floor outside the kitchen.

I hit the bottom hard that produced a sharp pain in my left ankle. I was down on the floor between the two doors. The heavy steps of Corbinian were coming faster and faster.

Hopping on one foot, I reached the door, pulled it open, shutting it behind me. I jumped inside the dustbin just as I heard the door fly open.

***

Walking toward the classroom a hand roughly whirled me around.

"Hey you fooking mick you look like a fooking darkie," Red McGregor jeered.

"I was moving some bituminous coal for Sister Corbinian."

"You are a fooking mess, boyo."

"Sure, I'm going to the loo to clean up."

"You look like you had a fight with the dustbin and the dustbin won." Red was right about the dustbin, it trashed me but saved me from far worse.

For the next two days, I asked girls on the other side of the yard fence where Colleen was. All they said was that Colleen is being punished. Today, she finally found her way to the fence. I can see by her sunken eyes and the way that she holds on to the fence that she is very weak. She tells me through the fence that separates the boys' and girls' yards that she is being punished for reading a book during Sister Mary Puss-face's catechism lesson. The beating Colleen received would have been enough, but Coll didn't cry. Crying is a demonstration of contrition for the good sisters.

"You are a bold, brazen hussy!" Sister Puss-face said.

That was when it got worse for Colleen. Sister Mary Puss-face dragged her to Mother Superior's office where she got another beating, this time with the riding crop. That beating made Coll cry. Mother Superior was not finished. She made Colleen kneel on the hard floor and recite Hail Mary after Hail Mary for a long time.

Coll said when she had fidgeted because her knees were hurting, Mother Superior who was sitting comfortably at her desk noticed her fidgeting. Mother Superior's punishment became even crueler. She made Colleen kneel on her fingers. That made the pain ten times worse. Even when Mother Superior left the room, Coll was too afraid to stand up fearing that Mother Superior would suddenly return and add something worse to her punishment. Still, Coll was able to ease the pain by pushing with her hands into the floor to lift her knees off her fingers. Until she tired holding her body over her hands it became a cycle of fatigue and pain. With her body weight on her hands, the pain would slowly increase until she had to raise her knees by lifting her weight again and again.

Fortunately, she was on her knees and fingers with her head down sobbing when Mother Superior returned with Sister Corbinian.

Mother Superior said, "Get up Callaghan! *Schnell!*"

Mother Superior turned to Sister Corbinian, "Put Callaghan on bread and water for the week."

Now the third day of a slice of bread and water had Colleen too weak to stand at the fence for more than a minute or two without holding on to the chain links for support. She was pale, paler than usual. I have to do something.

"Wait here I'll be right back."

As Coll sat in the dirt next to the fence, I took off at a run.

I broke off a green stick from the bush next to the stairs. No one was looking my way as I went around the corner to the ground level window there. Using the stick, I moved the latch to pry open the window. I rolled myself through the slot and dropped feet first to the floor. I was in the kitchen hallway. Quietly, I slid along the wall toward the pantry. All that scrubbing grease and slime in the kitchen now paid off. I knew the layout, where the cooks and scullery maids would be at this time of day. The cooks and maids were still there but they were eating at a table in the small room around the corner. They were the Magdalene Women. Women and girls. Some were teenage girls like Dotty who cooked, cleaned and did laundry for the nuns.

The Magdalenes were treated as badly as the orphans. Often, the nuns would beat one of them for a small infraction. Beat them with a wooden spoon or whatever instrument the nun could find or had.

After the thrashing, the poor woman would be sent to the rectory for confession of her 'sin.' The priest would grant absolution and penance. The sinner did penance in the rectory before she could return. Like us, the Magdalene women were underfed. So, they ate wordlessly with a ravenous quickness.

Now, I had to be quick too.

I reached into a pot with a long fork that was on the counter nearby. All that I got were two small potatoes. I put the folk down as I heard chairs and stools moving. Holding my breath, I moved toward the door that led to the dustbins. There were heavy steps moving in my direction. Looking in the direction of the sound, I groped for the doorknob.

Once outside, I ran to the fence.

"Here, eat this," I said to Coll.

I was about the add "Quickly" but it was unnecessary. In the time that I thought this, poor Colleen had finished one potato and was starting on the other. Then the whistle blew, and we had to return to the respective wings of the building, Colleen to the Girls' and me to the Boys'.

"Tomorrow morning, early, I'll have something else. Look for me here."

Colleen nodded, wiped her hands on her smock and turned away. I watched her until she turned and gave a little wave.

***

"Waddaya mean, you don't know this boy? This is Mikey. He's new," I said to the Magdalene woman who handed the meal plate to me.

"Mikey came in last night. Didn't you hear the horseless carriage? He's a new orphan."

It was Colleen's idea that she be called Mikey. Dressed as she was, we were positive that this would work. Thus far, I had remembered to call her 'Mikey' whenever the occasion presented.

The woman looked at Colleen, then at me as she handed 'Mikey' one of the new plates and big knife and folk that had been donated to St. Joe's by the nearby Navy station. The Magdalene woman was so pale that the blue vein between her thick bushy eyebrows was so visible as if it had been painted there. She was too tired to care. She ladled out some porridge and a piece of meat to the new boy, Mikey. Colleen held the tin plate with both hands along with the large US embossed knife, fork and spoon.

During previous night, using a soup ladle that I stole, I had dug a ditch, actually it was a short tunnel under the fence near a storage shed. There was no moon. I used a burlap potato bag to line the tunnel to keep dirt or mud at bay for Colleen. I covered the hole with a few pieces of wood, some newspaper then dirt to make it less visible. Then I spread the wet dirt from the hole all around the yard instead of leaving it piled up near the ditch. Now Colleen could slip into the boys' yard easily and without being seen or getting dirty. The work of digging kept me warm even though I could see my breath in the first gray light of dawn. I slipped back into the building, upstairs and into the boys' dorm.

My timing was good, but sleep would have to wait for another night. It could not have been a minute before the door to room opened. It was Corbinian. With quick steps she was at my bedside and my blanket was on the floor.

"*Raus! Schnell!*" Out! Fast!

Once again, I was in the scullery cleaning pots and emptying coal dust from the stoves. As I emptied the last coal pail into the one of the bins, I strained my eyes to see if Colleen was outside. There in the cold dim light was Colleen. Colleen was at the fence shivering. Using only hand signs, I directed her to the tunnel. I kept looking out for nuns and other boys and girls. It was another gray day. You could smell the rain that would be coming in on the east wind from the Atlantic Ocean. Dry brittle leaves rattled against the fence and scuttled across the yard.

Coll was so skinny that she slipped easily under the fence and through the tunnel. Alone in the kitchen for a few minutes, I ran to her with a burlap bag of boy's clothes. Being so skinny she stuffed her skirt inside the trousers as she dressed. She hid her long red hair under a boy's cap. She was ready for breakfast!

Her freckles looked so stark against her pale face. I led her inside the cafeteria and to the boys' area.

With our plates and utensils, we sat with Jimmy Hurley, Danny Dolan, Paddy Clarke and Liam "Squint" McGee. Liam had broken his glasses playing baseball last summer in the yard. He could hardly see without them. Squint mis-copied numbers from the blackboard during math class, getting the wrong answer and being called *dumkopt* by Sister Corbinian. He was never given glasses the whole time we were at St. Joe's. It would be years later before Squint got glasses. Even then, he continued to squint. Habit, I suppose. I had Colleen sit next to Squint.

"Who are you?" Squint asked.

"I'm Mikey," Colleen replied. "I'm new here."

"When did you get here?"

"Oh," she said, "Early this morning."

I put a forkful in my mouth to stifle a grin.

Chapter 4
The Bishop's Crook

Sean

King Alfonso XIII of Spain Gravely Ill with the Grippe

A bunch of us were at the blackboard desperately trying to do our sums. Little Tommy O'Flannery, Liam McGee and I stood in front of a pile of numbers that Sister Corbinian had written on the board for each of us. We were staring at the numbers hoping that in some way we could escape. We needed a miracle. With his tongue sticking out, Tommy was working on his sum marking the board. In front of his numbers, Liam blinked and tossed the piece of chalk from hand to hand. I had added up my first column of numbers and was starting on the second column when there was a knock at the door. An older boy opened the door, looked around for a moment, saw Sister Corbinian, handed her a note with a slight bow. She read the note then nodded to the boy. He clicked his heels and was out the door.

"Put your jackets on now. Stand by your desks," she ordered.

Liam and I looked at one another and smiled!

In a few minutes, the class was at the stairwell, and we began marching down. Behind, other boys' classes were forming up at the stairwell we just left. They followed us. We were led to the yard where the January cold penetrated our jackets and sockless shoes. Then we stood assembled in front of the main double stairs to the yard. The sisters wrapped in thick black shawls shouted at us to line up. We wondered what was happening. Tommy O'Flannery was shivering, and his teeth were chattering. Cripes, it was cold.

The door to the girls' wing opened. To our surprise, the girls were led out to the yard by Sister Hildegard. This was unusual. She led the girls to assemble in neat rows and columns a few feet from us. The girls were chattering with excitement. When the last line of girls formed up, Sister Hild inside.

Standing there, we became even colder. The frigid weathe. anyone from speculating about the reason for the full assembly.

In a few minutes, Sister Hildegard opened the door and hel Mother Superior. She slowly walked to crenellated balustrade, a bla …u wrap draped over her shoulders.

"Silence! *Ruhe!*"

Mother Superior, in her loudest voice, "The Cardinal, His Eminence Cardinal Farley, would be here soon to honor us, bless us and he would offer mass for our souls. You must behave perfectly, perfectly. Every day you will be responsible to clean and polish floors, walls, desks, everything. If you do it well and you practice your lessons, there will be good things. You will be getting a gift in recognition of your good work, if you are perfect."

The boys wondered and whispered about the surprise. Was it candy? Was it ice cream? Baseball gloves? It was more likely the 'gift' of the scrubbing the pews or saying only one Hail Mary instead of the whole rosary.

During the next several weeks, we were drilled in how we would sit, stand, kneel, line up in the best Prussian tradition. The children practiced saying, "Good morning, Cardinal Farley!" "Good morning, Bishop Cusack!" It had to be clear and perfectly synchronized. Tommy O'Flannery stuttered when he got nervous or things became too demanding. His stutter singled him out to Sister Eucharius who charged through the line of boys standing by their desks like a black and white panther as she slapped Tommy hard across the face.

"Do that again and I vill cane you goot."

Tommy's solution was simple. From that moment on, all that he did was mouth the words. He did not utter a single word or sound aloud to welcome the visiting dignitaries. Sister Eucharius never knew.

February 1918

Jimmy Hurley, Paddy Clarke, Little Tommy, Liam McGee, and I waited near the fence that was closest to the rectory. Ever since Danny Dolan became an altar boy, we would get to read newspapers. Danny would have yesterday's Sun, Tribune or Herald that Father Hoffmann or the Monsignor Fitzpatrick would have read already.

se newspapers gave us a peek into the world outside the chain links of .. Joe's. Every page was carefully read. We were starved for a glimpse of what the world had to offer. We read about President Wilson ordering an investigation of large ship building yard in Hogs Island, wherever that was. There was a shipping strike that had 50,000 men not loading ships despite wage arbitration. A renewed U-Boat war is expected. A six-hour artillery barrage by American forces in France resulted in a successful French raid into German trenches. A nunnery in Montreal burned killing 38 children just like us. That story rattled us.

We heard a call and then a handbell ringing. It was that nice Sister Catherine Vianny. She waved for all the boys to follow her inside where we lined up and were given brooms, pals of water, vinegar, and newspapers. Thus armed we followed her, Sister Eucharius and Sister Hildegard into the church sacristy where we began to scrub the floors and walls using water and brushes. This was the start of daily cleaning in preparation for the Cardinal's visit.

Tall, older boys like Jimmy Hurley had to work side by side with some of Red's boys. Kidney punches were traded daily. Jimmy got an idea to soap the floor around the wall that he was cleaning. After one of Red's boys slipped and broke his arm, the kidney punches stopped.

Cleaning windows was a good job. Put vinegar in a rag, wipe the grime off then use a balled-up piece of newspaper to wipe the window dry and clean. We had to be careful though. Little Tommy and I were cleaning windows but one of us always had to be on the look-out for Red's gang. We cleaned the inside windows first. Often when we are cleaning outside, one of Red's gang smeared something on the inside window. More kidney punches were payment. Vinegar toughened the skin over my knuckles preventing bleeding when fighting. Red's boys never figured that out. They would get caught 'red-handed'. Ha! Ha! I did not. Over the next three weeks this war became part of our daily chore.

Danny was excused from the work because he was an altar boy. He went off to learn Latin with Sister Vianny or to polish altar things. Still, almost every day he brought a newspaper for us to read and learn about the outside world. Sister Hildegard would give us great big slices of brown bread with butter as we worked. Danny would bring some sausages from the rectory. He was a good guy to have in our gang.

Three days before the Cardinal's visit, the boys were all paraded downstairs to the tub room. This place brought the shivers to me. My mouth got dry, my feet cold and I started sweating before we even reached the tub room doors. As I remember, it was a black and white tiled room with only one oil lamp. I was right about the colors but this day it was well-lit. Sisters Eucharius, Corbinian and Hildegard stood next to several boxes containing new clothes.

In turn we were measured. Then trousers, a shirt, socks and shoes were piled on to our arms. We were told to get dressed.

As we finished dressing, Sister Corbinian called each boy over to her box where she produced short woolen jackets that we had seen men wear in newspaper pictures and advertisements.

Dressed in the new clothes, we were inspected by Mother Superior. She nodded her approval and left. Then we were told to undress and pile the clothes neatly, and in order. Each boy's name was written on a piece of paper and placed on top of his new clothes. The clothes were the first that actually fit me since I came to St. Joe's. At that point, we redressed in our well-used and under-sized clothes. We marched out of the tub room to continue our school lessons. Of course, we did not see those clothes again until the morning of the cardinal's visit.

During our class that afternoon we were graced by Mother Superior. She stood in the front of the room and slowly looked each boy in the face as if she was memorizing the boys' faces for a reason known only to her. Her eyes lingered on mine. Unblinking, I returned the stare. Still looking at me, she said, "You WILL NOT damage or dirty these costumes. There will be serious punishment if you do. DO YOU UNDERSTAND!"

***

Helen Agnes Naismith leading 32 of The Hello Girls, Army Signal Corps board the troopship Celtic for duty in France

"Look here," Jimmy said holding the Tribune. "The old 69th regiment is fighting in France! The Irish of the Fighting 69th are part of the Rainbow Division. We'll show those Huns! The Irish will beat them soundly."

We really did not care. If it was not boxing or baseball, then we were not all that interested. Jimmy was thoroughly into news of the war. The Great War had been going on ever since we could remember.

"I cannot wait until baseball season starts again," said Danny changing the subject. "The White Sox can win this year's pennant and World Series; you can bet on it."

"I will betcha," I said. "How much?"

"Do you really think that any team can beat the Sox?"

"Do you have any money to bet?"

"I have a dime. A dime says that the Sox win the 1918 World Series."

"I will bet a five-cent piece to your dime"

"What? Why not a dime for a dime?"

"If the White Sox are so good then for every two cents that you bet, I should be able to bet only one penny. You want to bet a dime, so I'll put up a five-cent piece."

Danny mulled that over for a minute then stuck out his pinky finger.

"You got a bet."

I clasped his pinky with my own and said, "Bet."

Tommy piped up with, "Any good fights in the newspaper?"

***

Yesterday, the Central Powers and Russia signed the Treaty of Brest-Litovek thus ending the fighting on the Eastern Front. (New York Times)

I have seen too, too much today. As I lie here still awake, I hear the old German grandfather clock two floors below strike one. The day started normally with my boys taking on Red MacGregor's gang while doing our "Cardinal Chores." A couple of fists to the kidneys and an elbow thump or two, we had what we wanted. Importantly, I collected other things including ninety-five cents and a good jackknife. I doled out shares to the gang. I made sure that boys got mostly what they wanted. Danny Dolan got some candy while other boys got socks, a shirt, shoelaces and even a pair of shoes that fit Tommy O'Flannery. Tommy is the gang's mascot. He is the littlest one. Until I came along, Tommy was a regular sport for the MacGregor gang.

I hid the money. Ninety-five cents won't get you anywhere. I will need more for my plan for Mikey and me. One of the boys said that the city has a vagrancy law. If you have a job that is good, but you had better have at least five dollars in your pocket or the coppers haul you to jail. Mikey and me will need more money than five dollars. I have to find out the cost of the ferry. I will get us to Brooklyn and out of this prison.

I'm telling no one of my plan until I am ready. I will need Jimmy Hurley, Danny Dolan, Liam McGee or someone else to help but that is all. Maybe even little Tommy O'Flannery. Once I have everything ready, Mikey and I will escape. The others can come along if they want. What I am lacking is cash. Bejesus, after all this time all I have is $9.56. We will need more. Mikey is a girl. She needs nice things.

A new orphan had forty-two cents. I offered to protect him from Red and his gang for five cents a month. By the time he runs out of money I plan to have enough for Mikey and me living anywhere but here. When we are out, I'll put together a gang. Mikey has a good head for arithmetic, she can handle the do-re-me. Now, for what I saw.

About 11 am, one of the boys in catechism threw up. Since I was a 'favorite' of Sister Leila, she ordered me to clean up the mess. I got a bucket and mop from the cloak room. The cloak room had only Sister Lelia's black shawl.

As I carried the bucket of mess past the chapel, I heard noises, grunts and crying. Without opening the chapel doors, I looked through. There was Danny Dolan, one of my gang on his hands and knees. His altar boy robe was nearly over his head but his bare ass was out of his pants bunched at his knees. Monsignor Fitzpatrick was on his knees behind Danny. He was holding his cassock up with one hand and the other one was gripping Danny. He was rhythmically moving his hips back and forth. Danny was crying. Monsignor Fitzpatrick was grunting. Then, Monsignor Fitzpatrick let out a loud sigh.

At that point, Danny turned his head. As he did, he looked toward the chapel door. I froze then stepped back and away. I picked up the bucket and the mop and continued to the basement utility sink.

When we had lunch, Danny sat with us. He didn't look at me once even when I was talking about the Cardinal's visit for this afternoon. He got up to use the lavatory in the middle of his meal but did not return.

We had been told that our regular classes would continue until 4 o'clock when the Cardinal would offer mass. After mass, we would go to the dining hall then do chores or homework. The Cardinal, we were told, was very interested in Catholic education and would visit some classes. Then we were told that he would visit my American History class before mass. The boys always grumbled about going to Sister Eucharius' American History.

Actually, there was very little *American* History. Sister Eucharius often gave long rambling stories of German saints including the one for which she was consecrated. German saints could raise the dead. Then she would continue on how Martin Luther became a heretic who fostered crazy ideas like Protestant free-thinking and this led to even crazier ideas like democracy.

Today, the class almost stayed on American History, almost. Sister Eucharius' classes in American History often diverged into stories of Prussian grandeur, military and religious accomplishments. She let us boys know that George Washington was an ineffective general not like Von Molke who soundly defeated the French in the Franco-Prussian War in 1871.

"If it was not for Von Steuben and the French in 1781," she sneered, "the Englanders vould haf beaten the Americans und you vould be Englanders today. Von Bismarck united Germany unter Kaiser Wilhelm the first und beat the French. We ver paid reparations by the French and ruled Paris."

Sister Eucharius continued, "Wilson is a *dummkopf*. The Englanders are the enemy! Ve need Kaiser here in America. Our Zeppelins bomb London und there is nothing the Englanders can do to stop them."

I lean over whispering to Danny Dolan, "German gas bags." His shoulders shook as he chuckled behind his textbook.

"Vent the German Army marches into Paris, ve vill make them pay reparations. Wilson is no good, a *dummkopf*."

At that instant, the classroom door was opened dramatically by Mother Superior. After a theatrical pause, a large man in gold rimmed robes and a red beanie walked slowly into the room looking at us the whole time. This was His Eminence, the Cardinal of New York. He was followed by a bishop, Bishop Cusack who held a large gold shepherd's crook, then several priests and our own Monsignor Fitzpatrick.

We boys knew exactly what we were supposed to do, we had it drilled into us: show respect by counting to ourselves, *ein, zwei, drei* then, all together get up from the left side of our desks and chant in unison.

As if there was only one boy speaking, we said, "Good morning Cardinal Farley."

Then, once more silently counting *ein, zwei, drei,* "Good morning Bishop Cusack."

We were to remain standing until such time as the cardinal gave us permission to sit. Once again, we counted to three, sat in synchrony then quietly clasp our hands, as if in prayer, on our desktops. Pencils were placed in the desk top groove. Inkwells were capped and not in use all week in preparation. There would be no *dumme* or clumsy ink spill mess. We scrubbed the classroom daily for a week before. They gave us polish for our shoes and wax for our desks. St. Joe's never looked or smelled so good as it did in the days leading up to the Cardinal's visit.

With a slow, theatrical hand gesture, the Cardinal indicated for us to sit. We moved and sat as one. Sat waiting with hands folded in silence. He looked intently at Sister Eucharius then at Mother Superior.

Slowly, he turned and addressed the boys saying, "Criticism of the government irritates me, I would consider it treason."

Eucharius and Mother Superior just rolled their eyes.

Turning to the boys, "It is the duty of every Catholic boy to serve his country. You older boys should join the Marines, the Navy or the Army. It is your sacred trust. I am positive that you learned about the Revolution, the Mexican War, the war with Spain and now our war with Germany. Your allegiance, fealty and devotion to your government should be demonstrated."

He paused again looking briefly at Sister Eucharius, then back to us, he said, "Bless you and bless the government of the United States of America."

Mother Superior and Sister Eucharius bowed their heads but gave each other a sidelong glance. The Cardinal turned and introduced Bishop Cusack who held a curved staff or bishop's crook then introduced the ordinary priests who would be assisting him at mass. As the Cardinal raised his hand to give us his blessing, we slipped out of their desks and piously knelt. The blessing completed; Mother Superior opened the door. The Cardinal, the Bishop and the rest of the party left the classroom at a stately pace.

"Ve vill finish our lesson tomorrow," said Sister Eucharius. "You vill stand and ve vill go to church for the Cardinal's mass."

The mass was a long, tedious one with much standing and kneeling. The kneelers were hard wood making all that kneeling uncomfortable. Nuns walked the aisles like coppers, making certain that no boy or girl even tried to sit unless we were instructed. They had clickers that signaled a change from kneeling. The only sitting permitted was during the Cardinal's sermon. He talked about the Great War in Europe and praying for our soldiers and sailors.

The Cardinal ended by saying, "I prayed that peace would come by arbitration and diplomacy. It seems however that no permanent peace can be hoped for except by the defeat of German arms in the field or a repudiation of the Prussian autocracy by the German people. As Catholics in America, we owe unswerving allegiance to the government of the United States and it is our duty to answer with alacrity any demand our country makes upon our loyalty and devotion."

It was sometime later that we heard doors banging open and shut. Two of the Cardinal's priests searched the classroom, cloak room and broom closet. Surprisingly, they even went into the fifth floor where the Magdalene women slept. They searched the sheds in the yard and under the stairs. We heard that they were looking for Bishop Cusack's crook. They came up empty-handed. The good bishop died a month later without ever locating his crook.

That night, after lights out, I heard a loud sob. I slipped out of bed. I padded in the direction of the sobbing. In the faint moonlight, I saw Danny lying on his back, staring at the ceiling with tears running down his cheeks.

"Danny, are you all right?"

He did not answer, just shook his head.

"I can help."

"No, no, no you cannot h-e-l-p."

"Sure, I can. We're pals."

"No, no, no one can help me. I'm done."

"Aw, don't say that!" I heard someone in the room mutter something. I whispered. "We'll think of something."

"There's nothing, nothing, nothing…" Danny trailed off.

I patted his shoulder and tiptoed back to bed.

Colleen – April 1918

Despite Mother Perpetua's real intentions, ordering me to work in the kitchen was the answer to my daily struggle with life. It gave me the roadmap I needed to follow later on in life. The Magdalene women, especially Dotty were reasonably kind to me though they hid kindness well, lest Lelia or Mary

Puss face might catch them in the throes of acting like a human being. Vianny was always in my corner and somehow, she got away with it more often than not.

One afternoon, Sister Vianny turned away from a soup pot she was stirring, "I want you to take a more active role in the kitchen, Colleen."

I looked up from my inventory sheet and smiled, "Alright, what do you want me to do?"

"First, I want you to take over this soup."

She stepped away from the enormous pot and handed me the spoon. I smiled at her knowingly. Vianny loved to sit in the kitchen corner on a stool and put her feet up on the sideboard and read or muse on about politics.

She took up her seat on the stool and said, "Simply put Colleen, you need to learn how to cook. You need to leave this place and you will one day with some practical knowledge that you can use. I had instruction at an early age and quite frankly, I am blessed to possess it. It gives me the opportunity to work in here rather than one of the other menial tasks that our holy Mother Superior would insist on. You know how I like to sample the potatoes...," she smiled. I was mindlessly stirring the pot. "Taste the soup and tell me what you think."

I took a small teaspoon and dipped it into the swirling hot liquid. "It's good, I began."

"Not enough information! Tell me what you taste."

I dipped the spoon in again and tasted it. "I think hmmm. There is carrots and um..."

"Can you taste the carrot? Or is it that you can see the carrots?" she demanded.

"I'm not sure. I think there are vegetables in the soup but I, I don't really taste them..."

"The soup is a bit boring then, right?"

"I didn't say..."

She interrupted me, "What would make it more interesting? What should you add to it to improve the flavor?"

I looked at her questioningly. She shrugged in response. I studied the kitchen counter. There was an array of additional vegetables and some herbs, I picked up some parsley.

She shook her head, "Not yet. You must add fresh herbs last, or they will wilt into nothing."

Ok, so that rules out thyme or chives. I pointed to peas.

"Wait a bit on the peas lest they become mash. You can add them a few minutes before we serve the soup."

"Tomatoes?"

"OK, good choice, but don't put them in whole! Here chop them with a good knife"

I began chopping the tomatoes. When I finished, I scooped up the chopped tomatoes and dumped them into the pot. I stirred the soup smoothly.

"Taste it again," she said after I had added the tomatoes.

"Yes, it definitely has more flavor now, I can taste the tomatoes."

"OK, now what do you want to add?" Feeling empowered with the addition of the tomatoes, I searched the counter again. There was not much more there that looked promising. She strode over to the stove and picked up a small bowl.

"Salt, you need salt"

I said, "How much?"

"Put a little in the soup. Then taste it and you tell me!"

So, I learned that I could enhance flavor just by adding salt and a big soup pot needs a lot of it. But that is how Vianny taught you things. She made you think, consider alternatives and then test them. Kitchen duty gave me the opportunity to learn how to organize meals so that everything was ready at the same time, how to run a kitchen and how to cook. Before Vianny arrived, meals at St. Joe's were ridiculously plain, loaded with cabbage and potatoes and totally unseasoned.

Once Lelia was taken off cooking duty and Vianny took over things definitely improved. Lelia was the orphanage's vegetable and herb gardener. Unfortunately, on her new assignment, Lelia wasn't much better than she was in the kitchen. She knew nothing about gardening but once again Vianny stepped in.

Vianny got herbs plants from Mr. Abernathy, our green grocery supplier. Vianny knew about cooking with herbs and Mr. Abernathy liked working with Vianny and me much better than with grouchy Sr. Lelia. He gave us parsley, thyme and chives which we added to Lelia's garden. We harvested what we needed before Lelia got her fat arse over to the garden every day. We used the herbs in soups and stews and miraculously Perpetua never said a word. Maybe she liked her meals better and decided to not question anything. Vianny could make any meal no matter how meager taste better. One day she told me that she had a French grandmother who taught her how to cook in the hopes that she would find a husband and not become a nun.

(*Jersey Journal*, 5 October 1918.) *Explosions at a munitions factory in Sayreville New Jersey killed at least 100 people and injured hundreds more. A continued series of explosions forced evacuations in nearby communities. The factory held enough shells to supply the war for six months. Sabotage is suspected.*

Sean
St. Joseph's
After midnight 5 October 1918

Sister Hildegard turned on the new electric lights in the boy's dormitory earlier than usual. One benefit of the late Cardinal's visit was the electrification of the orphanage. She stood still waiting for us to wake up and quiet down. Once she had our attention, she placed her fingertips over the hole in her throat and spoke in that raspy way of hers. The boys were so quiet that I could hear and understand her even from my bed near the far wall.

"Boys, there has been a bad accident. Many people hurt. Many people have no place to live. They are coming here. We are good Catholics and will provide shelter. You must help by making room for our guests."

I said to Tommy O'Flannery, "She means move our beds closer, please."

I helped Little Tommy move his bed closer to Jimmy Hurley's whose bed was against the wall. Then I moved mine. There was barely room enough to stand between our beds.

All the boys happily shoved their beds to one side of the room. When the cacophony was over Sister Hildegard clapped happily and patted each boy on the head as her way of saying, "*Danke schon!*"

By mid-day, the first dozen or so of the refugees arrived at St. Joseph's. Some were well-dressed and had carpet bags while others were wearing bedclothes, robes or blankets. The men and boys were separated from the girls, and women with babies. I was glad because most of the babies were crying. Then sometime later a horse-drawn wagon delivered another dozen or so men, women and children.

We marveled at the boys' clothes, shoes and hats. Well, those who were dressed that is. I admired a boy's six-piece cap.

I overheard one of the new arrivals talking to another man.

"Where are you from?"

"Perth Amboy. You?"

"Sayreville."

"We were listening to the Denny Farrell Big Band Showcase on WOR when we heard the Gillespie Plant explosion."

"Oh, that plant has munitions for the war in Europe."

We pelted one the new boys with questions: "What's a W-O-R?"

"Why do you call it a big band?"

"Where'd you get that shirt?"

"My Ma gave it to me."

"How many shirts do you have?"

"You don't know nuthin'," the boy replied startled.

The two men continued, speaking loudly, "When did you leave your house?"

"Must have been about 7:35 last night. They hauled us over the new bridge to here in Staten Island."

"We heard the explosions in Perth Amboy but we were not told to evacuate until this morning, then we went over the Outerbridge Crossing too. My wife and me had no idea where they were taking us. It was bad."

The boy we were talking to had a nice cap.

"Can I hold your hat? It is a nice hat."

"Sure."

As I fingered the rich wool and the curved brim of the cap, I asked, "What happened?"

"There was an explosion, then another, another and another. One was so strong that it knocked my mom's looking glass off the wall." The boy took his cap from my hands.

"Then what?"

"Then policemen came knocking at all doors on our street, yelling for everybody to get out."

The bed next to me bounced, and Jimmy Hurley appeared at my side. He was bug-eyed with excitement. Well, this was the most exciting thing to happen since I came to St. Joe's.

"Must have been German saboteurs!" Jimmy said excitedly.

"How do you know that?"

"I read the newspapers. German spies infected some of our horses with a disease call Glanders or Ganders or something. German spies are all over Newark New Jersey. I know that from the papers."

"Could be," said the boy. "What is Glanders?"

"Some disease that makes horses sick. I guess."

Who cares, I thought.

"How do you get such swell clothes?" I interrupted.

"My father owns a furniture store in Jersey City. He sells hundred sofas and beds a week."

"What's a sofa?" Jimmy asked. The boy jerked his head back to see if Jimmy was trying to fool him.

"My name is Sean, Sean Callaghan. This crazy guy is Jimmy Hurley."

"Nice to meet you, my name is Charlie Yanowsky. I am a Jew."

"What?" Jimmy said. "I thought that Jews were only in the Bible. You mean Jews are real?"

"Well, Charlie is real," I said looking from Jimmy to Charlie.

The noise of everybody talking was reaching a peak as the door opened. Sister Eucharius appeared in the doorway. She rapped hard on the open door. Slowly, the room quieted down.

In a loud commanding voice, she said, "If du do not haf clothes. *Kommen Sie mit mir*!"

"Cripes!" Someone said. "She is a Hun!"

As if she had not heard that, she turned smartly and walked to the corridor outside the room. Men and boys who were nearly naked wrapped their blankets around themselves and followed Sister Eucharius out of the room.

Sometime later, the 'bomb boys' and men walked back into the dorm room. Jimmy christened the boys with the name, 'bomb boys'. When they returned these boys were wearing clothes that looked new. One boy recognized a jacket that had been too big for him when the Cardinal visited. Another recognizes the shoes that he had tried to fit into because they laced up high.

"SO, Mother Superior gave the Cardinal's clothes to these kids not us!"

The Bomb Boys seemed embarrassed. Some started crying.

Red MacGregor and one of his gang had one boy against the wall. I could not hear what was being said but I could see Red pushing the boy against the wall. Crying silently, the boy was undressing, taking off his new clothes.

I elbowed Jimmy, then looking at Danny and two others I jerked my head sideways toward the two around the crying boy. Quickly, we jumped from bed to bed toward the three near the dorm wall. Red must have heard us, he turned and put up his fists.

As Red pulled his right back to punch, Jimmy kicked at him. Jimmy missed, lost his balance falling backward on the bed. Red jumped on Jimmy. Then Danny jumped on Red's back. The other fellow with Red started to run as I jumped down from the bed to go after him. Leaping, I pounced on the guy. We went down to the floor. There was shouting, punching, wrestling, pushing until some big men started to separate the fighters.

One man was big enough to lift me off the boy with one hand and grab Red's pal with his other hand. We found ourselves both suspended, feet searching for the floor. I wiggled in his grip still trying to get in another punch or a kick. The man held us and laughed.

In a funny accent, the man said, "Stop or I will whip you!"

We stopped struggling in his grip and he set us down.

With his finger pointing at us, the man said, "You boys are devils."

Other men had intervened with Jimmy, Danny and Red. Another man was walking away with the crying boy. As the disorder settled to a noisy order, it became clear that we had been cheated. We could have clothes that fit us better only if Mother Superior Perpetua wanted to give them to us. Obviously, she did not. Now that I knew, Mother Superior lost some of her control over the situation. I would find where she stored the clothes that we had returned after the Cardinal's visit. I would steal them from her.

One of the orphanage girls holding hands with a smiling little girl came to the door of the boy's dorm. One of the men walked over to the little girl, picked her up, kissed her head. Still holding the girl in his arms, he turned back to the room. In a loud man's voice, he boomed, "Dinner!"

Men and boys collected in the corridor with a cacophony of voices then started down the stairs. That is when I noticed one of the 'bomb boys' who looked really ashen and coughing. No one knew it at the time, but *The Great Influenza* arrived at St. Joseph's Orphanage.

Chapter 5
The Pestilence

At 5:35 this morning, Allied Forces launched the strongest offensive of the war along the Courtrai front. The Grande Armee de Flandres pressed the German Imperial Army with a rolling barrage that crept 100 yards ahead of advancing Belgian and British troops (New York Times, 14 October 1918). *Allies Attack German defenses along the River Lys in Belgium*

Colleen
14 October 1918

One of the best things about working in the kitchen meant that not only did I get to eat but I learned to cook! And the most wonderful, unexpected thing that happened to me during my kitchen time was my discovery of some great writers. All due to Mr. Abernathy, our grocery man and meat purveyor. Mr. Abernathy and his helper, a thin-as-a-rail boy named Jimmy, delivered to the kitchen once or twice a week.

Until Mr. Abernathy, my reading was about saints. Mostly German saints. For example, Saint Eucharius could raise the dead. Saint Corbinian of Bavaria tamed the bear that killed his horse then rode the bear to Rome to visit the Pope. Saint Hildegard was an abbess and Christian mystic, who founded an order of nuns in Germany.

I do not remember how I learned that Mr. Abernathy loved to read. I think it was seeing a book of poetry sticking out of his coat pocket one day. I asked him about it.

"It's the latest collection of poems from William Butler Yeats."

I said, "I am bored reading books about German saints. Maybe, Mr. Abernathy, could you lend me the book in your pocket?"

He did!

Mr. Abernathy became my librarian of sorts. At first it was once a month when it was time to reconcile accounts. While skinny Jimmy stacked the cans and sacks of potatoes in the pantry, Mr. Abernathy sat with Vianny and me as we recorded delivery and payments due. Surreptitiously, he would slip me his latest favorite book. When he discovered that I devoured every word in less than a week, he would bring a new book when he picked up the weekly inventory list and order.

I was enthralled with Alexandre Dumas and his wonderful Count of Monte Cristo. I dreamt that like Edmund Dantes, I too would seek revenge one day when Sean and I were out of this place. I loved Dumas's The Three Musketeers; Edgar Allen Poe's Murders in the Rue Morgue, 39 Steps by John Buchan and Wilkie Collin's The Moonstone and of course, Sir Arthur Conan Doyle's Sherlock Holmes novels. Then Mr. Abernathy slipped Willa Cather's My Antonia to me. It became my favorite.

Of course, these books also got me into a peck of trouble with the Sisters of St. Joseph. I would place the book inside the catechism or history book in class and pretend to be piously reading along with the class. Instead, I entered a world of intrigue and suspense! Every now and again, I would get caught not paying attention. Sr. Mary Puss-face would be asking me a question about the catechism reading and I would not be able to answer. That gave me tons of writing homework. Lelia actually confiscated the Hound of the Baskervilles from me when she slipped behind me and saw that I was not reading my history book.

I was aghast. But I have to be honest with Mr. Abernathy. I explained how the book had become "lost" and I could not return it. At that, Mr. Abernathy just laughed when I apologized.

"Push-posh, don't you fret. I have another book of Sir Arthur's stories in my wagon. Let's get the victuals in first."

When I think of those years, the only joy I get is from memories of Abernathy and Vianny's kindnesses. Sean too, of course.

I also found a real happiness in cooking. Maybe it was because I spent so many years just plain being hungry. But I really developed a talent for it and of making a simple meal taste better with just a sprinkling of thyme leaves or a dusting of chopped chives. And it became a real resource for me as I got older.

Sean

10 November 1918

Germany signs an Armistice in Marshal Foch's railcar; Guns will go silent tomorrow at 11 am

At first, it was one boy, then two of the older boys that got sick with a fever. Just as it seemed like they were recovering, they began to sneeze. They became too dizzy to sit up for soup when Sister Hildegard tried to feed them. One boy looked like he got punched in the nose because it started bleeding.

That night, the older boy with the nosebleed died. By early morning, the other one stopped breathing. Rumors started that one of the young nuns on the girls' side died. Then we heard that one of the Magdalene women died. Suddenly, there were seven or eight more boys were too weak to stand or walk. In less than a week, five more boys died.

Nearly every morning, we would find a boy dead.

Jimmy, Danny, Liam, and I were ordered to carry the dead boy on a sheet. Down four flights and out to the far side of the yard. It was a cold November, every day seemed to be cloudy with the threat of rain, snow or both. The winds chilled us to the bone, as did the chilling effect of carrying dead boys we knew.

Sister Eucharius always escorted us on these carries. During one of these trips, we saw a longer body under a white sheet. Then turning, we saw six long bodies under sheets. A pair of gray feet stuck out from one. Eucharius saw us looking and said coldly, "Magdalene whores."

Immediately, I hoped that Dotty was not in one of those sheets.

Two men wearing white masks and carrying shovels stood by waiting for a signal. Then, Eucharius nodded to them.

To us she said, "*Kommt mit!*"

As we followed her back, we heard the quick grating sound of shovels digging in the hard November dirt. November 1918 was a long, cold, gray and terrifying month. Even the biggest, strongest boys died. Most were old enough to be released, sent off on their own by the orphanage but instead they were dead. The Great Pestilence, Mother Superior called it. Well, the Pestilence called many to their graves.

By the end of November, there were two dozen empty beds in the boy's room. Mikey had told me about girls dying too. My gang and me managed to grab a dead boy's clothes or shoes before Red's boys did. That was the easy part. Hiding the clothing from Eucharius or Corbinian was very tricky. Tricky, but I had the upper hand. The broom closet on the fourth floor was the perfect place. I knew when the Magdalene women were down to the kitchen. I took advantage of that time to steal up the stairs with the spoils of death. On my way back down at the top of the stairs, I paused to admire the kaleidoscope of colors of from the late afternoon sun pouring through the window. It was a small beacon of hope amid all this death.

By December, the grippe eased. Boys got sick but fewer died. My boys, Jimmy Hurley and Danny Dolan, came down with fever. They did not die. Sister Hildegard took care of them and the other sick boys, giving them milk with cinnamon. She started to give boys something she called 'salicin' which brought down fevers. I never learned where she obtained it.

Even though the death toll was decreasing, boys and girls continued to die. Again, it was sad that the older ones who were within days or weeks of being released died. They missed their opportunity for a free life. Death is no freedom.

In early December, Liam McGee said that we were carrying out only one corpse a week. The week before Christmas no one died. At Christmas Mass, we celebrated our 'deliverance'.

It was premature.

Colleen
Late December 1918

I have to admit it, I almost enjoyed Christmas time at St. Joseph's. It was as if the nuns, even the most intolerant and insensitive ones were more human somehow. Sister Mary Aloysius, aka Puss-Face and Sister Lelia actually seemed less angry. I have come to the realization that they were probably attempting to be kinder and gentler for a few weeks or days out of some vague religious fervor. But I relished the respite in their temperament regardless of the reason. We even got to sing Christmas carols at the beginning of math class. We chose the Twelve Days of Christmas because it was the longest song we could think of to delay the torturous sums and long division work awaiting us. Actually, I enjoyed math class. There was something comforting to me in the balance and order of arithmetic. I guess I enjoyed it because it gave order to my uncontrollable situation. I knew in my heart that one day, Sean and I would get out of this place and that everything would be alright for us. But until such time, I had to take refuge in what I could find, arithmetic, cooking and reading the wonderful books that Mr. Abernathy lent to me.

Mr. Abernathy brought homemade cookies from Mrs. Abernathy to Vianny and me when he came to pick up our order for Christmas week. I stuffed several in my pocket for Sean. The cookies had little red and green candied speckles, I knew Sean would love them.

It seemed like the terrible fever that raged over us for the past two months had subsided, maybe that was part of Christmas magic too. We all got up early Christmas morning like we did every day. And like every day at St. Joseph's we marched into the lavatory where a long brown wooden table held four basins of cold water. This was how we washed our hands, faces and any other body parts in preparation for the day. I did not know it then, but it was just another way for spreading influenza throughout the girls' dormitory.

Sean told me to stay on my own as much as possible to avoid getting sick. He had to help bury the dead; it was miserable work, but he never complained. I worried that he would get sick especially because he was in contact with those who had succumbed to the illness. The fear that Sean would become ill was more frightening than anything to me.

Sometime in the early part of January, I started to feel very tired. I thought it was just the sadness at all the death and illness surrounding us. Vianny made sure that I ate well. She feared that I would contract the illness too. She insisted that I have extra bowls of soup and thick crusty bread. I actually felt better after eating the extra food. But the fatigue always returned the next day and seemed to intensify a bit more each day. I remember starting my weekly inventory one bitter cold day in the middle of January; I was standing on a chair so I could see the top shelf in the pantry when I suddenly felt shaky, my eyesight dimmed, and I lost my balance. Sister Vianny was there and grabbed me to beak my fall. Then my world went black.

Sean—January 1919

Then, around mid-January, the grippe returned with a vengeance. Even I became sick, just a headache and muscle pain but no fever. I told no one that I felt sick. It was a good idea not to complain. This time Mother Superior moved all the sick orphans to the basement tub room in neat rows of cots. The tub room hadn't been electrified so oil lamps were used, day and night.

Liam and I were given mops and pails to clean the tub room. At first, it seems that there were too many cots in the tub room, not many sick orphans. Boy, I was wrong. Quickly, they filled up with sick boys and girls. They were fed chicken broth and Sister Hildegard's cinnamon milk until they started to vomit or bleed from their nose so badly that they could not breathe. The smoke from the oil lamps didn't help. The room was smoky, cold, damp and noisy with coughing, sneezing and moaning boys and girls.

In addition to clean up, I was still on Eucharius' corpse carrying crew. Eucharius was acting stranger than usual. She held long conversations with herself. She talked with von Bismarck and others that I could not follow because it was all in German. Perversely, she teamed Red MacGregor with me. I guess that we were the biggest and strongest boys left. More likely she probably hoped that the two of us would become sick and die as well.

We carried the dead up the stairs and out into the yard. No longer did the men in white masks wait for us to dig a grave. They arrived at first light of day to dig. A long narrow trench maybe thirty feet long, six deep and six-foot wide. At the end of the day, the men returned to shovel dirt and some white powder on the bodies that we had dropped there during the day. We would drop bodies in by emptying them from the sheet. We used the same sheet many times until it ripped.

On a dark rainy January day, I received the shock of my life. There were no classes. We were supposed to spend the day in the church praying for 'delivery from pestilence'. In the middle of a rosary, Red and I were pulled out of pew by Eucharius. We were to go to what she called the infirmary. I called it the 'Rude Morgue' after the story that Mikey told me about, it was called Murders on the RUE Morgue by Edgar Allen Poe. It was a waystation to the grave, not an infirmary.

Down the dark stairs, Red and I descended into hell. The infirmary was a pit of garish yellow light, smoke, and odors. The smell of blood, vomit and shite was enough to make a maggot gag. We covered our noses and mouths. But, after a while you did not notice it. I think the awful sights that we saw were more overpowering than the odors.

The suspended oil lamps cast pools of smoky yellow light revealing disorganized rows of cots. I saw Sister Hildegard waving to us from the other side of the room. I slapped Red on the arm and pointed toward Sister Hildegard. Moving as quickly as I could between the many cots, I reached

Sister Hildegard's side. She was wearing a stained white smock over her habit and was dabbing the fevered forehead of some orphan with a damp cloth.

When she took the cloth away, I saw the face that I never wanted to see down here.

It was Colleen!

Mikey! She looked so pale, so small, and so sick.

Sean
Sunday, 19 January 1919

Weimar Republic elections using proportional representation and allowing women's suffrage has 82% voter turnout: Social Democrats capture National Assembly

Sister Hildegard placed a clean cool compress on Colleen's forehead, as she did, I watched rivulets of water run into Colleen's beautiful red hair. I was cotton-mouthed with fear.

With dark circles under her blue eyes, Sister Hildegard looked pale, tired and sick herself. Painfully, she rose to her feet by grasping both my arms. Her fingers dug into my muscles as she pulled herself up. Being taller than me, I looked up into eyes that stared off into a far distance. They were not the bright intelligent eyes that I had seen many times before. She stood blinking like she was sending Morse Code. It appeared that she had some difficulty focusing.

But finding an inner reserve of strength, she said in that particular croak of hers, "Here take this, give it to her, she will get better."

She packed my left hand with a wrapped handkerchief. Still gazing off into some distance beyond the walls of the infirmary, Sister Hildegard shuffled off between the beds and up the stairs. Climbing up the stairs as though it was the side of a mountain, she pulled herself up using the handrail and pausing on each step. I watched until I saw her shadow on the wall at the top of the stairs, then it was gone.

I knelt next to Colleen. "Mikey, Mikey! I am here. It's me, Sean."

"Sean."

"Yes, it's me."

"Sean, I'm thirsty."

"I will get some water, Mikey. I will be back in a bit."

I threaded myself through the maze of cots, coughs and moans. Suddenly, Red appeared in front of me, blocking me.

"We have bodies to move. Where are you going, you stupid fooking mick?"

I did not say a thing as I gave him a sock in the kisser then stepped over him. This Scotsman never seemed to learn.

Colleen
Wednesday, 22 January 1919

Red Army occupies Ukraine (New York Mirror)

I awoke. The muscle pain and the fever were gone. Still, I was so, so tired. Someone was crying, painful sobs and gasps of deep sorrow.

But the heart-wrenching sobs made me sit up.

In the dim oil lamplight, I could see a nun and a figure bent over a cot nearby. The nun had her hand on the shoulder that shook with each sobbing breath and wail. My vision cleared as I sat there. But it was the crying that riveted my attention. It spoke of a terrible loss, of heartbreak. "Come," said Sister Hildegard, I recognized her voice, "Come with me."

There was no break in the crying as the figure stood. It was a woman, one of the Magdalene women by her costume. She fell into Hildegard's arms. The woman's wailing became muted by the folds of Hildegard's habit.

Gently and slowly, Hildegard led her away from the cot. The two figures passed close to an oil lamp.

It was Dorothy Gale!

Sean
22 January 1919

By this morning, Mikey's fever was gone. I must have fallen asleep next to her cot in the tub-room infirmary. As I stood up, the faintly pink light of dawn could be seen through the dirty cellar windows. The only sounds were that of boys and girls coughing, moaning as they tossed feverishly on their cots. There were several cots with deathly still occupants. Mikey was quiet but I could see that she was breathing, not coughing, not moaning, not feverous just sleeping like an angel, not with the angels. Whatever the magic potion was that Sister Hildegard gave me for Mikey, it worked. Now, as I stood there, I realized that I had to get her out of this room away from the dead and dying. I wrapped the still sleeping Mikey in her blanket, picked her up and carried her the four flights to the boys' room. Opening the door with my foot, the room had beds that were unused. One of the empty beds was next to mine. It had been Tommy's.

Tommy O'Flannery had died yesterday. He faded away very quickly. Two days ago, he awoke with a headache. Down he went to the infirmary. Yesterday at twilight, he stopped coughing, rattled as if he was trying to spit. Then Tommy stopped breathing. He was gone.

Already, Tommy's bed was stripped. The nuns had taken to either burning or boiling the sick ones' blankets and sheets. I did not concern myself with what they had done to Tommy's things. I put my sheet and blanket on Tommy's bed for Mikey. As I tucked the blanket around her, I could see even her freckles were less washed out. There was some pink on her cheek.

I hated to leave her alone, but I knew that it would not be long before I would be called to carry out the ones who had died overnight. It would be another day for Red and me to be on corpse duty. I was tired yet relieved that Mikey was getting better. Almost every kid who came down with the Spanish grippe died. As I looked around, I counted six boys asleep in a room of 50 beds. Not one boy over 14 was alive.

I had another problem. I knew that if Eucharius discovered Mikey in Tommy's bed there would be hell to pay. I had to get the sleeping boys up and moving to take away a reason for Eucharius to come here. I started waking a few who immediately knelt next to their cots praying. I laughed to myself. Prayers would not stop the grippe. Prayers did not even save some nuns, many had died.

For Mikey's sake, it would be important for me and Red to get working early today. I had to know where Eucharius was at all times. I could not let her discover Mikey in Tommy's bed. Then there was the problem of Red MacGregor.

Red was sound asleep in his bed. Empty beds surrounded his because the grippe had killed most of his gang. Was it strange that we should be paired to carry out the dead? Without a word, we had an armistice. We did not trust one another. The time for fighting was over, for now. I did not want Red to find Mikey. He would use it against me. I had better keep him busy. I walked to his bed and shook him.

"What? Go away. I want to sleep."

"Get up before Eucharius gets you up."

"I do not want to do this."

"Get up"

Throwing the blanket off, Red was still dressed even wearing his shoes to bed. As I did, he had slept in his clothes, too tired to get undressed. He sat there looking at his shoes as if they were not his.

"We better get going and find Eucharius before she finds us."

"All right, all right, you fooking mick."

"And stop with the fooking word. Eucharius will beat the bejesus out of both of us if you say it around her. I could do with a day without her beating the fook out of me."

Looking up, he smiled at me. "I like seeing her beat the fook out of you."

As he stood, he said, "Fine, I will watch my fooking tongue."

Together we started down the stairs. At the second-floor landing, we heard a voice coming from the nun's quarters. A voice was repeating something over and over, almost like a short prayer.

"By the rood of St. Peter, arise. By the rood of St. Peter arise. By the rood of St. Peter arise, take up thy bed and walk." It was Sister Eucharius' voice.

Red and I slid quietly next to the door of the nunnery. Red inched the door open a crack to look and I peered over his shoulder. There in the room was Sister Eucharius. Holy cow! She had Bishop Cusack's gold crook! She was using it to stroke a form under a white sheet so white that it dazzled in the morning winter sun.

"Arise, take up thy bed and walk, I command thee." Now Eucharius was louder. "Arise!" Louder still. "By the power of the rood of St. Peter, ARISE!"

She struck the body under the sheet hard, then placing the butt of the crook at her side lifted both her arms to the ceiling shouting, "My father! Why hast thou forsaken me?"

We heard a rustle of fabric like a nun's habit. Red and I silently stepped back from the door. Just then we heard Mother Superior's voice in a surprisingly gentle way say, "Sister, you vill gif me zie crook, *Bitte*." Please give me the crook.

Meekly, Sister Eucharius said, "*Ja, Grossmutter*." Yes, Mother Superior.

Red and I tiptoed to the stairs. We had not taken two steps down before the door opened. With that dreaded booming voice, we heard, "*Kommt herin!*"

Come here.

"Yes, Mother Superior," we said in unison.

Mother Superior waved her hand for us to follow. Entering the room, we saw two sheet covered bodies. Sister Eucharius was standing by the window with vacant eyes. She swayed right and left humming softly.

Mother Superior cuffed Red in the back of the head. She pointed toward a canvas and wood stretcher leaning against the wall next to Bishop Cusack's crook.

We loaded one heavy body on the stretcher. Red took the front stretcher handles while I took the back. It would be Red who would take the brunt of the body's weight as we descended the stairs. But the back-breaking job of keeping the body from sliding off was all mine. The dead kids weighed only a little more than the sheets they were carried in. This was a heavy body.

With Mother Superior leading, we carried our load down the stairs and out the side door. She turned to the gravel path that continued toward the church. This was a different route than the one we usually took with a corpse. The dead kids were buried in long trenches in the yard. This was the churchyard, sacred ground. We struggled with weight of this corpse. Both of us staggered, struggling to maintain a grip and desperate not drop the body.

A cold, damp, raw wind from the Atlantic blew Mother Superior's habit into black wings. She held on to the crown of her headdress as its black veil whipped wildly in the wind. We trudged past the rectory, past the thick row of hedges that bordered the churchyard near Carroll Street toward the church. Our feet crunched noisily on the gravel walk. I looked ahead as we passed old headstone after old headstone. There were two men digging a grave in the church yard. They tossed shovelful after shovelful of dirt in a defined pile. Looking past them, I saw another rectangular hole also with its pile of fresh dirt. The smell of earth wet, wormy, decaying plants and leaves was strong. Wordlessly, gathering her billowing habit, Mother Superior pointed. We placed the body next to the finished grave. With only a hand signal, we knew to follow her. Once back into the building, it felt good to be out of that damp cold wind.

Last night, we had carried bodies out until after dark. We missed dinner. No one saved us anything to eat. I was hungry, tired. Red must be too. I was not certain that I could carry another big body down three flights.

The second body was not as heavy as the first. Still, we struggled to lift it. This time, I went down the stairs first placing both handles on my shoulders as I faced down the stairs. The wood dug into my muscles, right to the bone. It really hurt but I could use one hand to steady the stretcher and the other to hold the handrails so as not to fall. At the bottom of the stairs, I turned slowly taking one handle then the other as it slid down my chest painfully. Then, I turned again to hold the stretcher behind me. We followed Mother Superior out the door back to the churchyard.

Both men standing by the second open grave, took their caps off, bowed their heads as Mother Superior, Red and I approached. The wind picked up as we set the stretcher by the grave. A rogue gust ripped the sheet off the body.

It could not be! I blinked, blinked again.

Hildegard!

One of the gravediggers tucked his cap under his arm as he squatted to cover Sister Hildegard with the sheet. Wind whipped the black folds of her habit, but Mother Superior was looking up, away toward the church steeple.

Sister Hildegard, Sister Hildegard who saved Mikey. Sister Hildegard who took care of me after that torture session in the tub room. Hildegard who had taught Mikey and me to read. Hildegard who took care of Danny Dolan and Jimmy Hurley during the first round of the grippe. It was Sister Hildegard who gave me medicine for Mikey that could have been used to save herself.

I cried. I cried for Hildegard, for Tommy, for the dead boys and girls. I cried for all of us. The hot tears running down my face only made me feel colder. Glancing at Red, I saw tears streaking his dirty face too.

Chapter 6
Rescue

Eight White Sox Players Are Indicted On Charge Of Fixing 1919 World Series: Cicotte Got $10,000 And Jackson $5,000 (New York Times, September 27, 1920)

Sean
1920
St. Joseph's Orphanage, Staten Island, New York City

Now that the Great War and the Spanish Flu were over, the orphanage still had many empty beds. The Spanish gripe killed a large number of orphans. Slowly over time, the dead were replaced by another, younger orphan. The gripe must have killed some mothers and fathers in the city. As a result, St. Joe's received a few new orphans but not many. Empty beds were silent daily reminders of our losses, so many unused beds.

We wore clothes until they were too ragged for the nuns to look at or we grew completely out of them. As I said, shoes were real bartering items as were socks. When shoes got holes, some would find a piece of newspaper that might have blown into the yard to insert to cover the hole. My gang had a reliable source of newspaper with Danny Dolan, the altar boy.

Usually, we read day-old newspapers. Jimmy Hurley, Paddy Clarke and Danny Dolan argued about baseball. We argued about the Scandal. The World Series Scandal. Squint had the boxing pages. He grunted something and kept eating his porridge.

Paddy Clarke said, "White Sox! They should be called Black Sox! Those bums don't wash their socks."

Jimmy fired back, "That's because Cominsky won't pay to have their uniforms washed."

"Who the fook is Cominsky."

"He's the owner of the Chicago White Socks."

"To me winning is everything, the Sox didn't try to win. Shoeless Joe Jackson was a hero to us. He was hitting great all season," I said.

"Lookee here!" said Jimmy slapping the sports page. "How can you call throwing the Series when Shoeless Joe was battling better in the Series than the regular season? Boys, Joe was battling .375 in the Series!"

"He was bribed to make it look good. This guy ain't no hero."

"Who? Who? Who? Who bribed him?" Jimmy retorted.

"Whaddareya, a fooking owl?"

"Who? Who bribed Joe, Gandel, Cicotte, Williams, Feisch and the others? Huh? Who has that kind of money? The king of England?"

"All I know is what I read and that all the confessions and records mysteriously disappeared. There's a cover-up and the Sox owner Cominsky may be behind it," Danny Dolan interjected.

"Ah, whatdayouknow," said Jimmy dismissively.

Colleen
October 1920

I continued to meet Sean at our place at the fence every day at recess. I usually got there before him. I always knew he had 'business' with the other boys to handle first but he never failed to meet me. Sometimes with a swollen lip or a blackened eye but he always came. Today, he was actually there first.

"Listen Mikey, I need you to do something for me."

The Mikey nickname stuck even though I didn't have to squeeze under the fence to go on the boys' food line anymore. I was getting extra food because of my work in the kitchen.

"What do you need Sean?" I was worried. Sean hardly ever asked for anything from anybody not even from me. He handed me a sweaty handful of coins.

"Hide this. We can use this when we get out of here."

"Where did you get…"

"Don't ask. Mikey, will you do this"

I said, "Yes of course."

"Put it in your pocket before someone sees."

"OK, I don't know where I can…"

Sean always prepared had already thought my hiding place through.

"Find a place up high in the kitchen pantry behind the door where even Abernathy's tall boy Jimmy cannot see, use a ladder."

I nodded and said, "Skinny Jimmy died of the grippe."

"Sorry to hear that," he said tightening his lips.

After a moment, Sean said, "Mikey, we need money to get by when we get out of here. This is not enough, but it's a start."

He glanced around as if he thought someone was watching our exchange at the fence.

"Please don't let the coins jangle in your pocket, Mikey. Get it hidden away quickly as you can."

Sean was looking over my shoulder. Then he touched my hand.

"Watch your back. Lelia and Puss-face are coming." With that, he turned and melted into the crowd of boys on the other side of the fence.

I was still at the fence when heavy heeled shoes crunched the dirt behind me then stopped. Silence.

"Having a little chat with your bold brazen brother?" Said a familiar but unfriendly voice.

Sister Mary Aloysius of the Holy Sepulcher, better known to Sean and me as "Puss-Face" due to the deeply etched acne scars on her cheeks. She glared at me with both hands on her ample hips. I kept my head down, hands in both pockets of my skirt and penitently walked past Sister Leila, keeping a good distance from Puss-face.

I quietly said, "Yes, sister, I was talking to my brother."

I walked slowly to a group of Mary Kate's girls. I maneuvered in the group to keep Sister Leila and Puss-face in view. The two seemed to be in a discussion and no longer interested in me. I excused myself from the girls saying that I need to go, you know 'go.'

Inside, I went immediately to the girl's lavatory. I enclosed myself in a stall and grabbed paper to wrap around the coins so they would not clink. My next subject was History with Sister Leila. I did not want her asking what was bulging in my pocket. So, I tried to make sure that my little bundle of coins was as flat as possible. I had three more classes, and a chapel prayer session before I could get to the kitchen pantry. Somehow, I made it through the rest of the school day until it was time to go to resume my kitchen chores for supper. I hid our treasure behind two sacks of flour.

Cleveland Indians beat the Brooklyn Dodgers to win Series; Cleveland wins 5 games to 2

Construction begins on Hudson River Vehicular Tunnel connecting New Jersey with New York City. Engineers Clifford M. Holland, Milton Freeman and Ole Singstad's design will connect Canal Street with 12th Street in Jersey City

Sean
12 October 1920

Hearing someone being whipped may be worse than seeing someone whipped. Your mind invents things far more terrible than the actual whipping. For the person being whipped, each time the lash strikes the whole body is jolted by pain. As the lash is being drawn back it pulls skin causing a second even more exquisite pain. Worse yet is listening to the whip singing back to hit once again. You hold your breath in the hopes of lessening the pain. It doesn't work. I know. I've tried it. It only makes a new drumming sound in the chest. That sound itself is painful.

I was in the broom closet hiding some money that I took from one of Red's boys. I'll get it to Mikey later. As I was counting up my hoard, I heard voices and heavy footsteps form the stairwell. Deciding that my best bet was to stay hidden in here, I pulled the door fully closed, not a moment too soon as the footfalls arrived at the fourth-floor landing.

I heard a body slam against a wall.

"Kneel *Du Hure!*" Kneel whore! Mother Superior's voice commanded. I heard the sound of cloth being torn violently.

"I've done nothing!" A voice I recognized as Dorothy Gale's said.

A loud smack followed with Mother Superior saying, "Succubus! Whore! You are the devil's temptress, his minion."

"Please Mother Superior I have done nothing wrong."

"You filthy *Hure!* You will be *strafen,* punished for your sins."

Then the whipping began. I counted at least fifteen or maybe twenty lashes. Mother Superior's voice was even and controlled as she punctuated each lash with: "Du Hure!" "Succubus!" "Satan's whore!" "*Du Schlampe!*" "Tramp!" "Slut!" "*Hundin!*" "Bitch!"

"*Grossmutter,*" Eucharius' voice said breathlessly. "I'm getting tired. Can I stop now?"

So Eucharius is doing the whipping!

"*Ja*, we will finish this later. It will give this whore of Satan time to repent."

With that, the two began to descend the stairs but Mother Superior paused on a step saying, "Ve vil be back *Du Hure*! You can be sure that you will suffer for your sins."

They continued down the stairs.

As their voices and steps faded below, I eased myself out of the closet. Facing me was an open door to a room. There, on the floor was Dotty. She was naked, face down, breathing in gasps. Her back was a mess of bloody stripes. I realize that this room connected to Eucharius' room. Racing inside, I threw open her closet, found a clean sheet and blanket.

I covered Dotty. I did not know what else to do. Then I thought of Mikey. Mikey would know what to do.

Gently as I could, I touched Dotty's blanket-covered shoulder. She flinched but did not turn her head toward me.

"Dotty, I am going to get help. Everything is going to be better."

I raced through Puss-face's room to the boys' dormitory then down the central stairs all the way to the kitchen.

Colleen

I was standing on a step stool next to the stove to give me the right height and angle to stir a large pot of vegetable soup for tomorrow's dinner when I sensed Sean. We had become so close that I usually could feel his arrival moments before he showed up physically speaking. Sean moved with quick soft steps like a cat. I half turned away from the stove and watched the doorway. He appeared a second later, but his usual lopsided grin was missing. Sean's face was tense, and I could see the red color high on his cheeks. This was a sure sign of his temper getting away from him.

"Sean! What is it?" I stepped down from the stool and ran toward him. "What's wrong?"

"Those fooking abominable nuns," he spattered. "They have almost killed Dotty. She needs help. She is bleeding!"

"Bleeding!" I gasped. "Where is she?"

"Come with me," he ordered.

I grabbed some white cloths we used for drying dishes and a bottle of brandy from the priest's larder. Soundlessly, we crept up the stairs. Dorothy lay on the bare wood floor of a narrow room. She had curled into a fetal position with a sheet wrapped tightly around her torso. I knelt down next to her and whispered in her ear.

"Dotty, we are here now. Let me help you."

Tears were streaming down her face and her breath was coming out in ragged gasps. Blood was spreading across the sheet covering her back. Sean and I turned her as gently as we could. Then I peeled the sheet back and inspected the work of Perpetua and Eucharius. In my mind, they were cruel, yes, but the beatings they inflicted on the children of this horrible place was unforgivable. Dotty was hardly more than a child herself. Her back was a scarlet mosaic of open welts that bled profusely. We gave her a sip of the brandy to help ease the pain. I looked up at my brother, "Sean get us some warm water and soap!"

He turned and disappeared down the hallway to the lavatory room. He returned with a small basin filled with water that sloshed over the sides and a bar of soap. The basin was so small that he had to make multiple trips back and forth the hallway to empty the bloody water and refill it with clean water. Each time, I tried to stem the flow of blood by holding the dishcloths tightly against her skin. When I felt I had cleaned the wounds sufficiently I was ready to try to bandage her up.

"Sean please take these cloths and rip them into three or four-inch widths. Now tie all of the strips together in sets of three."

I folded some of the torn cloths into squares and placed them on the deepest wounds.

"We have to wrap this tightly," I warned. "So the bleeding stops."

I gave her another sip of the brandy. Then Sean and I began wrapping the torn dish cloth segments around her thin torso. All the while, Dotty whimpered in pain.

Sean said, "We have to get her out of here. They said they were coming back. If they see she has been helped, all hell will break loose."

He looked squarely at Dotty, "Can you walk?"

In answer to him, she grabbed my arm and pulled herself shakily to her feet. I nodded to Sean, "Sean go back to the kitchen and light the flame under the soup pot for me. I will help Dotty to get dressed and ready."

"I have an escape route in the yard."

"What?"

"We can get Dotty to the fence where a tree came down then she can be on St. Mark's Place and out of here with no one knowing."

"I do not, not think I can climb a fence," Dotty said.

"Sean go to the kitchen! We haven't much time."

He vanished from the little room silently. I helped Dotty to the bed and she looked at me with wet eyes.

"Thank you for, for..." She started crying again.

I put a finger to her lips. "Dotty, sweet Dotty. You can thank us later at another place and another time. Because you are getting out of here tonight."

"My dress is ripped," she moaned. "I don't have anything to wear other than this kitchen smock." I heard the bells start chiming calling the sisters to prayer in the chapel. When the sounds of nuns tromping down the stairs subsided, I looked into the adjourning room to see an armoire standing open. It gave me an idea. I slipped into the room to get what I needed. In a few minutes, I returned, my arms full. "Here now, let's get you dressed," I said.

Sean

While I waited in the kitchen for Colleen and Dotty, my stomach rumbled so I decided to give the soup a taste. Then I heard a sound behind me at the kitchen door. As I turned, my heart froze. I couldn't move. I held the bowl of soup and a spoon. A nun was standing with her back to me. My mouth went dry and my hands shook. If hot soup splashed on my hands, I did not feel it. We had been discovered. Dorothy Gale had been discovered! Everything was falling apart. We are all in for it now! Mikey must have been caught red-handed with Dotty. Our stash of money would be found. Our escape plan wrecked. Mikey would not talk but Dotty was in no condition to resist another Mother Superior's 'interview.'

Then Mikey stepped from behind the nun with a wan smile on her face. As the nun raised her head and turned toward me, I steeled myself for what was to come.

"Hello, Sean."

I blinked, blinked again. The transformation was defying my imagination

Dorothy Gale was in the full habit of the Good Sisters of St. Joseph. I looked at Dotty, then to Mikey, and back to Dotty. Cripes! This is too good. My mind was working on a better escape plan than just making a dash for the fence. Dorothy would walk out with her head held high.

Colleen

When Dotty and I reached the kitchen, she was breathing hard. Her eyes were red rimmed and hollow looking, a part of her had died. I reached for her hand, it was cold to the touch. Sean nearly jumped out of his skin when he saw how Dotty was dressed. It was a perfect disguise, and I could not resist the irony of dressing her in a nun's habit!

It was too large for her of course. We had to hitch the skirt up, doubling the waistband several times so she would not trip and to keep the skirt from slipping off her thin hips. The head piece and black veil gave her a funereal appearance that deepened the dark circles and empty look of her eyes.

Sean said, "My God, Dotty you scared the wits out of me! Cripes, you looked like Perpetua. I thought that Perpetua had caught us all!"

I stepped back and realized Sean was right, she did look like Perpetua, if you glanced briefly or from a distance. Dotty was about the same height and held her posture in much of the same way. Dotty swallowed a groan, no doubt miserable at the very thought of resembling her nemesis. She slumped to the floor in a heap of flowing black. I poured a little more brandy for her and held it to her lips.

"How are we to get out? How are we to get away?" she whispered frantically. "Right now, leave that to me. You must get away, not us. If we must answer questions, we'll be sending them on a wild goose chase. We'll say that you were heading for the Outerbridge to New Jersey. Meanwhile you'll be on the ferry to freedom."

"But Sean, I thought that you and Colleen would be coming with me"

Sean and I exchanged looks. I said, "Dotty, you cannot be here another minute. They'll kill you."

Sean smiled that lopsided grin of his, "We will all be out of this evil place soon enough, don't you worry. But now we need to get going."

I said, "Vespers will be over soon. Then we will have Perpetua breathing down our necks. I think we can have a new escape route dressed as you are. You are not climbing over or under any fences."

Sean looked at me, "Right-o. I think the front door is the way to go."

With that, he took Dotty's arm and propelled her toward the passageway that led to the parlor and the front door.

"Mikey, you stay put."

"Not on yer life," I retorted.

I looked around the kitchen thinking we might need something for defense. I grabbed a large iron skillet from the sideboard. Usually, I had trouble lifting it but tonight it seemed much lighter. I followed Sean and Dotty as they marched through the hallway past the parlor and into the main foyer and the heavy wooden door to freedom.

Dotty's chest was heaving from exertion or panic, probably both. It seemed like her raspy breathing could wake the dead. I put my arm around her and pulled her close. She winced in pain.

"Sorry. But you need to calm yourself. Control your breathing. Don't be afraid. Breathe slowly and deeply. It always helps me when I am scared."

Sean said, "Dotty, just think about being out of here and away from these hellish nuns!"

He turned to the door and pulled the latch that held the bolt. It moved with a scratching sound. Ridiculously I said, "Shhhh…" He just grinned at me and yanked the bolt free. The door sung open. It was like a dream. The foyer was bathed in moonlight. All at once, I wanted to run through the door and keep on running. As if reading my thoughts, Sean took my face in his hands. He did not utter a word. But his eyes spoke to me, 'soon, Mikey, soon. Just not now.'

He took Dotty by the hand and marched her through the doorway and down the front path. I stood on the threshold and watched them go. Sean took Dotty's arm to steady her halting steps. Just past the communicating walkway to the far side of the garden and chapel Sean stopped. He was speaking in a low voice to Dotty. I could not make out his words. Then instead of continuing down the path Dotty knelt as in prayer. 'Pray later' I thought. The moonlight shone around them illuminating the path with a silvery light. Sean gently brought her back onto her feet. Then the two turned away and disappeared from my view. They were going in the wrong direction! Sean turned to me and signaled with his hand, telling me to wait. I stood in the threshold as each excruciating minute ticked by. Suddenly they reappeared on the pathway. Sean put both hands on her forearms and spoke to her. Dotty shook her head then Sean handed her a small white package. It looked like one of the white kitchen cloths. She clutched the little package to her chest. Sean turned on his heel and walked briskly back to where I was standing. Dotty turned to us, and I could see tears streaming down her cheeks. She raised her hand then turned and ever so slowly continued walking down the path.

I whispered to myself, "She is going to make it. We did it…"

Then disaster struck.

Sean

All right, my idea of brass was for Dotty to walk past Mother Superior's office right out the front door to St. Mark's Place. Then, it's only a short walk to the Staten Island Ferry. From there she could be in Manhattan out of this hellhole. Once there, we were sure that with our money and some luck she could make a new life for herself.

Dotty was trembling and sweating into the white triangle of her nun's headpiece. This escape plan might be too brassy. Mikey poked me, jerking her head toward Dotty.

"Sean, let's let her rest for a moment."

"Sure."

"I need to sit," Dorothy said as she slumped to the floor.

A full moon was rising in the east flooding the kitchen with blue light. The three of us sat on the floor in utter silence.

"Sean!" Mikey said wrenching me by the arm to look at her. "We have, have to get her out tonight but we can't carry her to the ferry. She needs to get there on her own two feet." Looking me straight in eye, she said, "For god's sake, don't make her any more frightened than she is."

Mikey stood up and poured more of the brandy into a glass for Dotty. The drink worked to bring Dotty around. Holding the glass of amber liquid for Dotty, Mikey turned to arch an eyebrow at me.

"Well?" She asked.

"Here's the plan. I will go through the passageway to the front rooms. If it is quiet, I will come back to help you and Dotty. If I get caught. I'll make a ruckus. You two will have to come up with another plan. If it is quiet, then we'll keep going right out the front door. Meanwhile, you keep watch from here to signal us of any trouble. Dotty and I will continue down the path toward the rectory and the churchyard. From there, Dotty will be able to make it to the street, then down the hill to the ferry dock without a problem."

"That sounds good. Does it sound good to you Dotty?"

She nodded, took another swallow from the glass, coughed then to our surprise, smiled, saying, "I won't be forgetting you."

I slipped silently from the kitchen and through the passageway to the front of the house. I returned a few moments later grinning. "Looks good, time to go." I helped Dotty to her feet.

"Mikey, you stay here."

"Not on yer life."

With that we were off to the races.

As Dorothy and I entered the gravel path between the trees and hedgerow, she paused, turned to wave to Mikey. I patted her arm to indicate that she should go on.

Dorothy whispered, "I have to say farewell to my Tommy."

"What?"

"My Tommy is buried here."

Tommy? Little Tommy! Dorothy? Holy Cow! I never guessed. She must be Tommy's mother.

Now I wondered if Tommy knew.

At Tommy's grave, Dotty knelt with hands clasped in prayer. There was no time for this. We retraced our steps to the front walkway. I pushed a small packet into Dotty's hand, "Here, here is some money that you will need." Dotty started to walk, slowly down the path to the street, I stepped back into the shadows of the tall trees lining the path. Suddenly a loud voice called out of the darkness, "Who is there?"

The light slipping from closing door of the church sacristy outlined a nun who was brandishing a walking stick. It was that fooking Eucharius!

"Who is that? Sister, Sister where are you going?"

Then with her robes flying like a terrible night bird of prey, Eucharius launched herself toward Dotty. She grabbed at Dotty's cloak to stop her.

Cripes! We are all going to be caught! I have to get Mikey out of here!

Too late! Mikey was running down the path.

Dotty continued walking briskly away and did not turn despite Eucharius' grip twisting her arm. But Eucharius tightened her grip forcing Dotty to stop. As Dotty started to turn shadowy clouds moved across the moon enclosing us in darkness. Dotty slapped Eucharius a hard right in the kisser! There was silence for a moment then a metallic ring. Eucharius dropped to her knees then fell face first.

Colleen

Coming around the path from the chapel was a dark figure. It was one of the nuns and it was evident that she saw Dotty. As the dark figure grew closer, I saw it was Eucharius.

She hastened her step. "Sister! Sister! Where are you going? What are you doing? Sister, Sister!"

Dotty did not turn and continued walking onward, faster now but she was no match in her condition for Eucharius. Now Eucharius could hustle when she wanted. I heard Sean mutter "no fooking way!" I was vaguely aware that Sean was running in my direction. But I was already out onto the path. Eucharius was closing the gap between herself and Dotty.

She was yelling now, "Sister! Stop!"

I ran as fast as I could toward the impending melee. Eucharius was just reaching out for Dotty's cloak. Dotty turned her head.

Eucharius exclaimed, "You!"

Dotty slapped Eucharius really hard. The slap stopped Sean momentarily. I caught up to the three of them just as Eucharius took hold of Dotty's arm twisting it. The little white package fell from Dotty's hand as Eucharius spun her. I raised the iron skillet in both of my hands and with all of my might brought it down on Eucharius' head. She dropped like a stone in a great big heap of black. Her headdress and veil askew slightly covering her face.

Sean picked up the white package and shoved it into Dotty's shaking hands. "Go! Go Dotty!"

Sean turned to me, grabbed the skillet from my hands and propelled me in a run back to the kitchen. Actually, I am not sure that my feet were touching the ground. We seemed to fly. Somehow, we made it back to the kitchen.

He hissed "Quiet."

Then he washed the skillet though there was no blood on it that I could see. He dried it thoroughly and returned it to the sideboard.

"Say nothing. Not a word, Mikey, Fierce Mikey." He grinned. "Finish the soup and go to bed. Say nothing. Not a word to anyone," he repeated. "Soup, then to bed with you."

He kissed my cheek and ran up the back stairs to the boy's dorm.

Chapter 7
Out of the Frying Pan

Colleen

13 October 1920

I was keeping busy organizing the pantry, cleaning the countertops, checking the kitchen inventory, anything rather than think about last night. But my thoughts kept returning to that terrible moment. Dotty escaped but, in the process, I hurt Eucharius, maybe even killed her. I never imagined I could do such a thing to another person. All at once, I knew that I hated Eucharius and she stood between Dotty making a clean break and Sean and I from being found out. Perpetua would relish punishing us to the extreme. I am sure we would be put into prison and since it was me that slammed the frying pan down on her head, I would suffer the worst punishment. I could be hanged for murder. I heard a rustle of nun's habit and looked up as Sr. Vianny rushed into the kitchen.

Vianny said, "Mother Perpetua found Sister Eucharius on the front walkway last night. She collapsed coming from the sacristy! One of the Magdalene women, Dorothy Gale, has gone missing!"

"Oh my God! How horrible," I exclaimed, trying my best to sound shocked at the news.

She looked intently at me. "Tell me, Colleen, do you know anything about Dorothy? Do you know where she is?"

I shook my head and said, "How is Sister Eucharius?"

She eyed me closely. "The doctor was called immediately as we feared she suffered a stroke. But it seems she lost consciousness. She has a severe headache, but the doctor says she was probably struck by something and she will fully recover. Mother Perpetua has accused Dorothy Gale of beating Eucharius as she made her getaway."

"Oh, Dorothy couldn't have, she couldn't hurt anyone," I stammered.

"I thought the same, though Perpetua is sure the culprit is Dorothy Gale. If not Dorothy then how do you suppose Eucharius got hurt?"

"Perhaps she stumbled and hit her head?"

Vianny searched my face. "No, the doctor thinks she was hit from behind. What do you know, Colleen? Was it one of the boys?"

"I really don't know anything at all about, about Eucharius. I admit I don't like her much but I am relieved that she is alright. She was hit from behind? Did she see anyone?"

"Relieved? That's an odd thing to say when you say you know nothing about her injury!"

I just shrugged. "I guess it sounds odd, but I really don't like to hear of anyone getting hurt or sick. Vianny, I used a poor choice of words, that's all."

Her eyes bore holes into mine. I turned and busied myself with the breakfast set up. Just then, Perpetua swept into the kitchen. She was looking straight at me. I thought, 'Oh God, she knows, she knows!'

Perpetua spat her words like knives at me, "Your pal Dorothy Gale has almost killed poor Sister Eucharius and now she is on the run. I have summoned the police and it is merely a matter of time until the criminal is apprehended and put into jail for the rest of her life. Where has she gone? Where is she hiding?"

I stammered, "I really do not know anything Sister." I looked at her squarely and set my jaw.

Perpetua hissed, "I don't believe you, girl. You know. I will beat it out of you if necessary!"

Vianny stepped between us. "I've spoken at length with Colleen about this terrible incident. She is not involved at all."

Perpetua turned on her heel but before she left the kitchen she turned once again to me. "If I find any proof that you are lying, if I find any proof that you know where Gale is…if I find any proof that you and that no good brother of yours is involved in this, beware, girl. You better pray that Sister Eucharius doesn't remember anything more about the events of last night. Because I know in my gut you are guilty. If I find one shred of proof, you will wish you were never born." She turned to Vianny and said, "And you would be wise to keep your busy nose of out this. Fair warning, Sister Vianny!"

Later that day, I heard some of the girls gossiping about Dotty. Apparently, someone reported that one of the sisters of the order of St. Joseph was seen boarding the early morning ferry bound for Manhattan. It was notable to the ferryman as the sisters rarely went out alone and almost never on the early 5 am boat.

Perpetua was filled with animosity toward Dotty whom she was sure had hit Eucharius. The police constable was called in to speak to Sister Eucharius and get a full description of the criminal, Dorothy Gale. But it was Eucharius in the end that got Dotty off the hook. I was summoned to Eucharius' room after the constable arrived. Eucharius, in her ditzy manner was holding her bandaged head moaning, fully enjoying all the attention she was getting. She was propped up in her bed with the policeman sitting in a chair next to her bed taking notes. I had just brought some soup for the injured patient when Perpetua stormed into the room.

"That wanton Magdalene woman will pay for hitting you in the head! She will pay for what she has done to you!"

"What? Who? What woman? You mean Dorothy Gale? She did not hit me. I am sure of it!" Eucharius said.

"What do you mean? Surely you are confused…"

"No, *Gross Mutter*. I am not confused. I know what I saw and the last thing I saw was Dorothy Gale in one of our sister's habits running down the path away from me. She turned and looked straight at me. I know what I saw. The next thing I knew I was falling hard then you found me. My head hurts so. Can I have another warm compress?"

The Policeman concluded much to Perpetua's chagrin that Eucharius stumbled and hit her head and that while Dorothy Gale had stolen a sister's habit and run away it was a smaller crime and not much worth his time. Truth be told, I think he didn't care much for Perpetua. And he was happy to have proven her wrong in her accusations. I could see it in his expression as he told her as much.

So, in the end, Dorothy Gale had indeed escaped the evils of the St. Joseph's Home for Orphaned Children. Sean and I eluded detection. I had not murdered Eucharius. But that moment of hatred that fueled me with the strength to hit her and knock her out was still there. And it frightened me. What kind of person was I?

Chapter 8
The Changeling

*Irish folklore: a deformed, imbecilic or ugly offspring of the fairies that is substituted for a beautiful human child

Sean
18 March 1923
Three Years Later
St. Joseph's Orphanage, Staten Island, New York

Unconfirmed report that Vladimir Lenin has died after suffering a stroke (WCBS Radio News)

This has been a good day. I was being punished for not being at bed count last night. I tried to slip into the boys' dorm room, but Puss-face Aloysius was waiting for me. After getting six or seven raps of a ruler across my knuckles, she gave me the good news—I would be cleaning lavatories on both the boys' and girls' dorms as well as on the classroom floor below. That would mean that I would not get to enjoy choir practice. That was just peachy.

I was on my knees cleaning under the sinks when the familiar thumping footsteps of Puss-face echoed off the lavatory walls. Turning toward the sound, I bumped my head on a pipe.

"Callaghan, stop what you are doing. You'll finish it later."
"Yes, Sister Aloysius," I said.
"Wipe that bold brazen grin off your face Callaghan."
"Yes, Sister, Aloysius," I said with deliberate pauses, hoping to bait her.
She pinned me with a stare, then said. "Come with me."

Out into the hall to the main stairs, then down we went to the first floor. The etched glass of the doors to St. Marks Place scattered light into hundreds of small rainbows. It must be cold and windy outside. Doors rattled with each gust. Puss-face knocked on the door to Mother Superior's office.

Oh, brother, this was not good, not good at all. Cripes, was lavatory cleaning not enough? What have I done to deserve this? I remembered the punishment Mikey had described when she was brought before Mother Superior. I gritted my teeth and followed old Puss-face into the office.

It was comfortably warm. A fire was crackling in a fireplace behind Mother Superior who was engrossed with papers on her huge oak desk. The flames outlined her with shimmering red, orange and yellow light. A boy dressed in fine woolens the kind that I had only seen in the papers was sitting a chair across from her. He wore mahogany brown herringbone knickerbockers, white knee-high socks, shiny black shoes, a wool jacket with a matching cap held in his hands. A light camel-colored topcoat was draped over the back of his chair. But that was not the most amazing aspect of this boy. What was amazing was he was eating or at least chewing on some food as he sat there.

I estimated that the boy must be about 11 or 12. He was taller than me. He certainly weighed more. What was this about?

The door to the office opened again. This time it was Mikey and Sister Vianny! With quick clipped steps, Mikey was at my side grasping my hand with both of hers.

Mother Superior looked up, "Callaghan and you too missy I want you to meet someone—your brother, Ian Callaghan."

Mikey looked up at me with a face that was even more surprised than when she entered the office. She blinked, blinked some more then swallowed hard turning to look at the boy in the chair. It was so obvious that he was surprised too. Our eyes flickered from one face to the other but not a word was spoken. That is when I heard a woman crying softly. A visit to Mother Superior's office would not be complete without someone crying.

The boy, our brother started to cry too. I followed the sound of a woman's sobs to a man and woman huddled together on a small sofa on the far side of the office near a set of double doors. The woman had on a wide brimmed hat, a fawn colored felt coat with a fur collar and black high-buttoned shoes. I could not see her face due to the hat. A man wearing a three-piece navy-blue suit with a gold watch chain linking one side of his vest with the other. A medallion on the chain flickered in the sunlight from the St. Marks Place windows. His maroon tie contrasted with a pearl white high collar shirt. Parted in the middle, his wavy brown hair must have been lustered by Brilliantine. These people are swells!

No one spoke. It was so quiet that the hallway pendulum clock could be heard through the closed doors. Tick, tick, tick, tick. The man stood assisting the woman to her feet. She still could not hold her head up such was the sobbing. Arm in arm they walked stately, even elegantly to our brother. Ian leaped from the chair clasping the woman, burying his face in the bosom of her felt coat.

"DON'T LEAVE ME!" He begged. "DON'T!"

"Be brave son. Be a brave boy. This is for the best. The Sisters will take excellent care of you," the man said.

Mother Superior arose slowly, ever so slowly from her chair. She nodded to the man. "It is best that you leave. We have everything under control. You *haf mein* word."

Her control of her Prussian accent was briefly lost. We had noticed that her accent seemed to be less in the years after the visit by the Cardinal. Anti-German sentiment during the Great War contributed to this, no doubt.

The woman peeled Ian from her coat, produced a silk handkerchief to gently wipe his face. Ian still reached out with both arms. She kissed his cheeks ever so gently.

"Don't go, please. Please!"

Moving quicker than I ever knew she could, Mother Superior had Ian's shoulders clasped with both hands.

"You should go," she said quietly.

The man and woman stepped to the office door. As the man opened it, the woman turned, lifted her head looking longingly toward Ian. It was a beautiful face. Brown ringlets framed a porcelain flawless face with the most beautiful green eyes. She blew Ian a kiss with a gloved hand, as the man escorted her from the room. The man closed the door behind them with a click.

Mother Superior had taken two or three steps back from Ian. Her eyes were two steel cannons searching for a target-me or...

Colleen

20 July 1923

The famed bandit and revolutionary Pancho Villa was assassinated in Parrel, Mexico (Arizona Republican, 21 July 1923)

Sean wanted us to 'break out' of the orphanage. I never really learned the plans because that bony nun took away his recess privileges and one week later, I was called into Mother Hilda Perpetua's office.

She looked me over like I was some insect and said, "Clean yourself up, girl. You are going to be seen for an adoption. If you look presentable maybe the fine German couple that I have coming tomorrow may want you, though I can't image why."

"I need to talk to my brother" I said.

Stone-faced, she glared at me, "Shut your nasty, vile mouth. You will speak only when I say that you can. You will talk to whom I say you can talk. Get out of here and take a bath."

I cried myself to sleep that night. I thought "What if they take me away and I never see my brothers again? What will happen to me? Who are these people? What will happen to Sean? And poor Ian, he is so young!" It was bad enough that we are orphans in this miserable place but being separated from Sean was too much to bear. At least, he'll have Ian.

My misery at the thought of being adopted by strangers did not last long. The next morning, I found myself back in Mother Perpetua's office. To my great relief, Sean holding Ian's hand walked into the room. He grabbed my hand and pulled me to his side. He said nothing just pointed with his chin. I looked from the Mother Perpetua and back to Sean. "Are we all being adopted?"

At this comment, Perpetua let out a raspy chortle. "No, you are not being adopted." With a wolfish smile, she said, "Seems your blessed mother wants you back, the lot of you."

Mother! Mother? Orphans don't have mothers.

21 July 1923

Sean

The day had begun as most days at St. Joe's, someone was whipped by Sister Eucharius for going too slow; we went to mass in the church; we ate a quick porridge breakfast then lessons. Catechism first and a few ruler raps across your knuckles. It was in math class that Sister Cecilia came to the classroom door and asked for me!

As I left the classroom all eyes were on me. All the boys were glad that it was not one of them being called. Being called to the door only meant one thing. Mother Superior and that meant pain. Red McGregor smirked at me as I walked past his desk.

What could they have caught me doing? Did they find the tunnel? Did they find the secret cache of clothes under the stairs? Could they have figured out that I helped Dotty escape? Somebody must have snitched. Who? What was this about?

At another classroom, Sister Cecilia collected Ian. As we approached Mother Superior's office, Sister Cecilia turned to smile at me. Was there a cruel smirk in her grin? I didn't think that she was as mean as the others but perhaps she was.

She opened the door to the office. I held my head high and walked over the threshold.

It must be worse than I imagined! Standing to the side of Mother Superior's desk was Mikey! This was holy hell to pay. I've done something that will get us a beating. What did I do?

"About time. Stand over there," Mother Superior said, slowly rising to her full height. "Let us finish this business."

In a sweeping movement of her habit clad arm like a flopping black wing, she pointed to a woman sitting on the plush chair opposite us. The woman was dressed in green with a cloche hat adorned with a long pheasant feather and a pale green scarf knotted at her shoulder. She held a brown leather handbag in her lap and her skirt just covered her knees. Shocking. Scandalous. Yet, the woman was dressed just like the pictures we saw in the newspapers. Holy Cow as Jimmy would say.

"Here," said Mother Superior. "Here is your mother!"

I think that I heard Mikey's jaw hit the floor. Ian looked to me with eyes as wide as a dinner plate. Mikey had taken a step back as if she had been struck. What? This cannot be. We have been here for 10 years. OK, Ian has been in St. Joe's just a few months but still…

"*Kommen*, introduce yourself to your mother," Mother Superior said pointing now to Mikey.

Mikey took hesitating steps toward the woman who took something out of her handbag. The woman opened a metallic object in her left hand. From the object she produced a circular pad that she used to dab on her nose and cheeks as Mikey slowly approached. Mikey's curtsy was Prussian-perfection as reflected by Mother Superior's chin thrust.

"I am Colleen Callaghan, Madame."

The woman continued to rub something on her nose with only a quick glance at Mikey. Then Ian stepped forward to stand by Mikey. He bowed formally with his right arm across his waist.

"I am, I am, I am…" he said nervously. "Ian, Ian Callaghan."

It was my turn. I glanced quickly at Mother Superior and smiled. As I turned toward the woman, I put on a serious face. I stepped forward. I stopped a foot closer to her than they had. After a three second count, I clicked my heels and with arms rigidly held at my sides, fingers aligned with the seam of my pants, I bowed. She looked up at the Prussian heel-click and we locked eyes. The steel-blue eyes showed no emotion. None. I did not get a chance to introduce myself though.

"What happened to this one? He wasn't cockeyed when I left him with you. Look at this changeling. Oh, never mind." She turned her eyes from me to Mother Superior.

Addressing Mother Superior, the woman said in a way that suggested that she was used to being obeyed, "How quickly can they leave? I have to be back at the Garden this afternoon."

"They will be quick, I assure you. Sister Cecilia will see to it," said Mother Superior.

All it took was a wordless look from Mother Superior for Sister Cecilia to tap us on our shoulders. She whirled in a quick about-face to the office door. We meekly followed.

Chapter 9
The General

Sean

July 1923

I started to refer to this woman, our mother, as The General. It was obvious the woman who was our mother was certainly used to being obeyed. Even Mother Superior oblige her. The General took the three of us out on a Staten Island street for the first time in years. Well, at least for Mikey and me it was.

On the pavement outside, I looked back at St. Joe's, puzzled at the abruptness of it all and a little afraid of the future. At St. Joe's, I knew the lay of the land. I knew what I needed to do get through the day to keep me, Colleen and Ian safe. Without saying a single word, the General took Colleen's hand and started us on a quick march to the St. George ferry landing.

The General snapped orders at the three of us as if we were her soldiers. Ian actually saluted her. I laughed. Mistake, that salute and laugh earned us both a smack in the face.

As we braced for the follow up slap, she said, "There will be no shenanigans boyos! We have a ferry to catch."

As we walked down the long hill to the ferry, I was amazed by all the sights and sounds on the street. I stared at the electric streetlamps that looked so different from gas lamps. Horseless carriages of different sizes and shapes labored up the hill while others charged down to the ferry landing going very fast. There were a few horse-drawn wagons but not many.

The women that we passed wore small hats perched like birds on their heads. Meanwhile, men were wearing bowler hats or skimmers and high collared white shirts with dark colored suits. The boys and girls we passed all looked different.

They weren't dressed much different from the orphans at St. Joe's. I could not say how, but they were just different. At the ferry, my mother paid her fare then insisted that we should ride for free since we were all under eight years old. I glanced at Colleen in silent communication to say nothing. Ian just looked confused. The ferryman in fare booth eyed us suspiciously then insisted that at least Ian who was the tallest of us must be eight or nine. That set my mother into an Irish shouting match with him. The three of us stood there watching, waiting, listening and wondering which of us would be chosen to get on the ferry. The shouting became louder and attracted the attention of the ferry's crew. Finally, a man who was dressed as an admiral came, pulled the ferryman aside leaving my mother to steam on her own.

Seagulls overhead began their own noisy argument. As noisy as the birds were, they were no match for General's voice. As for Mikey and me, we thought that Sister Puss-face was loud when she got into a rage. We were mistaken because the woman calling herself mother has a voice that would rouse the dead. If the man with the fancy sailor suit had not come along, I think mother's voice would have shattered the glass of the ticket booth.

The admiral returned.

"What county do you hail from me darling?"

"Kerry"

"'Tisn't this a fine thing! I'm a Kerryman too."

While I had no idea where Kerry was, they did. Maybe Kerry was a street name. Then the admiral offered the General his arm as led us past the red-faced ticket booth man. The five of us walked on the ferry. Once on board the ferry, the admiral turned and squatted in front of Colleen, "What is your name, you pretty colleen?"

"Colleen."

"No darling, what is your name?"

"Colleen. Colleen is my name."

He laughed, stood up, then tipped his hat to mother saying, "No rest for the wicked. I have to get this boat going. Toora-Loora!"

With that he took the stair to the upper deck two at a time.

Horseless and horse drawn carts were loaded in the center of the ferry. Passengers could sit on the wicker seats or stand holding a suspended leather strap. There were plenty of seats inside and the General took one. Ian noticed that some passengers were gathering at the opposite end of the ferry. We went to look. Mother, the General was uninterested, picked up a newspaper that was on the bench next to her.

"Hey Ian! Look at all the horseless carriages!" I said pointing to vehicles lining the interior of the ferry.

A man sitting by the railing said, "Sonny you sound like me dear old Ma. They are called 'motorcars' not horseless carriages. Where have you been since the Titanic sunk?"

I was about to say that I was in an orphanage for over ten years, when Colleen let out a sharp cry. The ferry abruptly pulled away from the St. George dock and into New York Bay. White knuckled, Colleen gripped a handrail for dear life.

"Issss the-the boat saaaa-sinking?" she stammered.

Ian and I laughed then we took her hands.

"We got you. You are safe," Ian said. He turned then pointed in the direction that the ferry was traveling.

"Look."

There it was Manhattan. Through the mist of the July humidity, we saw the skyline emerge. As the ferry plowed through the waves, we could see all the tall buildings. The buildings seemed to grow as if by magic rising out of the steel-gray water with sea gull cries filling the air. The birds whirled around the ferry, diving then hovering. The man who had made fun of me was standing at the railing of the ferry throwing breadcrumbs to the birds. The air was clean and fresh. The saltwater spray made me feel as free as the birds.

Almost too soon, a blast of the ferry's horn signaled docking at the ferry slip in Manhattan. We were swayed back and forth with the docking. The General appeared at our side; without a word she took Colleen's hand. The four of us followed the crowd off the boat and into Manhattan. We walked and gawked. Ian and I tripped over cobblestones because we were mesmerized by the buildings. I tried to count how tall they were by counting the windows. One was 32 windows tall!

"Hurry up you two!" the General commanded.

When the General led us down some stairs. I exchanged glances with Ian. He winked that it was fine. Then the noise and a rush of air blew into our faces. The green gates had a sign that read: South Ferry. There the General pushed Colleen under a wooden capstan bar to the other side of the green gates. She waved at us, and we did the same. She put a nickel in a slot next to a wood bar, then pushed herself up against it until she was completely through. A train roared into the station, doors opened, people got off and we got on the car for our first subway ride. There were men in suits wearing skimmers holding leather straps to steady themselves. Most were reading carefully folded newspapers as the train clattered and swayed. There was so much to see. We grinned at each other in excitement. Meanwhile, the General sat on a wicker laced bench ignoring us.

Chapter 10
Hell's Kitchen

In 1835, Davy Crockett said, "In my part of the country, when you meet an Irishman, you find a first-rate gentleman; but these are worse than savages; they are too mean to swab hell's kitchen."

Sean
21-22 July 1923

"I'll beat the bejesus out of you if you wake Mr. Connolly."

The General had led us three to the 45th street brownstone just off 10th Avenue. Then it was up to a third-floor walkup apartment. As she fumbled with a large ring of keys, she admonished, no really ordered us to be quiet.

Who is 'Mr. Connolly', I thought but did not dare ask. The General said, "That is an order! I will not be disobeyed."

Ian saluted her and got a hand across his face for it.

"Cheeky little brat!" the General said. "Silence!"

As she opened the door, Ian was fighting back tears.

We entered an airless front room and were confronted by the view of a big man sleeping on a sofa. He wore a thin white cotton shirt that had no sleeves, brown pants and socks. A pair of ankle boots were tumbled next to the sofa. I guessed that this must be 'Mr. Connolly'. With a hand signal, the General directed us into a small kitchen. There was a stove, sink, an icebox, a small table with two chairs set by a window that looked out across to another brownstone's windows. We stood in the kitchen silently. Mikey and I held our small paper sack of clothes while Ian held the carpet bag that his foster parents had provided him. Ian had more clothes than Mikey and I combined. It was his only legacy from those good people who had fostered him.

Looking from Mikey to Ian, she hissed, "Sit."

She did not even look at me. I correctly guessed that I would stand.

Wordlessly, the General took out a pot and began to cook something in it. She set out three bowls and spoons. She ladled a thick brown soup with some kind of meat into three bowls. She merely pointed to the bowls and said, "Eat."

Mikey and Ian sat and began eating. Since breakfast at St. Joe's, we had not had anything. There was no chair for me, so I ate standing up leaning over the small table. The meat was almost tasteless. The broth tasted good but then when you are that hungry, a boiled shoe might be delicious.

We had no sooner finished when the General appeared with a folded brown wool blanket.

"Clean the dishes and pot," she ordered Mikey. Then to Ian and myself she said, "You two this way."

As we walked through the front room, Mr. Connolly was still snoring loudly. She opened the door to the stairs. Ian and I were befuddled as she pushed us out the door. I had the blanket thrust into my chest.

"Get a job," she said slamming the door behind. Smart as a pistol shot, I heard the apartment lock bolt slam.

One blanket for me and Ian. Ian's face registered shock, fear. He looked around the landing and the stairs. This was far worse than St. Joe's. His foster parents had not treated him like this. I am sure that he had not expect to be treated this way by his real mother. Me, I had no expectations. Sure, I can take it. I can take anything. I took all that those nuns at St. Joe's could do. Those Prussians were meaner that cornered rats. If the Kaiser had a regiment of nuns, Germany would have won the Great War. Those damned nuns did not care if you were cold or hungry. They only cared if you did your chores perfectly, kneeled still and could recite the catechism word for word. If you had to use the lavatory, it was only with their permission.

There was a time back in the orphanage, when Jim Hurley pissed in his bed one cold winter night. There was never enough heat for the dorm room anyway. I think that it must have been a large chicken coop before the Church bought it. Jimmy asked to go to the lav, but Sister Puss-face said, "No."

When she saw that he didn't hold it, she ordered him outside to scrub his mattress. There was a light dusting of snow on the recess courtyard when Jimmy dragged his mattress and blanket out. He was wearing just a shirt and pants with shoes that were too big. We watched him from the boys' windows as he took buckets of water to the mattress and blanket then scrubbing them with a floor brush. We could see him shaking with the cold. When he returned, he used newspapers to cover the mattress and under the blanket to keep warm that night.

I used Jimmy's idea to keep us both warm in that stairwell. I found newspapers on the street outside the brownstone. I layered them under us and between the folded blanket. Jimmy's idea to stay warm worked in Hell's Kitchen too.

So, sleeping on the stairs with one blanket and newspapers bunched as a mattress under Ian and me wasn't the worst. At St. Joe's if you had too many demerits, the nuns took your blanket. Sure, you were cold. After two nights, it was easier to fall asleep. I went to sleep in that stairwell knowing that I had to do something as soon as day broke. I slipped into a dreamless sleep.

I slept until a sharp pain violently brought me awake. A man in canvas pants carrying a lunch pail stood over us. He gave me another kick to wake up. Ian awoke briefly then pulled the blanket over his head. Amazingly, Ian went right back to sleep. I was up. The kick made me sore and angry.

The man continued down the stairwell. Using the banister post, I pulled myself up without disturbing Ian. Then I followed the man down and out to 45th street. In the hazy light before dawn, streetlamps were still lit. I followed him. At 9th Avenue, the lunch-bucket man turned right. About halfway down the avenue he opened a door and disappeared. I walked up to the door that had a large green shamrock etched on the glass and a sign that read Limerick Bar & Grill. The word 'bar' was partially covered by a sign that proclaimed: PROHIBITED TO SELL, MANUFACTURE OR DISTRIBUTE ALCOHOLIC BEVERAGES BY LAW.

I walked past the door to stand in front of a hardware store. I waited for lunch bucket man to emerge.

After a while, I walked to the Limerick to look inside. In the low light of the tavern, I spotted my man as put his head back and poured whiskey down his throat. Using his sleeve, he wiped his mouth and quickly drank a mug of beer. He rapped on the bar. The bartender poured another whiskey, then refilled the beer mug.

After finishing those, the man bent over for the lunch pail behind the brass rail. I smiled as he almost fell over picking up the pail. I stepped away from the door.

When the man in the canvas pants lurched out of the Limerick, he turned right, then around the corner back on 45th Street heading west. I ran to the next street, turned and headed in the same direction. There was an alley about halfway that connected to 45th. As fast as I could I ran between the trash cans lining the alley to 45th Street and peeked out. He was walking unsteadily and would pass the alley soon. I stepped back and saw a broken broom. It was in my hand before I knew it.

As he passed the alley, I grabbed his sleeve and pulled with all my strength. I pulled him into the alley. He fell heavily against wall of a tenement building. As he slid to the alley dirt, I wacked him hard with the broken broom. His chin rested on his chest. I went into his pocket for coins. One was a gold piece and several silver dollars! This guy was rich. Then it happened.

A hand had me by the neck, squeezing. It felt like my eyes were going to pop out of my head. I still gripped the broken broom. Then with both hands I slammed it against his chest. I slammed it again and again. The grip on my neck loosened. Then I jammed my knee into his groin. He let go with a loud 'oof'.

I was shaking. I vomited.

A little later, I walked back to the 45th Street brownstone. In the pale morning light, I could see dirt and trash littering 45th street. Ian was on the stoop. He was shivering under the blanket.

I sat down next to him.

"Where were you?"

"I went to see a guy about some money," I replied.

"What? Who do you know to get money?"

"Well, no matter, I got some. Call it a loan but we don't have to pay it back."

"Who gives money to a kid?"

"A fella that I met on the street."

At that moment, the brownstone street door opened. The General stepped out, closed the door firmly behind her and started down the stoop without a glance or a word to us. Silence.

"I think we gotta get some work."

"I think I need something to eat," Ian replied.

The doorknob to the street door turned slowly. Then little by little the door opened. There was Mikey. She was holding two boiled eggs in her little hands.

Colleen
August 1923

I wish I could say we were happy being in that drafty apartment on Tenth Avenue instead of St. Joseph's. It was great being away from the nuns spying on you every moment and all those girls who really didn't want to have anything to do with me. But I did have my own bed there and at least I always knew where Sean was. Coming "home" was a totally different story. Sean was out of the apartment more than he was in it. I did not know where he and Ian slept.

In the apartment I found books by Horatio Alger, Jules Verne and Mark Twain. The nuns gave me a bad time for reading books, especially in class. They did not approve of my selections, often they called them "nonsense books." My mother gave me no leniency in that area either.

She told me in no uncertain terms, "Put that blasted book down, Colleen or so help me I'll shove it up your arse! Get out of this house and find yourself some work. You think it's easy for me to put food on the table for you and your brothers?"

"No, Ma, I don't know where to go for a job..."

"Get out, Missy and don't come back until you get one!"

In tears, I ran down the stairs and out onto the stoop. I sat down there and mused about my life such as it was. I had no friends other than Sean and Ian.

Behind her back, even Mother's cleaning crew at Madison Square Garden called her "the General", and the name fit her to a 't'. She came to America on the Lusitania as a young 17-year-old; but there was nothing naïve about her. Life in Ireland was extremely harsh and she took her first opportunity to escape it. Sometime around 1899 when Mary Margaret stepped out of steerage on Ellis Island, she married Thomas P. Callaghan, a sailor in the Geoghegan Steamship Freight Lines in New York City. While I know nothing of those years, I do know that Mary Margaret Callaghan had children by Tom Callaghan. Tom Callaghan was lost at sea during Hurricane Two of 1911.

Having children did not bring out a kinder, softer side. Instead, it provided her with her own makeshift miniature army. She was the female version of Dickens' Fagin, and she did expect her children to produce an income from whatever source they could find. However, we were a trifle too young to contribute to the household coffers. She decided the expense of children did not suit her lifestyle, so she packed us up and sent us to St. Joseph's Orphanage on Staten Island. I can only imagine the malarkey that she told to Mother Superior to take us in as 'orphans'.

Ian was the one that got the General into taking us out of St. Joseph's. When she heard that his foster parents were filing papers to adopt him, she decided that she would spring all three of us out. Of course, that meant putting us to work. I didn't know it then, but my dear Mother was the instigator for Sean joining the bootleggers. She seemed to wield her own power in these street gangs. I can only attribute that to something in herself, an insatiable desire to become one of the society ladies on the East side of town. Of course, that is something that would never happen; her Irish brogue was much too thick to converse with the ladies lunching on Park Avenue.

"Hey Mikey! What are you doing?"

It was Sean calling me from across the street. I crossed 45th. On my left, a few motorcars and trucks rumbled over the 10th Avenue cobblestones. Even as I crossed, I could see that he looked a bit disheveled, but his crooked smile made me smile right back. It's funny but that slightly drooping eyelid gave him a devilishly handsome look.

"I'm out to find a job. Maybe you could help me, introduce to me to the men you work for and…"

"Not on yer life! Not a good idea at all!" he said firmly. "Look, you are pretty and you can read and do numbers so good – why don't you get a job in a shop or something. You know on Fifth Avenue?"

"Sean, won't you help me?"

"Listen Mikey. I'll do anything for you. I only know things around here not Fifth Avenue. You can find work but not around the Kitchen. You don't know this place. I do. I do not want you working in Hell's Kitchen. This is one thing we both don't want. You stay clear of the guys around here. You hear me! If I hear that one of these boyos touch a hair on your head…"

"Alright." I stood and straightened my skirt. "I get it. I will find something to do outside of the neighborhood."

"Look in the Herald Tribune or the Sun. There are jobs for smart girls like you."

With that, he gave me a hug and said he had to be off somewhere and once again, I was on my own. I walked to the corner newsstand and looked at the papers there. I didn't have even a dime in my pocket. Art the little man inside of the newsstand watched me with his clouded eyes. Well, it seemed that he could 'watch' me. Art had been blinded by mustard gas in the Great War. He could identify every coin by size, feeling it, rubbing his thumbnail along the ridges on the coin's side. I marveled at those sharpened senses that allowed him to 'see.'

I said, "Good morning, Art. I am going to look at today's Sun."

"Well, Mikey are you gonner buy one?"

"No, not today, I don't have a nickel. Would you let me look at a newspaper? I need to check the want ads."

"Mikey, this ain't no library," he said with sightless eyes searching the sky over my head.

"I don't have more than two Indian Head pennies."

"Oh, today you don't have money huh?" He laughed. "You only bought one of my two-penny chocolates just yesterday."

I think that he could hear me blush.

"You want a paper?"

I looked at him with bright eyes but before I could answer, he just laughed and said, "I got yesterday's paper here. You can have it. Free. No good to me anymore. No one is buying yesterday's news now that it's history."

With arcane precision, Art reached behind his stool. He handed me a copy of yesterday's New York Times.

"Oh, thank you, thank you Art!"

He just rolled his head, laughed and slumped back on his chair inside the newsstand. He turned on a small wireless radio next to his chair and sounds of a Brooklyn Dodger baseball game drifted out of the small booth.

I took my paper and folded it carefully and placed it under my arm. I had seen men doing that when they purchased their papers, so I knew that was how it was done. I walked to 6th Avenue and then down to 42nd street to Bryant Park. I found an empty bench away from the rumble of the El, as its trains thundered their way to lower Manhattan. I opened my prized newspaper and devoured every word. I loved the advertisements and I felt so intelligent and worldly just sitting there. That is until a bowery bum sat down next to me and began spitting on the pavement in front of us. I got up and he laughed, I am quite sure at me. Any way I found a new seat on the steps of the New York Public Library and continued my literary sojourn into all things New York from the Times point of view. I thought what a great job! That's what I want to be, a reporter, like Anne O'Hare McCormick! She wrote about Benito

Mussolini and how she believed he would become the leader in Italy. How exciting, I would be not just a reporter but also a foreign correspondent!

It started to drizzle so I walked to the corner of Fifth and 42nd Street. It was just one block to Madison then the Vanderbilt entrance to Grand Central Terminal. As I stepped through the heavy doors, the rain began to come down like cats and dogs. On my left were a row of phone booths and the ramp down to the main concourse of Grand Central. If you had any money, you could continue down to the Oyster Bar and Restaurant. I realized that the phone booths were just what I needed. I entered one of them, sat down and opened the telephone book that hung inside the booth. I found the address for the New York Times. It was 620 Eighth Avenue. That was close by! On the floor of the phone booth, I saw a shiny nickel. As I examined the Indian head nickel, I realized I could afford the subway shuttle to Times Square and 7th Ave. It would keep me out of the rain. I couldn't believe my luck! I was really excited. I wondered what I needed to be a reporter. A notebook and pencil for sure. I could use one of the notebooks I had from St. Joseph's; that would work just fine. Walking down the ramp, I turned as if I was going to the Oyster Bar but turned left again at the 'Echo Archway' to the lower train track level then right to the Grand Central Ladies Room. It was all brown marble for the swells that took the trains from Westchester or Connecticut. I used the Ladies room and smoothed my dark red hair and surveyed myself in the mirror. I looked all right; I could be a cub reporter. Then I thought, why waste that nickel on a train ride? I retraced my steps to the Vanderbilt doors. To my surprise, the rain had stopped. The street steamed in the fresh sunlight while taxicab tires hissed as they drove by on the wet street.

I started my trek back to the westside to The Times main office. I did a lot of walking that day, but that is not unusual. That is what you do in the City. Unless you take the subway or are really rich then you can hop in a cab. Anyway, it was nearing lunchtime when I entered the hallowed offices of The New York Times. I asked for the employment office and the receptionist waved me to the stairwell, "Go down one flight and turn right," she said already turning her face and smiling at a tall man standing in front of her desk. I followed her instructions and found myself standing in front of the door marked Employment. I stood there for a moment trying to think about what I would say when the door suddenly opened. A tall man bolted from it almost knocking me down. He had his seersucker suit jacket swung over his shoulder and a straw hat in his hand.

"I am sorry," he said, helping me back to my feet. "Are you here for the staff lunch order?"

"I, er no, er," I stammered. He eyed me more closely.

"Looking for work?"

"Yes sir, I want to be a reporter"

He chuckled and said, "Experience?"

"What, Oh, I, er, I read and write quite well" I said.

"I am sure you do. Are you Irish, Honey?" He smiled. "What's your name, Irish?"

"Colleen Callaghan." At that my stomach rumbled. Unfortunately for my embarrassment, it was very loud. He laughed again.

"Have you had breakfast? No, of course you haven't. Come with me, Irish, I will buy you a cup of coffee."

He took my arm and turned me around and propelled me toward the stairs. "But I want to apply for a job!"

"I am the guy who hires here. So, you can apply over a cup of joe. I am hungry and need a sandwich so you might as well come along, and you can tell me all about your ability in reading and writing."

"You have me at a disadvantage, you know my name."

"Allow me to introduce myself, I am Robert Arthur."

He held out his hand. I gravely took it and said, "I am Colleen Callaghan and I want to be a foreign correspondent."

"Let's discuss this over lunch. I prefer Horn & Hardart. The food is good, and one does not have to wait for a waitress to waste your lunch time." Then grinning he said, "Is that acceptable, Miss Callaghan?"

"Sure is!"

The Horn & Hardart Automat was a terrific place. A sign read: Service to New York since 1912. There were no waitresses, it was all self-service. Horn & Hardart was decorated in the latest Art Deco architecture. Everything was coin-operated. There was a woman who changed your quarter, fifty-cent piece or dollar to nickels. For a nickel you could not buy a better cup of coffee. For a couple of nickels more, you could have a chicken potpie that was delicious. There were all these little drawers with glass windows so you could see inside. Each drawer had a sandwich or a slice of cake or a piece of fruit; all you had to do was insert a nickel, turn a crank and the window unlocked miraculously and it was yours! Mr. Arthur noticed me staring at a sandwich behind one of those little glass windows. He said, "How about a ham sandwich, Miss Callaghan?"

I was starving and wanted to wolf it down. But felt I should eat properly as I was on a job interview after all. Mr. Arthur allowed me to eat my ham sandwich uninterrupted. It was absolutely delicious.

Then he said, "Hmm, a foreign correspondent, hmm. What languages do you speak?"

I swallowed the last bite of my sandwich and murmured, "English…"

He smiled. "That's not much help in Berlin or Madrid. Now, is it?"

"I guess not, but I am sure I could learn…"

"That's true, but it wouldn't pay me to hire you while you were learning now, would it? How old are you, Miss Callaghan?"

"I'm old enough" I retorted.

Mr. Arthur did not give me a job as a foreign correspondent. In fact, I didn't even get a real interview. What I did get was a beautiful ham sandwich and glass of milk and along with that he sent me to see a friend of his on Wall Street. It seems the Stock Exchange was looking for a page to go on the floor and give information to the brokers. It was not exciting in the way that being a New York Times reporter would be. But Wall Street was certainly fast paced and I was thrilled getting any job. Besides, it gave me the momentum to use my head a bit. Even though a page merely delivers information; I could easily calculate the monetary value of stocks that rose or fell. I found this ability of mine in of all places my hell on earth, St. Joseph's Orphanage. Walking from the bus on my first day on Wall Street I thought back to my start in the kitchen at St. Joseph's.

Sister Catherine Vianny was in charge of the kitchen, and she was actually very kind to me. Sister Vianny arrived a few months after my initial stint as Mikey on the boys' food line. She transferred in from a convent in Philadelphia and I guess she had not been taken in with the hard line that Mother Superior Hilda Perpetua commanded. Vianny saw that I was a bit of a loner, so she put me to work in the kitchen. Now, this was a great place to be as I was always a hungry and there always seemed to be a scrap of bread or, dare I say it, a smidge of butter just waiting for me. Anyway, I was supposed to help with clean up, taking stock of the children's food supplies for ordering. It was the bookkeeping in particular that Sister Vianny found quite boring.

There was a special pantry for the nuns. The nun in charge of placing both food orders, Sister Lelia was a total turd. She held the purse-strings making the payments to Mr. Abernathy our greengrocer and meat purveyor. I did the books for both the good sisters and the outcast orphans. It was easy for me.

Sister Lelia came swooping in, her black rosary beads clacking loudly against her thick thighs made bigger still by the voluminous folds of her black habit. Her pince-nez spectacles hung by a black ribbon. She taught literature and poetry. The poet William Butler Yeasts and Gerard Manley Hopkins were her idols. Yeats wore a pince-nez so she affected the look. She was a nervous sort and was continually fidgeting with her stiff white starched neck collar and bib.

"Vell, Missy! Where's the food inventory for this week?" she said in her nasal voice that floated a faint Germanic accent.

Respectfully, I solemnly handed her the sheaf of paper where I had printed a neat list of flour, porridge, tea, sugar, potatoes, ham hocks, beef, cabbage, beets and onions, soda crackers and milk. She glanced at the paper then back at me, "Vell, dot's it zhen?"

I nodded in reply and off she went.

Later that afternoon when the food order arrived, I was still in the kitchen helping with the mid-day dishes. Mr. Abernathy, the grocer and one of his young helpers, a skinny boy named Jimmy arrived with our order. He placed the cartons of food on the long worktable in the kitchen pantry and said, "Good afternoon, Colleen. Where is Sister Lelia?"

"I'll go fetch her. I expect she is in the chapel." I passed through the small vegetable garden and down a stone path to the Chapel of St. Joseph. Sister Lelia was not there but happily, Sister Vianny was.

I said, "Sister Vianny, the grocer is here with the order."

"I expect he wants to get paid," she said, "and that is Lelia's job. She was here just a moment ago, come along, Colleen. Let's go see how much we owe. Mr. Abernathy."

We walked hand in hand back to the kitchen to find, Lelia there, near-sightedly counting out seventeen dollars and seventeen cents onto the worktable. "Much obliged Sister. See you next week" and he was out the door with Skinny Jimmy following in his wake.

Sister Lelia called for Dotty to carry in the large box of victuals to the nun's pantry. Vianny surveyed the foodstuffs that remained. She shook her head, "We might as well try to make soup with a stone."

Undeterred, Vianny and I worked on the orphans' dinner trying to make the most of our meager supplies. We became very creative too. As an avid gardener Vianny added herbs to the tiny kitchen garden plot and changed our otherwise dull cooking routines.

Two days later I was up to my elbows scrubbing dishes in the large kitchen sink when out of nowhere Mother Perpetua suddenly appeared in the kitchen scullery. Mother Perpetua pulled me away from the stack of dirty dishes knocking me across the kitchen floor. I skidded to a stop right before my head and the worktable were about to collide. Tears clouding in my eyes, I looked at her. Did she know about me getting food on the boys' food line?

"I told Sister Vianny not to trust you. *Dumkopf!* Your little pea brain is incapable of doing a proper inventory."

Sister Vianny rushed in at that moment and helped me to my feet. "Mother Superior—" she began, but Mother Perpetua was not going to listen to her.

"Don't interfere with me! This little hussy ordered too much food and caused Sister Lelia to spend too much money. What did you think, Missy? Did you think you would steal our food? We don't ever need thirty-seven dollars of food for a week to feed you brats!" She shook me violently, her mouth a tight scar.

Sister Lelia came into the kitchen at that moment, "I found my spectacles *Grossmutter.*"

As Mother Perpetua shook me as a cat does a rat, Sister Lelia said in that peculiar nasal voice "I knew I should have checked her inventory list more closely."

Moving in front of Mother Perpetua and Sister Lelia, Sister Vianny held up her hand, "If there is an error in the inventory count for this week, it is my sin. I did the inventory. Colleen merely handed it over to you."

Sister Lelia and Mother Perpetua whirled to glare at her. Then Mother Perpetua said in that low, rumbling Prussian voice of hers, "Go to confession Sister Vianny. You are lying to me, and I know it. You hate this job. I gave it to you to teach humility. It is true, you have sinned. It was you who choose this brat to take stock of our food supplies. But I will not have you try to cover her sin, her crime."

101

"I did not order thirty-seven dollars' worth of supplies!" I said loudly, then thought, oh my God she is going to hit me again. Mother Perpetua, stood very still, slowly, deliberately turned her two Prussian-steel gray eyes on me like twin cannons.

"Girl, if I ever hear you address me unless I ask you a question, you will wish that God had not given you a tongue."

Turning back to the two nuns, "Sister Vianny to confession. *Schnell*! Sister Lelia, wash this girl's mouth out with soap."

Then she said, "Afterward, Sister Vianny you will take this brat to Abernathy's and get our money back. I don't care how you do it, just get it done by super time. But you go after her brazen mouth is cleaned out."

Whenever I think about that afternoon, I can still taste the harsh carbolic soap. Lelia, I think, enjoyed scrubbing my mouth out with soap and she even chuckled at the foamy mess that spewed from my lips as I cried. Afterward Vianny took my hand and together we walked to town. I had not been outside of the confines of the Orphanage for years and I briefly considered making a run for it. But where would I go and how could I go without Sean?

When Sister Vianny and I entered the Abernathy Produce Store, it felt great. Despite the red rash on the lower half of my face from the harsh soap, I could smell the freshly baked bread and there was such a big pile of beautifully red, shiny apples. Cheeses hung in mesh bags from hooks overhead. The smells were, were...It all smelt wonderful. I smelled freedom.

Sister Vianny approached one of the two boys standing behind the counter and asked, "Is Mr. Abernathy here?"

It was Skinny Jimmy, he looked at me and Sister Catherine Vianny surprised, questioningly but said nothing.

"Yes, madam. I mean Sister. I'll get him. He's just around back."

Wiping his hands on his flour dusted apron, Mr. Abernathy came right out to us. He spoke to Sister Vianny immediately.

"I did not realize when Sister Lelia paid me that she over paid. She gave me twenty dollars too much. I put her payment right into my pocket and did not check it because, of course, I trust Sister Lelia completely. It was not until this morning when I was doing my books for the week that I realized her mistake. I was going to send Jimmy over to the convent this morning with the money."

Later that evening, Sister Vianny came into my dormitory. She told me that she had straightened out the situation with Mother Perpetua. I was in her "good graces." Silently, I doubted that I would ever be in Mother Perpetua's good graces. I knew that mean Prussian nun much better and longer than kindly Sister Catherine Vianny did. She said that Sister Leila confessed that she was not wearing her spectacles when she counted out the money for Mr. Abernathy. I had my job in the kitchen back again cleaning dishes and Lelia was assigned to chapel and garden duty where wearing spectacles would not matter much. Now it was Sister Vianny in the kitchen and the pantry in charge of pots, pans, utensils, and dishes. As a matter of course, Sister Vianny would be ordering food and paying Mr. Abernathy from here on.

Winking at me, Sister Vianny said, "You know, I cannot stand the inventory counting up and I am no good with numbers, so I will make you a deal. I will do most of the cooking, you take care of the rest. I will teach you how to make soup from a stone if necessary. We will have the Magdalene women do the scrubbing."

I smiled though my face still hurt from Lelia's hard mouth scrubbing.

"Deal."

Chapter 11
Irish Need Not to Apply

Sean

November 1923

"Hey Callaghan! You can go," the jailer said.

"Great. It's about time."

I gathered my coat and hat on my jail cot. Being in the Tombs, as the New York City jail was called, was pretty good. Sure, jails are noisy and stink. But the food was good but not as good as the meals that Mikey produced in the last years at St. Joe's. Now that was good eating.

I had been arrested for stealing food from Briamonte's delicatessen on 9th Ave. I was clumsy and new to this thing, but I was starving again. The General had said that if I could not contribute to the rent then I could not eat in that fooking apartment. She said that I should go to Wall Street to be something called a 'runner' since most of them had been killed in the bombing a few years before. Well, I walked to Wall Street from 45th only to find several cleaner and better-dressed boys awaiting interviews at J.P. Morgan. I waited. I waited for a long time.

Finally, a tall man in a gray flannel suit waved me to come through the mahogany gate that surrounded a flotilla of dark oak desks. His footsteps echoed on the gray marble floor and off the massive Corinthian marble columns that supported the vaulted ceiling far above us. At the desk with a nameplate that read, 'Peter Montgomery', we stopped. He pointed to the man sitting at the desk who was moving papers from one tray to another. I stood there while Montgomery banged a hand stamp from an ink pad to papers on his desk. After a dozen or more papers had been dutifully stamped, he raised his head from the papers, raking me up and down with his eyes, twice. He grunted, sat back in his chair but did not invite me to sit.

"You boy, you're Irish are you?"

"My mother and father came from Ireland but I was born here…"

The man interrupted, "Well, even though our Vice President, Mr. Joseph P. Kennedy is Irish, we do not hire Irish, Irish like you."

"I would like the chance to work and show you that I am quick and…."

"Yes, yes, I've heard this from you Micks before. Then I have to chase you down at some speakeasy. All you Irish are the same—beer and free boiled eggs. Well, there is no free lunch here at J.P. Morgan."

"I can prove that I am different…"

Again, he interrupted saying, "You will not do. We do not want your kind here at J.P. Morgan. Good day!"

"But…"

"Good day," he said pointing toward the mahogany gate behind me while looking at something on his desk.

With my hat in my hand, I turned to leave, then l looked back to see Montgomery with the telephone ear-piece in his hand and the other hand pressing the lever twice. "Hello, Annie please connect me with Mr. Montaigne. Thank you, I will wait."

He looked right through me as he said that. It was a dead-cold look as if I was not standing there.

By the time I walked back to 9th Avenue and 45th, I was so disappointed, tired and hungry that I could not think. That is when I noticed a group of women entering Briamonte's Deli across the street. With that many shoppers, the grocery man would be busy and not notice me.

Quickly crossing the street and with the merry tinkle of the bell over the door, I slipped into the delicatessen. The smell of sharp cheeses was overpowering, intoxicating. I put an apple, two potatoes and a can of beans in my arms as I moved toward the back of the store. I stuffed them in pockets while working my way through the women who were shouting their orders to the man behind the counter. But his eyes must have been on me. Nearing the door, I saw an unsliced loaf of bread, I grabbed it. Once outside I started to run. I ran right into the blue uniformed copper. The delicatessen's door burst open with the grocer shouting, "Stop! Thief!" I wiggled free, ran but the copper's Billy club caught me in the back of my knee, down I went. The copper had me by the collar while he dragged me kicking to the lamppost with the green police call box. A few minutes later a paddy wagon arrived. I was hauled off.

Now, three days later and at least fed I was leaving jail. But it was not just a warm bed and bread that made my first incarceration worthwhile. I learned there was money to be made if a boy was willing to take some risks. You had to know the right people. There was a Dutch guy and a man named Johnny or Joey Noe who ran a bootlegging gang in the Bronx. I had an address and names in addition to being able to say that, "Vinny Coll sent me."

Vinny Coll had been arrested on the same day with a Sullivan Law charge for carrying a Harrington & Richardson vest pocket .32 revolver. He was sprung the next morning but not before giving me a good tip. Getting arrested was not all bad.

The introduction that Vinny Coll gave was to the Schultz Trucking Company in the Bronx. Located a stone's throw from Yankee Stadium, Schultz Trucking was well located. I walked from the elevated subway stop past other shipping and transport companies. A truck bearing the name Schultz rumbled over the cobblestone street toward the MacCoomb Dam Bridge. I watched it cross to turn left on the Harlem River Drive. Around the corner, I could not have missed it, a large sign proclaimed, "Schultz Trucking Company." I entered a side door to receive a meaty hand on my chest from a colored fellow who was the size of the door. Keeping his hand on my chest, he ran his right hand up and down my sides and my back.

"Whatcha y'all want?"

"I want to see Joey Noe."

"Who sent y'all."

The colored fellow sounded Deep South not South Bronx.

"Vinny Coll sent me."

"Why dint y'all say so fursest. He be in the office over 'chair." He dusted some dandruff from my shoulders as he took the baseball glove sized hand from my chest. Together we strolled across the trucking floor watching several men roll heavy barrels being loaded on an idling truck. The place reeked of diesel fumes and beer.

The Negro politely knocked on the solid wood door, waited and a voice said, "Com'on in."

"Mistah Dutch, there's a boy 'cheer that say Mistah Vincent sent 'im."

"S'he okay, Bumpy?"

"Yes, Mistah Dutch. He okay." Then Bumpy stepped aside and said, "Y'all can go on in then."

At two desks were Joey Noe and his partner, Dutch Schultz. Together they ran beer in the Bronx and were expanding into Harlem and the East side according to Coll. Schultz was a German Jew who was tough, smart and had a reputation for violence. He was not much taller than me, but he seemed taller. With a soft almost chubby face with wide set eyes, Dutch wore his light brown hair short, a comma of hair falling over his right eyebrow. His partner and friend, Noe was taller, maybe six foot tall, dark complexioned with raven Brilliantine slick black hair parted slightly off center. Noe had bushy eyebrows. He could hood his eyes that that of a hawk. Both men wore dark brown suits. While Noe wore sharp purple silk tie, Schultz wore his shirt tie-less. It was cool in the office. A window was open to a cool summer breeze assisted by a black cage-fan.

Neither spoke, they just looked at me.

"Vinny Coll said that I might find a job working here."

Silence.

Schultz stood. "Coll sent ya, eh? I'm Schultz. This here is Joey Noe. We run this, this business."

Schultz walked right up to me.

"You ain't got much to you. Betcha can't pick up a beer barrel."

"I don't know Mr. Schultz, never tried to."

"Can you drive at least?"

"I haven't learned to."

"That's good. You ain't learned bad driving. OK kid, go wait outside. I'll be witcha in a minute."

My driving lessons began that morning. Learning to ease off the clutch pedal was hard. Schultz kept me in first gear just easing off the clutch, moving forward, pushing it in then repeating the process over and over. Finally, he let me speed up and shift into second gear. At a street corner, I stalled the auto. At the next corner, I punched my foot on the clutch pedal as I stepped on the break. I didn't stall again, ever.

He demonstrated the trick of using the handbrake as a way of not stalling on a hill. Before long, I was driving the cobblestones of the Bronx at a good clip. As I eased the auto to a stop outside the Schultz Trucking, he said, "You learn quick."

I learned more from Schultz, but he was not the only teacher. Dutch Schultz taught me how to drive a truck, but it was his bodyguard, Vinny Coll who taught me about guns. Vinny was Dutch's bodyguard. He preferred the big .45 Colt automatic from the Great War but frequently carried a Vest pocket revolver. He had one in his topcoat, and another tucked in his waist held there by his suspenders. In a closet on the trucking floor there was an arsenal that included a Reising Model 50 submachine gun in .45 caliber, a lever-action 30-30 Winchester model 94, a 12-gauge Remington Model 11 auto-loading shotgun and a Springfield bolt action in "thirty-aught-six." The Springfield had a bayonet stud on the barrel.

"A gun is a tool. You choose the right tool for the job, for the situation and the guy. The Reising is needed when you could be facing several guns or you gotta do a job quick. A shotgun is great if you hafta be quick, not so accurate."

"When do you use the 30-30 or the 30 aught 6?"

"They're for long range, say 100 or 200 yards. I used the 30-30 when this welsher tried to run in Van Cortlandt Park. The Winchester made it an easy job. They take practice. Hey, even pistols need practice to hit the guy and finish him. There was this guy who fired eight shots at me from twenty feet. He missed with every bullet. I didn't miss with my first."

"When do I get a gun?"

"When Dutch or Joey says."

Colleen 1924

The job of a page on Wall Street was simple, hectic, confusing at times but always exciting. The air was electric with a strange combination of static energy and sweaty, noisy stress along with a strong aroma of ink and paper. Tickertape machines whirled incessantly informing brokers of minute-by-minute changes in stock prices. But buy and sell orders from clients necessitated getting messages quickly to the stock exchange floor by pages running as fast as possible to deliver them.

I loved the energy and the pandemonium of the whole place. I would leave the relative quiet of the City just waking up and within a few minutes of arriving at the Exchange, I would be totally immersed into its madness. It was intoxicating and frightening! There was no denying the adrenalin rush I felt as I dashed to the floor calling out in loud voice for whichever broker I needed to find before the price of the stock changed. The brokers were usually quite rude, yelling at each other and at me to speak up which was next to impossible with the noise that enveloped the place. At the end of the day, I exited into the busy New York City streets which seemed almost quiet in contrast.

All of the pages had to report to the pages meeting room every morning at 8 AM sharp. It was a large room painted a faded yellow color with a few chairs scattered around and one long wooden table in the middle. There were hooks on one wall where we hung our coats and hats. We signed in on a log pinned to the wall by the door and put on bright red vests so the brokers could easily see us on the exchange floor. Then we pushed our way to the long table in the center of the room to get a cup of coffee before the bell announced the opening of the market. Sometimes the brokers would come in for coffee as well and a few were actually quite nice before the frenetic day began. It was an exciting place and I was treated as an equal there. We were all message runners! No one was special. I liked that.

Before I left our small apartment on Tenth Avenue, I always drank a cup of hot tea with milk and sugar. But I loved the hot, steaming coffee at the Exchange. It was part of the daily ritual, and I relished it as an integral part of the day. I found out soon enough that you had to force your way through the crowd of pages to reach the table before the coffee or milk and sugar ran out. So, I made it a rule to arrive early before all the other pages amassed into the room.

Early one February morning, I was leaning against the wall in the vacant pages room holding my coffee cup in both hands which were still stinging from the cold wind outside. I blew on the hot coffee in a vain attempt to cool it. The door open and a young man with sandy blonde hair walked in. He had not noticed me, and he headed straight for the coffee urn. He poured himself a cup and took a big gulp choking a bit as he swallowed the hot brew. He turned and coughed again. I continued to watch him over the brim of my cup as I softly blew on the hot liquid. He must have unconsciously felt my stare so he finally noticed me.

"Oh, I did not see you there. Good morning. Coffee's pretty hot, isn't it?"

I said nothing just continued blowing on my coffee. He walked toward me and extended his hand. He wore a starched white shirt and blue necktie under his brokers' jacket.

"My name is Jim Baker."

I shifted my cup to my left hand and shook his extended one saying, "I am pleased to meet you, Mr. Baker." His handshake was firm, warm and dry.

"Jim," he corrected. "What's your name, Miss?"

"Colleen."

Several pages started to drift into the room. A few were making a bee line for the coffee pots.

Jim Baker smiled at me, made a quick little bow with his arm across his waist and said, "Miss Colleen, the pleasure is entirely mine."

Just as quickly, he left. Looking at the door as it closed behind him I thought about how blue his eyes were and how nicely he smiled.

The meeting room was filling up quickly and the pages were pushing their way to the coffee urn. Suddenly there was a clatter as several porcelain cups fell to the wooden floor, the noise of the day had started.

The next morning when I opened the door to the pages room. Jim Baker was already standing at the coffee table.

Jim said, "How do you take it?"

"I beg your pardon?"

"Your coffee, how do you take it?"

"Oh, with milk and sugar."

"One cup of joe, white and sweet. Should've guessed!"

He poured me a cup added milk and one lump of sugar. He raised his eyebrows in a question.

I caught on. "Two lumps please."

Another cube of sugar was ceremoniously dropped into the cup. He handed it to me.

"You look very nice today, Miss Colleen."

I looked down at my navy pleated skirt and white blouse. It was the same outfit I had worn yesterday and would be the same one tomorrow. Each night I washed the blouse in the kitchen sink and hung it to dry in the bathroom, ironing it when it was still damp. It was the best way to smooth out the wrinkles. He looked very nice in expensive looking pleated gray flannel trousers, white shirt and a bright red tie. I looked at his shoes. They were polished and gleaming. My brown loafers were scuffed and worn. I used a dab of Crisco fat to cover the scuffs. Hopefully, it made them look polished. But I had spent too much time in skimpy rags at St. Joseph to feel embarrassed at my appearance.

I lifted my chin and said in a clear voice, "Thank you."

When I met his gaze, I was surprised at the warmth there. It was as if his compliment was real and not at all a put down.

He was there every morning thereafter. By the end of the week our conversation had moved along from coffee and the weather. He told me that Charlie Chaplin was in a new picture show, and he was sure I would enjoy it. Now how would he possibly know what I might enjoy? I didn't know what I enjoyed! He asked me to go with him and said he would pick me up at my apartment. I said I would meet him at the theater instead and my friendship with Mr. Jim Baker began.

Jim and I began to see each other often. I usually found him leaning against the wall next to the coffee urn holding two cups of steaming coffee as I entered the break room every morning. On weekends, we went to the picture show or to dinner. He was always a perfect gentleman. But I never let him pick me up or drop me off at my apartment. I did not want the General to see him. I got wise to her pretty quickly. If she thought there was a buck to be made, she would go for it. I knew in my heart she would get a load of Jim in his nice gray flannels and shiny shoes and she would try to rid him of his wallet. Instead, I would meet him by the clock in Grand Central Station and we would set off from there.

While Jim's wardrobe was always neat and fashionable, he never made me feel badly as I continued to wear the same blouse or sweater over and over again. I was able to add a blouse or two and a warm sweater over the first couple of months of employment, but it was all due to some good finds at the secondhand store. The General took half of my wages every week, smirking.

"Thanks for the rent."

And with that, new clothes were just not in the cards for me.

Sean – December 1924

Vincent Coll was looking over his arsenal while rubbing the barrel of the shotgun with an oily rag. Looking almost dreamily, he said, "I need a Thompson. They are real 'typewriters' with fine oak stock, drum magazine and a handy front pistol grip. I hear that they are easier to control than the Reising."

When Coll drove with Dutch and Joey anywhere there was a shotgun under the backseat blanket rope. Coll liked driving Dutch and Joey. He liked it better when I took the wheel and he sat next to me with the shotgun at his feet. He said, "I'm learning the business. Business is good."

Coll's business was eliminating problems for Dutch and that meant bumping off the competition. Coll was the executioner for the Beer Baron of the Bronx.

Collee – February 1925

On Saturday afternoon, I met Jim at the clock in Grand Central at 2 pm. He said, "Let's go for a skate."

I took a step back and stammered, "I don't have skates."

"Neither do I" he laughed. "We'll rent them."

"But, but I don't know how to skate. I've never skated."

"Then I will have to teach you." He took my arm leading me to Vanderbilt Avenue where he hired a cab to take us to Central Park. Jim instructed the driver to leave us off on Central Park South. From there, we marched to the Wolman Rink inside the Park.

He was wondrously athletic as he skated around showing me the fundamentals. And I was wondrously awkward, wobbling and fumbling as I vainly attempted to stay upright on the ice. After my fourth fall flat on my ass, he took pity on me. He stopped laughing and helped me up.

Grabbing my hands, he said, "Your hands are freezing! Let's get a cocoa and warm up."

He skated holding me upright, so I somehow made my way to the edge of the rink and the railing. Holding on to the railing for dear life, I managed to haul myself to the exit gate.

As we sat on the bench removing our skates, he noticed a friend of his.

"Alistair! ALISTAIR!"

A tall handsome man in a chesterfield overcoat was strolling with a tall, slender woman on his arm. She was wearing a bright red cloche hat with a matching long red coat. He waved at Jim, said something to the woman then the two headed in our direction.

"Well, Jim old sport, fancy meeting you."

The woman looked at me intently. Her eyes widened, "Colleen! Is it really you?"

Jim looked from the woman to me. "Colleen, I see you already know my friends."

I blinked back tears that were forming quickly, "Dotty, Dotty. It's so very good to see you!"

Dorothy Gale let go of the handsome man's arm and rushed to embrace me. Then she excitedly introduced me to her companion, her husband, Alistair MacMillian. After a brief conversation, the men suggested we go for a quick bite. We returned our rental skates and left the Park.

As the four of us sat down in the lounge of the nearby Plaza Hotel, Dotty explained, "Colleen and I are old friends, childhood friends."

She rightly surmised that I did not want to share my childhood history with Jim. Perhaps, her own story was also unshared.

Grabbing my hand across the table she continued, "How is Sean? I've thought of you both so often. I hoped and hoped that I would see you again."

Alistair took Dotty's other hand and said, "Sean? Who is Sean? Should I be jealous?"

"No, my darling, Sean is Colleen's brother and he and Colleen helped me through a very tough time in my life. I will always be eternally grateful for their kindness." Jim and Alistair exchanged quizzical looks.

"And that is all we will say about it!"

"So now Miss Colleen tell me what you are doing with this rogue!" Alistair laughed.

Ignoring his question, Dotty turned to me saying that they had a beautiful home on East 54th Street and her own cleaning lady who comes once a week to clean and polish everything.

"Can you believe it! Me with my own cleaning lady!" She insisted I meet her for lunch at Central Park's Serpentine Restaurant on Sunday, just us girls.

As we were leaving the Plaza, she whispered to me, "Please ask Sean if he will join us on Sunday."

We met at the Serpentine Restaurant on the lake in the Park at noon. Sean was not able to come; 'some pressing matter' I explained. Actually, I had not seen him in the last two days.

We talked or rather I talked about Hell's Kitchen and how tight things were. "What can I do to help you and Sean? I owe everything I have today to you both."

"Dotty, you don't owe us anything! St. Joe's was an awful place. We were glad to help you get away."

"What happened after I left? I worried for months that the police would come and arrest me!"

I told her about Eucharius' recovery and how Perpetua suspected that we were involved with your disappearance. She blamed you for Eucharius' injury and called the police, but the final analysis was that she must have fallen and hit her own head.

"I did not see what happened to her. When I heard a clunking sound; I turned around and she was falling."

I interrupted her to explain the 'clunk'. "Remember that big cast iron frying pan in the kitchen?"

She raised an eyebrow, "You?"

"Yes, and to this day I wonder at how I could have done such a thing. I was filled with a sudden strength and consumed with hatred for everything at that awful place."

"Colleen to the rescue! Something like a brave cowgirl in the cinema, saving her sister from a Simon Legree. Those nuns ruined my faith."

"Yes, I know how you feel. I cannot bring myself to go to Mass."

"But let me tell you the rest of my story. After Eucharius fell, all I heard was Sean's voice telling me to run. I got away as fast as I could, and I made it to the Ferry dock. I had to wait in the darkness until 4:45am when boarding began. I thought for sure I would be arrested but nothing happened. When I arrived in Manhattan, I used the money you and Sean gave me to buy some clean clothes. I found a room in a boarding house in Kips Bay. The proprietress was kind. She helped me to recover from my wounds and helped me find employment. I started to work for a rich lady on the upper East Side who wanted a girl to help with her children. One evening her husband brought home his young protégé, Alistair MacMillian. He is the most handsome man I have ever seen and Colleen, he is the kindest man. We got married a few months later and my life is like a fairytale."

"That is really wonderful." I tried to smile for her good fortune.

It wasn't long before she pulled the rest of the story from me. How we were shocked to find out that we had a brother, Ian. Then how our less than saintly mother showed up one day and delivered us into the slums of Hell's Kitchen. From one hell to another.

Dotty and I continued to meet for lunch frequently. She always paid the bill and absolutely refused to let me chip in. She was the one who put the thought in my head about cooking for a living. She reminded me that at St. Joseph's, once Vianny and I got the run of the kitchen, the meals improved greatly.

"Even with the merest of provisions, suddenly the meals actually tasted good. You are wasting time running messages to the Exchange floor you should be cooking!"

6 November 1925

Wall Street Journal: Dow Jones has a record closing at 159.39

Sean

"Sean! Sean? Where did you get all this money?"

"Listen Mikey, you just hold on to it. When you open your restaurant someday, you'll need extra. Just make sure the General doesn't get her paws on it."

Mikey, Ian and I were sitting at our table near the back door of Chumley's on Barrow Street. With its peat fireplace giving a comfortably warm glow, it was easy to see that Prohibition was good for business. Chumley's didn't serve bathtub gin either. Chumley's served good booze. You entered Chumley's through a Barrow Street courtyard near the corner of Bleeker. At the back end of the courtyard was the old carriage door with the grated small slide window. You knocked twice, paused then knocked twice more. The window would slide back then a voice would say, "Whaddayawant?" The reply was "Farmer John sent me." With that the door would open to the cheerful noise and smells of the speakeasy. The other door, the 86 Bleeker door was only for escape if the joint was raided.

Farmer Sullivan, the unofficial 'mayor' of Greenwich Village had both Republican and Democratic politicos on his payroll. Sullivan was standing at the bar. At this distance, the scar that ran from his mouth to his ear appeared to be a smile. "The Farmer" was not a smiling man. Sullivan was not above plugging someone who crossed him or even annoyed him. He had a special distaste for the Italians who ran the Fulton Fish Market. If, and it was rare, if Chumley's was raided, the bartender would yell "86!" and the patrons would escape to, using the 86 Bleeker Street door. The Farmer would stay right where he was to greet and pay off the coppers. They would leave a little richer and the patrons of Chumley's would drift back into the cozy speakeasy.

I was sipping my gin with my feet enjoying the warm peat fire. I turned to Ian and said, "How you doin'?"

"Sean, I'm doing swell in the Men's department of Best & Company on Fifth Avenue. Even got this apartment with another clerk right off First and 38th. I'm not mooching off Colleen anymore. What have you been up to?" Ian asked as he sipped his gin.

"Oh, this and that."

"You look like you could use a good night's sleep."

"I'll sleep when I'm dead."

"Stop talking like that! Now you must tell me. Tell me where you got the money," Mikey interjected.

"It fell off a truck."

Chapter 12
Ratner's Deli

Sean

March 1926

I was rolling beer barrels on a truck for delivery when who walks into the joint Jimmy Hurley and Liam "Squint" McGee. Quick as a cat, I jumped from the truck bed to the floor. They were a sight to see.

"How did you two find me?"

"We bumped into your brother, Ian while we were 'borrowing' things from the swells on Fifth Avenue."

Squint said, "Ian seems to be doing good. We were about to borrow his wallet when Jimmy recognized him."

"So here we are!" Jimmy said looking over my shoulder at the rows of beer barrels. "Didn't think a Jewish guy would hire an Irish Catholic!"

"Dutch don't care if you are a mick, dago, Negro or what. His driver is Vincent Coll who was born in Ireland. We work with Bumpy Johnson and his Negros. They speak in a drawled out way but don't be fooled they can move fast as Jack Johnson the boxer."

"Are they brothers or something?"

"Not as far as I know. Jack Johnson used to own the Club Deluxe in Harlem. You love this, now an Irishman, Owney Madden owns the joint, calling it the Cotton Club. We still deliver beer to it just as when Jack Johnson owned it."

"Think we can get a job here, with you with Schultz Trucking? We almost got pinched by a copper while we were borrowing wallets from swells at Grand Central Terminal."

"Schultz is expanding into Manhattan so, yes, he could use the likes of you, both of yer. Where's Paddy Clarke these days?"

"Paddy's 'up river' in the slammer."

"What happened?"

"We were doin' fine pinching swells at Grand Central then Paddy got greedy. He robbed a payroll clerk in the Graybar Passageway, ran out to Lexington Avenue and right smack-dab into two coppers who were strolling Lex. Now he's in Sing Sing."

"We decided that Grand Central was getting too much attention from the coppers," Squint grunted.

I said, "Let me introduce you to Mr. Noe and Mr. Schultz."

With the two trailing me, I knocked on the Schultz Trucking office door.

"Who's it?" Schultz shouted at the knock.

"It's me, Sean, Mr. Schultz."

"C'mon in then."

Schultz was closing a desk draw as we entered. After introductions, Schultz walked over to Jimmy and Squint. He looked them over. Still looking at them, he asked me, "You vouch for them? They are boys I can trust? I only need boys that I can trust."

"I've known these guys since I was a kid. You can trust them"

Schultz walked back behind his desk. Turning back, he seemed to have another thought.

"Sean, see if Bumpy Johnson is still here. If he is, ask him when he's heading back to Harlem. Take Squint and Jimmy witchya. I need you to do a job for me in lower Manhattan, at Ratner's Deli."

"Sure, Mr. Schultz."

***

The three of us were crammed in the back seat of the Durant A22 four-door sedan with Mr. Johnson, as Schultz insisted that we call him sitting next to his driver, Moses.

With his arm draped across the back of his seat, Mr. Johnson said, "Mr. Dutch say, 'Take them boys to the 125th Second Ave IRT El. I say sho nuff. Me and Mr. Moses be going to our bank nearby. Yo boys look snug as a weevil in a cotton gin."

"You own a bank, Mr. Johnson?"

"Yo making fun of me boy?" Bumpy shot back.

"I, I thought that this fine motorcar costs, so you must be rich."

"Boy, I ain't no fucking rich." He paused, tucked his big upper lip into his mouth before saying, "Thanks to Mr. Dutch and his main man Otto 'Abba Dabba' Berman, I got me a good policy racket goin'."

"Is that the same as 'numbers', Mr. Johnson?"

"Boy, yo' don' know whether to scratch yo' ass or check yo' watch. Listen, here be the racket: yo' get some poor coon to pick the last three numbers of the racetrack handle, yo' know, the total money they haul in on race day. If he picks the numbers right it pays 600 to 1."

"Holy Cow! That's why guys play the numbers!" Jimmy said. "But wait, how do you make any money if you are paying off that?"

"Boy, when Jesus axed if you want brains, did yo think he say 'trains'? No! We're not paying nobody off! Mr. Dutch and Abba Dabba fix it so nobody wins. I gots bookies in barbershops all over Harlem. They be getting runners to bring the betting slips and money to my bank. I moves the banks to keep the poll-lease busier than a long-tailed cat in a room full of rocking chairs"

"Mr. Johnson," Squint asked. "Do you know why Mr. Schultz has the name, Dutch? Who is the Abba Dabba guy?"

"Boy, you ax more questions than the Three Wise Men can answer. Mr. Schultz's folks from Germany. When he say Germany in German, most folks think he say 'Dutch'. His main-man be Otto Berman, he called Abba Dabba. He can do crazy magic things with numbers. He make Mr. Schultz rich and now he be helping me be rich too."

"What do you do to help Mr. Schultz? I'm sure that he and Berman don't work for you for nuthin."

At that point, Moses made a sharp left on Second Ave, weaved between the elevated subway posts to the curb.

Mr. Johnson said, "Yo get the train to Rivington. Ratner's be only a block away."

Climbing out of the sedan, we chorused. "Thanks, Mr. Johnson."

Bumpy leaned over Moses to say out the window, "Watch out for that crazy bedbug Siegel."

Ratner's Deli on Delancey Street was busy with people dressed even more differently than I had ever seen. Men with long black and gray beards, dressed in long black coats, wide brimmed black felt or fur circular hats. Most had long curls on either side of their face that reached their stiff white-collar shirts. Women and girls wore long skirts and sleeves.

Ratner's Kosher Deli was alive with voices in a language that sounded like German but was like no German I've ever heard. The menu was on a long chalkboard behind the tall display case. Dutch had asked me to return with a 'pastrami sammish on rye'. That's what I ordered. Two pastrami sandwiches on rye with mustard.

Casually, I asked the clerk as I paid, "I'm here to see Mr. Lansky about a truck."

The counterman shrugged his shoulders up to his ears saying, "Vell, see Mr. Siegel."

He jerked his head toward the back of the deli. Scanning the crowded tables, I noticed the one with a man wearing a double-breasted brown suit with polished brown brogues. His suit jacket was unbuttoned revealing the butt of a revolver under his left arm. That made me think of Bumpy's words to watch my step with Siegel in particular.

After the formality of a complete pat-down, Siegel opened the door to a back room of Ratner's. It was a speakeasy! The smell of the beer and the hooch was unmistakable. The place was filled with a low murmur of voices. Siegel pointed to a table in the back with a lone occupant, a very nattily dressed man. That must be Myer Lansky.

He stood as Siegel introduced us. Lansky pushed his wavy hair back then extended his hand to me. Lansky was shorter than I and I'm not tall. I guessed that he was just about five feet, not much taller. Polite, soft-spoken with a firm handshake, Lansky's eyes bored into mine as he said, "Dutch sent you boys?"

"Yes, sir, he did."

"Do you have something for me?"

I handed him the envelope. With a mere glance, he dropped it next to the coffee cup and the newspaper on his table.

"Benny, see to it that these boys get what Dutch needs."

With that he sat, picked up his coffee cup, shook out the newspaper and never looked up. Our introductions were over. We grabbed our pastrami sandwiches and left.

Under the Williamsburg Bridge was the Lansky-Siegel Garage. A ten-foot-high chain linked fence marked the borders of the garage, but it was the two men with not-so-hidden sawed-off shotguns that was our sign that it was the right place. While one who looked like a beer-barrel on piano-legs unlocked the fence the other one kept his eyes sweeping over the three of us.

"Mr. Siegel called, says that yose need of a truck. Dere's some," Mr. Beerbarrel said indicating with his thumb. "Do youse know hows to drive a truck?"

"I do."

"Dat's good. Mr. Siegel likes to get his trucks back and not all bunged up."

"I'm a good trucker. What about that one? Can I take that one?" I said pointing at the truck with wooden doors.

"Sure, sure dat's a Star Depot Wagon. Dat's one you can."

As we pulled out, I said. "Boys, this is going to be the start of making good money. Lots of good money."

Chapter 13
Left Holding the Cheese

Sean
Hell's Kitchen
April 1926

When I knocked on the 10th Avenue apartment door, I was hoping to see Mikey. Instead, the General opened the door.

"Well, well, my prodigal son returns. Do you have any money?"

"Well, 'hello' to you too. Mother."

"Are you employed?"

"Why?"

"Well, Mr. Connolly is unemployed due to his health."

Looking over her shoulder, I saw Connelly in a familiar place and health, on the couch and unconscious. I could smell the booze from the door.

With a grip like pliers, the General pinched my arm to get my attention away from Connolly.

"Can you get a car or better yet a truck?"

"Maybe" I replied slowly, wondering where this was leading.

"I need you to pick up some cheese for me." She handed me a revolver.

"What do you have in mind, Mother?" She gave me the plan.

"In that case, I need two more revolvers."

***

I travelled to Ratner's on Delancey again.

"Youse boys goin' out on yer own?" Siegel asked.

"Yeah, I need a truck."

"I'll cut you a deal if you give me 50% of the loot."

"How about 25%"

"Lookie here kid, doncha want the truck? Make it 40% and I won't even charge ya rent."

It was a good deal especially since I had no money to rent the truck. Ultimately Bugsy Siegel would get more than 50% but let me continue.

I put together a gang, adding a fellow from the Schultz Trucking, Izzy Redmond. Izzy has a good handle on hijacking trucks. Squint, Jimmy, and me were new to this racket. That night with Jimmy and Squint under blankets in the back of the truck we took the Christopher Street ferry to Jersey City. From there we took the Lincoln highway south. Just before dawn, we were positioned on the road waiting for the Philadelphia ferry to land at Palmyra in Jersey.

When the ferry docked, we watched the Brotherly Love Dairy truck rumble off. It was exactly as the General predicted. We followed the truck in pale morning light down the still dark road. Izzy at the wheel of our truck, said that the road was nice and quiet. He suddenly accelerated to pass the dairy truck. Our truck was now in front by a dozen yards when Izzy slammed on the brakes while turning to position our truck across both lanes. Just as our truck stopped, Squint leaped out of the back with his revolver. Izzy came around from the front as the Brotherly Love skidded to a tire-squealing halt inches from my door.

I had to climb over the stick into the driver's seat. Meanwhile Izzy, Jimmy and Squint pulled the diary truck driver and his companion out at gun-point. Izzy climbed into the driver's seat of the diary truck with Jimmy climbing in next to him. Squint fired two shots as the driver and his companion ran for their lives. He missed both of them, but the effect was good.

Izzy driving the Brotherly Love Dairy truck was in the lead as Squint and I followed. We drove the Burlington Pike south. At route 30, Izzy turned and headed east through the pine barrens of New Jersey. Up ahead was a sign for Eli's Restaurant. Izzy slowed at Eli's Restaurant, but we could see it was closed. We continued. Just past the restaurant, Izzy turned on to a dirt road that he must have known. I followed in his truck's dust. In the middle of nowhere, there was another dirt road crossing the one we were on. Izzy stopped at the dirt road intersection. There we transferred as much of the cheese as we could fit into the 'Bugsy truck' as we had started to call it. All of New York called Benjamin Siegel, "Bugsy" since he was crazy. Crazy as a bedbug that is. After that we put some branches and bush to conceal the Brotherly Love Dairy truck. The four of us crammed in the cab like sardines, we were soon back on route 30 then headed back to the City.

By noon, we were really hungry. We pulled the truck up to a roadside diner in Howell. As we approached the diner I saw a face sitting near a window that looked familiar. Although I could not place him at first, I finally remembered him, Charlie the Jew Yanowsky. He was one of the boys who came to St. Joe's after the German sabotage bombing in 1918. While the boys ate in another booth, I sat with Charlie and his buddy, George Keeler. Keeler was busy shoveling apple pie into his mouth. Charlie was famous for running his gang through the Jersey City – Hoboken freight yards. He asked what brought me to Jersey. I sketched out our heist.

He whistled, "I woulda liked in on that caper."

"There's still an opportunity. We left a fair amount of cheese in the Brotherly Love truck off route 30. You're welcome to it."

"Really, you couldn't haul it all?"

"All you have to do would be a drive to route 30 near the Eli's restaurant in Winslow. You can have what's left and even the truck."

He looked at Keeler who had his mouthful of pie. Keeler nodded. We shook hands. We all left the Howell Diner driving in different directions.

Sometime later, I learned that Charlie and George nearly got pinched by some local coppers as they were picking up the goods from the Brotherly Love Truck. Charlie was always funny around me from then on. There was no brotherly love between us.

By midnight, we were back in Hell's Kitchen. I awakened the General to come down in her bathrobe to inspect our load. She hardly had looked at all. Then she directed me to deliver the cheese to 'a friend' at the Landmark on the corner 46th Street and Eleventh.

Evidently, this was some really pricey cheese. The guy at the Landmark couldn't pay for it all. So, we drove down to the Lower Eastside. That's how Bugsy got his 40% plus some cheese.

Ratner's had a 'special' that week. It wasn't kosher.

Chapter 14
Lend an Ear

Sean

1 June 1926

Paddy Clarke had the bright idea to rob payrolls. He 'bumped' the payroll delivery in the Graybar Passage of Grand Central Terminal but ran right into two coppers on Lexington and 44th. Paddy got sent up to Sing Sing, where he met Danny Dolan who was already doing time there.

Squint, Jimmy, and me couldn't believe our eyes when the two walked into the Ear on Spring Street. The Ear was right off the docks on Spring Street. It had been built around the time of War of 1812 by a freed slave James Brown, an aide to George Washington during the Revolutionary War. It could have been the oldest bar in the city. Its neon sign "Bar" only illuminated as "Ear," hence the name. I guess that a joint called the Ear didn't catch the eye of Prohibition Agents. Both the Ear on the Westside and McSorley's in the East Village were never raided. Out of 'kindness', I suppose.

Tommy the bartender gave us all a round of drinks. We had a few more before someone suggested that we needed something better to look at than Tommy. Taking no offense, Tommy blew us a kiss as we left.

The boys and I took Paddy and Danny to the Café Fey on West 45th to celebrate their release. Danny had his eye on one of the Café Fey chorus girls. She was eyeing him back plenty.

"Yeah, pinching wallets at Grand Central was good for pocket change but then I noticed that one guy that I was about to bump had a holster and gun. I followed him. He was making a payroll delivery. He had a regular schedule of payroll deliveries. It was an easy grab-and-run," Paddy said.

"Yeah, but you ran right into two coppers" Jimmy laughed.

"So, so, so maybe I didn't plan the get-a-way too good, still," Paddy said. "Still, it would have been some real do-re-me."

Payrolls have real dough. So do banks. That's where the money is as Willie Sutton would say. Robbing banks like Willie the Actor was too tricky for lugs like us. Delicatessen and store robberies got me 'chump change'. It was nickels and dimes just like the store 5&10. I was making steady money with Dutch and Noe but only enough for me. If I was to get Mikey and Ian started, I had to have a lot more cash.

With Paddy, Danny, Squint, Jimmy and I in two stolen cars, we hit the Geoghegan Steamship payroll. We covered our faces like the cowboys in the Tom Mix flicks. The payroll office was on the second floor. We crowbar-opened the locked back door. In a minute we had the payroll. We were in and out before the Steamship workers arrived for the day. The only thing that went wrong was Squint's revolver went off accidentally. The guard was hit but it didn't kill him. Having two cars must have confused the coppers because it was a happy ride to our Bleeker Street hideout.

After splitting up the dough, we celebrated at the nearby White Horse Tavern on Hudson Street. The White Horse served good bathtub gin in coffee cups for the benefit of the coppers. I was having a swell time until I saw someone emerge from the side room heading for the piss-room door near the head of the bar. It was none other than my step-da, Danny Connolly. He was drunk as a lord. A little later he was weaving his way to the street door. As he shambled by, he looked at the four of us with glazed bloodshot eyes. There was no recognition. Connolly stumbled out of the White Horse toward 11th Street.

I watched Connolly while the boys talked about going to Madison Square Garden for a prize fight. As we sat in our hole-in-the-corner table looking out on Hudson Street a Brinks Armored Truck rumbled over the cobblestones outside.

Danny Dolan slapped me on the arm then pointing with his chin indicated the Brinks' truck.

"We would need more than a crowbar to get into that!"

"Yes, yes we would."

That started me thinking. We could get our hands on some really good cash. We could get several payrolls at once. But how could we get into the armored truck, past two guards with their Thompson guns? There was also the little problem of a clean get away.

Solutions for problems often arise from unrelated circumstances and events. So, it was with the Brink's heist. I brought home a flapper from the Cotton Club. We had danced the Charleston and the Black Bottom until my pins got tired. She was a noisy broad, in bed and out.

"Seanie, Honey, can you take me for a different ride," she said saucily. "I want to go to Coney Island."

"Don't call me Seanie, my name is Sean."

"Sure, will you take me to Coney Island?"

"Doll, now where's Coney Island?"

"Brooklyn, sweetie. Dontcha know?"

"Cripes, I ain't been to Brooklyn except to where the Dodgers play, Ebbet's Field."

"Sweetie pie, it ain't much farther from Flatbush where the Dodgers play and the Wonder Wheel at Coney Island. Please, pull-eese, pull-ese take me!"

Before I knew it, I am packing her into the roadster that I bought with the money from the Geoghegan heist. All across the Manhattan Bridge and on to Flatbush Avenue, the broad was clutching my arm excited as a school kid. She was making shifting into gear something of a challenge.

"That's Junior's Restaurant!" She pointed to the corner restaurant. "They have the best cheesecake. We should stop on the way back."

"Why not right now."

"Don't be all wet. Let's get to Steeplechase Park quick."

I smiled in reply. Then a Brink's Truck turned right in front of us. I followed it all the way to Church Street where it stopped, The Dime Saving Bank was on the corner. Two guards jump down from the back door one with Thompson sub-machinegun, the other guard had a satchel in one hand with a revolver in the other. On the pavement, pedestrians parted to give them easy access to the bank.

On Ocean Avenue there was another Brink's truck. It hit me. Brooklyn offered more getaway options. Manhattan was too busy, too few side streets and too many coppers. I hadn't seen a copper on the street except for directing traffic, not even a paddy wagon.

The amusement park was crowed and noisy. Surprised, we did not wait long to ride the Wonder Wheel. From the top of the rotation of the Wheel was a view far out on the Atlantic. After that, the broad dragged me from one silly ride after another.

Pretty soon I got wise, I bought only one ticket, for her. Watching her long legs hike up her frilled skirt as she climbed on the Steeplechase horse was entertaining for me. It was her next ride that got me thinking. The ride was a motorboat ride. An enormous tub had a capstan with a miniature motorboats on each spoke. As the boats circled, it came to me that a motorboat would make a good getaway 'car'. When you think about a heist, you have to plan the getaway first.

Ever since getting nabbed at Briamonte's, I planned all my jobs with a clean getaway first. Then I planned backward to the job. The next problem was the Brink's route. Drivers made it difficult, always changing routes, locations, times and days.

For weeks we trailed the Brink's truck using two different cars sometimes three. One car would follow for a time, then fall back letting the second or third would take over the trail. We couldn't find a pattern or a regular schedule. It was maddening. Then, it was Danny Dolan who figured it out. Ice cream, it was ice cream. In the meantime, I have to spend some time to learn how to operate a small boat. I took up flounder fishing out of Sheepshead Bay while the boys shadowed the Brinks. Each morning, I drove my roadster across the Manhattan Bridge then straight on to Sheepshead Bay. Operating a boat out on the Bay was easier that driving a Schultz truck.

It was on one flounder fishing trip that I discovered an abandoned dock on Breezy Point. A hard surface road was near the dock. That would be very useful in the plan. Now all I had to do is leave a small truck at the dock. It would be a three step get-away plan, car, motorboat then truck.

16 July 1926

Brighton Beach Judge Jones Again Orders 'Not Guilty' in Rum Trial Verdict of Mrs. Canaday and Two Others—(Brooklyn Eagle)

It was fooking hot. Hot, for Cripes sake! We had grown beards as a disguise. My beard was itchy with sweat. Dressed in all white as a Polar Bar ice cream man, Danny Dolan stood under the lily-white umbrella telling ragamuffin kids with nickels for ice cream to scram.

Danny was on the opposite side of Cropsey Avenue from Squint and me. We were sitting on the King David Old People's Home loading platform pretending to be workers awaiting a delivery. Boxing in the ice cream stand, on the corner of Bayview, Jimmy was behind the wheel of a Model T. Paddy Clarke sat sweating in his four-door Birmingham on the other corner, Bay 32nd Street. It would not matter which direction the Brink's truck took.

This had been our routine for the past two days. We were all getting a little 'antsy'. My rear was numb from the wood on the loading dock and my hand was sweaty on the revolver in the brown 'lunch bag.'

It had rained earlier. The air smelled of steaming cobblestones. From the loading platform, I could see that Jimmy Hurley's head was down. He was nodding off. Squint was sprawled out on the platform but within range of my foot if he started snoring.

Then, out of the fog of the evaporating rain the Brinks Truck appeared. Danny rang the bells on the ice cream hand-trucks push rail. It was our signal. Jimmy's head snapped up. I couldn't see Paddy Clarke because he was around the corner but I heard his big Birmingham engine crank into life.

It began perfectly. The Brinks guard climbed down from the box to get ice cream. Squint and I slipped off the loading platform then walked very quickly to the open side door of the Brinks. The second guard left the door connecting the driver and shotgun seat of the truck open. He was going to get an ice cream too. His uniform shirt was soaked in sweat. Squint and I were at the door before the guard knew it. With Squint's revolver pressed into the guard's forehead, I relieved him of his Thompson gun. We pulled him off the truck as I stepped up holding both my revolver and the Thompson on the driver. Meanwhile, from the icebox of the hand truck Danny had produced a shotgun instead of the ice cream that the guard had ordered. He too was relieved of his Thompson. We ordered all three face down on the cobblestones.

Jimmy had Cropsey Avenue blocked with the Model T as Paddy roared up alongside of the Brinks with the Birmingham. Danny held his shotgun on the two guards and the driver. Squint and I loaded bags of cash into the Birmingham. One bag was very heavy. I dropped it and the bag ruptured silver dollars all over Cropsey Avenue. We finished loading the Birmingham and I jumped in next to Paddy. Squint and Danny ran for the Model T. Squint stepped on the running board to open the backseat door, Danny ran around to the other side for the shotgun seat next to Jimmy. That's when things began to go haywire.

Jimmy must have popped the clutch as the two stepped on the T's running board. Squint fell. Danny held onto the door swinging away from the car. He was holding on for dear life. Squint lost his grip on the Thompson. The gun skidded over the cobblestones far from his grip. Jimmy stomped the T's brake.

"Furgettaboutit!" He screamed at Squint. "Get in the fuckin' car! Get infor Christ's sake!"

Squint and Danny jumped in. Looking back, one of the Brink's guards was up now, sprinting for the Thompson left on the cobblestones. Our Birmingham turned left on Bayview with Jimmy's car only yards behind. Jimmy had the Model T making the turn when a burst of the Thompson bullets shattered the rear window.

"Turn left here! Go! Go!"

There was another burst from the Thompson as the T turned the corner right behind us. With Gravesend Bay shimmering in the morning heat on one side and the back of the King David, we raced to the end of the street.

"Cripes! Cripes, Sean! This is a dead end!"

"Pull up over there!"

Sirens could be heard screaming in the distance, as the Birmingham screeched to a stop at the bulkhead.

"Get the money and let's go!"

I climbed down the ladder to the speedboat that bobbed in the brackish water below. I pulled the lanyard to start the motor. Nothing! Nothing again! Cripes! Then on the third try, the motor coughed oily smoke and started. Paddy was starting to pass bags of cash down. Jimmy appeared bug-eyed and sweating. He climbed down with a bag of money in his teeth. He looked like a modern pirate.

"That's the last of it," Paddy shouted. "Hurry."

Then Squint appeared at the top of the bulkhead carrying Danny over his shoulder like a fireman. He had no sooner had his feet on the boat's deck as I untied the boat and pushed off the dock. As I steered the craft into the fog of the bay, I saw Danny's wounds, one in his head and the other his chest. I raced the boat toward open water and Breezy Point.

If it wasn't for Danny Dolan, this would have been an exhilarating boat-ride, better than anything at Coney Island. We bounced over the bay with the boat creating a refreshing breeze. None of us were refreshed.

With each breath more blood bubbled froth from Danny's chest. His head wound covered Squint with blood as he cradled Danny in his arms. Then, the bubbling stopped.

"Dan! Danny! Danny!"

We looked at Squint as he held the dead man. Looking past Squint, I saw the dock and the truck not too far off. Squint stood suddenly. Not a good move in a small boat.

"Squint, buddy sit. You're rocking the boat."

Squint stood as the boat plowed the bay toward the dock. Squint was in a rage. His face was vividly bright red and his neck veins bulged ominously. He started to yank at one of the money bags. Then from out of nowhere a shotgun blasted. It tore a hole in the side of the boat. We looked around for where it came from. I saw the drawstring of the bag that Squint had been tugging on was snagged on the trigger of Danny's shotgun.

"Dint ya put the fooking safety on!" Paddy said not as a question.

"What's a safety?"

"Forget about the fooking shotgun and plug the fooking hole with something," I said. "Everybody slowly get to the other side of the boat!"

Jimmy nearly fell overboard as the boat motored forward.

"Careful!"

We were still a ways off the Breezy Point pier. Now the hole was just above the waterline at least weren't taking on any more water.

"Cripes!"

I was standing in about three inches of cold seawater. My feet were freezing but my thoughts were racing.

"Everybody listen, we won't have much time to offload the dough. This boat is sinking. At the dock grab a bag and get ready. You'll get off from the front. That will keep us afloat for enough time."

Anxious eyes turned toward the boat's front as Jimmy, Paddy and Squint each picked up a Brink's bag. Danny's body lay in the seawater sloshing the deck.

I slowed to ease the boat up to the pier. Jimmy grabbed the post of the dock flinging a bag on to it. He was smart. Jimmy held on to the rope attached to the boat as he climbed up. Then Paddy and Squint passed bag after bag of money to Jimmy before they climbed out.

I turned the boat to point it out into the Great South Bay. What to do? I opened the gas can to spill gas into the seawater sloshing at my feet. As I climbed up on the dock, I slipped the motor into gear. Ghostly, without anyone at the tiller, the boat carrying Danny Dolan's body moved away from the pier. I struck a match tossing it into the boat. It caught fire. The fire spread as the boat moved farther into the Great South Bay off Breezy Point. The small boat was completely aflame a hundred yards off as it sunk.

We gave Danny Dolan a Viking Funeral.

Chapter 15
The Mad Dog

Sean

19 September 1926

I got to know Owney Madden of the Cotton Club while I was there to arrange the delivery of Schultz's beer. Madden had been with a gang that had done well, now he was legit. Well, kinda legit being the owner of a famous speakeasy.

Over a Scotch, Madden told me of his glory days with the Gopher Gang and fights with the Hudson Dusters. He had done nine years in Sing Sing for killing a Duster. When he was paroled in '23, the Gophers had broken up but one of his pals, Larry Fay was running booze out of Canada for his club El Fay on 45th. He had a floor show run by the film star Texas Guinan. Madden also had a taxi company that sometimes picked up 'customers' in Canada. By customers, he meant booze.

"Listen boyo, I did my time. I kept my mouth shut. I earned respect. When I got out of Sing Sing, my gang was gone. My money vanished. Larry Fay got me on my feet. He has a good head for picking the right jobs. Help yourself to that Scotch." Madden said in a brogue that was rich and sweet to the ear.

"Me and my boys are doing a number of small jobs but…"

"But you see that's not enough."

"I did fine with the Cheese Heist but…" I didn't mention the Brink's, things were still too hot.

"No buts boyo, you want more."

Madden was eyeing the chorus girls lining up for a rehearsal, "Fear pays. Get 'em to fear you and things happen," he said waving his hand in a grand sweeping gesture. My eyes travelled around the club's walls, stage and tables.

With the palm trees and palm fronds you could imagine being in African jungle.

"First rule, find a good boyo to be your muscle. Second, make an example of some other gang's muscle, put a few slugs in him but finish him. The Hudson Dusters tried it on me. I had my boyos pay 'em back for those eleven slugs that I took. I made fookin' sure they weren't comin' back at me to finish me off."

"I have three good boys with me."

"Good start. Before Sing Sing, I was earning $200 a day. Now I make double that and even more. Last, have a second or third line of money. I have a taxi company that does more than deliver customers to the Cotton Club. For some reason the Prohibition coppers don't see a taxi as transportation for Canadian rye and Scotch."

"Good advice Mr. Madden, I was thinking of how Vinny Cole makes money..."

"Cole is the worst kind of muscle. He's mad as a dog with rabies. He's too crazy. Like a mad dog he'll have to be put down someday."

A few days later at the Schultz Trucking, Dutch waved to me from the office door. I tucked the pencil behind my ear and the trucks and destinations clipboard under my left arm. I was being trusted with more responsibilities. Dutch was good to me.

As I entered the office, Vinny Coll and Johnny Noe were there. Coll stood up. Johnny Noe glanced up from his book work then put his pencil down. Dutch closed the office door behind. My mouth went dry, cripes, what did I do?

"Hey, I'm not in trouble, am I?"

Pursing his lips, Noe said, "Nah, we just need you to drive Coll over to Arthur Avenue." He said 'avenue' the Bronx way, av-van-a. "We need him to convince a guy not to buy from Diamond."

"Sure," I said. "I can drive Vinny."

"Good." Noe shoved two twenties and an ignition key across his desk to me.

"Here's a lit'l somethin' extra. The wheels are around the corner, a Chevrolet. You and Coll can get started. You wait for Coll keeping the engine goin'. This guy opens up his joint about four, maybe five. I wantcha to be there before he arrives. Make sure he's alone, then Coll will convince him not to buy booze from Diamond. You pick up Coll, get rid of the wheels in Harlem. Can you do dat?"

"I can, Mr. Noe."

"Get somethin' to eat then youse and Coll take the Chevrolet to Arthur Ave-ven-a."

Coll climbed in the Chevrolet wearing an Army trench coat with the collar up. It was a windy cold Bronx day with hardly a cloud. The Chevrolet did little to keep out the cold. As Coll sat the snout of the Reising Model 50 stuck out from under the coat like a short metallic leg. Coll closed the Chevrolet's door, turned toward me and dropped a pistol in my lap. I jumped, hitting my head on the car's felt ceiling.

"Whatsamatta? You're acting like it's a snake. Ain't you ever seen a Savage auto? It's a great gun, gots nine shots of .380."

"No, I was just surprised. Cripes, you coulda handed it to me."

As I was instructed, I kept the auto idling in the alley across from the Arthur Avenue restaurant. Actually, I was not sure which restaurant because Arthur Avenue seemed to have dozens of restaurants, butcher shops and cheese shops. They were all Italian restaurants and stores. The smells were making me hungry even though I had had lunch only two hours before.

On the way to Arthur Avenue, Coll kept up a steady stream about how good he was and his side-business. Actually, it was several businesses. "I make some money working jobs for the Eyetalians, you know Sal Maranzano. Sometimes, I snatch some rich people then I gets their rich daddy to pay me to bring 'em back, you know, alive."

It started me thinking that Squint, Jimmy, and me should be doing some jobs to make money for ourselves not Schultz Trucking. I was trying to think up some jobs just as the streetlamps came on. These electrical streetlamps don't need no lighter or gas, they just work. I remember looking out from St. Joe's some nights to see the lamplighter step up on the pole peg with lit wick on a stick to reach and light the gas lamp. That was a long time ago.

I was startled from the memory by the rapid thunder of .45 rounds exploding from Coll's Reising. Across the street a man and a woman danced like violently jerked marionettes as .45 slugs slammed into them. Then Coll appeared, fired two or three more rounds into the man and calmly waved to me.

I put the auto into first and popped the clutch. I stomped on gas while wrenching the steering wheel to turn on the avenue. I skidded to a stop right in front of Coll. Instantly, Coll flung the Chevrolet's back door open. As he backed into the seat, he fired another burst from the Reising.

"Go! Go! Go!" He shouted over the seat, as he slammed the door. I sped up the avenue toward Fordham Road.

"Turn here" He commanded. I turned left. I could see the elevated subway ahead. "Turn right under the El!"

Holy craps! I could already hear police sirens.

"Good, we have the light! Turn left! Hurry!"

The tires screeched as I cut in front of a truck heading south under the El. Coll had me turn at almost every corner. Police sirens did not seem any closer but then again not too far behind either.

"Cripes Coll are you mad, crazy or what?" I said as turned a hard left on to Fordham Road. "Is that what you call 'convincing him'? Cripes!"

"Well, he ain't gonna buy from Diamond ever again."

I heard him slam another box magazine into the Reising. The sirens sounded louder. Then I saw his eyes in the rear-view mirror. They were as cold and unfeeling as the eyes of a rat.

"Turn right ahead at Morris then left at 190th. We have to get some distance."

"Got it," I said. It felt like the Chevrolet went on to two wheels as I turned on Morris Avenue.

The pursuit sirens faded then came on strong behind and on our left. It must be two or even three cars. They were close. Ahead, the intersection was blocked by a truck. Coll must have been looking over my shoulder.

"See that space between, turn!"

"What space?"

He slapped on my shoulder, "Here! Turn hard!"

I turned into an alley between buildings knocking over several trash bins. Laundry lines of underwear and sheets flashed overhead. I slammed on the breaks to avoid hitting a wall, backed up then turned to drive next to a gap-toothed wooden fence that separated the tenements on 190th street from the ones on the 189th. A police siren echoed off the tenement walls. The siren continued past the alley.

"Stop here."

With the hot ticking engine running, we sat in the alley. In the rear-view mirror Coll's eye were wide. His pupils were wide too. It was almost as if his eyes were black not blue. Coll began to grin.

Sirens sounded farther away.

"Wait here. I'm goin' to look see." Coll opened the door; he was out and running down the alley soon out of sight.

Then, I notice the Savage pistol under the clutch pedal. It would block the clutch. As I reached for it, the passenger door was flung open by Coll. I sat up sharply with the Savage in my hand but banging my head on the steering wheel.

"The coppers are off chasing the wind. We can get out of the alley easier that way." Coll pointed.

"Hey, whassamatta you!" A female voice from above shouted.

Coll stepped back, pointed the Reising upward then I heard a window slam down. Coll smiled and was still smiling as he climbed back into his seat. On190th, we continued heading west toward the Harlem River. Coll had me turn on to Webb Ave, I could see the bridge to Harlem. Then as we were crossing the University Heights Bridge, he yelled "Stop!"

Coll jumped from the car with the Reising barely concealed by his coat. He wiped it down with a rag while holding it with the folds of his coat. A moment later, I saw the weapon drop from the bridge down to the dark waters of the Harlem River. Turning back to the vehicle, Coll wiped his hands on the rag and it too was thrown into the River. Casually, he climbed in next to me.

"Let's see who's playing at the Cotton Club. We can ditch the car on the way. Take St. Nicholas downtown."

I put in the clutch and drove. It was even darker now with streetlamps providing pools of yellow illumination as we drove on St. Nicholas Avenue. When I glanced over at Coll, the streetlamps flickered on a face that was contently smiling. This man is crazy and very, very dangerous.

When we reported back to Dutch about Arthur Avenue, he become really pissed.

He yelled at Coll, "I tole ya to convince him not to buy from Diamond. He ain't buying nothin' from nobody; he's dead."

A week later, two detectives walked into the Killarney Rose on Webster Avenue where Coll, Squint, Jimmy and I were having a boiled egg and a beer lunch. We were tossed against the bar wall but only Coll and I were hauled off in the paddy wagon. Coll was charged with first-degree murder of the couple on Arthur Avenue. I was charged with accessory to murder. Murder in the First carried a death penalty. Coll was unimpressed. He said nothing so I modeled him. When I was questioned, I shrugged, played dumb and said nothing.

It paid off. Dutch and his lawyer Richard "Dixie" Davis parlayed some deal to get the charges dropped. An eyewitness disappeared and three others developed memory problems.

Coll and I were given our wallets, and other personal things that they took when we were arrested. Before walking out into the sunshine. I was suddenly overtaken with a hunger for Chinese food. When I mentioned that to the Schultz's lawyer Dixie Davis, he laughed.

"Sure kid, I'll take you to Hong Fats on Mott. You have been eating the crap they serve prisoners all week. And you've been smelling all that great Chinese from the nearby restaurants. Just let me finish up the paperwork."

Davis with his glasses perched on his 'Gallic nose' was intently reviewing every word of the papers in front him. Although Davis was only an inch or two shorter than me, he must outweigh me by twice. The buttons on his double-breasted suit were threatening to pop off any minute. As Mikey once described him, he looked as though he was pregnant and over-due by several weeks. With a Lucky Strike in the corner of his mouth, smoke making him blink, he worked through the release forms. Scanning each line with his fountain pen poised in his right hand. He was on Dutch's payroll doing a great job keeping Dutch out of jail. We were on Dutch's payroll too. Dutch has this real fear of being locked up. He expected everyone would abandon him to rot in jail while they took his money. Not so with Coll, being in jail was not a problem for Coll.

Dutch took care of his gang. He paid us a regular salary, we don't get a percentage of the take. As I learned, other gangs paid on a percentage of the take on a job. But Dutch paid us regular. That means we have a guarantee of cash, even if a job don't work out.

Dutch had a job waiting for me though. It was a doozy.

Chapter 16
Cityboy

Sean

28 February 1927

Outside of Stowe, Vermont

It ain't true. They say when you are about to die that your whole life passes through your mind. It ain't even close to true. The muzzle of the heavy police special was pressed into the back of my head. The sound of the hammer being thumbed back made me jump.

"Stay still, you bastard. It will go easier," the voice growled.

Liam and I had been given the job of picking up a shipment of Canadian beer and Scotch from a line house in Highwater, Quebec. It was just over the border. As a matter of fact, the La Bounty line house was half in Canada and half in the US. There were a number of line houses along Rue Montee de La Bonne Chance. That means good luck street. This time our luck ran out.

The job went like this. I was given a packet of money, some spending dough and two Colt hammerless, one for Liam and one for me. I decided to call Squint by his real name, Liam to see if it would stick. I had found an eye doctor on Lexington Avenue who gave him glasses. I thought that Liam would stop squinting.

Even with the glasses, Squint was still squinting. We were to meet one of Dutch's friends in Troy, New York. Once I got there, we would get directions and our Vermont contacts. Stowe, Vermont would be our hideout until we got the Canadian hootch.

"Mordecai Friedman runs a deli for the goyim workers in Troy. Give him the envelope for his trouble. Speaking o'witch, dontcha trouble Mordecai. Mordecai is a 'hat'. Don't annoy him about what he's wearing."

"What do you mean a 'hat'?"

"Mordecai is very religious. He wears his yarmulke and observes a kosher kitchen. He is a good friend of my mother's, especially after my father died. He has an old stable that will keep my truck away from nosey coppers. He has connections in Vermont, to the Canadians and other things you might need. Mordecai will give you directions and who to contact in Stowe. Are you good?"

"I'm good."

"Good. Get on route 9 early, it's a long road north to Troy."

With that he handed me a piece of paper with an address.

"Take Squint with ya."

At 4 am, Liam and I climbed in the Schultz's truck. The make of the truck was Graham, a big one-and-a-half-ton truck. We headed for Broadway and Route 9 North. We drove under the elevated subway until it ended at Van Cortlandt Park. A couple of miles later, we were outside of New York City for the first time in our lives, if you don't count the Jersey Cheese trip.

It seemed as if the temperature dropped by the mile. As the sun set, it got even colder in the big Graham. By the time we crossed the Hudson River into Troy New York, we were damned cold. I was driving at the time. I stopped at Friedman's Deli at 268 River Street. Liam's breath steamed in the truck's headlamps as he knocked on the door. The delicatessen was dark, but I saw a light in the window above the shop. A figure appeared in the window. A minute later a light came on in the deli.

Mordecai Friedman was dressed in a flannel bathrobe that covered his knees. He had two long Clara Bow like sideburn curls that merged with his dark beard. The glowing tip of the cigarette in his mouth bobbed as he spoke to Liam. Then, Mordecai handed him a big O ring of keys with one key held out. Mordecai went back inside the deli locked the door with a loud click as Liam walked over to the double doors of what used to be a stable next to the deli.

Using the key, Liam unlocked the padlock on the doors. He swung one door wide for me to drive the Graham inside. The garage was one of the cleanest and neatest that I had ever seen. Liam ran a finger across a work bench then held it up for me. Clean. Who cleans a garage that well? A side door opened, and a silhouetted Mordecai appeared in the doorway. We followed Mordecai to his apartment above the deli.

In the kitchen, Mordecai's wife ladled out two piping hot bowls of soup for us. She disappeared into another room. My fingers were so cold that I warmed them holding the bowl a few minutes before I picked up the spoon. Liam's glasses were all fogged up by the steam from the soup but he did not seem to care. Liam finished his bowl by drinking directly from it.

In his bathrobe, Mordecai sat opposite us, smoking. He had a pinched narrow face with large eyes hooded by thick black eyebrows. When I sat back, he took it as a signal to begin.

"You finish? Gut."

"Yes, thanks!"

"So," he paused pulling in a lung-full of smoke. "Arthur gave you something for me?"

I walked over to my topcoat for the envelope that Dutch gave me. Mordecai rested his cigarette on his tea saucer with his left hand then took the envelope. His right remained in the bathrobe pocket.

"So here's the spiel..." He began.

With his heavy accent, we had to listen carefully as Mordecai gave us directions for our job in Vermont. He may have been speaking English but he was hard to follow his words. I asked him to repeat things several times. Mordecai did not seem to mind, he flicked cigarette ash into his teacup saucer and repeated what he said until Liam and I nodded.

We would meet some local boys, the Sabotski brothers of Stowe who knew the roads. Both were real *mensches*. They would drive across the border into Canada with us to talk French. They would help arrange the shipment. The Sabotski brothers would make sure that we didn't get any schlock, only high-grade booze. Together, we would pick up the shipment drive it south back to the City. Our truck would be loaded with the booze and the Sabotski would then continue south as decoys for any nosey coppers. We were to return to Mordecai's place to spend the night with the truck hidden in Friedman's garage. Man, I hope that I got this right because his accent made it hard to follow.

As he finished, his wife appeared with blankets and two pillows. We slept on a rug in the front room with snowflakes whispering against the windows.

Sometime before dawn, I heard Mrs. Friedman putting some coal into the stove. As I poked Liam awake, she set out two cups and a pot of steaming tea. A few moments later, Mrs. Friedman put out a small plate of what she called *latkes* with a cup of applesauce. Mordecai appeared from the bedroom. He struck a match to light his first cigarette of the day as he sat down.

"What's with you goyim? Eat!"

With that he picked up a *latke* dipped it in the applesauce and popped it in his mouth.

"Eat."

As we ate a sleepy little boy dragging a stuffed bear emerged from the other room. The boy climbed into Mordecai's lap. As Mordecai stroked the child's hair, he reviewed our directions and made us repeat them back. As soon as the last *latke* disappeared, we all stood. Mordecai held the boy in his arms then nodded toward the door to the stable.

Then it was back into the Graham for Liam and I. Liam adjusted the choke after two attempts to start. Then with a rattle and shake the Graham sputtered to life. I opened the stable doors to a dark street. The Graham's headlamps made two tubes of yellow light that had crystals of snow drifting through. Liam drove out, turned on the street then waited as I closed and locked the doors.

A brilliant cold, sunlight filtered through in the eastern tree line as we crossed into Vermont. Following the Mordecai directions, we turned on to route 7 at Bennington, the long narrow road north toward Stowe and Canada. With Liam at the wheel, I was mesmerized by the Vermont scenery. It was so different from the City. Pine trees dripping with icicles edged snow-covered farms that had black and white cows, dozens of cows. As a city kid, this was like nothing I had ever seen or ever imagined. As the sun rose higher, I had to tilt my cap to shield my eyes from the reflected sun off the snow. Cripes, it was cold. I had my gloved hands tucked in each armpit. Liam complained that his fingers were getting stiff holding the steering wheel. I took over driving at Wallingford.

It was after sunset when I drove the Graham through the town of Stowe. Using the Graham's headlamps, I slowed to read mailboxes. First one farm then another, we crept along the road at a speed so slow that we could have walked. Then there it was, Sabotski Dairy. The road to the Dairy Farm was only a single lane between fence rails. At the end of the lane was a small farmhouse with a steep-sided roof. Oil-lamps were lit in a window on one side of a covered porch. I backed the truck up to the middle of a hitching post in front of the farmhouse using the lamplight to guide me. Snow was piled chest high on either side of the walkway. An anemic gray twilight seemed to intensify the cold. A wind made funnels of powdery snow dance in front of the truck's headlight then off into the darkness. I turned off the Graham and the darkness of a moonless night closed in. I opened the truck door to a blast of frigid air that knifed through my topcoat. I was stiff from both the cold and driving the Graham. Moving like men forty years older, Liam and I hauled our cheap suitcases from the back of the truck. Then the farmhouse door opened, flooding the walk with a shaft light silhouetting a gal in the door frame. The light behind her gave her a halo, a halo of blonde hair. Hotsy totsy!

At that very moment, I went from standing upright to lying flat on my back. My suitcase went flying off into the snow. The blonde appeared in the corner of my vision. She was squatting at my side chuckling.

"Poor City Boy, you would think that you could walk a few yards without falling."

"I did not fall. I am enjoying the view," I said, as I looked at this picture-perfect milk maid. Her coveralls and wool shirt did little to conceal her shape. With one hand extended to me and the other holding her wind-tossed hair, she said. "Let me help you up."

"Sure."

I took her arm as she pulled me to my feet. I felt her muscle strength doing the work. I was not on my feet long. Just two or three steps and I was windmilling my arms and falling pulling her down on top of me.

"City boy, you are pretty fresh. We just met."

"Sorry, it must be my shoes."

"Bet that you say that to all the girls."

"Only the ones I like."

"Don't you think it would be polite to introduce yourself?"

With her on top, I did not want to get up, I said, "I am Sean Callaghan."

"Pleased to make your acquaintance Mr. Callaghan." She laughed resting her chin on her hand using my chest as for an elbow rest.

"Call me Debbie."

With that she jumped up. Then with that strong grip, Debbie pulled me to my feet. She did that with such easy strength that I bet she could go nine rounds with Max Schmelling without breaking a sweat. I had much to learn about the Vermont farm-girl.

She showed us to a small room with a single bed off the kitchen, lit a kerosene table lamp, said, "Goodnight."

I kicked off my shoes as Squint sat on the other side of the bed. As I pulled the blanket over me, Squint who was still in his topcoat sitting on the bed said, "Sean, you didn't introduce me. So, when you do could you introduce me as Liam?"

"Sure Squint. Now put out the lamp."

"I'm not kidding."

"Fine, it's Liam. 'Night Liam."

"'Night Sean."

Liam blew out the lamp.

Chapter 17
North to the Linehouse

Sean

Heavy caliber gunfire awoke me. I rolled off to the wood floor, then elbow-crawled to the door. My topcoat holding the .38 Hammerless was on a peg board on the back of the door.

Coat, pants and shoes on, I was outside on a covered porch bobbing and weaving like a punch-drunk Golden Gloves boxer. There was another heavy caliber gun blast. I had the .38 in my hand. As I rounded the corner of the porch, there was Debbie in a red-black checked wool coat, green woolen trousers tucked into knee-high boots ejecting a spent cartridge from a bolt-action rifle.

"Cal!" She yelled into the hillside to her right, "I'm ready for the next!"

"Yell 'pull' when you're ready." A high-pitched voice from the hillside replied.

"I said I was ready. Fine. Pull!"

A moment later a tractor tire with a wooden center rolled off the hillside starting a bouncing roll across the open field. In one smooth effortless movement, Debbie had the rifle shouldered, swinging the muzzle left ahead of the rolling tire. She fired. I thought that she'd miss it, but the tire went down as if it was struck by a sledgehammer.

"Cal, I'm good. I'm finished practice. You can come on down for breakfast now."

"That was wicked good shooting Deb." The voice from the hillside said.

"Thanks."

She turned. She froze. Even at this distance, I could see that her eye caught the revolver in my hand. Still with her eyes on mine, she worked the bolt on the rifle. A spent shell disappeared in the snow.

"Well, good morning, Mr. Lazybones. The day is nearly over."

With the rifle in the crook of her left arm she strode across the shin deep snow that crunched under her boots. She stepped up on the covered porch, she opened the rifle action, briefly glancing into the chamber.

Without looking at me, she said, "That little peashooter isn't any good for deer hunting."

"I wasn't sure what was going on out here. So, I brought it out."

"Can you hit anything with it?"

"Never fired it."

"Are you joking?"

"No, I have never fired a gun. Even this one."

"Well, Cityboy, we'll have some shooting lessons after breakfast. Now, I don't see a hammer on it. Can you drop the cylinder? For safety sake."

"Why?"

"Because if you fall, and you do fall, it's likely to go off." She put a cold-pink hand on the barrel of the Hammerless pushing it off to the side, "Now you be careful where that muzzle is pointing Cityboy. Never have a muzzle pointed at anything that don't need shooting. May I?"

Muzzle down, I handed Deb the Hammerless. With her thumb sliding the cylinder release forward she dumped out the .38 rounds into her palm. She raised her nearly white-blonde eyebrow rolling the rounds under her thumb.

"You loaded six rounds." She paused, then she said sternly, "Never load six rounds, only five. Leave the empty cylinder under the firing pin so that when you fall you don't shoot yourself or someone else."

"I'm pretty good at staying on my feet in the city, it's just this damned snow and ice here."

Before Debbie could reply, a large, bearded man stepped up on the porch.

"You must be Mr. Callaghan, I am Cal Sabotski."

I turned to the high-pitched voice that was coming from a blonde giant. Cal Sabotski towered over me by about a foot. The voice and the man did not match. The voice was that of a little boy but it was emanating from the mouth of a bearded giant.

"Just call me Sean."

"Oh, that is how it is pronounced, Shawn, not 'seen'. You look cold Mr. Callaghan, let's get you inside for some hot coffee and pancakes."

Inside I met the third Sabotski, "Little" Joe. Of course, he was not little either. Joe Sabotski had a deep baritone and baseball glove hands that covered mine as we shook. His huge hand was the size and toughness of Lou Gehrig's mitt. I eyed the frilly apron that he was wearing.

"Oh, this is my late Mom's apron. Since I do all the cooking in the family. I wear it in her honor."

"Sorry to hear that she is gone."

"Mother and Father died in the Great Flu. Between Cal and I we raised Lit'l Debbie and kept the farm going." At that Debbie punched him in the arm. "Who are you to call me 'little'?"

He just smiled. "The farm barely keeps us fed and covers some expenses. I figure that the farm made almost $300 last year."

I was paid $300 last month alone by Schultz Trucking, but I didn't say so.

"Thanks for helping us, putting us up for the night and all."

"Listen mister, we don't do this out of the goodness of our hearts. We need a few more Holstein so the extra money we get from the Canada line helps. Besides, it's more fun to play with the immigration and Prohibition agents than all this farm work."

"We're up early every day to feed, water and milk the cows," Cal said.

"It's a good thing that there's three of you for that work. I thought that work in the Bronx was tough, but this is a really long day for a little dough and keeping food on the table."

"Shucks, we do alright. There's plenty of venison and rabbit to be had. We have Mason jars full in the cold cellar. We just need two or three more cows to have some cheese and milk to sell and keep the barn warm. That's the ticket to farming success," Joe said.

"Cows to keep the barn warm? I don't get it."

"Cows have a higher body temperature. With two more cows, the barn will stay about 40 degrees even on the coldest night."

"Stop flapping your gums and get back to the stove. Time's a-wasting," Deb chastised Joe while setting the table. "If Mr. Callaghan can wake up his buddy, we can get them started on their own work."

"I'll get Liam up," I said.

Dressed in his barncoat, mittens, woolen forage cap and driving the mule-drawn wagon, Cal Sabotski looked comfortable with the cold. My topcoat and sweater barely kept me from freezing. Liam and I sat next to him as the pair of mules pulled us from the Sabotski's lane and turned on Vermont route 100 heading north. Looking south, I could see there were a number of automobiles parked in Stowe's main street. One was a yellow Meany cab right outside the hardware store. Well, well, we weren't the only ones from New York. As the mules plodded along there was open farmland on either side of the road. It felt decidedly colder. The wind whipped up snow from the fields as if it was snowing from the ground instead of the sky. The wagon offered no protection from the cold and the wind-driven snow. I could feel Liam shaking with the cold on the bench next to me. Although the idea of keeping the Graham truck in the barn away from nosy coppers seemed like a good idea, the Graham's cab would have blocked the wind. Cal said that the immigration agents at the border wouldn't care about a mule-drawn wagon, but a truck with New York plates would. I was starting to regret this mode of transportation. Mules were not the quickest means to get to the linehouse. At this rate, we would be frozen dead by the time these mules got us to North Troy, forget about making the Canadian line.

"Cal, is there someplace warm or where we can buy some warmer clothes?"

Cal turned to look and said, "Lord, you boys look cold. I think that Mr. Liam's teeth are about to start rattling like an unlatched door in a wind."

"Well, there's an extra saw-buck in it if you can get us somewhere quick."

"Can do, Mr. Callaghan. Can do," he said as he whistled to the mules and slapped the reins.

He steered the wagon around a turn and uphill to the town of Johnson. It was named for the woolen mill and furniture producer. The Johnson Mills store was 'just the ticket' as Joe Sabotski would say. There were racks of good woolen coats. Liam and I outfitted ourselves with thick red and black-checkered mackinaw coats with big collars, and hoods. Cal convinced us to buy deerskin fur-lined mittens and woolen caps. He suggested heavy wool socks but they were too thick for my shoes. While keeping the mackinaws on, we paid for our Vermont warmth. I picked up our topcoats to leave, they felt light-weight and thin. Just putting on the Johnson Mills mackinaws made us feel better.

Back on the wagon, it was still cold. But now dressed for it, it felt like a cold Bronx day instead of the Yukon during the Goldrush. The road northward was a thick wild forest of snow-covered pines. The dense stands of trees sheltered us somewhat in the open wagon from the wind.

The mules pulled us along the road and over a small bridge into North Troy. As the wagon trundled onward, neither Liam nor I were shaking with the cold. North Troy Vermont had just one Main Street called Railroad Avenue. There were several snow-covered cars outside a guesthouse we passed. Cal said that the Journey's End was a meeting place for bootlegging moneymen. Most likely the snowy cars were driven by guys like Liam and me but from Boston, New Haven, or Providence. North Troy was like a Klondike gold rush town. People, cars, trucks and wagons similar to ours crowed the snowy streets. It was busier than Arthur Avenue in the Bronx on a Saturday in June.

Cal turned to us so that only we could hear, "The moneymen work out of North Troy. They stay at one of the guest houses, most in Journey's End and rarely go out of town. They pay local boys to drive over to the line houses in Highwater. With a load of hooch, they run the immigration gauntlet. Most get through and some don't. Some get caught by the US immigration boys who then steal the hooch, lockup the boys then go selling the load to the moneymen themselves. The boys who get caught get nothing but a few days in jail with a fine usually. With Dutch, it's different. We usually get the hooch out, but one time we got caught. Unlike the moneymen, Dutch heard and even had a lawyer help us. Dutch made sure that we got our money even though we got caught. That's something. Lil' Joe and me came up with a plan. We're not going to get caught a second time. Now we have a better way to get the hooch out of Canada."

Then, suddenly it seemed we were back on a wilderness road to Highwater. The mules pulled us through pine forests well-sugared with snow and over a wooden bridge. Cal leaned into the reins as the miles past under the wagon. The road seemed to get narrower before it opened up to a series of long buildings on either side. There must have been a dozen as far as I could see. I had expected a sign saying "US-Canada".

Chapter 18
Copains

Sean

    The very first linehouse was the La Bounty on our side of the road. The La Bounty straddled the US-Canada border with a US flag painted on the south side. On the north side was a red flag with a union-jack in its corner a shield in the red field. I guess that was the Canadian flag. The La Bounty was a long low roadhouse with a foot or two of snow on its steep sided roof. Cal hitched the mules and threw an old army blanket over each. There were several cars and one truck parked there as well. All were dusted white.

    We opened the door to heat, noise, voices, blue smoke and the smell of spilt beer on sawdust. Cal had to bend over to get through the door, so did Liam. I just watched my head. I stepped to the side of the door to allow two drunks speaking French to stumble out into the cold. I let my eyes sweep the room through the fog of cigarette and pipe smoke. The La Bounty was warm, melting the frost from my new wool coat with that distinctive wool smell.

    As I scanned the room through the smoke, I spotted a familiar face from New York. Through the blue haze, there was Legs Diamond and three of his boys sitting at a table near the bar. Cripes! I elbowed Liam nodding my head toward the Diamond table. Liam's eyes widened. I let my eyes drift back to Diamond. Judging by the way he acted, he did not seem surprised to see Liam and me. That was not a good sign.

    I pulled off the mittens and put my hand on the .38 in the chest pocket of the mackinaw. Cal stepped in front of me blocking my view of Diamond. Turning to me from Diamond, Cal smiled thinly.

    With his hand over my chest pocket, Cal quietly smiled, "We're all friends here. Don't want an international incident. We have an armistice here. This is strictly business."

A large bear of a man walked up to us, stopped, threw open his arms.

"*Bon jour, mon ami!*" Hello, my friend! Taller than Cal, he clasped Cal in a hug then holding his shoulders put Cal at arms-length saying, "*Comme cais va?*" How's it going?

"*Bien, mon ami!*" Well, my friend!

The giant had a thick brown beard with a long gray vertical streak on the right side of his face that went from the corner of his right eye to his jawline. He wore a pale blue wool watch cap with a red pompon that resembled a cherry on the large cupcake that was his head. Both he and Cal were over six feet tall. They grow big men in this part of the world.

"*Maurice, faire de connaisance mes copains,*" said Cal. Maurice, meet my friends. Subtly I slipped my right out of the mackinaw chest pocket and extending it toward the big man.

"*C'est Sean et Liam,*" This is Sean and Liam, Cal said.

"*Ravi de vous recontrer tous les deux.*" Delighted to meet you both. The man called Maurice replied taking my hand in a firm clasp pumping it as though I would spout water. He did the same to Liam.

Cal had already informed me that Maurice Faustin was one of the owners of La Bounty and our key connection to get the booze. Maurice led us to a table on the "American side" where four men were playing some game with black wood pieces. The table was back in a corner. Diamond could not see us nor we him. I looked for one of his boys to wander around, but no one did.

Maurice shooed the players away from their game with a wave of his hand then pulled out a chair. They gathered up their game and moved to another table without a comment.

"*Veuillez vous asseoir.*" Please sit.

The four of us sat and immediately I understood the reason that Cal Sabotski drove us here, he spoke French smoothly and effortlessly. We negotiated for two big shipments of hooch, Scotch and Canadian beer. As Cal negotiated, I casually tilted my chair back to bring Legs Diamond into view. Diamond's eyes were drilling into the wall that concealed Cal and Maurice. Then the eyes were on me. I stared back and he glanced away.

Through Cal, we negotiated with Maurice for the better part of an hour. I managed to get the concessions and agreement for more business just as Dutch wanted, maybe a little better. Then we listened as Cal explained the smuggling plan and route. We would take Chemin Rodrique to the Missisquoi river, then

Canadian route 243 or Rue de Masonville that became Railroad Avenue on the US side. Then on Vermont 105 until it became Route 101 to Stowe and on to New York. There were no alternate routes and that meant that coppers could swoop at any point. We needed a better plan.

Cal translated this to Maurice. He pushed back his chair, got up and disappeared into the blue smoky haze. Cal leaned across the table to us, "Maurice is good for his word, so we must be too. He was at the Battle of Vimy Ridge where he took out a German machine gun nest by bayonet. The Canadians took the ridge methodically. They kept at the Huns by bayonet and trench knife when they ran out of bullets. These Canadians are tough. He was wounded later in a German counterattack. Maurice is an honest, fearless, tough guy. Above all there is no man that I would rather have in a tight spot. He takes care of his *copains*. I admire him."

Maybe five minutes later Maurice returned with five glasses of Scotch and another French Canadian who wore a tam-o-shanter named Georges. While Liam and I sipped the Scotch, Maurice, his companion and Cal spoke quietly in French. Maurice and Georges took out Gauloise cigarettes. I struck a match. They leaned into the flame but as I was about to light mine, Georges blew it out.

"Jamais trois," he said flatly. Never three.

"A German sniper would have time to shoot the third man on a match," Cal explained.

With his cigarette wedged in his teeth and smoke closing his left eye, Maurice produced a pencil, drew some squiggly lines on the table talking excitedly with interjections from the Georges. In another minute, Maurice tossed his pencil to the table while pushing his chair back. Picking up the pencil as a pointer, Cal quietly explained the plan in English. It was simple but it should work.

***

Later, the Sabotski boys, Deb, Liam and I sat at their farmhouse table with a Bottle of Johnny Walker. As he worked gun oil into the action of his Winchester '73, Joe said, "Usually, we call this time of year, Mud Season. The snows start to melt then it snows or rains but more rain than snow and it turns roads and fields into icy cold mud."

"I've noticed a ground fog this morning."

"Fog 'eats' the snow in a way that the rain cannot. It makes mud. The fog does make it easy to slip close to deer and add some venison to our larder. Would you be interested in deer hunting?"

"I've never been hunting."

"Deb, did you hear this, Mr. Sean hasn't ever been hunting."

"If you are thinking of taking him hunting then the Cityboy needs some shooting lessons. You should have seen how he was carrying that little pocket revolver."

"Do you have a hunting rifle Mr. Sean?" Joe asked.

"No, there isn't any hunting, well, deer hunting in the Bronx."

"If you'd like, we could take your truck down to Mr. Parker's Hardware to get you a deer rifle."

"I know nothing about deer, rifles or hunting."

"Well, Cityboy I bet that I can learn you about deer," Debbie said, "and more."

A few hours later in Parker's Hardware store on Main Street, I was the owner of an 1898 M98 Mauser and a box of fifty 7.92 rounds. Joe had looked over a few rifles then whistled when he picked up the Mauser. Some doughboy must have brought it back from the trenches of the Great War. The Mauser's beechwood stock had numerous nicks and deep scratches but the bolt handle, bolt and receiver were shiny and clean. With the bolt open, Joe had inserted his thumb into the receiver while looking down the barrel. The light reflected off his thumbnail showed a mirror like spiral of twists without a blemish. Joe was excited as a child about the rifle. I paid Mr. Parker fifty dollars for the rifle, its military sling, a box of 7.92 and the box of .38 ammunition for the Hammerless.

As the Graham lumbered over the ice, slush and mud of the driveway of the Sabotski Farm, Debbie stepped out of the cow barn in coveralls. She made coveralls look like a dress that a swell's gal would wear. Her blonde hair was tied back with a black ribbon. The broads at the Cotton Club and other joints wore their hair short. Not this gal. The flappers at the Club Madrid looked like they just were released from St. Joe's, thin as toothpicks. Not Deb. Her coveralls did not conceal her figure. A wide belt accented her hips while her coverall bib with a flannel shirt under actually emphasized her bosom. This gal was no flapper toothpick.

"Let me see your new popgun Cityboy." She smiled.

I reached behind my seat, picked up the Mauser by the stock and handed it to Debbie. She did a closed-mouth jaw-drop as she hefted the Mauser. Working the bolt and performing the same thumb light trick Joe had done, she looked down the barrel. As she closed the bolt, she looked at me from under blonde-white eyebrows.

She whistled, "Fine firearm Cityboy. How much did it set you back?"

I was distracted by how her breasts moved under the flannel shirt.

"I said, how much did this cost you?" She bent to get her face between my eyes and her flannel shirt. "Oh, all together $50 with some bullets for the .38 too."

Still holding the Mauser, she turned quickly striding toward the barn. "*Viens avec* moi! Follow me!"

I'd follow her anywhere.

Over the next hour, I learned how to shoot. We had placed a dozen soup cans alone a rail fence about 100 yards from the back of the barn. The cows in another field were unconcerned by rifle fire. Before long I had the cans spinning off the rail into the field beyond. I had some difficulties with becoming a 'marksman' as Debbie called it. Shooting requires breath control and concentration. Deb stood close behind me instructing. Very close. I had to really concentrate, especially with Debbie's hot breath in my ear giving me direction and the feel of her pressing into my back. I was willing to shoot all day if she would continue to be my instructor.

"Let me have that pocket pistol of yours."

"Of course." Of course, I wanted my shooting lessons to never end.

With a flick of her wrist the cylinder of the Hammerless was opened. Debbie loaded three rounds then carefully closed the cylinder. She strode briskly to the middle of the field, stopped, turned sideways, extended her right arm with the revolver, fired all three rounds that knocked three cans off the fence railing.

"Now you, your turn Cityboy."

I slung the Mauser diagonally across my back and walked out into the gray light of the field as Debbie re-positioned the cans on the railing. As she walked back, she was loading the Hammerless. Smiling at me, she closed the cylinder into the revolver's frame.

My first shot hit the railing splintering the wood but the next two hit the cans. Opening the cylinder, I removed the spent shell as Debbie placed soups cans on their side on the top of three posts. I saw only the circular end of the can. She walked back then standing really close, picked up my left hand and place three .38 rounds into the palm.

"Here is your final exam for marksman. I expect you to get them all."

"I'll try."

"There's no trying Cityboy, just doing."

I turned. I fired, fired once more and again. Each time a can flew off the fence post.

"Go pick up those cans and meet me in the barn" She smiled and gave me a kiss on the mouth.

We spent the rest of the day in the hayloft with Debbie teaching me. She was the best teacher.

***

"Cityboy, you are the most unusual deer hunter, although that shot at a running deer was very good for a nimrod. But I have to ask, why did you shoot it in the head?"

Debbie and I had the farmhouse to ourselves. Joe and Cal were in North Troy doing some final preparations. They dropped off Liam to buy another truck. We would be moving a lot of booze in the next few days.

"Well, a head shot is a quick kill. Why?"

"Mmmm," she said lying next to me in her feather bed. Taking the cigarette from my mouth, pulling a long slow drag, she exhaled, "Because most hunters want the head for a trophy. But since you're a Cityboy, I guess that it doesn't matter. Thanks for getting some venison for the table."

"What does it taste like?"

"You find out tonight." She laughed. "We need plenty venison meat to make it through the winter. It's a long winter here in Vermont."

"Long winter nights in Vermont can be fun"

Debbie punched me in the arm, "Am I hearing you? You, a Cityboy become a Green Mountain boy?"

"Well, I do like these long dark winter nights…"

With that, she dropped the cigarette into the Moxie bottle at the bedside.

"Well, Cityboy how about another roll in the Green Mountain hay?" She said as she gave me the best view of her yet. Firm breasts with erect nipples, a narrow waist accenting those hips that I found with my hands. She straddled me.

Then Debbie leaned over huskily whispering into my ear as her breast rubbed my chest hair, "Let's find out how quickly you reload."

Chapter 19
Cold Feet

Sean

At 3 am the next day, the Graham was difficult to start in the frigid cold. I was in my mackinaw and Cal in his heavy Filson barncoat. We wore heavy gloves and Canadian style knit caps. I had mine pulled over my ears. The moon was still up casting a silvery blue light on the snow. With Cal at the wheel, we drove the long dark road north. Dense pine forest lined the road making it appear like an unlit tunnel. The Graham rumbled over the planks of the Missisquoi River bridge. The rapids of the river below could be heard clearly even with the truck's heavy engine and the clatter of the bridge boards. Out of the corner of my eye I saw Cal glance at me.

As we turned on Route 101, we went into a skid which Cal deftly controlled by taking his foot off the gas and steering in the direction of the skid. We entered the dark and silent outskirts of North Troy. On Elm Street, light from window in the Journey Guest House was the only indicator that someone was awake. Cal turned left on to Railroad Avenue leaving the sleepy village. North Troy vanished in the darkness behind. The Graham slipped into the dark tunnel of pines again. Cal continued past the La Bounty where Railroad Avenue became Route de Masonville to Highwater, Quebec.

Highwater was the preferred site for Canadians to move liquor to the line houses and ultimately to the American bootleggers. It was another dark village along the Missisquoi with a rail line between the buildings on the street and the river. A light appeared in the road ahead. Cal slowed the Graham.

Like a huge bear standing in the middle of the road, Maurice Faustin was holding a tin lantern. Signaling directions with his lantern, he led us down a narrow path to a barn-like building next to the railroad tracks.

Even before the Graham's lights picked them out, red embers of several cigarettes indicated that we were not alone. As though on a signal, the men smoking by a barn took one last drag then flicked the still burning butts into the snow near the tracks. Cal turned the truck around and backed up slowly with only Faustin's lantern for a guide.

"I'm going to leave it running. I'm taking no chances with it not starting."

I climbed down from the truck and Cal did the same. Suddenly, Faustin appeared. Once again Cal and I was given a bear hug.

"Mes copains! Bonjour!"
"Bonjour, Maurice."
"Viens avec moi, mes copains."

We followed Faustin inside where several lanterns showed stacks of liquor crates and jugs of Molson beer. Emerging from the shadows, Joe Sabotski appeared holding a bottle of Laphroaig Scotch. He smiled broadly. Grinning myself, I took it from him, pulled the cork and took a swig. It was a smooth burn. Just the ticket for a cold night's work. Already, men carrying heavy crates shuffled past us to our truck. As we shook hands, I handed Maurice the envelope of money I had.

Faustin counted the money, leaving a small pile of bills on a desk in the corner. Then he put the envelope with the majority of the money into his own mackinaw. Joe clapped Cal and I on the back before disappearing into the darkness. Faustin was grinning like the Cheshire Cat. He said something to Cal who replied in French.

"He's going with Joe and will meet us later," Cal said.

As we walked back to the Graham, one of Faustin's 'copains' was putting up the tailgate. As we passed him, Georges still wearing his signature tam-o-shanter cap clapped Cal on the shoulder.

"Bonne chance, mes amis." Good luck my friends.

Cal slipped the still running Graham into gear, driving south to North Troy. He grinned at me as we drove past the La Bounty linehouse. We were back in the States. The moon was down. Only a few stars in the indigo sky punched icy holes in the night. There was no hint that dawn would be breaking soon.

Suddenly, headlamps pinned us. Coppers! Cal stomped the brakes. He climbed down to stand in the light. I sat in the cab as Cal handled the situation.

158

The coppers' flashlights searched my face then the back of the Graham. Surprisingly, they backed their truck into the forest to allow us to pass.

Once again, we drove into North Troy straight past Elm Street. We were not following the first plan by taking Elm to route 106 south to Stowe. The Graham rumbled over icy gravel road. If we had moonlight, then we could have made out the Missisquoi River between the pines. Cal stopped the Graham in an open area off the road. We were on the high bank of the Missisquoi. The dark outline of the river bridge was barely visible below. Cal set the brake and reached into his barn coat pulling out a pack of Chesterfields. After he wedged a cigarette between his teeth, he offered me one. He struck a match. The flame touched my cigarette tip with that distinctive crackle.

"I'm going to keep the engine running," he said still holding the lit match.

As the flame touched Cal's cigarette, the window glass on the driver's door exploded. Instinctively, I opened the door, leaping to the snow only to slip falling as another explosive flash roared in the darkness. I crawled to my feet slipping and stumbling toward the pines. I dove headlong over a mound of snow into the pines as another pistol shot snapped past.

I slid down a steep embankment headfirst, gaining speed. I put both hands in front to protect my head as shadowy pines flashed by. Suddenly, something more solid than snow flipped me over. Now, I slid sideways on my back. Then the ground under me was no longer. Everything seemed to slow down. I turned in the air, put both hands against my head, bent my knees to meet the impact that I knew would follow. It did. I bit my tongue as I hit. I crashed through river ice to my knees. Freezing water ran into my shoes taking my breath away. The shallow Missisquoi river's edge was damned cold.

On my hands and knees, I crawled back to the river's snowy bank. As the sky above the river was showing the first faint twilight of dawn.

I heard voices coming from the bridge.

"Did ja hear that?"

"He musta jumped ina river."

"He won't last long. Furgetabout 'im. Let's get the booze and getoutahere."

I couldn't feel my feet. I waited, listening while my feet became a distraction of pain. Truck doors slammed. The Graham's headlights moved, came overhead but not down the embankment. The lights backed away, then swung away into the night and into the pines to the north.

I waited until the Graham's engine noise faded away. The only sound was the whisper of wind blowing powdery snow from pine boughs. The river ran south. South to the next bridge where Liam would be waiting. I took the rocky shore along the riverbank because I did not want to chance getting ambushed up on the road. I thought of calling for Cal but keeping quiet was my best option right now. I stumbled and cursed my way to the second rendezvous. It was a brutal grueling walk. Each step punishing my feet the way Sister Eucharius did when she beat my bare feet with a ruler. I took the beating then, I can take this now.

A pale cold dawn was breaking through the pines on the opposite bank, still I nearly walked into the bridge abutment. I lurched over snow-hidden rocks and tree limbs, trying not break a leg or ankle. Walking along a river in the Vermont darkness requires your compete attention. After some time, I realized that I could see better. I was at the bridge. My feet were frozen but the rest of me was sweaty under the Johnson mackinaw. Cautiously, I climbed the embankment using the bridge buttress both for cover and as a handrail. To the east on the opposite site of the Missisquoi a gray light was brightening into dawn. Long shadows of the pines stretched across the Missisquoi from the other bank. I slipped from one shadow to another, as I climbed the embankment. Before pulling myself to the bridge deck, I stopped and listened. Nothing. I climbed up to the bridge deck. My own shadow preceded me.

Set back in the shadowy pines, there was a truck. Was it the truck Liam bought? I pulled myself up straight. With the hammerless in my hand, I approached the truck. The driver's door was flung open. I dropped to one knee. I aimed at the head that appeared.

"Sean, 'sat you?"

Liam. I relaxed. I limped toward the truck as if my feet were bricks on the ends of my legs. Liam was silent, eyeing me quizzically from behind his thick spectacles. I climbed in the truck's cab.

Briefly, I explained what happened at the North Troy bridge.

"I think Cal is dead and whoever did it, they weren't from around here. They sounded like Lower Eastside boys."

"Cripes, Sean, this is bad. This is really bad. Bad."

"Sure, it's bad but If I don't' warm up my feet real soon I think that they will fall off."

"I have a blanket," Liam said reaching behind his seat.

The shoelaces were frozen stiff as was the shoe leather. As I pulled the shoes off then the wet socks. My feet felt as cold and solid as my frozen shoes did. Liam handed the blanket to me. I struggled out of my mackinaw. Unbelievably, I had worked up a sweat in my walk. As I took my coat off, the chilly air enveloped me, so I wrapped the blanket around my shoulders. I shoved my feet into the warm arm pits of the mackinaw. Liam thrust a Lucky Strike between my lips then scraped a match across the floorboard. It sparked, sputtered then burst in to flame in his cupped hands. I sat back drawing the warm smoke into my lungs. He shook out the match. Then Liam slapped me on the arm.

"Look Sean, there's Cal!"

"Holy Mother of God!" I stabbed out the cigarette.

Cal or his ghost calmly walked toward us. How had he escaped? I had some of his blood splattered on my mackinaw. There he was walking toward us in that barncoat that he wore. The cold dawn sunlight silhouetted him in a halo of blowing snow. Something was wrong, very wrong.

It wasn't Cal. This guy had a heavy police revolver in his hand.

As I opened the truck door, I was greeted by a gun barrel pointing at my right eye. There were two men in long dark topcoats, holding revolvers at me. One taller than the other relieved me of the Hammerless then smirked when he saw my bare feet in the snow.

"Boss, whatcha want me to do?" The shorter one squeaked.

Then Liam appeared from around the back of the truck. Another guy was pushing him with the barrel of a shotgun.

"Go look in the truck for the hootch. Let's see if these boys have anything besides pancake syrup!"

"Wha?"

"Go look!" Said the man in the barncoat backlit by rising sun.

"Yessir boss."

I knew who our killers would be. Legs Diamond and his gang. Diamond was really cheesed off at Dutch moving into Harlem and upper Manhattan. Our own maple syrup trick for the coppers was also played out on Diamond when he highjacked the Graham. That really, really cheesed him off.

"Well, Diamond, you should go into the maple syrup business," I said with a smirk.

Legs Diamond walked up to me. He wasn't taller than me. Without a word, he slapped the barrel of his revolver hard across my cheek. That pain distracted me from my feet.

"Funny man. Smart guy too, eh? Thinking about a vaudeville routine."

"There's nuthin' in dis truck. Nuthin, Mr. D."

Diamond's eyes narrowed. "So where's the hootch, Mr. Vaudeville?"

My cheek was on fire with pain despite the icy wind. The blanket that I was wrapped in blew in the wind. That's when Legs Diamond saw my feet.

"Whatsamatta, smart guy. Someone steal your shoes and the hootch?"

"Yeah, yeah that's the ticket. Some other gang got the drop on us before you."

"Do you think I'm knuckleheaded to believe you?"

"Johnny, you and Ernie take these clowns down to the river for a swim. Artie, you come with me," Diamond said as he walked away.

"I'm going to kill you, Diamond. You can bet your numbers on it," I yelled at his back.

He paused, turned and said, "Mister Vaudeville, your days of being a tough guy are over, over."

I had lost all feelings in my feet again as the two goons pushed us toward the Missisquoi. My mind was racing on how I could turn the tables on the two behind us. Then the heavy Police revolver pressed into the back my head.

"Say your prayers Mr. Vaudeville. Stay still, it will go easier on you."

From behind, I heard quick steps crunching on the snow, then a thump, and a sound like someone dropped a large bag of potatoes. I braced myself for the bullet as a heavy hand gripped my shoulder.

"*Copain, c'est moi. Comment ca vais?*" Friend, it's me. How's it going?

Incredibly, I turned to see Maurice Faustin! One of Diamond's boys was lying at Faustin's feet. In Maurice's hand was one of those wicked looking trench-knives with the brass knuckle handguard. The blade dripped with bright red blood as did the spike on the butt-end of the handguard.

"*Allons y, depeche.*" Let's go, hurry.

A few feet away, the guy who was marching Liam to the river was lying face-down with a bayonet sticking out of his back.

Maurice wiped the trench-knife on the dead man's topcoat. Georges was pulling a long bayonet from the other body.

"*C'est fini*, Georges Martel?" It's finished

"*C'est tout,*" came the reply. That's all.

"*C'est la guerre,*" Maurice shrugged in that Gallic way, "*N'est pas?*" This is war, isn't it?

"*C'est la guerre,*" I said. "*C'est la guerre,* Legs Diamond."

It had been a terrible start to the day. While I sat in the truck trying to warm my feet, all I could think of was Debbie. How would she take it? Maurice, Georges and Liam dragged the two bodies into the woods then used pine boughs to brush away our tracks.

We found the Graham in the woods near the ambush site. The tailgate was down with one of the maple syrup barrels in the brush nearby. Cal's body lay in the snowy tire tracks. His body stripped down to his farmer johns and socks. Bitter winds had blown his bloody shirt and coveralls against a pine tree. Some of his clothes must have been used to wipe his blood and brains from the Graham. Diamond's boys didn't want a mess in the truck they highjacked.

Maurice and I wrapped Cal's body in a blanket placing it in the back of the Graham. Then I climbed into the seat next to Liam. He started the Graham. With Maurice and Georges in the following truck, we turned south toward Stowe and the Sabotski farm.

Debbie was inconsolable, as was Joe. Maurice cooked up some soup, but they weren't having any. Maurice, Georges, Liam and I ate the soup in silence.

"*Mon ami, votre pieds?*" Maurice asked.

"Your feet," Georges translated.

"My feet?" Even this far from the fireplace, the pain in my feet was as though someone was holding them over a fire.

"We saw much of trench-foot in the war."

"Let Maurice do medicine on your feet. He is very good."

The small toes looked purple, while the bottoms of my feet were ghostly white. Even walking on my heels was painful while the rest of my foot was itchy and tingling. The Missisquoi may have saved my life, not my feet.

Maurice put a large soup pot filled with water on the stove. After a while he tested the water with his elbow. He set the pot on the floor next to my chair. As he looked at my bare feet, Maurice made a clucking sound.

"*Mon dieu, mon dieu.*" My God, my God.

Gently, he eased my feet into the pot of water. I stiffened as the water closed over my feet. It was torture. My feet were burning, on fire.

"Patience, *mon ami*," Georges said looking over Maurice's shoulder. "We have saved many feet from being amputated, from gangrene."

Afterward, Maurice dried my feet. Then he massaged each foot with some oil from the kitchen's pantry.

"*Merci*, my good friend," I said.

Later, a noisy Model T rattled to a stop at the Sabotski hitching post. Another one of Maurice Faustin and Georges' *copains* appeared at the door. After a discussion all in French, Maurice announced that he was required at the La Bounty. He and Georges said their farewells through the door to Deb and Joe.

The Model T rattled and whined to life. As they drove off, a deathly silence descended on the farmhouse. Not a complete silence. Deb's chilling, wracking sobs and a ticking Seth Thomas pendulum clock in the hall added to my guilt though there was nothing I could have done.

Our two trucks parked in front of the hitching post were filled with the hootch that Maurice and Joe had smuggled by boat down the Missisquoi. The Sabotski brothers had concocted this plan by moving the booze by river preventing any interception by the coppers. Once Joe arrived with the booze on the US side of the river, we loaded our trucks. The plan worked perfectly with one horrible exception. The murder of Cal by Legs Diamond's gang.

Liam and I should have left for the Bronx by now. Our job in North Troy was over but I could not leave Joe and Debbie like this. Liam and I tried our best. Until we realized that it was our presence that was making it harder for Deb and Joe to deal with their grief.

The last time I saw Debbie was in the side mirror as I drove away from the farmhouse. Her blonde hair was being tossed by the wind as she stood on the porch wrapped in a blanket. The wind whipped up a fog of snow blown from the cow fields. Just as the truck dipped across to the road south, I looked again. She was gone.

I never saw her or Joe again. On subsequent jobs that took me to the Canadian linehouse, only Maurice and Georges remained. Often at the La Bounty and in a crazy mixture of French and English we talked over a beer or Scotch. He heard that Debbie married a fellow and moved to South Thomastown in Maine where he took up fishing and lobstering. Joe Sabotski remained in Stowe, ran his dairy farm but would not have any truck with bootlegging. On one trip to Stowe, I overheard two men talking about a local

"Joe" who was killed while delivering milk and cheese to Boston. I asked if it was Joe Sabotski.

"Yeah, it was Sabotski, Joe Sabotski. His truck skidded off a bridge. We heard that he drowned."

Chapter 20
Colleen's Education

Colleen
1927

Over the next year, I saw a lot of Jim Baker. Despite the difference in our ages, I was falling in love with the guy. But this worried me to no end. After all, he came from a completely different world. His was a world of well-appointed apartments, butlers, maids and a 'cottage' in West Hampton, Long Island. From the pictures on his desk, it was a multistory palace. As F. Scott Fitzgerald wrote, "Let me tell you about the very rich. They are different from you and me."

Jim knew nothing of my early years at St. Joseph's. He certainly knew nothing of our small tenement flat in Hell's Kitchen, or my dear ole Ma. I never invited him further west than Seventh Avenue. Jim was always a perfect gentleman. On a street corner, he kissed me good night, but I never felt any pressure from him to go any further. I must admit, I thought about going further but I really wasn't sure what that all entailed. I was not a sheltered girl by any means, but I was not very well informed either. In the end, it was Dotty who helped me through my growth from child to woman.

Dotty and I met for lunch at Chock Full O'Nuts on Eighth Avenue. I munched on my tuna sandwich while I got grilled by Dotty.

"Sooo, what's happening with you and Jim? Seems like you two have been seeing a lot of each other lately."

Buying time, I wiped my lips with a paper napkin then took a sip of coffee. I swallowed then said, "I really like him, Dotty."

To that, she smiled, "Yeah so, that's good. Isn't it?"

When I didn't reply, "You look so somber, Colleen. Why 'so pale and wan fair lover'?"

"I mean I really like him, but I don't know, I don't know what…I don't know how to, you know, let him know. I think I want to marry him."

"Marry him! Colleen you are so young. How old are you?"

"I am sixteen, almost seventeen," I said a bit more defensively than I meant to.

"Alright, alright but Jim's what? Twenty-five? Twenty-six?"

"He's twenty-four," I muttered into my coffee in answer to Dottie's question.

"Oh, only eight years difference." Dotty arched an eyebrow.

"Not a big deal besides I want to be his wife." That rocked Dotty back in her chair.

"Being a wife is much more than being a girlfriend."

"You know, I'm just not sure what wives do. My mother slept with Mr. Connolly and I could hear them breathing and panting. I even heard my mother cry out; I thought he was hurting her. I was going to go into her room, but they quieted down, and laughed. I was kind of afraid to even knock. My mother gets really mad when I ask anything. Somehow, I instinctively knew I should not interfere. Anyway, she is not much of a role model wife."

At that, Dotty grabbed my hand, "Let's get out of here. Let's take a walk."

As we walked toward Fifth Avenue, Dotty said, "Look, Colleen, I am glad you have feelings for Jim. But you are really young." When she saw me getting ready to protest, she put a gloved finger to my lips. "Let me explain a few things."

She proceeded to give me an education about a man and woman in love. I listened silently as we walked. I felt my face growing redder with each step. I was grateful that we were side by side as I did not want her to see my awkwardness with the subject.

"Being a wife is so much more. You should be dedicated to helping each other no matter what happens. You have to help him by making a home. With all that love making, you have to be prepared for childbirth. Then motherhood. Being a parent is no easy task."

She stopped walking abruptly. Neither of us talking for a few minutes. Then, I said softy, "You are thinking about your Tommy. The child you lost at St. Joseph's, aren't you?"

"Yes, 'tis one of my greatest sorrows."

After another moment, she said, "Recently, my doctor told me I could not have any more children. But Colleen, you have to think about what it means to be a mother. A mother not at all like your 'own dear sweet ole Ma' as you call her. You have to be ready to be a good mother."

Her words struck me. I knew nothing about babies, childbirth or raising children. My years at St. Joseph's Orphanage taught me to hide away, be secretive, to hate and scorn those who hated and scorned me. My only friends were Sean and Dotty. Well, Vianny and Mr. Abernathy were always kind to me. Kindness that's it. I have to learn how to be kind, trusting, supportive and to teach my kids like Vianny taught me to cook. And like Mr. Abernathy taught me to love to read. I have a lot to think about.

Two days later, Jim Baker took me to the cinema. We went for an ice cream soda at a near-by lunch counter after the picture show. Seated next to Jim, I watched him in the mirror behind the counter. He was thoroughly enjoying his chocolate soda. I put down my spoon and swiveled my stool, so I faced him. Looking somewhat surprised, he turned.

"Is something wrong with your soda?"

"No," I replied in a firm voice. Then in a much softer voice I asked, "Jim, do you want to make love to me?"

I thought he was going to choke. He coughed, gagged then wiped his lips with the white cloth napkin.

"Colleen, you never cease to surprise me!" He took my hands in his and raised them to his lips. "You are not like any girl I have ever known."

He turned back to his chocolate soda. I did not move. I was annoyed.

"You did not answer me. That was not an answer."

He swiveled to face me.

"The answer is yes. Yes, I do. Very much. But you are way too young. You need to wait. And I hope you can wait." I stared into his clear blue eyes. "Because when you give yourself to a man, I don't want it to be anyone else but me."

I blushed at that and lowered my eyes.

"Finish your soda and I'll walk you home."

I always parted from Jim on Seventh Avenue. I did not want him to know where I lived. He pulled me close and kissed me with greater force than he had on any other goodnight kiss. I walked home feeling butterflies in my stomach and just a bit wobbly on my feet.

But after that date, he backed off. While we continued to see each other at work in the break room each morning, our dates tapered off to once or at most twice a month.

"Not going to the picture shows these days? Your hoity-toity Wall Street boyfriend has lost interest in ya!" My mother thoroughly enjoyed being critical of me.

I just ignored the remark and got dressed. I was meeting Dotty for lunch in about an hour from now and I wanted to get out of the apartment and away from my mother's caustic tongue.

I met Dotty at our usual coffee shop, Chock Full O'Nuts on 8th Avenue. I secured two stools at the end of the counter and ordered coffee while I waited for her. Dotty slipped onto the stool next to me as I stirred milk into my coffee. It is very important to get your coffee just right.

Satisfied with color of my coffee, I turned to her "Hi Dotty!"

She gave me a little hug, "We need to talk!"

"Oh, oh," I said, "What's up?"

"Let's order first," she smiled.

Over soup and sandwich, Dotty seriously said, "You know, I've told you over and over that you need to do something with your life. Being a page for the Stock Exchange is fine. I mean it gives you a steady paycheck, but it doesn't pay much."

"That's true enough," I replied. I still harbored dreams of being a reporter for the Times.

"Colleen, you have a talent that you are not using. I've told you about this before." She paused, "Be a chef."

"You mean cooking?"

"Yes. Cooking!"

"That all fine and well," I said. "But it's quite another thing to be hired as a cook since I have no real training. And besides, most of the big restaurants hire men as their chefs."

"Yes, I know this. In fact, Alistair and I discussed this, just last night."

"Really? You and Alistair were talking about me last night?"

"Oh, 'tis true. You and Sean come up in conversations more than you could guess!"

I took another bite of my ham sandwich. Patiently, Dotty eyed me over her coffee cup.

"So, what did you two decide about me," I asked with a slight note of sarcasm in my voice.

"We decided you should own your own restaurant."

"Oh, now why didn't I think of that! Being paid as a page, I could buy a restaurant."

Ignoring or not hearing my continued sarcasm, Dotty, said, "Yes, we do think that is the answer for you. And we are very interested in being investors in a restaurant, your business."

I put down my sandwich. I studied her face.

"You are serious."

"We are very serious."

"I, I don't know what to say! Besides, Dotty, I don't know anything about running a business! It's very kind of you and Alistair but I don't know anything about running a kitchen with waiters and waitresses. I would need to buy food, silverware, plates, linens, while managing costs and creating menus. I don't have any experience in any of this. I'm sure there is more that I don't even know about that would be involved."

"But you see, listen to yourself. Colleen, you are already organizing your thoughts regarding this! You managed pantry inventory, food preparation and costs at St. Joseph's while creating menus out of the blue."

I just stared at her. "You are serious, aren't you?"

"Yes! I am. No kiddin', yes! WE are very serious." She touched my arm in a gesture to silence me. "I had a very sad life that was continuing to drag me further down after my Tommy died. I thought of killing myself until Mother Perpetua decided that she should be the one to kill me. I was dying. Dying inside and out. That is, until you and Sean saved me. And at the very time that I needed the most help, you both were there. You and Sean took enormous risks to help me escape that awful place."

"And now I want to help you escape a mediocre life. I found help. I found Alistair and I live a very comfortable life. I'd like to think had I been able to be a mother, I would find ways to help my children lead the best life that they could. I want to help you and Sean. I know Sean gets involved in some more nefarious activities, but I think he would step in and help you, maybe even work with you. That could help him too. You two are a great team. Regardless, I want to help you. And Alistair agrees."

"I don't know where to begin."

"Come to my house tonight. Talk with Alistair. He can help you make a plan."

I stared at Dotty in disbelief. Was it really happening? Was someone really stepping into my life to really help me? This was something out of Horatio Alger story. I would have a 'worldly but good-hearted patron.' I wanted to get out of my mother's Hell's Kitchen apartment, away from that drunkard husband of hers, her daily scrutiny and criticism. But most of all I wanted to live on my own and be as far away from her manipulative rancor as possible.

"OK, I'll come to your house but only on one condition."

"What condition?" Dotty eyed me suspiciously.

"I'll make you two dinner."

Chapter 21
Dottie's Restaurant

Colleen

Two weeks later, I sat on the stoop in front of my mother's brownstone apartment, waiting for Sean. It was almost nine o'clock and Sean usually stopped by to check in on me and Ian. He had no desire to see our mother, the General. To accommodate Sean, Ian and I usually waited on the brownstone's stoop to see him. Tonight, I was alone on the steps. Tonight, I told Ian that I had to speak privately with Sean first.

The streetlamps cast a warm yellow light that softened the sins of the street. It was early September and while the day had been pleasantly warm, the night had the beginnings of an autumn chill in the air. I wrapped my sweater more tightly around my thin body.

"Mikey! What in blazes are ya doin' out here? You'll catch your death of cold."

"Waitin' on you Sean," I smiled at seeing him.

I was always happy to see Sean. He sat on the stoop beside me. Reaching for his shoulders, I gave him a hug. Something on his side, something hard, cold and metallic pressed into me. I ignored what I knew it was.

"Where's Ian?"

"I need to speak with you. I wanted to speak with you, only…"

"What's on ya mind, Mikey?"

As we sat, I told him about Dotty and Alistair's offer. How Alistair had helped me formulate a plan. I told him about how Alistair said that I could run the business and what I needed to do to get a lease and hire employees.

"He told me I need to get a business license and to conform to health requirements to make and serve food to the public. And he told me how to figure out my costs for food and how to price the meals I would serve."

As usual, Sean listened intently to me. He did not interrupt. He just let me talk it all out. All the while I spoke, he stared down at his hands turning them this way and that. The streetlights cast shadows but I could see him thinking.

"So, what do you think? Sean, am I crazy to think I can do something like this?"

He raised his eyes to me and I was surprised to see the look there. He looked sad, I said, "Sean, what's the matter?"

He took a deep breath, "Mikey, I am so sorry! It shoulda' been me to do this."

"Oh, Sean you need not apologize to me. This is a dream that they are proposing. I knew it was a silly dream. But it was fun for a while to imagine it could actually happen."

"Mikey, you don't understand. I believe in you. I know you can do this. You know so much more than you think. I just wish I had thought of this first. I am ashamed that I didn't think of this for you. I am ashamed that someone else is gonner give you the money to do this." He pulled me into his arms. "But know this, I will help you any way that I can."

"Sean, this is just a start. I have more investigating about what I need to do. I need to find out exactly what the business license and health department fees are. Most of all, I need to find a good location. Alistair said that the most important thing to be successful is location, location, location!"

Sean gave me his big lopsided grin. "Well now, that's something I can do for ya!"

Only four weeks later it was whole lot colder outside, so Ian and I were sitting on the inside stairwell waiting for Sean. It was too cold to be on the stoop. He yanked open the door and seeing us he opened his arms for us to both rush in.

Laughing he said, "I've got news!" He looked from me to Ian. "I know you want to keep this confidential but it's cold as a witch's you know what outside. So, let's sit here and I'll tell ya both." Sean, lowering his voice, turned to Ian, "Ian now, you got to promise not to whisper a word of this to anyone. Most especially, not a word to the General."

"I promise," Ian said immediately.

"No, a promise is not enough. Ian, my boy, raise your right hand; you must make a vow to me and Mikey."

Puzzled, Ian looked at me.

I said, "It's OK, Ian. But you must make the vow."

He slowly raised his right hand, Sean said, "Repeat after me. I do solemnly swear," Ian repeated Sean's words. "That I will not tell another living soul what I am about to be told. Most especially, I will not tell the fookin' General."

In a whispered tone, Sean began. Sean had all the information we had discussed, about leases, licenses and City fees. He even found a location in Yorkville that he thought I might like. We made a plan to go see the location tomorrow afternoon. I couldn't be happier.

"One thing, Mikey. You gotta be 18 years old to sign a lease." My smile faded; I was about to turn 17. Did I have to wait a year?

"I was thinkin' that Alistair could sign for it."

I thought about that, but I did not want to ask for more help from Alistair and Dotty. They were prepared to do so much for me already. "I guess so." Then I turned to Sean, "You can do it! You can sign for me. Can't you Sean?"

His eyes twinkled, "It would be my pleasure, Mikey. You bet I can!"

"Let's talk to Alistair and Dotty."

Ian had to study for an examination, so it was only Sean and me to tell Dotty and Alistair about the Yorkville location for our restaurant. At Schraff's on 59th Street, the four of us celebrated the partnership over a Salisbury steak dinner. A dinner that Sean insisted on paying for. I told Alistair and Dotty about the site in Yorkville and how we were planning to remodel the vacant *Hofbräuhaus* restaurant there. Sean explained about the workers that he had pulled together to start the construction once the business license was in hand. Sean estimated we would have it by the end of the week.

Alistair listened carefully then said, "Wow, I'm impressed. This is pretty fast! I've known colleagues who've opened new businesses and it's taken a few months to get the license. What about the City fees?"

"That's all handled," Sean assured him, "I have friends with connections to Mayor Jimmy Walker."

Alistair and Dotty exchanged a look, Dotty said, "Sean, you are a miracle worker!"

Sean did his best Will Rodger's 'aw shucks' grin.

"This is great!" I said, "Sean and I have even chosen a name for the restaurant."

"I am not surprised! You two never let any grass grow beneath your feet," laughed Dotty.

Alistair said, "I like the location. Yorkville is a stable area and generally pretty safe. So, what's this name?"

I took Sean's hand. "We've decided that we will call it 'Dottie's'."

He smiled at Alistair and Dotty's shocked expression. "You've helped my sister not just financially but with learning about what she needs to do. It's the least we could do. Besides, He turned to Alistair, calling it 'Alistair's' sounded way too hoity-toity for the Yorkville folks and the likes of us. Hope you don't take offense."

"None taken. I agree. It does sound too posh. Besides, naming after my beautiful wife is perfect."

Dotty said, "But I owe you and Sean so much. You need not name your restaurant after me!"

"Too late," I said, "it's been decided!"

After much reflection, I knew in my heart the reason that everything fell into place so quickly and why so many of the City fees were affordable. It was Sean of course. He was helping to run a major bootlegging operation in the City. That required a number of public officials and coppers to 'look the other way.' There seemed to be no limit in his growing influence. While I wanted to tell myself this was a positive thing, I knew that it wasn't. He didn't have the respect or admiration of the City officials; it was fear and bribery that propelled them to get in line and issue a business license. The bank manager allowed Sean to sign for the lease even though he had not even a nickel on deposit. I knew all of this without even asking. And I let him do it all the same. Dottie's was becoming a reality by hook or crook.

Chapter 22
Dottie's Library

Colleen
1927

"A restaurant or bistro, not a speakeasy," I said.

"Mikey, hootch will fill tables. Make your customers come back. Yorkville types need beer to wash down their pork chops while the Wall Street swells have to have their rye or scotch."

"What happens if we get raided? The place doesn't have another door like Chumley's."

"With a few hundred bucks, we could build something like the 21 Club, a rotating bar."

"Sean, the place doesn't have enough square footage. We would lose tables. Let me think about it. Don't do anything just yet."

At Union Square, opposite Klein's Department store was an open-air marketplace. A man at the farm stand had a sack of books at his feet while he waited for the greengrocer to weigh his purchases.

He looked at my metal folding carriage. "Excuse me, mam' but where did you get that?"

"This? I found it at a Yorkville Household shop on First off 82nd."

"I need one of those."

"So, let me ask where did you get those books? Looks like you've got a lot of classics there."

"I got them at The Strand Bookshop two blocks down on Broadway."

***

At the Strand, I was like a kid in a sweetshop. The Strand Bookstore was floor-to-ceiling with books. Better stocked than most public libraries. Mr. Abernathy would be in heaven here if he wasn't there already.

So many books, novels, poetry, history and art books! A clerk glided a ladder with wheels affixed to a brass rail near the ceiling to bring down a Walter Scott that I had my heart set on for years, Rob Roy. It was a thick dusty tome. Then I asked for Tolstoy's War and Peace. The clerk on the ladder slid to another part of the tall book rack. Adeptly, he did a fire pole slide to the bottom of the ladder.

"Here's your Tolstoy but let me check it. It feels too light."

"Too light?" I puzzled.

"Oh, shoot! Another glued and hollowed out book. The boss is not goin' to be happy. We must have gotten about a hundred books like this. Sorry Miss."

"Wait! Yes, I'll take this one and I'll even take all the other hollowed out books too."

Dottie's would have a 'library'. My customers would order something to 'read' while they awaited their meal service. Dottie's would have a literary theme decoration that would be functionally a speakeasy bar. Problem solved. Sean loved the idea.

Construction on the restaurant, Dottie's, proceeded without a hitch. The construction crew would not dare to be late or call in sick. They worked from 8 am until 6 pm every day except Sunday. A family owned *Hofbräuhaus* had previously been on this site so it already had a good-sized kitchen. I have no idea why they closed considering Yorkville was home to a majority of the City's German-American residents. And, I didn't consider for one moment that an Irish-American owned restaurant might not work out in the neighborhood. It was simply that Sean said this was the right location and that was that.

City inspection proceeded right smack on time and before I knew it, we were planning a grand opening. Sean had procured tables and chairs, linens and china. Things just seemed to appear in big wooden crates every day. I noticed more than once that there were paper documents tied onto the wooden crates stating the date of their arrival at the Port of New York. Several had scratched out names and business addresses on the affixed labels. Penciled in next to each crossed out address was my name and Dottie's address. Evidently, Sean had made some deals to redirect the cargo hopefully paying for it all as he said he would. But again, I had my doubts.

In addition to bootlegging, Sean was an up-and-coming union boss for New York's busiest Westside port. It didn't take a lot of thought as to how all these goods were arriving on my doorstep. And, as always, I put the thought out of my head. Sean was helping me; helping us all get out of the arms of poverty and out of Hell's Kitchen. That was all that was important.

We opened on a Saturday night. To my surprise, we were packed. That was probably Sean's doing. It created a challenge to get food out and, on the tables, quickly. Even with a new wait staff and inexperienced busboys somehow, we managed. Of course, Dottie's stood out compared to other restaurants and speakeasies. The 'library' was quite unique. As our guests lingered over their literary choice, it gave us ample time to perfect the food service. Sure, we served good food, but our 'library' was really the draw.

Dottie's had a special dining room with built-in bookcases on two walls. We referred to the room as the 'library'. On the lower shelves were books of all kinds, even schoolbooks. It was the books on the middle and top shelves that had a special feature. Each book was hollowed out in the center providing just the right space for a flask. Some contained Beefeater gin, Canadian rye or scotch even cognac. They were our top shelf books. Of course, we also had a 'low price-point shelf' that contained just some cheap old hooch.

I created a special menu for books that gave a brief veiled description of the book contents. Meanwhile, the wait staff would add the necessary additional information that thirsty New Yorkers craved. Just like the Strand, waiters then climbed aboard the library ladder to select the requested volume. It was easy as pie. Even the ladder-gliding waiters became a draw. In the parlance of the speakeasy it was better than "Joe Sent Me".

Soon, customers knew what book contained what flask. Our regulars began to order a steak and baked potato with The Complete Works of Sir Arthur Conan Doyle. Gin, if you please. Or perhaps it might be Shakespeare's, Scotch – As you Like it! Oh, and the customers did like it a lot! When the cops would come by every now and again, they must have thought that our tables were filled with bookworms. There was no head librarian schussing noisy 'readers' either. Dottie's was a good bit noisier than the New York Public Library or any other library for that matter.

Ultimately, the jig was up, so to speak. Word got around town about our special library. But in the end, it didn't matter much because Sean had some 'influence' with the cops that rounded on us periodically. I took note that several of them stopped by after shift to open a good read like <u>The Maltese Falcon</u> Canadian rye or another Dashiell Hammett bourbon story.

I spent my 17th birthday waiting tables, cooking and scouring dishes but I was loving every minute. Wall Street tycoons and Prohibition had made dining out a way of life for the well-heeled New York crowd, politicos and even for mobsters. Sardis opened the same year on West 44th Street. The Broadway types and the Italian mob loved it. But Dottie's got a real mix of the Italian, German and of course the Irish sitting right next to the Park Avenue smoothies. Sean made it known that Union bosses would be well treated and they would all dine in peace at Dottie's.

Unlike Sardis, where fights broke out frequently between rival Italian gangs, Dottie's atmosphere was live and let live. Even when Sean was off on one of his escapades, he made sure that a tough looking group of union dockworkers (cleaned up and in their Sunday best) were seated at the bar drinking 'coffee' and 'reading' books. Funny, but on more than one occasion, I had to turn books right side up. Poor lugs obviously didn't know how to read. One fellow became our basement-bartender mixing Manhattans, Rob Roys, and Martinis for discerning diners. I picked up several more copies of Walter Scott's novel, <u>Rob Roy</u>. We referred to his mixed drinks as inter-library loans.

But the union guys were at Dottie's as insurance and security. I was well protected. And if anyone started to get out of hand these longshoremen were quick at a troublemaker's table. They would either frog-march the miscreant out or pour oil on the troubled waters with a twelve-pound hand on a non-cooperative customer's shoulder. Usually, whispering some forecast on what would happen if they did not quiet down was enough. Another owner might have been off put by all of this. But not me.

I grew up in a rough environment headed by some of the most wicked women who portrayed themselves as servants of God. Then I moved into Hell's Kitchen. So, this seemed perfectly normal to me. The Twenties were supposed to be hard times for bootleggers but in reality, it was a boon! Every night my little restaurant was crowded. People waited anxiously for a library table. Oh, it was heaven!

After the cold, hard, and downright mean early years of my life I suddenly found myself in a good place. Dotty started me on the dream and gave me my first bit of seed money to open a restaurant. I put it in the bank immediately as I did not want Mother to find it. Then Sean gave me money – lots of it – to open this restaurant on Second Avenue in Yorkville. My kitchen experience at St. Joseph's taught me an important lesson. I learned to cook without the heavy Germanic methods. I offered simpler fare: roast chicken and steak, fresh vegetables and potatoes! I am Irish after all; there isn't a potato dish that I don't like. And at my restaurant, I made all kinds of potatoes. We found a good friend in Miss Dorothy Gale in those awful years at St. Joseph's. And quite frankly, I wanted to never forget how inhuman those 'Sisters of God' were to all of us. They were especially cruel to Dotty.

It seemed only right that she is recognized in some way. In quiet moments I could think about this lovely young woman who faced hardship with such grace. Finding her again that cold day at the skating rink and renewing our friendship was a turning point in my life. She gave me the seed money I needed to open the restaurant and more importantly she gave me hope when she suggested that I become a chef. But of course, it was Sean, my guardian angel who somehow found the rest of the money I needed to make this dream of running a restaurant possible.

When we opened the restaurant, speakeasy actually. Our name for it was an obvious choice, *Dottie's*. I don't really know where Sean got the money and all that equipment to help me keep the place running on a day to day basis.

I must admit, I never asked. Often a truck from the Bronx would make a surprised delivery. Sean suggested ways to quickly hide liquor if we were raided. Lucky or well prepared, Dottie's was never raided.

When we walked out of the orphanage, we had nothing. So, for Sean to come up with such a large amount of money I knew in my heart it had been stolen or at least, illegal. But I wanted to be on my own. I wanted to be away from my mother and her dinky stifling apartment on Tenth Avenue. I wanted out of Hell's Kitchen. It was important to me to start anew.

Chapter 23
Texas Guinan

Colleen

Dottie's took off! To my continued surprise, my little restaurant was hailed by the Daily News and the Post as a refreshing change from the usual Yorkville fare. The well-heeled Eastside crowd filled my tables and ordered lavishly. Dottie's was noted for its kitchen, not just the 'library' service at the tables. The fact that all this occurred during Prohibition is all the more amazing. Sean kept me in good supply of good Canadian whiskey, Scotch, and Bourbon. As I said, we were never raided, not even once. Of course, having customers such as Mayor Jimmy Walker and his Tammany Hall cronies helped. I greeted all the customers, but not the way my friendly competitor "Texas" Guinan did.

Texas ran the Salon Royale on the Westside on 53rd Street. Her real name was Mary Louise Cecilia Guinan. She would say things like, "Hello suckers" to her customers! She was quite a gal. With her brunette curls, Clara Bow lips and ever-present ermine boa, Mary Louise or 'Texas' as she preferred to be called was the embodiment of the woman of the Roaring 20s. She had been in vaudeville and acted in the flickers, *Girl of the Border, Soul of the West* and *Moonshine Feud*. In the cinema, she was a gun-toting cowgirl who was a match for all the bad guys. Her speakeasies, she 'owned' several, were raided often. That did not bother Texas one bit. They could never prove that she actually owned the speakeasy. Often, her picture, accompanied by her scantily clad chorus girls graced page four in the Daily News. The charges were always dropped.

We met at her 300 Club on West 54th shortly after Dottie's opened. She became my speakeasy mentor and sometime friend. It was Texas who said that Dottie's had to expand or move to a larger space.

"Sweetie, I know that you don't need a stage for some chorus chicks as I do but you need a bigger joint. With a bigger joint you can fit in more of those meat and potato men."

"Dottie's doin swell but it is tough on the kitchen staff…"

"Sweetie, with more tables come more do-ray-me, if you catch my drift?"

"Where would I go? Would my crowd follow me? I'm not a showman like you, you're famous. I mean Walter Winchell writes about you. Even if you and your chorus girls get arrested in a raid, you're in the morning papers."

Texas took another pull on her Lucky Strike and in her west Texas drawl said, "Sure I did vaudeville, singing my heart out to the crowds, it's my way of beating the padlock boys. I need the papers to keep me in the morning news. Pictures of me and my chicks being locked up brings in those meat and potato men with big Wall Street money throwing that money around my clubs. They know how to find me."

"But how would they find me if I relocate?"

"They sniff out the hooch. As long as you have hooch they'll find y'all."

She lifted a bejeweled arm to look at her new Swiss watch. Blinking through the blue haze of smoke, she said, "Sweetie, I have to be moseying along. You should get along on home too. Think about going big. It works for me."

Taking the cigarette from her ruby lips and crushing it out in a coffee cup, she embraced me in a Texas bear hug. Then holding both my shoulders in her strong hands, she said, "We gals have to stick together. We got the world lassoed. We have New York in our saddlebags!"

I walked out of her Club feeling completely out of my element. Texas was a smooth, fast-talking woman. But I also knew Texas was right. If I had a larger restaurant with a bigger kitchen, I'd make more money. Of course, I make four times as much on the booze or the hooch as Texas called it than I do on the kitchen. Yet, it is my food that keeps customers coming back. I'm not like Texas, so I need to make sure my food is good, really good. Sean makes sure that I get the booze that Dottie's needs and keeps the other bootleggers from muscling me.

One of my well-heeled diners, told me that some big investors were buying stocks on the cuff.

"They don't pay for the stock up front, they say, 'put it on the margin. I'll wire the money when it's called." Well, I can't pay for my food or my payroll on margin. I have to pay on delivery.

I run a great kitchen and I take good care of my staff. Customers ask me to compliment the 'chef' not knowing that's one of my hats too. Maybe I should be louder and sing my own praises or wear big hats and ermine boas like Texas. No, I still prefer my own quiet style. That is my comfort zone. Besides wearing a boa would just keep flopping into the soup pot.

When I told Sean I needed a new location so I could build a bigger restaurant he just smiled at me. "Mikey, I knew you were a winner! That's swell!"

Miraculously in two days' time, the landlord told me that the establishment next to Dottie's was suddenly going to be vacant. It was a bookkeeping company, and its space would double the size of Dottie's nicely. I stopped by the next day to talk to the proprietor.

"Hello," I said to the receptionist, "is Mr. Packard available? I am Miss Callaghan from Dottie's next door"

"Oh, Miss Callaghan…I will check." She got up from her desk and walked to the back of the office, closing Packard's door as she went in. She returned in just a moment with a regretful smile.

"He is so busy. We are preparing to pack up and there is much filing and paperwork to be completed."

"Oh," I said, "I just wanted to wish him well and to find out where you are moving to."

The receptionist hesitated a moment. Just then, Packard emerged from his office, seeing me still standing in the vestibule, he called out, "We do not wish to tell you where we are moving to, Miss Callaghan. Louise, please come into my office, now."

He turned on his heel and disappeared into his office once again. Mr. Packard had always been so cordial to me before but now he is dismissive and rude. I think he had been solicitous in the past because he wanted to do our books, so he went out of his way to be especially nice. This was a decidedly different attitude toward me. Initially, I wrote his behavior off as anxiety about his move. But later I suspected that Sean had something to do with Mr. Packard's sudden decision to close up shop next door to Dottie's.

While it appeared that Sean was influencing those around me in order to help me, my mother was sticking her nose into my business, not in a helpful way. She would stop by in the middle of the afternoon while we were getting ready for the supper service and complain of poverty.

"Colleen, I'm short ten dollars for the rent this month" or "Your poor mother needs a winter coat."

Even as she told me these lies, I could read her eyes. I have always believed the eyes are the mirror of the soul within. She looked as if she was laughing at me as she fabricated a new story to exact money from me. I would give her a five or a ten just to get her to leave me alone. I had no love for this woman who gave me birth. She robbed me and Sean and Ian of a childhood. And while she destroyed our early years, when she had Sean highjack a truck, she set him on a path with no return.

It's kind of crazy to understand that while I had no love for my mother, she was the central figure of our family unit as dysfunctional as it was. My younger brother Ian was working as an assistant in a men's wear department on Fifth Avenue, Best & Company. With the fine clothes that his foster parents had given him he talked his way into a good job on Fifth Avenue. He dressed well and spoke like an Upper Eastsider.

I was working day and night doing whatever it took to make my restaurant profitable. I cooked, I even cleaned pots, I managed the wait staff and the books. I wanted Dottie's to be more than a speakeasy. I wanted a restaurant.

Each night, I gussied myself up to welcome our supper guests as the hostess. Dottie's guests were an eclectic group of people. On most nights my tables were filled with German immigrants living in Yorkville. Other tables were filled with Eastside swells, Sean's bootlegging buddies, even the City's municipal officials and police. Giving into my mischievous side, I occasionally seated City politicians next to bootleggers. It was amusing to watch Mayor Jimmy Walker try to pretend that "Dutch" Schultz was not sitting at the next table. Running a restaurant during Prohibition was not boring, far from it.

But Sean struggled every day dealing with the lower than lowlifes on Tenth Avenue, the Bronx and on the docks. Loyalties shifted, rivals became partners, pals became enemies. His was a violent shadow-world. But no matter what, he checked in with me almost every night. Most of the time he came to Dottie's just before closing, finding me counting receipts, saying "good night" or shutting down the kitchen. He would sit at the bar nursing a whiskey while I locked the door. Sean would ask me about my day. He never talked about his day or nights. He'd ask if there was something that I needed, for myself too. On the rare instances that he was too busy to come by, he would call me.

"I'm going to visit a friend in Vermont to go hunting," Sean said on the phone one night. Or he was going fishing with someone he called the "Dutchman" in the Catskills for a few days. Once he took a railroad trip to Florida returning a week later with bags of oranges for the restaurant. Then as always, Sean looked out for me, just as he had so many years ago at St. Joseph's. When I told Sean about Mother's coming around to my restaurant, he blew his top.

In a strange way, I liked giving her a few dollars only if it would show her how wrong she had been about us. She was wrong to abandon us the way she did. As kids, we were a burden financially; I can understand that. But more than a financial obligation, she left us at that awful place because she did not want the drag of young children while she was on the hunt for a new husband. But I am grateful for the mental acuity all three of us inherited from her and our father, whoever he was. We might not have had formal education but we were street smart, and learned quickly. We were imbued with a common sense that served us well.

Chapter 24
Getting Ahead

Colleen

Sean was on a trip to Canada or was it Phoenicia? I can't remember. His trips were so frequent, I could barely keep track. Usually, he would return with barrels of booze and crates of hams. Once, he even brought some deer meat, venison.

That evening, as my dock worker pals were sitting at the bar thumbing through a Sam Spade or pre-mixed Manhattan, I heard a familiar voice. Jim Baker was standing at the *maître d'* podium asking for me. He had been out of my life once I quit my job on Wall Street. My time was totally consumed with getting Dottie's open and running the business these past few months. I thought of him often, but he really had no way of getting in touch with me since he did not even know where I lived. And it seemed my miserable Mother was probably right; he had lost interest in me. But all at once, there he was standing just a feet away.

"It took me almost six months to find you. Your younger brother Ian is the one who told me where you were and what you were doing."

"Ian? How did you find Ian? I never told you about him."

"Well, Colleen, you never told me much about yourself and your family at all."

I shrugged "There isn't much to tell."

"No? Then what all this?" Jim's used his well-manicured hand to indicate Dottie's. "I'm told you are the owner! Anyway, I waited outside of your apartment on West 45th, for weeks just for a glimpse of you. I kept seeing this kid who resembled you. It was your brother Ian. Then I took my time before I approached him…"

"My apartment?" I was devastated. "You went to my Ma's apartment on Tenth Avenue?"

He blinked. "Colleen, I followed you home a couple of times, so I knew where you lived."

"You did that…"

"I wanted to be sure you got home safely. When I realized you were walking west past Times Square into Hell's Kitchen, I knew I had to follow. I kept my distance discreet, as it was clear you did not want me to…to…"

I finished the sentence for him, "To see where I lived."

With that I signaled one of the waiters over and asked him to bring me The Thin Man and two coffee cups. In a minute, the waiter was back with the book and two cups and saucers. Jim looked at me quizzically. But he looked impressed, when I produced a hidden flask then poured a measure of gin into his cup and mine.

"Look, Colleen, I told you that you are unlike anyone else I know." He indicated our coffee cups. "Totally, unlike anyone I've ever known. I've looked for you because, because…we belong together."

He reached across and took my hand. "I hope we can see each other like we did before."

I glanced around the room. Sean's dock pals were eyeing us carefully.

"Well, maybe not like before," I laughed. "I discovered that gin is pretty good, don't get me wrong I still like ice cream sodas." But raising my cup to my lips, "I've got a taste for this stuff too."

It was like our time apart never happened. One year later, Jim and I got married. It was a modest wedding. His family did not want to have anything to do with me or Sean. That was fine with me. They lived in a big brownstone on Riverside Drive and were as white bread as they come. His mother was one of those puritanical types. A holier than thou who believed Prohibition was righteousness and that booze was the way of the devil. So, when Jim introduced me to Mother and Papa in their spacious 'conservatory room' with a Steinway grand piano and a view of the Hudson it did not go well.

The shock on their faces when I told them that Sean Callaghan was my brother was comical. Our visit was short. His Papa claimed that they had a previous engagement to attend. As we left, I saw the dining room table was set with candles lit.

They disowned Jim and wanted nothing to do with us as a couple. We got married in City Hall. That was fine with me, I could care less about getting married in church. I know Jim was disappointed in his family's reaction. He did want a good Episcopalian church wedding. But I assured him that marrying a Catholic, even a bad one like me was not going to get him in the Episcopal Church's good graces. We found a cute little apartment in mid-town, midway between Wall Street and Yorkville.

***

A few months later, sitting at the bar, nursing a whiskey while I counted the night's receipts and cash, Sean said, "Mikey, we need money to finance college for Ian. He's gonner be a lawyer." He placed a fat envelope on the bar in front of me.

I almost laughed out loud at his grin. Sean was so proud of Ian; you'd think that Ian was an attorney already. My restaurant was doing well. We had enough to pay for his first year's tuition and books at Fordham. I secretly hoped Ian would indeed become an attorney as I had a nagging suspicion that Sean would one day need his help.

"Yeah, but we will need more than just this, Fordham Law is pricey."

I always worried when Sean started talking about expensive stuff. It usually meant he would be going away on one of his 'trips'. And these trips were always dangerous. He would come back exhausted, beat up and bruised. But he would always hand me a wad of cash. "Stick this away for me, Mikey," he'd always say.

Ian had started Fordham that September and he did us proud, oh yes! He studied hard and was first in his freshman class. He was living with Jim and me in my two-bedroom apartment in mid-town.

It was important that we kept Mother away from Ian. In many ways he was so much younger than Sean and me. He would make excuses for her ignoble actions even though her true self always emerged in the end. He craved love and acceptance from her. After all he had experienced a good family life for his first formative years. It wasn't until the foster family had applied to adopt Ian that they were forced to bring him to St. Joseph's.

Then Mother Perpetua and our less-than-sweet-ole Mother decided to spring all three of us from our hell hole. But of course, Perpetua might have put two of us out regardless, since I was turning 14 and Sean 16. For Mother, it was a big win. We could be employed and that meant we could be useful to her at last.

But Sean had other ideas about Ian. He wanted Ian to have the time to study and attend school without the need for a job to support himself. Of course, Ian being true to his blood would not oblige. If he could not get an outside job, he would work at Dottie's. Bussing tables, mopping floors helping me with the receipts and just being useful. It did not matter how late he worked, he would come back to the apartment and open his books on the kitchen table and study for a few more hours before going to bed. He was smart. He had the gift of seeing people for who they really were (everyone except Mother) and he had a remarkable memory. He could read something and remember it exactly, word for word, number by number. He began to help Sean keep track of shipments of hooch. That had to stop before he entered Fordham Law.

I am getting ahead of myself.

Chapter 25
Depression

Colleen
24-29 October 1929

For the next couple of years, I busied myself with running Dottie's. Sean kept me focused on the restaurant. Alistair and Dotty pitched in too. Alistair arranged a number of catering jobs in and around Wall Street. Between running the restaurant and these catering gigs, I was darn busy.

One Thursday morning, I stopped into the president's office at the Bank of New York. Thanks to Alistair, I had been engaged to cater a luncheon for the chief executives and other mucky mucks that afternoon.

"The timing for the luncheon has been changed," he informed me.

I need to step up the start time by two hours! My staff was just sitting around the bank's kitchen smoking. I got them up and into motion. Within five minutes, we had the truck unloaded and began the dining room set up. The staff had polished every piece of silverware so that it gleamed. The samovar and silver servers were dazzling in the sunlight pouring through the windows. It would make the just the right touch of formality and elegance to the meal.

At 11 am, I saw men wearing expensive suits handing their hats and fawnskin gloves to the coat checker. Dorothy's husband, Mr. Alistair MacMillian was at the door personally greeting these important men. They solemnly entered the Dining Room as though it was a mortuary. I realized our work on this beautiful meal was for naught. The heads of every banking house from Chase National, National City and J P Morgan paid no mind to either the silverware or the food. Before the meeting began not one scone, profiterole, or éclair was touched.

In hushed tones, the leading men of the major banks offered suggestions to Mr. Richard Whitney, the VP of the Stock Exchange. In the few hours since the opening bell, the Stock Market lost 11% and the ticker tape was already hours behind. Investors had no idea what the stocks were doing. Mr. Whitney sat at the head of the table, then signaled to one of waiters to pour him a coffee.

With a total lack of expression, Mr. Whitney listened to each banker talking in turn. Across from Mr. Whitney, Alistair fidgeted.

Then, Mr. Whitney stood. The room went silent. Even the wait-staff stood in dread silence for Mr. Whitney's words.

"History, as I learned at Harvard is about leadership. Our strategic leadership will prevail, but it needs action, specifically symbolic action. Action can bring order out of the emotional contagion of chaos and panic. To do so, a leader needs resources and support. Support of men with the gumption and determination, men such as yourselves. I will need your resources behind me. Immediately, with your financial backing, I will be on the floor of the Exchange to purchase a substantial block of shares in U.S. Steel. Then I will bid on other blue-chip stocks, symbolic action that will allay the fear on the trading floor. Just as it did for the Panic in Aught Seven. I will be your Sir Gawain who will preclude the Green Knight of Black Thursday from any further games, chaos and panic."

"Hear! Hear!"

The bankers rose from their seats around the board room table to give Mr. Whitney an ovation. I wasn't quite sure what was happening. But Alistair clapped so enthusiastically that his silver hair shook like a lion's mane. Little did I know, I was witnessing history, the crashing of the New York Stock Market.

I could not have guessed that in less than ten years, Mr. Whitney would be arrested, sentenced to Sing Sing Prison. He was a criminal. His deeds were worse than anything Sean had done. Whitney dressed in a thousand-dollar suit robbed with a stroke of a pen. More people died, became unemployed, and homeless because of his embezzlement and speculative 'investments'. After he was paroled, Whitney who was banned from any Wall Street work became a gentleman farmer in Far Hills, New Jersey. Holy cow, I guess that some crime does pay.

The crash of the market delivered a blow to Dottie's too. It seemed that only the bootleggers and politicians had money to spend. My restaurant was becoming their hangout. Sean kept me supplied with booze and kept me with enough money that paying the rent was not a problem but I still had to let some of my staff go. I was back to cooking, hostessing and waiting tables.

One dark November night, Sean walked into Dottie's and immediately pulled me aside.

"Mikey, we need to talk."

Unmoving, I said, "So talk" But looking at his face I could see there was something bad happening.

"What is going on?"

"Not here. Let's go into your office."

My mind flew. "Ian! Is he OK?"

"Ian is fine. It's not about Ian."

"Then what?"

He propelled me into my little office in the back of the restaurant closing the door behind us.

"Sit."

I steeled myself and sat down. I wiped my now sweating hands on a kitchen towel that I had thrown onto my desk earlier that evening. If it wasn't about Ian then it must be something wrong with Sean.

"Are you in trouble?" He solemnly shook his head, no.

"Oh God, Dottie's. Are we going to lose the restaurant?"

Sean sat on the side of my desk. "It is Dotty, not this place."

"What do you mean?" I swallowed. My throat had suddenly gone dry. "What happened?"

"One of my boys, Bernie was working a deal out in Oyster Bay for the past couple of days. He told me…Mikey, Dotty and her husband were found dead last night."

I stared in disbelief at Sean. "Oh no! Are you sure? Are you sure it was them? What happened? How did they…?"

"They were found dead in their home last night."

He continued, "Bernie's cousin, Joe is the MacMillian's driver. Alistair and Dotty were supposed to go somewhere last night. When they didn't answer the door, Joe looked through the window. All the lights were on so he could see. Joe saw they were both dead in the living room. She was on the floor. He was slumped over on the couch. Blood everywhere…"

He stopped short realizing that I did not need to hear all of the gory details. I sobbed and Sean pulled me to my feet into a bear hug. My heart hurt. I flashed on the years of sadness and pain that three of us experienced at St. Joseph's. I thought about that awful night when Sean and I helped Dotty to escape. I wished it was not true that somehow someone made a mistake. But of course, it was true. Dorothy Gale MacMillian was gone.

**

As for Jim and myself things were terrific for a while. Then Black Friday in 1929 happened. The stock market crashed. Life changed dramatically. While Jim kept working at the Exchange, it wasn't the same. He became moody and irritable. Jim stopped coming to Dottie's to chat with me while I closed up. Then it began. He started gambling in high stakes poker and more than once Sean had to stop a fight between Jim and some of his poker pals. One night, he didn't come home at all. Sean was out of town so I didn't find out what happened to Jim until the next day when one of Sean's guys knocked on my door to tell me that Jim was in St. Vincent's Hospital on West 12th Street.

I immediately went to the coat closet, as I reached for my hat and coat, Sean's pal gently closed the closet door.

"Mrs. Baker, uh…Jim er, your husband. He didn't make it."

I stared in disbelief. Shocked. Gut punched.

He continued, "Jim was in a high stakes game. He got ina' a beef with one of those sports he plays poker with yer know? They really got into callin' each other cheats and stuff. This sport din' take it. No guns or knives but then the sport was a big Polack. He din' need it. He went at Jim like Joe Palooka. What I hoid, he whooped in several roundhouses to Jim's noggin' and a mean upper cut that may have snapped his neck. Anyway, Jim was probably dead before he reached the hospital."

So, my rotten Irish luck continues. I lost the one guy that I really loved and who actually loved me. I identified Jim at the St. Vincent's morgue then went home. But, before I could finalize funeral arrangements, Sean blasted into my apartment like a freight train on fire. He packed up my stuff leaving all traces of Jim behind and moved me uptown to a big two-bedroom apartment in Yorkville just a few blocks from Dottie's. Fresh start. As always, he was there for me. He made sure I was at work and he made sure I stayed off the gin. Once again, my dear brother Sean saved me.

Chapter 26
Fishing and Hunting

Sean
Phoenicia, New York
23-27 April 1931

"Let's go trout fishing," Dutch said to me out of the blue.

The next thing I knew, we were checking into the Phoenicia Hotel in the heart of the Catskills Mountains. I flopped on the bed, but Dutch had other ideas. He pulled me to my feet, out of the hotel and across the Main Street to the Forkert Brothers store. The main characteristics of Forkert Brothers' Dry Goods was a clean cedar smell, neatly arranged stock in glass cabinets. And I might add, it was distinctly German. Dutch was happy as a schoolboy in a sweetshop. He hungrily yet meticulously went from display case to display case. He picked out things that I had never seen before, asking a lederhosen wearing boy about item after item.

Dutch took my fedora off replacing it with a green felt Tyrol hat with what looked like a shaving brush pinned to the hat ribbon that was made of a braid of bird feathers. He bought three bamboo fishing rods with reels and a box of bugs that had fishhooks. The bugs weren't bugs but bird feathers wrapped around the hooks to resemble bugs.

"My Papa would take me fishing. You don't have a Papa, so I take you."

That did not pair up with what I heard about Dutch at the Schultz Trucking. Word was that Dutch's father abandoned the family. That Dutch's Papa was no father. But, if this is the story that Dutch is telling, who am I to say differently. After all, there was a time I did not know that I had a brother or even a mother.

"Thanks," I said. "I'm going to grab a pair of warm socks, my feet are freezing."

"You do that, it's on me. Take our packages back to the hotel while I pay Little Herman here," Dutch said, as he took a large roll of bills from his hip pocket.

Next morning, Dutch had me up at dawn. Dutch showed me how to fly-fish on the Esopus Creek that ran next to the town. After a few snags in tree branches, I used a sidearm pitch like the Yankees' Gordon Rhodes to cast the line. Dutch and I caught several trout that we brought to the hotel for dinner.

That evening, we sat in the Phoenicia Hotel dining room that was a magnificent, vaulted room with a large fireplace. Fittingly, the fireplace had a huge moose head mounted over it. The room was decorated with plates and crests of several German towns, Munich, Dortmund, Bremen and more.

Dutch shared his Canadian beer with the other diners. I ate trout almandine for the first time. Dutch showed me how to open the fish like a book to remove the skeleton and head in one piece, like a cartoon cat.

What started as a fishing expedition, ended as a hunting trip. On Monday, we drove out of Phoenicia up the Stony Clove Road past a small lake by a large boulder.

"That's the Devil's Tombstone." Dutch laughed. "Turn right here we'll drive through the 'Eyetalian Alps' down to the 'Irish Flats'."

Dutch was correct. We passed one Italian named place after another before the road dropped into a steep and narrow mountainside road with a treacherous drop to the Schoharie Creek below. Dutch said the locals call a creek, a 'crick'. With white knuckles, I gripped the wheel, not relaxing until we crossed a rickety bridge with the road leveling into the town of Palenville.

"Let's stop here for lunch," Dutch said pointing toward an open field in front of Griffin's Irish House. "Let's see if the Irish can cook."

I was about to say that my sister was a fine cook. I mean, her restaurant was more famous for the food than the booze. I didn't say nothing. We went in, sat at the bar and ate thick liverwurst sandwiches with mustard and onions, washing them down with some hard cider, the locals called it 'Dutch-courage'.

"I like that, Dutch-courage." Dutch laughed.

We sat at the bar joking with the owner-bartender named Jack who had a sweet-rich Irish brogue. A large cathedral radio behind the bar interrupted the music with an announcement about King Alfonso of Spain who was abdicating. We sat drinking more Dutch-courage as Dutch and Jack Griffin discussed the events in Spain. Was King Alfonso XIII abdicating or just going into exile? Would there be a civil war in Spain?

As we ate, Jack, changing the subject, said that Gov. Roosevelt just vetoed the medicinal liquor bill.

"That means Prohibition will be around for a long time."

"Ain't nobody thinks any different Jack," said Dutch.

We were the only men in the joint until this little guy, much littler than me, waddles in, looks at Dutch and me and be-lines over. Dutch squats down as the little guy whispered something. Dutch handed him a few bills from his hip pocket roll. Dutch stood up.

"Thanks Willie," Dutch said as the little man climbed up on a bar stool next to us. Dutch looked me in the eye, "Let's drive."

I paid the barkeep as Dutch walked out into the April twilight.

By dark, we were on a road called Heart's Content Road just off State Route 32 in Cairo, New York. We checked our revolvers.

"Do you think Prohibition will end soon?"

"Yeah, what I think is that Roosevelt is really for Repeal. Hoover is too conservative. He won't end the Depression or end Prohibition. The economy is in the shitter. He wants business to keep wages where they are. Then he tells the unions not to strike. He raised taxes then signed the Smoot-Hawley Act that started a tariff war. We are lucky that Canada didn't place a tariff on booze, or we would be out of business."

"Yeah, but if they repeal Prohibition then we will be out of business."

"We can get into the numbers like Bumpy Johnson. Maybe protections. Me, I'm favoring working on unions. The G-men and coppers only bust heads of strikers. We can be union sluggers against the owners' strikebreakers."

"Running booze down from Canada is one thing. I'd like to run it from ships right to the Westside docks. We can haul more booze in one boat than a dozen trucks."

"For now, we do really good hustling beer and hooch," Dutch said. "The bible-thumping Protestants won't let Prohibition die.

Dutch stopped talking. In the quiet, I could hear a little stream running southward to the Hudson River and New York. Then Dutch opened the door and he stepped over to a nearby bush. He peed, buttoned up and climbed back in.

I said, "So, what are we doing here?"

"We goin hunting."

"Hunting? Hunting what?"

"Legs Diamond. Let's put some daylight into Diamond."

"Do you know where Diamond is?" I asked.

"Yes, my little friend said that he'll be at the Arastoga Roadhouse a mile or two away. You ready?"

"You betcha I am." I started the roadster.

Our headlamps punched a tunnel of light as we drove. The Arastoga Roadhouse appeared in the lights. To enable a fast getaway, I backed the roadster in next to the front door. Leaving the roadster's engine running, we quickly opened the door to the roadhouse.

Inside was a large mud room studded with coat pegs. My eye went immediately to a Filson barncoat. It was Cal Sabotski's coat. I cocked the hammer of my double-action revolver. Dutch and I pushed open the double doors to the Arastoga dining room.

"Hello Diamond, it's me, Mr. Vaudeville!"

***

Diamond somehow survived.

I put three slugs in him. I even put one in his hard head as he shot back. He missed both me and Dutch. We didn't miss, yet he lived. The Arastoga was the second time that Diamond was gunned and lived. Back in '27, he had been shot in the chest but the docs at Bellevue Hospital pulled him through.

Months later, I had another chance, when Noe and Schultz tried to have a peace parley with Diamond at the speakeasy Club Madrid. Joey Noe waited outside on 54th street while I covered from a third-floor window. It was an ambush. Diamond had it planned. As the car pulled to the curb, Diamond, Arnold Rothstein and Lou Weinberg shot Joey Noe first. Joey was able to get off a few rounds, all missed. I could only see their muzzle flashes as the roof of the sedan obscured the shooters. Even with the Mauser I was only able to hit Weinberg, not Diamond.

Then sometime later at his suite at the New York Hotel Monticello, another mob shot him five times but still didn't kill him either. At this, Dutch said, "Ain't there nobody that can shoot this guy so he don't bounce back?"

Funny, it was the Albany coppers who finally put the s.o.b. down on 18 December 1931 after he beat an upstate bootlegging and kidnapping rap. It was going into competition with the Albany coppers' protection insurance racket that did him in, finally.

Things started changing. Prohibition did not last as long as Dutch predicted. Bad luck. Bad luck too that I got pinched for bootlegging. Convicted, I was back in Sing Sing Prison on 1 December 1932.

Whoever said that 'politics make strange bedfellows' has never been in prison. Talk about strange bedfellows! There are the guilty-as-sin, the railroaded innocent souls, and the ones who make prison their life. Of course, the majority are blacks, recent immigrants and poor guys who pissed off the local coppers. There weren't any WASPs or bankers or Wall Street types, just guys from tenements and slums.

I took up handball to pass the time. Then, the 'small world' thing happened. Red McGregor was delivered with the 'fish' one day. That's what we called the new arrivals. We started playing handball together and teamed up against some guineas who also got busted for bootlegging. It was after a game that Red and I started talking.

"Booze makes good money for the 'speaks'. It ain't so bad, it's getting it there without getting highjacked, shot up or pinched that's the problem."

I said, "I think that I got ratted out to the cops. This copper O'Boyle had a small army of blue wool waiting for me at the docks. I was surprised that he didn't shoot and keep it all for himself."

"Listen, the papers have been headlining the Repeal. The end of Prohibition is just weeks or days away."

"Then we're fooked unless we can find another racket."

"There's always the numbers."

"That's a five-and-ten operation, I'm looking for something that can make real dough while not bringing the coppers sniffing."

"There's always boosting a truck or a train."

"The docks have been good, the loading and unloading has things go missing for smart guys."

"How do we get on the docks? I ain't doin' no bailing hook work."

"No, it's union work. Organizing the longshoremen. We can get their dues, insurance dough, shape-up gifts along with loan sharking and numbers."

"Longshoremen are suckers for loans and numbers."

"I know this guy who can get us into the Westside docks. The guineas have the Eastside, Brooklyn and Staten Island but it's all Irish on the Westside, perfect for us to take over the docks."

PROHIBITION ENDS AT LAST!
DECEMBER 5, 1933

Dutch Schultz didn't last long either. Mayor LaGuardia of New York City made the city too hot for him. Dutch moved his headquarters to Newark, New Jersey. Even that was not far enough. He was being indicted by New York DA Dewey for tax evasion. Just like Al Capone. Like Capone, it looked likely that Dutch would go to prison. Dutch didn't want to spend a minute behind bars. To avoid it, he wanted to kill Dewey but the mob, 'the Commission' led by Lucky Luciano, Joe Bonnano and Lepke Buchalter disagreed. Killing DA Dewey would bring too much heat on all the rackets. Well, they also wanted Dutch's rackets. Dutch suspected that, so he planned to kill Dewey anyway.

The Dutchman had good cash-producing rackets in the Bronx and Manhattan that Buchalter and Luciano planned to divvy up. Dutch knew this. He also knew that both New York's Mayor LaGuardia and Dewey were not going to let up on him. Dixie Davis, his lawyer, had convinced the New York City judge that Dutch could only get a fair trial upstate. His tax evasion trial was moved to Malone, New York. After he beat that tax evasion rap in Malone, Dutch saw the writing on the wall. I'm pretty certain that his lawyer Dixie gave him the low-down that Dewey was now even more determined to pin another rap on him that would stick.

Still cautious, if he didn't kill Dewey, got convicted and ended up in Sing Sing, Dutch hid some $7 million in the Catskills saying, "I'm keeping the money in my head." He knew Owney Madden's story. Madden did his time, got out of Sing Sing broke and his gang all split-up. If Larry Fay hadn't taken Madden under his wing, Madden would have been selling pencils on a street corner. Dutch was having none of that shite. Suspecting that Bugsy Siegel or someone else would take over his operation if he was jailed, Dutch did not want to get paroled into poverty.

Moreover, Dutch did not want to go upriver in the first place. For that, Dewey had to go. He planned to kill Dewey at Dewey's upstate farm in Westchester. Unfortunately, somebody ratted the plan to the Commission. The Commission had to stop Dutch from bringing too much attention on the rackets. The hit on Dutch was sanctioned. Lepke Buchalter's Murder Incorporated sent two gunmen, Mendy Weiss and Charlie 'the Bug' Workman.

On the night of the 22nd of October 1935, Dutch and three of his key guys went to dinner at the Chop House on East Park Street in Newark, New Jersey. Dutch left the table at the Chop House to go pee. At the table were Otto 'Abba Dabba' Berman, Abe Landau, and Bernard 'Lulu' Berman. Realizing that Dutch wasn't at the table, Charlie 'the Bug' Workman went into the bathroom looking for Dutch. As 'the Bug' entered the men's room, he opened fire. At the same time, Mendy shot each of the three at the table at point blank range. Lulu Berman and Landau returned fire as Mendy Weiss backed away still shooting. Unwounded a panicked Mendy Weiss fled in the getaway car, leaving his partner, Workman to fend for himself. After plugging Dutch, Workman departed by a back door, escaping on foot for Brooklyn. Determined not to be found shot in a bathroom, Dutch staggered to the table where the others were bleeding. He collapsed but not before asking for someone to call an ambulance.

All four lived to make it to the hospital but three died of blood loss shortly after arrival. Not the Dutchman. It took him twenty-two hours to die. Shot in the gut Schultz died of peritonitis. Drifting in and out of lucidity and hallucinating wildly, he spoke with the cops, his wife, even a priest. Yeah, Dutch had converted to Catholicism to cozy up to Luciano, for all that got him. He babbled all sorts of nonsense that a bedside cop stenographer wrote down.

That was Dutch's revenge. It drove Dewey nuts trying to figure out the nonsensical meanderings of the dying Dutchman.

"Who shot me? No one." Was his most lucid of the thousand words that the police stenographer recorded. Gut shot, Schultz had a torn liver, spleen, gall bladder, large and small intestines. A blood infection set in resulting in the fevered delirium ravings.

"George, don't make no bull moves."
"Oh, mamma, mamma, please don't tear, don't rip..."
"Mother is the best and don't let Satan do you too fast."
"Yo can play jacks and girls do that with a soft ball and do tricks with it."
"Hey Jimmy. The Chimney Sweeps. Talk to the Sword. Shut up! You got a big mouth!"
"Please come help me up. Henry. Max come over here. French Canadian bean soup. I want to pay. Let them leave me alone."
"I'm keeping it in my head."
"Get ahead, you don't want the Devil's Tombstone."

Word on the street was that Dutch had driven to the Catskills to hide his money for a rainy day. He had lunch at the Phoenicia Hotel then drove up 214 along the Stony Clove Creek to Devil's Tombstone. Like a pirate, he supposedly buried that treasure chest of gold, cash and jewels. But I felt sure that Dutch had hid his money in Phoenicia.

Murder Inc. had strict rules about hit teams. You don't leave anyone behind to be caught and traced back. Weiss was lucky that Murder Inc. did not kill him for leaving Workman at the Chop House. For Murder Inc. considered leaving a fellow gunman at a scene a mortal sin. Weiss claimed that Workman had returned to the bathroom not to finish off Dutch, but to steal the three grand in cash on him. According to Weiss as he waited in the getaway, there was more gunfire. He further lied that he thought maybe Workman had been killed. So, fearing that all the shooting would have the Newark cops swarming on the Chop House, Weiss made a run for it. That got him off with Buchalter but not with Workman.

In 1941, Charlie 'the Bug' Workman was charged with Schultz's murder. Years later, Abe Reles, also an enforcer for Murder Inc. ratted out Weiss, Buchalter and other killers to Brooklyn DA Willian O'Dwyer. Weiss along with Buchalter were convicted for a different murder and executed in Sing Sing 4 March 1944.

I was supposed to meet Dutch that night. Not at the Chop House though. Glad that the Dutchman changed it for drinks later at the Hoboken Clam Broth House or I would have bled out on the Chop House floor with the others.

Chapter 27
Westside Docks

Sean
10 December 1936

England's King Edward VII Signs Instrument of Abdication to Marry
American Divorcée Wallis Simpson

As the newly minted President of ILA Local 364 Terminal Checkers and Platform Men, I decided to leave work early. I called Ian at the law office where he was doing his clerkship.

Doris, the firm's secretary, said, "Mr. Callaghan isn't here, Mr. Callaghan. Mr. Callaghan went to the 14th street office for a contract meeting. Do you have that number, Mr. Callaghan?"

"Is it the Gramercy or Chelsea exchange number?"

"Yes, Mr. Callaghan, Mr. Callaghan's number is Gramercy 9—"

"I have it, sweetie, Thanks."

"Sure thing, Mr. Callaghan, I will leave a message for Mr. Callaghan that Mr. Callaghan called. Anything else, Mr. Callaghan?"

"Nothing else, Doris." And I hung up.

I should make book on the times that Doris says "Mr. Callaghan". I mean the broad punctuates her sentences with 'Mr. Callaghan'. I'll have to ask Ian if he finds it complimentary or annoying. As I picked up my topcoat and fedora, Paddy Clarke put down the Racing Form, stood, and put on his coat.

"Kinda cold out, Mr. C."

"Not to worry, I have good merino wool socks. I won't freeze. Get the car, Paddy, we are going uptown."

No one goes out to dinner before 5 in New York, so when Paddy and I walked into Dottie's, only the waitresses and the bartender were in the joint. A pretty brunette with an armload of napkins stepped out of the storage room next to the coat check, seeing us she said, "Velcome to Dottie's."

She put the napkins down on the hostess podium, "Ve open for dinner at 6."

"Oh, that's fine. We can have a cocktail while we wait."

"You can have a drink at the bar or a table in the library while you wait. Can I take your coats and hats?"

She patiently waited as Paddy and I shrugged off the topcoats. As I handed her my hat, I locked into her gray-green eyes. She disappeared into the coatroom then returned with two coat check tickets. Wordlessly, she picked up the napkins and resumed setting tables. I noticed that the brunette had Paddy Clarke's attention too.

"Nice joint, how come you ain't never brought me here before?" Paddy said, eyes still on the brunette.

"Paddy, Dottie's is a long way from the pier. Look, if I wanted to grab a quick bite, we would have gone to the Viaduct on 10th. Besides, this is my sister's place. It's too good for a lug like you."

We walked to a table for four against the wall of books. I took a seat in the chair that backed up to the wall. I had read how the western lawman, Wild Bill Hickok, got shot from behind. While I hadn't heard anything specific, I don't take chances. I knew that the Italians were not above taking me out for reasons only they knew. Sure, they held all of the Brooklyn docks, Fulton Fish Market and lower Eastside docks, but they weren't above expanding by pistol. Paddy took a chair to my left.

"I like the steaks at the Beatrice."

"Dottie's has great steaks too. My sister picks them out personally. I think that her steaks are as good as those at the Homestead Steakhouse off 14th street or the Beatrice."

Then looking back toward the entrance, I saw the brunette look in our direction. She had a handful of utensils with snowy white napkins draped over her forearm. As she looked up, I caught her eye.

"Excuse me, Miss, when do you expect Miss Callaghan to be here?"

Setting the table next to ours, the brunette said, "She kommen about six. She was here early. She had an appointment, I think."

"Are you German, Miss?"

"*Ja*, yes."

"Have you been in the States long?"

"Five years. My father brought me, my brother and my stepmutter here in '32. I became an American this past September. I am a citizen now." She smiled, her accent fading in and out as she spoke. I could see that she was struggling to sound American.

"Why did you leave Germany? Were you looking for work?" Paddy asked.

"My father was employed but my brother could not find work. Many, many German boys could not find work."

"Unemployment is bad here too," Paddy said.

"We had to leave Germany. In August '29, my mother was killed by Brown Shirts led by Goebbels. She was walking home with some schnitzel, noodles and wurst when she was shot." Her gray-green eyes welled with tears.

"Sorry to hear that. Is your father still alive?"

"Yes, he works at Schiller & Weber now, as a butcher. In Deutsche…Germany he was a university professor. He was a professor of Chemistry in Berlin. He made enough money. Things changed when he re-married in '31. My father married a Jewish woman. She is a good woman and mother to *mein*…my broder and I. His university wanted him to join the Nazi Party. At first, he ignored the Nazis until he lost his temper with Party-proselytizing colleague. After that bad things happened." She swallowed hard, blinked back tears and said in a quietly firm voice, "Then my father lost his tenure at university. At the Potsdamer Platz, there were Brown Shirt attacks on Jews. We fled to Denmark then France to book passage to New York. We came here to become Americans. My father is trying to get a teaching position at the Hunter College here."

"Oh, what a story." I was amazed. She was like an open book. Telling the two of us everything about her and her family, only minutes after meeting us.

"I graduated high school last year. My father wants me to go to Hunter College for a degree in Biology. He is a professor of chemistry, in Germany, he was. Maybe here someday." She sighed.

"I heard the Olympic Games were good and unemployment is going down in Germany. It isn't here. Hitler is doing good things for Germany," Paddy interjected.

She was silent for a moment then with fire in her eyes, she said, "Hitler is not good for Germany, not good for anywhere! In 1933, Hindenburg made him

206

Chancellor. There was the Reichstag fire! Hitler who you think is doing good, used the chaos of the fire to ban all opposition parties. Meanwhile the Nazis had only 44% of the vote. Then Hitler got the members of the Reichstag to pass the Enabling Act that allows him to make laws without their consent. *Yersteth du mich*! You understand!"

She took a breath, then said, "My father read that Hitler had over 25,000 'Un-German' books burned. Books burned! To a university professor, that is the greatest offense of all!"

"Look at all the things that FDR has done here. Isn't that the same?" Paddy said. "Unemployment is still high. There are a lot of guys on the dole."

"Hitler reduced unemployment by conscripting men into the *Wehrmacht* and establishing the *Luftwaffe*."

"Wehrmacht? Luftwaffe? Speak American."

Patiently, slowly with the hint of a smile, she said, "The Nazi Army and the Air Force." Then she added, "In May of 1933, Hitler banned all trade unions."

"What? That is un-American!" Paddy said, reeling back in his chair.

I smiled and said, "You have to understand that my friend and I are union organizers. So that Hitler banning unions touches a nerve. Thank you for giving us the lowdown on Hitler."

"I am so sorry that I was so rude. I shouldn't be yelling about Germany and Hitler. I will tell Miss Callaghan and resign."

"You will do nothing of the sort. I am Miss Callaghan's brother and I say that you will stay on as long as you like."

She colored, covered her mouth then bowed slightly saying, "I had no idea, Mr. Callaghan. I mean no disrespectful behavior."

"Ah, you're just passionate."

"You know my name, what's yours?"

"Heidi Rupp."

"Please to meetcha, this here lug who doesn't know what's goin' on the world is my pal, Paddy Clarke."

At that moment, the restaurant's door opened with a blast of frigid air as Mikey appeared wearing a camel hair cashmere coat with a fur collar, she pulled the door shut. Her cognac leather high-heeled boots clicked noisily on the wooden floor as she pulled off brown calfskin gloves.

Heidi helped her with her coat then motioned with her head toward Paddy and me. Mikey's eyes went wide as she took me in. Quickly rushing over to the table, she threw her arms around my neck just as I started to stand.

Then she stepped back taking my shoulders in both hands, asked, "You are not usually here this early. Are you good? Are you in any trouble? Or are you just hungry?"

"No, no, Paddy and me are just looking for a warm place with good food. Naturally, we thought of Dottie's. Didn't we?"

"Sure, sure, that's right, warm place, good steaks and drinks. That's the ticket as you say boss," Paddy agreed.

"Where's Ian?"

"He had some business at the Lawyers Trust on 14th. Couldn't be here. Ian really wants to earn that Fordham Law degree. I won't argue. So, Mikey, what's good on the menu?"

"We have a Chateaubriand with twice baked potatoes with haricot verts or a Montauk bluefish with rice and green peas…I can request that the chef do something else if you prefer."

"Chatoobreeze, is that a steak?" Paddy asked.

"Yes, Paddy," Mikey smiled. "What about you, Sean? I know that you like to catch bluefish off Breezy Point but a cold night like tonight calls for a steak, don't you think?"

"Sure, I'll have the Chateaubriand, rare please."

"*Mais oui!*" Mikey replied as she stood. Mikey loved injecting French into anything she said. Often, she remarked that French sounded classy. I would wonder from time to time about Maurice and Georges. They spoke a version of French called Québécois. Would she think that Québécois was classy?

Mikey walked to the hostess podium as a beautiful blonde dressed like Ginger Rodgers joined her. They conferred briefly then Mikey disappeared into the kitchen. The blonde glanced in our direction then disappeared out of sight.

Paddy whistled under his breath, "Did you see that strudel? Man, this place has some good-looking broads!"

"Paddy, while we're here don't refer to any broad as a 'broad'. My sister prefers 'ladies' or 'girls'. This ain't one of Texas' clubs."

"WooHoo!" Paddy exclaimed. "I remember Texas and her chicks. Boy oh-boy they were some cuties in her reviews. Did you hear, she died in Canada back in '33. Texas ran some great clubs."

"Texas Guinan was quite a gal. She always had something funny to say like 'an indiscretion a day keeps the Depression away."

After dinner, Mikey sat with us as we had a Scotch, and she had a cup of tea. As she swirled her sugar cube into the hot tea, I could see she was still working, with her eyes at least. Looking at a table not far from ours, she said, "See the man in the gray flannel suit with the sharp silver tie?"

"Yes."

"That's the famous Broadway critic, Ward Morehouse. He lunches at Sardi's but does his interviews at the 21 Club. I put my best waitress, Heidi on his table. If he likes the food, drink and service we could be in his column tomorrow. I heard that he was in town for an interview. See the man with the mustache on his right? That's Eugene O'Neil, the playwright. His new play 'Ah, Wilderness' is premiering at the Provincetown Theatre on MacDougal. I'm surprised that they came here. Morehouse likes to interview in the Theatre District, you know West 52nd. He doesn't usually travel east of Fifth Avenue. Wait a minute, Heidi is heading toward the bar. I'll be right back."

Mikey was weaving her way through the dinner guests, meeting-and-greeting as she subtly slid up to the bar. She conversed briefly with the bartender then turned her attention to Heidi.

Mikey took her time getting back to our table, sat crossed her legs and causally threw her arm over the back of her chair. There was a hint of a satisfied smile as she said, "Morehouse is a food-hound and wanted to give us a try and he has been flirting with Heidi since he sat down." She gave me a knowing look.

Before I could say anything, she chuckled, "Heidi can manage that man. Fine." Then picking up her cup, "What new with you Sean?"

"Well, I see that you looked cold even with that cashmere coat. What would you say to a nice sable or mink?"

"Oh, I didn't know those kinds of coats fell of trucks too. Maybe you might help it fall off a truck." Her eyes sparkled with amusement, "Sean, Dottie's is doing fine. We have a good location, rent is great by the way, and we have loyal customers. Now, if Morehouse writes a good review of Dottie's, we could be taking reservations from the swells that the 21 Club turns away. What I mean is that while I appreciate it, I really don't want or need a fur coat."

"As you wish, sis. To change the subject, would you object to me taking one of your waitresses out sometime?"

That turned her around to look me straight in the eyes.

"Let me guess, our blonde bombshell hostess Carole Ransavage, our answer to Ginger Rogers…"

"I was thinking Heidi."

That got an eyebrow to her red hairline. "I knew it," she chuckled.

Chapter 28
Lost Hat

Sean
5 January 1937

It was nearly 1 am when I turned off my desk lamp at the Varick Street office, locked the Hudson Street door thinking that a nice Scotch at Dottie's would be just the ticket. Cripes, it was cold. My New Plymouth sedan started with a shiver. As I drove up Hudson toward 14th, I saw the first snowflakes glowing in the streetlight. By the time I turned the Plymouth east on 14th, the headlamp beams had big wet flakes in them. Not many were driving tonight, that made the drive easy despite the weather. Even finding a parking spot in Yorkville just off Second Avenue was easy.

After turning the engine off, I reached for the glove box extracting the Iver Johnson revolver. One can never to be too careful. The dusting of snow that the radio reported was more like heavy wet snow. I turned the corner on Second Avenue as icy pellets hit me in my face. The radio said it was 28 degrees but let me tell you it felt much colder. I pulled the brim of my hat down to shield my face. Then, I heard something that made me straighten up. I slipped my hand between the buttons of my topcoat to the revolver wedged in my waistband.

Two men were pushing a woman against the trash cans lined up outside an apartment building a few doors from Dottie's. They were saying something to her that I could not make out in the blowing wind. However, the wind did carry the sound of the woman slapping one of her assailant's faces. She wasn't taking any guff from them! The three struggled knocking over trashcans. I took my hand off the revolver opting for the leather-wrapped leaden cosh in the right pocket of my topcoat as I slipped up behind the two guys.

Over the sound of the howling wind and rolling trashcans the woman cried out. That's when my cosh came down on the nearest neck. He went down to the pavement. The other one whirled around and deflected my cosh with a trash can lid. Then he brought it into my face knocking me to the pavement.

My fedora was off into the snow and wind as he came down with me. Holding my right shoulder down, he cocked his right for a haymaker. The woman's arm came out of nowhere to hook under his right to roll him. Now on his back on the pavement, he wrenched his arm from the woman's grip. I rolled to my knees next to him. He grabbed my topcoat collar as my right brought the cosh across his forehead. His hand fell away to the pavement.

The woman was kneeling on his right arm. Her hair was whipping around her face. Snow and hail nearly blinded me as I stood up. I could hear her breathing hard as I brought her to her feet. She pushed me away. Her shoulders shook. Looking past her, I saw that the first man was rolling, moaning and holding his shoulder. The man that we stood over was not moving. Cripes! I didn't hit him that hard!

I have to get moving. I did not want any coppers' attention.

"Are you okay? You're safe now."

I looked around quickly. Not a person to be seen on the avenue. No lights in the apartment windows. No witnesses. Not even a truck or car driving on Second. Just whirling snow.

"Come with me, you're safe, I take you home."

I offered her my hand. Her fingers slowly closed on my hand. I led her around the corner to the Plymouth was parked just a few yards away.

I unlocked the passenger door, she climbed in. The Plymouth was still warm. It turned over easily. Punching in the clutch, I put it into first and eased out into the street. Out of nowhere my door was wrenched open! One of the two goons tried to pull me out of the Plymouth. He had a grip on my topcoat. Even as we accelerated down the street, he held on. Whirling my left around his arm, I slammed my palm into his elbow hard. He screamed as he fell away from the Plymouth. I pulled the door closed as I turned right on Second. Over the noise of the wipers and the engine I could hear the woman beside me crying.

I turned right at 55th and headed west toward Third and Lexington avenues. There was no traffic. Immediately after I turned on to Lex I pulled over, pulled the hand brake and jumped out. There was a storm drain there. I dropped the cosh into the drain and quickly returned to the Plymouth. The pellets of frozen rain that hammered the windscreen were collecting on the wipers. Barehanded, I cleaned frozen snow off the wipers before getting back in the car. Good to be out of the weather.

The woman was trying to push wet strands of hair from her face with shaking hands. I reached with shaking hands over the seat for Canadian striped blanket that I had picked up during my bootlegging trips to Quebec. It was a good Hudson Bay blanket. I draped it over her head and shoulders wrapping it around. Her cold fingers clamped on my arm.

"*Danke, danke shon.*" Thanks, thank you.

"*Nichts Zu danken.*" Nothing to thank me for I replied without even thinking. All that German from the orphanage wasn't gone.

She turned to me. The streetlamp provided just enough light to see that the woman next to me was Heidi.

"Do you have a handkerchief?" She asked.

I fished out a white handkerchief from my suit jacket pocket. She took it, and noisily blew her nose.

"Keep it I have more."

I continued to drive down Lexington toward Grand Central Terminal and 42nd Street. The snow on Lex was plowed into furrows by passing cars and buses.

"What happened back there? Who were those men?"

"They…they were late customers. Miss Callaghan wanted to close up early tonight because of the storm. But they had been drinking beer at the bar. When I informed them that we were closing they noticed my accent. They started to speak *Deutsch*, German, asking me if I was a Bund member. When I said that I would not have anything to do with the Nazis and the Bund, they became angry, started shouting."

"Then what?"

"Miss Callaghan and the bartender heard. They insisted that the men leave. They drank the last of the beer and left. I thought that that was the end of it. Maybe an hour later, we closed up. We all left together but Miss Callaghan and the Harry the bartender turned left on the avenue, and I continued on alone." Heidi took a deep breath. "As I turned the corner, I saw the two on the other side of the street. I quicken my pace but they crossed the street and they were coming up fast so I started to run. But they were faster. They pushed me up against the wall calling me 'Bolshevik', 'un-German', 'red', and worse. I cannot repeat it. With every word, they spit in my face…it was horrible. I thought that they would kill me as the Brown Shirts had killed my mother."

She began to pull the blanket snug. As she smoothed her skirt down over her legs, she looked at her knee.

"Look, the injury to my knee is bad. It's going to swell up. I'm a mess. I cannot go home looking like this my Papa would have a *Schlagenfall*, a seizure."

The Plymouth handled well, skidding only slightly in the heavy wet snow as we headed downtown. Staying in the tracks of autos that had been down the avenue while applying the brakes gently, I avoided skidding into the intersections at red lights. All the driving on snow and ice in Vermont and Quebec paid off tonight.

Turning on to 23rd, the Plymouth started to fish-tail. As I had learned in Vermont, if you took your foot off the gas, avoided the brake pedal, steered smoothly into the direction of skidding then you avoided a spin out.

The lights in Madison Square Park were hazy with the falling snow. The Flatiron Building loomed ahead like some great ocean liner in an Atlantic storm. As I drove, I tried to comfort Heidi. I rattled on about driving in Vermont as opposed to Manhattan, then about Madison Square Park where the Garden had been before it moved uptown to 49th. None of it drew a comment or even a word from Heidi.

Finally, Heidi startled me with, "Where are we going?"

"My place on Bank Street. You can clean up, get warm then I'll drive you home."

"Oh."

"I have a telephone. You can call your father to say that you're going to be home soon. Or whatever you want. We'll take care of any cuts, lumps or bruises. If necessary, or if you prefer, I could take you to St. Vincent's Hospital. They have good nurses and doctors. Want me to take you there?"

"No, let me see how bad I look."

We were in luck, there was no one parked in front of the awning at 110 Bank Street.

Heidi was in the bathroom while I went to each radiator to open the valves to warm up the place. The radiators banged and gurgled as the hot water surged into them. I shook off my coat and Heidi's hanging them to dry on the oak coat stand near to the radiator. I really liked my fawn-colored fedora that one of those goons knocked off me. I fingered the felt on my dark brown fedora, the companion to the fawn one and hung it on the coat stand. The Iver-Johnson revolver was placed in my favorite spot behind canned beans and soup in kitchen.

I knocked on the bathroom door, "Need something?"

"*Nein,* I am fine."

There was a loud knock on the apartment door. I thought about retrieving the revolver. I hesitated. There was another hard rap on the door. So, without anything in my hand went to the apartment door. I felt naked, vulnerable. As I looked through the peephole was I glad that I was empty-handed. Detective O'Boyle of the New York Police was holding his gold badge to the hole. Cripes.

"Open up Callaghan!"

"Gimme a minute, eh?" I said looking around the room for anything that he could latch on and put me in lock-up. This was not the weather to get my lawyer, Joel Friedman out of bed so he could spring me. I opened the door to O'Boyle and two burly boys in snow-speckled blue wool. They pushed past me into the apartment.

While the two blue wools stood near the door, O'Boyle casually walked around the front room as if he was thinking of taking over my lease. He strolled turning on the Tiffany lamp next to the sofa. He lifted the sofa seats.

"Nice warm and cozy Callaghan," he said looking at the bedroom door, then said to one of the blue woolies, "Johnny pat down Mr. Callaghan would ja."

The biggest blue wool came up to me as I raised my arms in a Y. Cripes, the copper had hands as big as Lou Gehrig's mitt.

"Hey, easy on the merchandise."

"Shaddup, spread your legs!"

"You aren't one of those Nancy-boys are you?" I said as he glared daggers at me.

"He's clean, detective."

"I'm as clean as your Sunday shoes."

"Callaghan did you lose a nice fedora? I found one that has your favorite haberdasher's label in the hatband." O'Boyle fingered the brim of the hat on the coat stand.

I did not reply. A noise from the bedroom interrupted O'Boyle's train of thought.

"So, who's hiding behind this door?" He said as he drew his Police Special. The blue wools did the same but the big one had his muzzle pointed at my face. I tell you I have seen subway tunnels that looked smaller than that .38 barrel.

O'Boyle flung open the door to an ear-piercing scream.

Heidi was in bed with the covers pulled to her chin. She let out another scream. And another. Holstering in his revolver and waving his hand back to the blue wools, he turned with a smirk on his face.

He walked up to me, saying, "I didn't know that you were entertaining. How long have you love-birds been here?"

Heidi said, "We have been here all evening. Now get out! Leave us!"

"Fine, lady, sure, sure." He was so close to me that I smell the cigarettes and beer that he had for dinner.

"Callaghan, you wouldn't have been uptown and busted a few heads tonight, would ja?"

"We have been here all night! Now go!" Heidi shouted from the bedroom. O'Boyle closed the bedroom door, probably so that he wouldn't have to hear Heidi.

"You had better watch your Ps &Qs Callaghan because I am keeping you in my prayers for a long stay upriver."

"You just do your rosary for your own soul."

With that O'Boyle was at the apartment door motioning for the blues to step into the hall. O'Boyle touched his hat brim, never taking his eyes from mine as backed through the door and closed it. I waited for him to change his mind. I waited a long count of ten before turning the lock.

I heard the bedroom door open, "Have they left?"

"Yes!"

"Good, *my Gott* that reminded me of Gestapo thugs."

I turned. Heidi was completely dressed, and her hair combed. She had some rouge on her cheeks and a smile on her lips.

"I got some shoe dirt on your sheets. I am sorry."

"Nothing to be sorry about."

She curled her finger for me to come over to her. As I stepped close, she took a quick step toward my chest and hugged me hard. The hair was still

216

damp, but it smelled clean and nice. I raised her chin and looked into her eyes. "Kiss me," she whispered. She tasted sweet like strawberries in summer. It seemed that the kiss was everything in the world. When she pulled her head back, her gray-green eyes bored into mine, searching.

Separating, she went over to the table and picked up the telephone. Speaking in German for a few minutes, those gray green eyes of her never left my face. She replaced the handset then wordlessly taking my hand, she turned and led me into my bedroom.

"I told Papa I was staying with a good friend from Dottie's. I will be home after the storm."

"Yes, after the storm," I said as I loosened my tie while watching her unbutton her dress.

Chapter 29
Reformation

Sean

I began to spend less time at the Varick Street ILU Local 268 office, especially on days that Heidi had off from Dottie's. Things between Heidi and me were terrific. She is a swell gal. I have had my share of gals from the Vermont farmer's daughter, to speakeasy flappers. Heidi was different in a way that I cannot put into words.

For us, it was 'making love' not just sex or a quick bang. I had feelings for her that I never had before, ever. She would climb on top of me and I would get lost in her. She was gentle yet strong, and vocal too though her utterances were entirely in German. She let me know what she wanted when she was ready and when she came, there was no doubt.

After one session, she lay on her side stabbing out her cigarette in a glass ashtray I snagged from the El Fey Club. She looked at me with those incredible eyes of hers.

"I have applied to go to Hunter College for biology. Papa taught chemistry in Berlin and my mother was a teacher of small children, but I want to do research to find a cure for polio and tuberculosis."

"Holy cow! That's a dangerous job. TB kills and polio cripples while it kills. Are you sure?"

She turned placing the ashtray on the bedside counter. Then she rolled back to me, "It has been my dream since I was a little girl. Tuberculosis took my cousin, my aunt and one of my mother's friends. I hate tuberculosis. There was a boy in my class who went to Baden Baden one summer, he came down with polio and slowly smothered. It was awful."

"Heidi, do girls do this kind of work?"

"*Dumkopf!*" She sat up glaring at me with a hint of a smile, "Madame Curie, Lady Montague were scientists! Fraulein Maud Menten described the toxins of Streptococcus and Salmonella. Girls do great work in science! I have to complete my studies to be prepared for working with my heroine, Dr. Isabella Morgan. Dr. Morgan is a world-renowned bacteriologist and virologist. If she comes to New York's Rockefeller Institute, then I would love to work with her if I can. If anyone can find a vaccine for polio, Dr. Isabella Morgan can!"

I saw passion and intensity in those beautiful green-gray eyes.

"Changing the subject," she said, "Tell me about your work."

I gave Heidi the honest story including my time in Sing Sing for bootlegging. She let me continue without a comment or judgement. I described the dockworkers hiring and my 'benefits'. Heidi listened intently, smoking her Lucky Strike, while balancing the El Fey ashtray on her bare leg.

When I finished, she turned her head, blew smoke away then stabbed out the cigarette saying, "What is shake up?"

I smiled saying, "It's s-h-a-p-e ups, Heidi."

"How does it work?"

"Early in the morning, longshoremen assemble on the docks in a horseshoe shape to be picked for work that day. The pier boss sends around the hat for donations. Then he picks the crew to work the pier that day. The guys who put a few bucks in the boss's hat get the work while the others go home or to some gin mill."

"Those donations aren't donations. They are bribing the pier boss for a job."

"We call it a donation. The longshoreman makes his money back by the end of the day."

"Are you a gangster?"

"No, no, I am a union leader."

"Then why are you allowing, how did you say? Shake ups?"

"Shape ups are how longshoremen get hired."

"But that makes your longshoremen temporary workers. They do not get picked unless they make a donation. What if they need that money to pay to rent, put food on the table or take care of a sick child."

"Well, then the guy could get a loan for two points of vigorous or vig as we call it. Say he gets a $50 loan. If he pays it back next week with the vig, he owes us $60 but if he doesn't then the next week, he'll owe $72 on a $50 loan," I explained.

"Your longshoremen would be better off if they went to a bank for a loan," Heidi replied.

"These guys can't get a bank loan. They have nothing to offer as collateral."

"That's because they can't depend on getting a regular paycheck.

Why don't you do as your sister does, give a schedule? Hire more or new people during busy times but have a schedule based on skill, seniority and make sure that they get a decent wage. Those men work hard for their families."

We had several pillow talks similar to this one. Heidi had a way of making me think about things differently. When Dutch Schultz gave his gang a regular salary, he had a ready crew who worked hard and loyally. Sure, Vincent Coll was the exception. He was not loyal. He was crazy. If scheduled hours and regular pay worked for bootlegging; it should also for dockworkers. I began to make changes. Most of the Pier 51 longshoremen groused at first but when Liam posted a weekly schedule and hired extra crews for larger shipments grousing gave way to grins. No shape-ups. What really changed was regular pay at the end of the week. Word spread.

It wasn't long before some of the other ILWU officials heard and came by Varick Street to try to convince me to return to the 'union-way.' Then two MacGregor muscles showed up on Pier 51 while Liam and I were collecting dues. We had stopped loan-sharking and shape-ups weeks before.

"Hello Callaghan, Red ain't happy and he ain't happy that other piers and other shops are making trouble because of you." A cold wind forced them to pull their hat down over their ears. While Liam and I wore gloves the MacGregor boys had their hands in their topcoat pockets. One boy, the big one with a bulbous red nose took a linen handkerchief from his left pocket to blow his nose noisily. His right stayed in the topcoat.

"Red wants you to go back to the old ways and he wants it right now, or else, if you gets my drift"

His right hand remained in the topcoat pocket. Both of these lugs were big thick, brawny, and taller than me and Liam. As our stare-down continued, I saw several dock workers put their bailing hooks on their shoulders and crossed their arms to watch. This was as entertaining as a Golden Gloves match to them. I stepped just to the big boy's left. The cold Hudson River churned with a gray-white chop in the winds. Liam was still. Cold light reflected from his eyeglasses into bulbous nose's eyes. He put up his left to shield from the glare.

"What's it gonna be Callaghan? Red wants this done today."

Liam moved fast, with both hands he pinned bulbous nose's right inside his topcoat pocket. The pistol report caused the guy in front of me to turn toward his partner as I grabbed his right sleeve while placing my leg behind his. With my right arm stiff I slammed it against his left ear. I pivoted while pulling on the sleeve. He worked to free his gun from his topcoat pocket. He still trying to free the pistol as he found himself falling backward off the pier. Even before I heard the splash, I was rushing toward Liam and his opponent. Blood was bubbling from bulbous nose's shoe. Liam dug the pistol from the man's topcoat flinging it over his shoulder into the Hudson. Splash.

The big guy I sent for a swim flailed his arms wildly; he screamed, "Help, Help! I...I can't swim."

One dock worker threw him a hawser. As he struggled to grasp the hawser, he disappeared under the water then he came up sputtering. Then someone threw a life-ring from the dock steward's shack. Big boy splashed and thrashed; he was no Johnny Weissmuller. When big boy took hold of the life-ring, a dockworker pulled him toward the boat ladder at the end of the dock. It was all that he could do to pull himself up the ladder until at last, he was lying on the pier shaking with cold. Meanwhile bulbous nose who was shot in foot was loaded on a luggage wheelbarrow. He looked damned pale, paler than the linen handkerchief he used to blow that big honker of his.

Liam and I passed through a crowd of dockworkers who slapped us on the back as we walked by. Boy, I need a drink.

Chapter 30
The White Rose

Sean

1937 was a politically tumultuous time. Resistance groups began to spring to life in Germany. Frank von Papen leader of the Catholic Right negotiates the Concordat with the Vatican which prohibited clergy from taking a political stand. However greater resistance to the Nazis was led by the Catholic Left Wing and trade unions.

Dr. Mildred Harnack, visiting professor from the University of Berlin who is famous for translations of various works of literature into German will be speaking at Hunter College. Her lecture, "The German Relation to Current American Literature" was a guise to inform Americans about conditions in Germany.

"Sean, I want you to come with me to a lecture at Hunter College tonight."

"Aw, sweetie, you know that I ain't book-smart. You go. College ain't for me."

"Sean, Sean, *Schatzie* this is different. This is a lecture about world news. This will be things that we do not hear on the radio except for the few times that we can tune into the BBC. You will find it interesting."

Heidi was in her first semester at Hunter and the kitchen table was loaded with a tall pile of books on Biology and Chemistry. She studied in the mornings. Heidi was an eager learner. She was intent, focused and obviously determined. She was getting A grades even in her English class. Of course, she didn't take German as a 'foreign' language.

"Sweetie, if you really want me to go I will."

"Great! Papa is going too. I will introduce you."

Cripes, it's meet the parents night! Well, better sooner than later. Now it seemed sooner.

* * *

A bow-tied man with mane of wavy silver-gray hair who looked perfect Hollywood casting as 'the professor' introduced Dr. Harnack, "Dr. Harnack received her doctorate from the University of Giessen. Recently she published a German translation of Irving Stone's biography of Vincent Van Gogh and is working on a translation of Walter D. Edmonds' <u>Drums Along the Mohawk</u> into German. Her lecture this evening: 'The German Relation to Current American Literature,' will be both informative and enlightening."

Heidi's cheeks were flushed with anticipation. She hung on every word that Dr. Harnack spoke. It was as if every word was directed to her. As for me, I had a hard time following all the literature, proletarian-revolutionary, Weimar republican, Social Democrat, Catholic Centre Party and German communist party or DKP references that Dr. Harnack made. As a labor leader, I don't like the Reds but if the Nazis are 'socialists' isn't that the same? Also, Nazis banned unions. Dr. Harnack was confusing me.

Harnack concluded with, "In '33, thousands of books were burned in an "Action against the un-German spirit." This atrocity happened in the Germany of science, music and art. Over 25,000 books were burned! This included Ludwig Renn's brilliant novel *Krieg* and Erich Maria Remarque's *Im Westen nich Neus*, published here as *All Quiet on the Western Front*. Their descriptions of the horrors experienced by the common soldier in the Great War transcend politics and national state. In his *Sun Also Rises*, the American writer Ernest Hemingway provided the reader with the post-war struggle of the former combatant who searches to find meaning. In Germany, we struggle to keep the sun from setting on art, on science, on the worker, and on love. As an American who loves literature and loves my adopted Germany, I implore you to throw off the shackles of capitalist isolation, resist the rise of dictatorships and social inequities. America must help Germans resist the Nazis before it is too late for Germany, Europe and America. Thank you for your kind attention to my little lecture."

The bow-tie professor sitting on the stage rose stiffly. As he walked to the podium where Dr. Harnack was standing, I thought that the last time he must

223

have bought those clothes, I was still in St. Joe's. Between his high collar shirt, ribbon-like bow tie, wide lapel suit jacket with those "Oxford baggy" trousers, he was a relic. The professor, if that what he was, harrumphed, coughed and grasped the podium with both hands as if to steady himself.

"Thank you Dr. Harnack for the most insightful, scholarly and humanistic lecture. This concludes our program however you are invited to stay for coffee with Dr. Harnack. We can offer fine pastries generously donated for this program by Dottie's restaurant on nearby Second Avenue."

The lecture was only sparsely attended, maybe fifty seats were filled out of two hundred. At the coffee and pastries table only a dozen or so attendees remained. As I was pouring coffee from the urn Heidi squeezed my arm excitedly.

"There she is! I must speak with her."

"Go before she leaves. Do you want me to bring over a cup?"

"No, no, my hands are shaking. I have to introduce myself to her. I'm so excited to meet her."

"Go ahead, sweetie," but Heidi was already halfway across the room to join the small group around Dr. Harnack.

I sensed that someone was behind me as I fixed my coffee. I turned and a tall man extended his hand to me. "Mr. Callaghan, I am Ernst Rupp." I was prepared to meet him even though I was somewhat unready at that moment. Ernst Rupp was a trifle taller than I. He dressed impeccably in a dark brown wool suit, an old-style high collar white shirt, double breasted vest, and bow tie. Looking every bit like another college professor, he extended his right hand to me, I put down the coffee cups wiping my hands on my trousers I shook his hand firmly. I noticed that Mr. Rupp's trousers' crease was pressed to a razor's edge as if he had never sat down in them. Mine looked as though I had been driving overnight from Canada.

"Pleased to meet you, Herr Rupp."

"Ernst bitte, please call me Ernst." His English was clear despite his accent. Then he turned to a woman and a young man standing beside him. "Permit me to introduce my wife Ruth and my son Hans."

"I'm very pleased to meet you both."

A stylish comma of brown hair from under her cloche hat almost covered a white scar on Ruth's forehead.

"Did you enjoy Dr. Harnack's talk?" Ruth Rupp asked her eyes boring into mine.

"She lost me a few times but in general I found it interesting."

"Dr. Harnack gave us all a warning about the anti-intellectual Hitler and his thugs," Hans Rupp interjected. "Hitler and the Nazis must be stopped."

His voice was filled with a passion that I had heard from Heidi many times.

But it was Hans Rupp's steel-blue eyes that told me much. They had that intensity that I have seen in the soapbox preachers. It was a religious fervor.

A match flaring in the back of the auditorium caught my attention. I saw the two men lighting cigarettes. I followed their gaze. Their eyes were locked on Dr. Harnack and the people around her including Heidi. I made an excuse about going to find a men's room.

I headed straight to the door to the back of the auditorium where the two stood smoking. Moving fast I had the barrel of my revolver in one man's back before he knew it.

"I'll plug ya if you or your pal here move."

With my left, I reached under the suit jacket and found what I expected, a pistol. Relieving him of his luggage I did the same with the other guy. He had a nice pistol too, a Walther. Both pistols were tucked into my trousers' waistband. I could always use a new pistol. Two pistols were even better.

"You boys expect these bluestockings to shoot?"

The two merely eyed me contemptuously, smiling thinly.

"Let's step into the hallway, shall we? I want to have a little chat."

One of the things that prison can teach is how one man can control two at the same time. Once in the hallway, I spun them to face the wall. I relieved them of their wallets while keeping my revolver pointed.

"Fritz, hello Fritz!"

The man whose driver's license read Fritz Julius Kuhn only grunted. I quickly glanced at the license in his pal's wallet. He was Gerhard Kringe of 86th Street here in Manhattan.

"Fritz, I thought Fritz was just a doughboy word for Hun. Well, then, the things you learn when you go to a Hunter College lecture!"

"We are just members of the Friends of the New Germany. We are only here to let that Red bitch know that she cannot tell lies about the new Germany."

"Zat true? What about you Gerhard? Are you just another bookworm?"

"Fuck you, you Jew-lover!"

That earned Gerhard Kringe a smart rap across his face with my revolver and when Fritz Kuhn turned, he met my left fist slamming in his breadbasket. As his pal Gerhard slid to the floor, Fritz clutched his belly but did not move a muscle. I noted with satisfaction, a darkening stain spreading on Fritz's trouser front.

I relieved both wallets of a few dollars to donate to Dr. Harnack's cause and pocketed the "German-American Bund" membership cards. Then I tossed both wallets down the hallway.

"Go, fetch!" I said stepping back from Kringe and Kuhn.

Kuhn helped the dazed Gerhard Kringe to his feet. He was going to need a leech or two to drain the blood from the shiner I gave him. His left eye was nearly closed already.

The two Nazi bastards picked up their wallets then like two war-wounded Huns stumbled away.

The sound of a door opening made me slip my revolver into my shoulder holster. As I turned, Hans Rupp let the auditorium door close quietly behind him. At my side, he said quietly, "I know them. They were with Heinz Spanknobel who was one of Rudolf Hess' agitators. Spanknobel was deported in October. '33 because he failed to register as a German agent."

"You Jew-Bolshevik!" One of the two screamed from down the hallway. "You are a kike communist!"

I shouted back, "I know some Jews could teach you some manners. Now get going before I feel the need to see how good your pistols work."

I clapped my left on Hans' shoulder, "Let's get back to our pastries and coffee, shall we?"

Hans' face broke into a broad smile. "We shall Mr. Callaghan."

As I followed Hans Rupp, I fingered the two Bund membership cards thinking that I should go to Ratner's for lunch tomorrow. I thought that Meyer Lansky and Bugsy Siegel would have their own methods of dealing with these Friends of the New Germany.

A few days later, Ian's secretary Doris said in her distinctive voice as it crackled in my telephone's earpiece, "Mr. Callaghan, Mr. Callaghan wants to schedule a meeting with you. Mr. Callaghan wants me to inform you that Miss Rupp and her brother Mr. Rupp will also be present. Mr. Callaghan has the meeting scheduled for 1 pm tomorrow. Can I inform Mr. Callaghan that you will be attending, Mr. Callaghan?"

"Sure Doris. I'll be there."

Promptly at one the next day, Heidi, Hans and I arrived at Ian's office. Around a small conference table, Heidi described the reason for the meeting.

"My stepmother is terribly upset. Her sister in Berlin is sick with consumption and is deathly afraid that the whole family will be picked up by the Gestapo any day now. She knows that to get the whole family out would be impossible, besides she is too sick to travel. In her letter, she begs Ruth to help to get her six-year-old daughter, Hannah to America. Ian, you have help us to get the necessary papers to get this little girl out of Germany."

"While I can get papers and a visa for little Hannah but you'll need an American citizen to escort the girl," Ian said.

"Fine, I'll go to Berlin to get her myself."

"You're not going anywhere, especially Germany without me!" I said.

"Sean, I know that you will worry. You don't speak enough German, you're not fluent. Besides you won't be able to blend in."

Heidi reached for Hans' hand across the table. "Hans and I can get it done quickly but I will need you to arrange return passage on a ship for the three of us."

Two weeks later, I watched Heidi and Hans board the ship to Germany. I was filled with dread.

Meanwhile, Red MacGregor was still giving me a hard time regarding my use of scheduling longshoremen instead of shape-ups. Then there was the Joey "Socks" United Seafood Workers deal. Joey "Socks" Lanza ran the Fulton Fishmarket on the lower East side docks. He needed an extra load of fish for meatless Fridays at my docks while his pier was getting re-planked. That was another source of contention between Red and me.

"I don't want those fucking Eyetalians muscling in on our docks."

"Red, you are beginning to sound like Farmer Sullivan. Remember what happened to Sullivan when he pissed them off. The Italians shot him dead. They ain't muscling us, if they are asking. And the Italians are paying us. Besides it's temporary."

"I don't trust those guineas."

"Our docks are too far across town and uptown for him at Fulton Fish. He trucks the fish load from our pier to the Market. This is good business. We

227

need good relations with his gang. Joey Socks works for Lucky Luciano. Remember when Dutch Schultz was uncooperative? Remember what happened? Also, we might need the Luciano gang's help sometime."

"I think it stinks."

"If it stinks then we'll renegotiate with Joey Socks. This is easy money."

Liam and I drove to Delancey Street. I spoke briefly with Lansky and Siegel. Before we left, I gave them the two German-American Bund membership cards. Then we headed back to the Westside. I smiled to myself thinking of Siegel and Lansky visiting East 86th Street Bund Headquarters.

Despite the head-cracking that Siegel and Lansky did, the Bund grew in New York and nearby New Jersey. The Bund expanded their influence across the US with summer camps and parades for American kids of German descent.

Sunday, 2 January 1938

Japanese Military Bombers Kill Hundreds—Montana Standard, Butte, Montana

7,822,912 Reported Jobless—The Courier, Waterloo, Iowa

Borax Asks Congress to Curb Trusts; Hundreds Slain as Foe Bombs Canton—Brooklyn Eagle, Brooklyn, NY

Roosevelt's Annual Message Gains Interest—Morning News, Florence South Carolina

Hitler Named "Man of the Year" by Time Magazine

Hans Rupp wired me from Maastricht for money to return. He had made his way to Maastricht in the Netherlands where I wired him the money to get to Southampton and sail on the Queen Mary. In turn, Hans wired that he alone would be returning to New York. Alone.

Return NY on Queen Mary STOP Alone STOP Details on arrival STOP Hans

Alone! What the hell happened! Where the hell was Heidi? I hadn't heard from her or Hans in over two weeks. I was getting a bad feeling. My feet go cold when that happens. I guess I never fully recovered from that first trip to Vermont so long ago. My feet were freezing despite good merino wool socks.

228

I drove my Chevrolet to Pier 51. As ILU President, I could drive right on the dock. There were some press and photographers including Movietone at the dock. I knew that Clark Gable was arriving on the Queen Mary too.

The dockworkers were working on the cold, windswept pier unloading baggage and some freight. I stayed in the Chevrolet to be out of the cold wind until I saw Hans Rupp.

There he was. He looked cold, dispirited and thin. His woolen topcoat hung on his frame as though it belonged a much larger man. He looked as though he had nothing to eat for weeks but I knew he would have had full meals on board. I wired the captain's first mate to wrangle a cabin for Hans, so I knew of all the amenities that the ship had. So why did he look so bad? More importantly, where the fook was Heidi?

I stood in the Chevrolet's open door waving my hat as I called to him across the windy pier. Startled by hearing his name called, Hans' head jerked up. I called again. Then he looked in my direction. He stood frozen in place for what seemed to be a long time. Finally, he picked up his one suitcase, leaned into the wind and started walking with clipped steps to the Chevrolet.

He opened the back 'suicide' door to toss his bag on the seat. Then he climbed in beside me. His bloodshot eyes scanned my face then as he closed the car door, he said, "Please, let's go."

"Hans, where's Heidi. Why isn't she with you! What the fook happened? Where is Heidi?"

"Sean, Heidi didn't make it. Heidi is dead."

I stomped the brake. I slammed my hands on the steering wheel. "Fook! Fook! I knew it! I knew she shouldn't go. Fook!"

"Sean, I am heartsick, heart-broken. Please let me tell this story only once. Please take me to my father's flat. I will tell you, my papa and mother everything."

I slammed the Chevrolet into reverse with screaming tires then shifted into first gear. The Chevrolet had a heater but it barely kept my feet warm. Picking up speed, I had the Chevrolet in third gear as we headed across 14th Street. We passed Ian's office on the corner of Ninth, as we drove east-bound in silence.

I turned on Third to head uptown. In the rearview mirror I saw my own eyes brimming with tears. I funneled my sadness into fury. My chest tightened as I gripped the steering wheel with an iron grasp. I had expected the worst, but this was even more terrible than my fears.

***

"Heidi is dead. Heidi was murdered by the *Geheime Staatspolizei*, the Gestapo by order of Reinhard Heydrich," Hans said.

I gritted my teeth and looked up at the apartment's tin ceiling as Ruth Rupp burst into sobs, and Ernst groaned, "*Mein Gott,* not again, not again, not again!"

"Hans, start from the beginning."

"All right," Hans said. "Give me a moment, although I spent the entire five days on the ship thinking about Heidi and what went so wrong."

The three of us sat stoically as we listened. Meanwhile, the traffic noise on York Avenue was filling the front room's silence.

Ruth Rupp set the teapot, cups and saucers on the table. She poured three cups. Only Hans took one. Neither Ernst nor I touched a cup. After one sip, Hans began.

He said that they should have realized that the Nazis had become far more dangerous when they were in customs in Bremerhaven. They went through every piece of clothing in their luggage. He was body searched by the KRIPO, the criminal police. My idea of concealing the money in the clothes that Heidi was wearing worked. Even under the Nazis, the KRIPO was respectful of women. They learned later that the Gestapo has no such scruples. There were Gestapo in leather coats roaming the train that they took from Bremerhaven to Hamburg checking papers. Hans saw two Gestapo search and manhandle a woman before dragging her off the train.

In Hamburg, they met the White Rose Resistance contact at the Emil Wolsdorf tobacconist shop. He warned them that they risked a severe beating if they did not stand and perform the Hitler salute when any Nazi demonstrations occurred. As if on cue, there was a parade outside of brown shirts with the new German swastika flag. Even inside the shop, they did the Nazi salute as it passed.

Hans recited a new German prayer that they learned from the White Rose contact, *Lieber Herr Gott Mach mich stumm, Dich itch nich nach Dachau komm.*

It translates to: 'Dear Lord keep me quiet so that I don't end up in Dachau.' Even this did not intimidate Heidi and Hans. They remained determined to liberate Hannah from Germany. Things were worse than what we heard on the radio or saw in newsreels.

The next day they checked into the Hotel Adlon in Berlin. They were even more uncomfortable there than in Hamburg. It seemed that Hans was the only man not wearing a uniform or a black leather coat. Though Heidi was unfazed, Hans was afraid.

One of their first stops in Berlin was with the FAUD. *Freie Arbitter* Union or Free Workers' Union that distributes anti-Nazi literature and assists escapes of anti-fascists and Jews from Germany. The FAUD forged papers for Hannah. Of course, that took a good portion of the money they had smuggled into Germany. Heidi still had over a thousand marks left. All was going according to plan until Heidi took a large satchel of anti-Nazi leaflets.

Later, they took the number 15 trolley to the Tiergarten, Berlin Zoo to meet Hannah and her father in the monkey house. As planned, Hannah was holding a white balloon as she stood watching the chimps. After a tearful goodbye with her father, they left the Tiergarten with Hannah in hand.

The three took the trolley back to Potsdamplaz. As they stepped off the trolley, Hannah stumbled skinning her knees. That's when things went bad.

Heidi took the sobbing little girl across the street to the Woolworth Five-and-Dime to replace her torn knee stockings. While Hans went into the Apothecary for children's aspirin, astringent and a bandage. That was the last time he saw Heidi and Hannah. The three were to meet in front of the Apothecary for the next trolley. Hans waited at the trolley stop but after the second trolley passed, and Heidi and Hannah did not appear he went into the Woolworth store. There was no sign of his sister or Hannah. He asked a clerk who pulled him into a small office whispering, "Gestapo took them."

Evidently, Heidi had placed a small pile of leaflets in the newspaper rack near the door. Two Gestapo men came into the store right after Heidi and Hannah. They must have seen her place the leaflets. They pulled her and the little girl through the side door to the Columbus Haus. The Gestapo have the two upper floors there. The clerk said that often he heard screams coming from those floors. He also told Hans that he had heard a woman's screams minutes after Heidi was taken.

Hans left immediately. He did not dare to go back to the Adlon Hotel. Instead, he waited at the Potsdamplaz tram stop hoping that the Gestapo might release Heidi since she had her American passport. Then he realized that letting more than two trams pass without boarding would draw attention. He went to the Emil Wolsdorf tobacconist that was next door to the Apothecary instead. There he called his contact in Hamburg he needed another contact, one in Berlin. The Hamburg contact asked for the booth's telephone number saying that someone would call in five minutes. There were only two phone booths in the Wolsdorf. To keep the booth while he waited, he held the switch down with his shoulder and pretended that he was speaking to a girlfriend. He waved a man off while he spoke to his imaginary sweetheart. Then the phone rang. A voice instructed him to go to the café in the Tiergarten zoo, order a beer and sausage but buy a bouquet to place on the table. His contact would be wearing a white rose. As he left the booth, the man outside glared at him but said nothing as he left. His only hope was that man was not Gestapo.

Hans walked briskly to the Tiergarten while picking up flowers from a street vendor. At the café, he ordered food, but his stomach was in a knot. He tried to eat. He was choking, trying not to cry. Then a woman dressed in a gray heavy woolen coat entered. She was wearing a jaunty hat with a white rose pinned to the hatband. To his surprise, she walked right up, kissed Hans and called him 'Schatzie.' She whispered for him to smile, look happy and let her take his arm as they left the café. She said she would take him to a flat. Meanwhile her friends would try to learn what happened to Heidi and the little girl.

As they left, she nodded to a large Slavic-looking man finishing his sausage and cabbage. The White Rose woman said that he was her guardian in case they were being followed. They caught a taxi on the other side of the Tiergarten and took it to a promenade along the river Spree. Sitting on a bench, they tried to look like lovers. The girl took off her hat, plucked the white rose from its hatband and tossed it into the River Spree.

She said that they would be picked up to be taken to a safe flat while her comrades tried to find out what was happening to Heidi. On cue, a sedan pulled up. At the flat, Hans was given a change of clothes and some personal items. That evening, the Slavic man from the Tiergarten café briefly appeared at the flat saying that two Gestapo men showed up at the café only minutes after they departed. He moved them via a back door to another flat that was across the street. It was on the fourth floor on the street-side. After knocking twice then pausing he rapped a third time. The flat door was opened by a very pale and gaunt man. The three entered the flat. The woman who had never introduced herself said that this man, again no name, would take care of Hans for the night. Then the White Rose woman and the Slavic man left. Hans never saw either again.

About 3 am, Hans was awakened by the sounds of cars coming to a sudden stop on the street outside. Two Mercedes-Benz had pulled up in front of the building across the street. Six Gestapo emerged from the cars, split up into pairs. Only one pair entered the building. Two Gestapo disappeared into the dark alley while two remained leaning against one Mercedes-Benz lighting cigarettes. Then Hans was pulled away from the window by the gaunt man. He hissed that Hans stay well away from the windows and against the wall. From their position, they could hear the sound of splintering wood accompanied by breaking glass. In the shadows they listened and watched until the Gestapo departed.

In the morning, another nameless man arrived at the flat. Once again, Hans was handed off to a new stranger who risked everything for a person he had never met. This man had a Hasselblad camera and a gold Nazi party pin. He snapped Hans' photograph and abruptly left. Hans stayed there for two days. Then one evening two new men arrived. They came with the news. Heidi was dead. Heidi's body had been found in the Spree. One of the men told Hans that at the Hotel Furstenhof, he had overheard two Gestapo men laughing and joking about a 'red slut' in 'protective custody' that was personally interrogated by SS Gruppenfuher Heydrich.

Hans wanted to see Heidi's body but was told me that it was too dangerous. Heydrich's Mercedes-Benz 320 convertible had been observed going and coming from Columbus Haus. The White Rose people would see to her burial.

That night another man and a woman smuggled Hans out of Berlin by hiding him behind a false wall in the car's trunk. Just on the outskirts at Hallensee, the car was searched thoroughly. One of the Gestapo using a knife almost found Hans as he hid behind the wall. The car was allowed to continue. At Michendoft, they were stopped once more. This stop was easier as the driver and young woman passed themselves as Lebensborn Aryans traveling to Aachen to find a discreet hotel. The Nazis have this program, Lebensborn for pure Aryans to have more babies. The policemen must have been KRIPO not

Gestapo. They laughed as they congratulated the driver for his choice of an Aryan maiden. They made lewd comments and crude jokes.

In Kassel, Hans was transferred to a truck carrying manure. It smelled terrible but at least he could ride with the driver because he had been given papers, a German passport and a Nazi party pin.

Surprisingly, they had little trouble crossing the frontier into the Netherlands at Maastricht. As the truck crossed the Meuse into the Netherlands, Hans took off the Nazi Party pin. He was about to throw it into the river as the farmer grabbed his hand. The farmer said that he would need it in the future.

A few cobblestone streets from the River Meuse and the German frontier, the driver stopped the truck in front of a café. They went into the Café D'Ingle. After getting coffee and a boiled egg, the farmer asked the waiter if Maastricht had an American Consulates office. It did.

At the American Consulate, the driver asked for Hans' phony German passport. Without so much as *'Auf Weidershen'*, the farmer was back in the truck and gone.

***

I know. I know that I should have stopped Heidi from this dangerous idealistic rescue in the heart of Nazi Germany. Now she was dead because I didn't go with her. Her death was my fault.

In a blind fury, I left Rupp's apartment in Yorkville. I don't know if I said goodbye or just left. My next recollection is some nelly spilling beer on me at the Whitehorse Tavern on Hudson Street. With one punch, I broke his nose then I went bananas. It took two bartenders to stop me from killing him. I do remember leaving the Whitehorse after dropping a pair of twenties for the bartenders.

Chapter 31
Retrieved Reformation

3 January 1938

President Franklin Delano Roosevelt's State of the Union address: "...the people of the Americas must take cognizance of the growing ill-will, of marked trends toward aggressions, of increasing armaments, of shortening tempers— a situation which has many of the elements that lead to the tragedy of general war."

The next morning was appropriately gray, cold and rainy. I sat in the Pier 51 checker booth nursing a bourbon 'hair of the dog that bit me.' Out of nowhere, two longshoremen barged in demanding to speak with me. You know what those crumbs wanted? They wanted me to change their schedule! I pulled my revolver from the desk, jumped to my feet and slammed the bigger crumb against the wall riveting him there with the revolver barrel drilling his forehead.

I didn't kill him, but I fixed those crumbs and anyone else who had similar ideas. Pier 51 and all my piers went back to the 'shapeup' that day and every day thereafter.

***

"Close the fooking door, Jimmy! It's fooking cold out there!"

I was sitting at the shack's small table counting the morning's take while Paddy and Liam read the papers. Jimmy closed the shack door then tuned to warm his hands over the potbelly stove. On a chair near the stove, Paddy noisily resumed reading his Racing Form for Hialeah.

"Boss, we gotta do somethin' about Pier 56," Jimmy said while warming his hands over the franklin heater.

"What's with Pier 56?" I asked.

"It's Gerry Toomey's boys. They've been hustling some of our longshoremen for sharking."

"What? The look on your face says, that ain't all"

"No," Paddy interjected lowering the racing form. "I was tole that Gerry Toomey's gang have been in the Viaduct after shapeup here. Our boss-loader was robbed a day ago. He thinks it was one of Toomey's boys."

"The other day, our numbers controller told me that some Jersey guys were selling on 9th Avenue. It can only be Charlie "The Jew" and his gang from Hoboken. They ain't over here 'cause they like a ferry ride. They looking to expand their operation. Charlie wants the numbers on the docks. Toomey is looking to expand his operations to our piers."

"This could be a war on two fronts!"

"For Cripes-sake, we have good times going. We have a deal with the Italians, Joey "Socks" has the Fulton Fish Market with Mike Clemente controlling the rest of the East River piers. They've agreed, the Commission agreed," I said slamming my fist for emphasis. "They agreed that we have the Westside docks and truck loading. Yanowsky should be in Hoboken and Jersey City not here. Meanwhile Toomey should be satisfied with passing-the-hat around after shapeup. So, if I'm hearing you two right, it's time for us to show 'em who's who on the Westside. In the meantime, let's squirrel away those Thompson guns. The cops are hot for those irons. Let's wait until the heat blows over."

Liam pushed up his hat, took off his glasses and began to polish the lenses with his suit pocket silk.

"Let's pay 'em a little visit."

***

The bitter cold wind bit into my face while the winter sun rising over the buildings made my eyes tear up. Jimmy and I crossed Tenth to the corner on the east side as trucks rumbled over the cobblestones around us. We paid no attention to anything but the doors of the Viaduct Bar & Grill.

As we entered, my eyesight was spotted the way you get when some reporter's flash bulb blinds you. That made me uncomfortable, vulnerable. I blinked several times to accustom my eyes to the darkness of the Viaduct.

My vision slowly returned yet I kept the handkerchief around my nose and mouth as I ordered rye and soda for Jimmy and me. Only when our drinks arrived did my eyes recover. I put the handkerchief in my pocket.

I dropped a Liberty silver dollar but ignored my drink. Jimmy was already scanning the tables of longshoremen who didn't make today's shapeup. I put my back against the bar as Jimmy had. There was Toomey. Right where I was told he'd be. He was seated only two tables from the door with his policy slips and two of his boys. The guy has some brass balls.

I just pinned him there with a stare. He returned the look then said something to his boys. They laughed. The sound of screeching car brakes interrupted the laugh.

Silhouetted by the glaring winter-white sunlight, a man with his porkpie hat pulled low burst into the Viaduct. It was very quick. One of Toomey's friends dove to the sawdust covered floor. Toomey reached for something in his pocket but not before the man in the porkpie hat opened fire. Wood splinters, from chairs and tables hit by gunfire, flew in all directions. Jimmy and I just stood there. His revolver kept blasting. Then all that could be heard was groans and sounds of men crawling in the sawdust.

As the smoke cleared, the man in the porkpie hat was nowhere to be seen. A sedan door slammed. Tires screeched on the cobblestones. The reflected light of the sedan's windshield flashed on the Viaduct' window. As it was roaring off on Tenth, the bartender's head appeared. I tossed him another Liberty silver, downed my rye and walked into the cold.

I promoted one of my policy runners to work the Viaduct. Another runner who emigrated from Germany was placed in the Hudson Hoffbrau Haus on the corner of 14th to run the policy racket for those boys. Things were almost settling down on the piers and with the numbers. Now, it was time to get Yanowsky to swim back to Hoboken or get a cement overcoat.

Sean
January 1938

Even across the Hudson on the Westside, the bar in the White Star Hotel in Hoboken was known as a bucket-of-blood. Every shapeup on the Hoboken piers brought un-hired guys into the joint for a beer-and-a-ball or what some people call a 'boilermaker'. After three or four, somebody always looked at another guy the wrong way. It was any excuse for a fight to relieve the rages within. The fight always included broken beer bottles, bailing hooks, knives that mingled blood with bar floor sawdust. Fights were daily events at the White Star.

I was dressed in my camel hair topcoat with the black felt collar, fawn brown fedora and kidskin gloves. Jimmy and Liam were similarly dressed except their topcoats were black, wore porkpie hats and kept their hands in their overcoat pockets. We stood out like sore thumbs in this joint.

A bartender was polishing a glass as Jimmy asked, "Where's Charlie the Jew?" Saying nothing but with his eyes intently on me, the bartender nodded his head toward the room off the bar. We walked around the long end. Liam stayed at the end of the bar as Jimmy and I continued.

The man next to Charlie Yanowsky, nudged him to look up from the Jersey Journal. Charlie casually put his arm over the back of his chair making sure that I saw his shoulder holster.

"Well, well, what brings yous to the gateway to the west?"

"Want to have a little business talk with you Charlie."

"What's to talk about? I heard 'bout Toomey and his pier 56 crew." With Jimmy still standing, I turned around the chair opposite Charlie and straddled it. I sat saying nothing. Our eyes locked. I slowly methodically pulled off the kidskin gloves finger by finger. A wall clock somewhere ticked loudly. Still, I said nothing.

"Ain't thinkin' of coming over here are ya? Joisy ain't for yous. Last time we talked, yous left me holding the cheese. Nearly got me thrown into the lock-up in Linden because of it."

"No, just thinking about the Newark Chop House and Dutch Schultz. If Dutch had just listened, then maybe he'd still be pulling in some money instead of being on the wrong side of the daisies."

"So whad'ya sayin'?"

"Saying that you can avoid having some daylight put into you if you…"

Yanowsky's man jumped to his feet, his chair clattering behind him. He was pulling his pistol. The .38 Special in Jimmy's hand roared knocking the guy back. Down to the floor. Twitching, the guy's blood mixed with the sawdust.

Charlie hadn't even flinched. His hands never moved. Maybe, the .38 in my hand kept him from being dumb and dead. His eyes were still on mine. The clock ticked.

"So, if I hear yous correctly I should fish on my side of the Hudson and yous fish on dodder-side."

Chapter 32
The MacGregors

Sean

February 1938

He was alone. I could see that. He wore a long black overcoat and black porkpie hat. His head sitting on top of the massive frame was kid-size making him appear comical. But there was nothing funny about the guy. He may have been alone, but he was one of those men who didn't need any backup.

I closed the Union Office safe with today's shape-up money. Then slipped my .38 Special under the Golden Gloves flyer on the counter just as the big man pushed open the Pier 51 ILU door.

"Com'on in why dontcha."

"You Callaghan?" The voice was resonating in that huge chest.

"Who's askin'?"

"Mr. MacGregor sent me."

I watched him closely. His meat hooks hung relaxed as his sides. The nose on the guy had been pommeled nearly flat and his left ear was a cauliflower. There was no tension, almost boredom like a guy waiting on the A train subway platform.

"What does Red want?"

"Mr. MacGregor wants Mr. Callaghan to come to his office with me."

If MacGregor was still cheesed off with me about the shape-ups, he would not be above to having me shot. His guys are hot heads, they have hair-triggers. I'll pick my own place and time to talk, not him. A quiet place.

"Well, we'll tell Mr. Callaghan when he comes in."

"Ain't choo Callaghan?"

"No, we just look alike. I'm Knobby Walsh."

"You think I'm punch drunk? You think I can't read the funnies. I know 'Joe Palooka', youse thinkin' youse funny?"

"I never fun with Mr. MacGregor. You just tell him that Mr. Callaghan will meet him at his 14th Street office later."

"Mr. MacGregor wants it now, not later."

"Unfortunately, it will have to be."

"Mr. MacGregor ain't feelin' so good and wants to go home to rest."

"So, what's the rush? We'll get a hold of Mr. Callaghan and set it up for when Mr. MacGregor is feeling better."

"But he wants it now." I picked up the telephone, put the earpiece snug against my ear while holding the mouthpiece close, I asked the operator, "Ring Chelsea 7-4571." Both the big man and I locked eyes. Then Doris Connelly's nasal voice stabbed my eardrum.

"Hudson Legal, Callaghan, Friedman and Bloom. To whom am I speaking?"

"Hi Doris, is Mr. Callaghan in?" I pressed the earpiece hard against my head.

"Mr. Callaghan, Mr. Callaghan is with a client, Mr. Callaghan. Can I…" I cut dizzy Doris off, "Doris, is Mr. Callaghan available?"

"Just a minute Mr. Callaghan."

"Just ask Mr. Callaghan to call Pier 51 when he is finished."

"Sure thing Mr. Callaghan, I will have Mr. Callaghan call you."

"Thanks, Bye Doris."

I pressed the earpiece hook down to end the call before Doris blabbed something that could be heard by the big guy. Still holding it down, I put the earpiece on the hook. Looking at the big man, I shrugged.

"Sorry, Mr. Callaghan is in a meeting."

"Mr. MacGregor ain't gonna be happy."

"You just tell him that Mr. Callaghan will meet with him as soon as he can."

Without another word the giant was out the door and moving quickly down the pier to Tenth Ave. As I watched him, I tossed my keys to Paddy Clarke.

"Paddy, lock up the shop." Then I turned to Jimmy. "Jimmy, you follow the big palooka and call me at the Hoffbrau Haus."

Jimmy was already out the door as I reached for my camelhair and fedora.

That afternoon, Paddy pulled the Pontiac Silver Streak up behind Jimmy's Buick Model 48 on a quiet street in College Point. I climbed out of the Pontiac. As I did, Jimmy rolled down his window.

"Good work Jimmy. You trailed him here."

"Uhuh, Red left his office only a few minutes after Joe Palooka must a given the bad news. Red looked like shite, coughin' an' wiping his nose with a big handkerchief."

"What's this place that Red's in?"

"I think it's his sister's. From what I heard Red moved in with her after she threw out the drunken-bum husband. I've been hearing that he smacked her and her daughter around."

"I remember that Mary Kate was a pretty tough cookie herself back in St. Joe's. She and her hyenas were a thorn for my sister. She don't need Red to protect her."

"So, Red's been in the house the whole time since I followed him here."

"You and Paddy keep an eye out."

"Sure thing."

I climbed the concrete stairs to a platform enclosed by a brick wall. A man I hadn't seen from the street put down his newspaper and quickly strode over to me.

"Who are youse?" he asked, as he relieved me of my .38. He was quick and efficient.

"Callaghan, Sean Callaghan, I'm Mr. MacGregor's business partner."

"I hoid of youse. Lemme see if Mr. Mac wants any visitor. Don'tcha move."

He opened the house door keeping his eyes on me all the while he shouted over his shoulder.

"Mr. Mac dere's that Cockeye Callaghan at the door. Wants to see ya."

A woman's voice said, "You are too sick to see anybody."

"For Christ's sake, I wanta hear what he has to say. Bring him in Moe."

I tried not to smile seeing Red MacGregor in a fluffy bathrobe with his nose as red as his hair. Seated at a kitchen table, there was a steaming cup of tea in front of him. A shapely blonde in a silk robe was fussing with something on the stove. Red was noted as a ladies-man with a new bombshell on his arm nearly every week at the Cotton Club. This must be his dish-of-the-week. Even with this view she was a real looker.

"Get Mr. Callaghan here a cupa."

"Sure Hamish."

'Hamish'. I never heard MacGregor called anything but 'Red' or 'MacGregor.' Moe the muscle had followed me around the center stairs into the kitchen. There was a large well-appointed comfortable looking living room that I noticed before passing through a dining room into the kitchen.

"Sit. I don't want to look up. My neck muscles are killing me."

"You ought to have a doctor come by," I said, pulling out a chair.

"Fuck doctors, now what do you have to say Callaghan?"

"Dropping the shapeup was, was not a good idea. So, I have the shape up going again."

"I tole you that you dumb mick."

"Yeah, well fook you and the horse you rode in on."

I sensed that Moe the Muscle was right behind me. Not good, I don't have a back-up pistol on me. This was turning out to be a bad idea. I need to just blow out of here before Moe the Muscle gets any bright ideas.

The good-looking blonde set the cup of tea for me. She looked familiar.

"Hey aren't you, Mary Kate? Mary Kate MacGregor?"

"Well, aren't you the bright one," she said.

"It's been a long time since St. Joe's," I said, remembering that Red had mentioned that her husband Tommy Maginiss had been found floating in the East River. Around the docks, the talk was that Tommy Maginiss had been thrown out or barred from several cat houses for getting too rough with the broads. Lucky Luciano ran most of the girls in Manhattan. I'm sure that he did not appreciate that his merchandise was getting bruised. Naturally, just as I would have, Red protected his sister. Luciano protected his broads. The Italians liked to put their problems to swim with concrete boots. They don't like floaters. Tommy was a floater. It wasn't the Italians that took care of Tommy.

Anyway, that made Mary Kate a widow, a widow in a silk dressing gown. A silk dressing gown that I'd like to explore.

"So, it has, it has been a long time" she said brushing back a stray curl that she wrapped around her index finger. Her blonde hair, parted on the left, was set in full lush waves. Very chic, as my sister would say. Even in a silk bathrobe, Mary Kate looked like a cover of a movie magazine, a cross between Jean Harlow and Carole Lombard. I could imagine Mary Kate without that bathrobe.

"So, what else Callaghan?" Red interrupted my imagery.

I could hear Moe was breathing noisily. Then I heard him shifting his feet. Oh, shite, before shooting some hit men or as I like to call them torpedoes settle their feet while others adjust their grip on their pistols. Well, most torpedoes did. Only Vincent Coll did neither. He just plugged you.

"Hamish, don't you think that Mr. Callaghan looks like that movie star."

"What?"

Mary Kate glided around the table to stand behind me, right behind. She was now between Moe and me. As she flecked off something from my shoulder, she said, "I think he looks like James Cagney. Don't you?"

Hamish Red MacGregor blew his nose noisily, muttering, "In that fucking Irish way of his. Maybe."

"I want you to finish your tea Hamish then take yourself off to bed."

Mary Kate had both hands on my shoulders. MacGregor's chair complained as he pushed himself back. He stood slowly coming to full height. He eyed me.

"We'll talk more when I'm feeling better."

From behind me, Moe took several steps toward MacGregor.

"Lemme help ya boss," he said trying to take MacGregor's arm.

"I don need no fucking help. You just help escort Callaghan out."

MacGregor shuffled out to the center hall. A moment later I heard his feet on the stairs. It reminded me of the two of us climbing the stairs exhausted after carrying out several dead boys and girls during the Influenza at St. Joe's.

Mary Kate still had her hands on my shoulders. I felt the warmth right through my topcoat. She squeezed my shoulders briefly then took a step back. I stood. I turned. Only inches from me, Mary Kate's steel blue eyes searched mine.

Maybe she was an inch shorter than me but those inches were well put together. We stood like that for a moment then to my surprise, she hugged me. Stunned, I put my arms around her. I could feel my heart racing. I guess that Mary Kate could too.

"Good to see you Sean after all the years," she said into my camelhair shoulder. "Will I see you again?"

"I don't see a reason not to."

"Find a reason."

Mary Kate's hands and arms released me, not her eyes. Then I heard steps or really, skipping steps from the center hall stairs. Thump, thump, pause, thump, thump. A girl of about eight or nine merrily hopped into the kitchen. Mary Kate turned to the girl.

"Elizabeth, did you check on your uncle?"

"Yes, mother. Uncle Hamish is tucked in and snoring already."

"Good. Now escort Mr. Callaghan here to the door."

"Of course, mother. Follow me, Mr. Callaghan."

Outside, Moe handed my .38 back. The cylinder was empty.

Elizabeth smiled, "Nice to meet you Mr. Callaghan. Uncle Hamish talks about you. Bye!"

With that she whirled around and disappeared back inside leaving me and Moe.

"Youse have a nice day."

"Youse too Moe."

For the next few days, all I could think about was those steel blues of that blonde Carole Lombard girl, Mary Kate MacGregor. Finally, I called Red. I said that I wanted to talk but it wasn't about business.

When I arrived at the house on College Point, Moe greeted me much the same way, except this time he took my topcoat, fedora first, then my .38 before leading me to Red. Wrapped in a blanket, Red still looked like shite. With dark circles under his eyes, he looked as bad as one of the nearly dead during the flu pandemic. Not wanting to spend more time than needed with him, I got to the point.

"What the fuck do you want?" He asked.

"Red, I want to date your sister."

"My sister?"

"Yes, I want to date Mary Kate."

"You don't need my permission. You need my sister's."

"See, we're partners in the union and on the docks. I want to be straightforward with you."

"Sure, if my sister is willing, who am I to say 'no'?"

"So, you're fine, if she's fine?"

"Sure, now leave me the fuck alone."

That evening, I called her on the horn. She didn't sound surprised. Mary Kate suggested that she needed to get out of the house for a trip into the City. Would I take her to Bonwits? Of course, I would!

When I arrived at the MacGregor's, Moe directed me to the sitting room to wait for Mary Kate. As I thumbed through the *Life* magazine on the coffee table, a happy Elizabeth skipped into the room.

"Mr. Callaghan, so nice to see you again."

"Nice to see you too Elizabeth. Do you know if your mother is ready yet?"

"Oh, no, she is very fussy about her make-up, but she should be down in a jiffy." With that she announced, "I'll run back upstairs to make sure that she knows you're here."

Only a minute or two later, the sound of stiletto heels on the stairs announced Mary Kate's entrance. She wore a tight-fitting blue wool dress with fur-trimmed collar and cuffs. She looked like she was poured into the dress.

"Wow!"

"Oh," she battered her eyelashes at me then walked to the hall mirror to pin on her hat. It was one of those highly fashionable hats that she pinned to one side that gave her a sophisticated Myrna Loy look. At her side, Elizabeth studied her every movement.

"Are you going somewhere Mother?"

"Mr. Callaghan is driving me into the City for some shopping."

"Mother, you are going to the City? The City! Can I come? Can I?"

"Don't you have homework?" Mary Kate said not stop adjusting her hat in the hall mirror, "Why am I paying all that money for your education? Don't you want to get into Mary Louis Academy?"

"I've finished my homework and studying. Can I come too? Oh, Mother, please, please…"

Turning to me, looking into my face, and as she hurriedly pulled on her kidskin gloves, Mary Kate said, "It's up to Mr. Callaghan. He can decide."

"Please Mr. Callaghan, take me too!"

"Of course, Elizabeth can join us. It's only a shopping trip."

The words weren't off my tongue before Elizabeth bounded back up the stairs with, "I'll be ready in a jiffy!"

That's when I received my first glare of warning from Mary Kate. The North Atlantic in January wasn't as cold as the steel blue of those eyes.

"She's a nice kid. Be a nice trip to the City," I said.

"The City" is what people in the other boroughs called Manhattan. It didn't matter that it was all New York City. Sure, there were nice places in Jamaica or Jackson Heights in Queens and Bay Ridge Brooklyn. The Bronx had Fordham Road shopping. Staten Island had, Cripes, I don't care what that fooking island had.

I had a really difficult time keeping my eyes on the road with Mary Kate sitting on the bench seat, dangerously close to me. Her Chanel No 5 was an aphrodisiac but that was like taking coal to Newcastle. An aphrodisiac that I really did not need. Want maybe, didn't need.

Mary Kate said, "If you drive straight across Fifty-ninth all way to Fifth, then we could go first to Bonwits on Fifty-six then stop at Bloomingdale's on the way back."

"Sure doll, I'll find a place to park near F.A.O. Schwartz on 5th. Ain't Bonwit-Teller's just a bit ritzy?"

"Bonwits carries the best frocks, from France you know."

This was going to be an expensive first date.

Several hours later and several hundred bucks poorer, the three of us were back at the house on College Point with armloads of boxes and bags. Elizabeth was obviously thrilled. I received a hug from her that could have broken a longshoreman's neck. With her bags, she took the stairs to her room two at a time.

Uninterested in Elizabeth, Mary Kate piled her bags, and boxes on the living room couch draping the Bonwit-Teller garment bags over its back. Each dress that she tried on provided me with many opportunities to feast my eyes. A burlesque fan-dancer would have cost me less but I didn't care. Now as she sashayed to the corner liquor cabinet, I could tell that she knew that my eyes were on her ass.

She turned profile and asked, "See anything you'd like?"

"Matter of fact, I do."

Looking over her shoulder, she smiled, "I meant rye, gin or scotch."

"Scotch, neat."

Mary Kate poured herself a gin and vermouth in a martini glass, dropped in an olive then poured my scotch. But she left the drinks on the butler's cart. She crossed the room, lifted the lid on a cabinet that held a Victrola turntable-radio combination. She selected a big 78 record and gently set the needle. Cab

Calloway's "When you're smiling" filled the room. I heard only the whisper of her silk stockings as she walked to the butler's cart.

"I didn't know that you liked Cab Calloway," I said.

"You ought to get to know me better."

"I'd like that, say how about you and me taking in Cab Calloway at the Cotton Club some night."

"That would be fine."

Mary Kate handed me the scotch. As she settled down on the settee opposite me, she kicked off her heels. Then she folded both legs up on the settee. My eyes travelled those long legs to the line of her stockings' top peeking out from her skirt. She lifted her martini to me.

"Cheers."

March 1938

I saw Mary Kate several times after that. She was intoxicating. I found myself hoping that she found me intoxicating too. As often as I could, I made excuses to leave the union shop to drive to her place on College Point. Working the docks from pier 56 to 51, we were pulling in good cash from union dues, shipping companies 'donations', the numbers and sharking. Naturally, there were miscounted shipments or things that fell off a truck that I could bring to the restaurant. Other things needed to be fenced.

I had Liam do the enforcement jobs. Jimmy took over the dues and shape-up donations. Paddy Clarke took care of the sharking and any fencing that we needed. That left me time to woo Mary Kate. The boys razzed me as being dizzy with a dame.

When Jimmy suggested that we take in the Golden Gloves matches at Madison Square Garden I was all in. Mary Kate had blown me off that night saying that she wanted to spend it soaping in a bubble bath.

I hadn't been to the fights in a while. This was the Golden Gloves' Semi-Finals. Jimmy said that the Garden was nearly sold-out. But I have connections. Owney Madden was still promoting fights. I was able to get seats, ring-side seats. I invited Red along but he said that he had other business that evening. Only Jimmy and I went.

The Garden was packed that night. There were no big contenders, except for Barney Ross. The welterweight fights were usually good, better than featherweight matches. Tonight, the card had a featherweight class, Henry

Armstrong matched against the World Welterweight Champion, Barney Ross. As Ross was taller by two inches and weighed almost ten pounds more, I expected a short fight. What a fight it was! Armstrong won in a spectacular unanimous decision. Have to keep my eye on this Henry Armstrong.

After that fight, we went to Jack Dempsey's Restaurant on 8th just a block away. The steaks were tender yet well-marbled and the beers cold. Jimmy and I lingered at the table talking about the fights over some scotch. It was a good night and one great fight. I picked up the tab.

At the coat-check, Jimmy tipped the girl who winked at Jimmy as she wished us a good night. It was a warm night for March. It suggested that winter might be over, but we knew better. We slung our heavy topcoats over our shoulders as we stepped out of Jack Dempsey's.

"Cripes my feet are cold."

"It ain't that cold Boss."

"Do you hear that?"

"Hear what?"

"Stop, listen! Somethin's not right."

Jimmy pulled out a pack of Lucky Strikes, "Here Boss, this'll calm ya. Why do you have the heebie-jeebies?"

As he closed the matchbook cover to strike the match, I saw the nose of a sedan poking out of the alleyway across the street. I looked up and down 8th. The street was completely empty. Jimmy lit my Lucky Strike then his. Only thing standing on the pavement besides us was the corner cigar store wooden Indian. I heard a clutch pop. Then the sedan screeched out of the alley. I pulled Jimmy to the pavement as bullets shattered the cigar store windows. Even the wooden Indian took a couple of slugs. The sedan sped downtown.

We both pulled our revolvers, but we had no chance of hitting the fast disappearing car.

"Lesgetoutta here!" Jimmy yelled.

"Now, who else wants me dead?"

March 1938

The next morning, as Paddy Clarke handed me a steaming cup of coffee. He said, "Boss, we heard that the steamer that will berth on 56 has a shipment of very expensive Russian furs. We heard that the furs would bring in over 20 Grand."

"You were supposed to find out who tried to put some daylight into Jimmy and me."

"I was tryin'. That's how I heard of the Russian furs. Asking about action."

Then, Liam added. "This is the first time anything expensive from Russia will be on our docks."

"Why's the Russians shipping furs? Up until now, we never heard about anything other than a silver samovar or caviar shipment. This is the first time I heard about Russian furs," said Paddy.

"Don't you read nothin' but the sports pages? There's a civil war in Spain. The Russians are sidin' with the Republicans fighting Franco's Falangist Army. The German's are supporting Franco. That's Nazi money. I guess the Russians need the money to buy guns, so they're unloadin' furs." Jimmy was always a news boy.

We were sitting in the ILU office on 14th playing cards as we did most days. Today, we had started the game after counting the sharking vig and trucker donations. The day's take was good and I would need my cut. Mary Kate has expensive tastes and loves going to high falutin' clubs. The money we could pull in by jacking the furs would be long green.

"I call," said Padric, the new guy to the Union Office.

"I have a pair of aces and eights, a deadman's hand."

"I have a bicycle of ace, deuce, trey, four and five," I said.

"Damn!" Padric said throwing down his cards.

As I swept the pot to my side of the table, I got back to the Russian furs, "When is the Russian fur boat supposed to dock?"

Padric asked. "What's the name of the boat?"

Liam snapped open the Shipping News, took a pencil from behind his ear and with his pink tongue held between his teeth squinted through his glasses at the paper.

"Found it! It's Saukko, out of Finland," Liam said. "I'm on it, Boss."

"When?"

"Should be in by the end of the week."

"Now who's the hauler?"

"Lemme find out, Boss!"

Jimmy was out the door.

***

250

"Mary Kate, would you like a swell Russian sable fur coat?"

"What girl wouldn't!"

I ran my hand down her silky back and squeezed her firm ass. We had been at the Cotton Club at its new digs in the Theatre District. The show featured the canary, Lena Horn. Mary Kate loved her "Sweeter Than Sweet" accompanied by Cab Calloway's orchestra. After that, it was a nightcap at the Waverly Inn. Then it was easy to push her into my Village apartment bed.

The boys were right, I was dizzy for this dame.

"When can I have my sable?"

"In a few days."

"Maybe that's all I'll wear from now on. Would you like that?"

"Only if you model it for me, only."

With that she took me in her mouth. Naughty girl, she kept her eyes on me the whole time.

***

It was nice and dark on Tenth Avenue at 4 am. The streetlamps cast a hazy light as a cold mist drifted off the Hudson. Across on Bethune, we waited for the truck loading to finish. Liam in the back seat had done some preliminary work paying off the driver. The driver was well greased to get 'roughed up' by us to make it look smooth for any copper later. Paid well.

Waiting in the Buick, my feet were getting cold. I was getting that same bad feeling. The calendar may be calling it Spring, but the weather wasn't too spring-like. I should've worn my merino socks.

Wordlessly, Jimmy who was the wheelman elbowed me just as the truck's headlamps lit up.

"Wait. Wait," I said. "Let him start up Tenth toward the Garment District. We'll take him on 15th. Then we can stash the truck until the heat blows over."

The fur truck's headlights swept by us as it turned uptown rumbling over the cobblestones. Jimmy turned the Buick's headlights on only after the fur truck was a full block ahead. It continued around the bend at Horatio. As we turned the bend the fur truck was nowhere in sight. It had disappeared!

We were in the Meat Packing District. Even at this hour it was busy with workers in blood-stained white coats carrying partially butchered cows in all directions. No fur truck anywhere.

"Turn here, at Gansevoort Street!" I shouted.

Even with multiple meat trucks crowding loading docks, I was able to spot the fur truck. It was surrounded by a dozen armed men.

"Pull over! Quick! Douse the lights!"

The three of us were out guns ready. Jimmy ran crouched over to a meat truck standing between us and the fur truck. With his revolver at his side, Jimmy stepped on a meat truck's running board to look through the driver's side window. Meanwhile, Liam and I crouched behind the meat truck engine for cover.

"Holy cow!"

"What? What do you see?"

"Our highjack is being highjacked!"

"We can't let that happen," Liam said as he racked a cartridge into the pistol's chamber.

"Hold it!" I said. "How many guys are there Jimmy?"

"Christ! Maybe a dozen with rifles and shotguns."

"Can you make out anybody?"

"Boss, come look."

Pulling myself up by the trucks sideview, I joined Jimmy on the running board. He was right. A dozen men with rifles and shotguns surrounded the fur truck. Rule one in a gun fight: Never bring a pistol to a long gun fight. Even if we had the Chicago typewriters, Tommy guns, it wouldn't have mattered. We were outnumbered too.

We had been robbed. Cripes! Then one guy stepped into the streetlight. The sonofabitch was lightning a cigar. Charlie Yanowsky! If that wasn't enough, his torpedo George Keeler was cradling a Thompson.

We followed them across the George Washington bridge to Jersey but it was a trip for biscuits, a complete waste of time. No point calling for some more boys. Everyone knew that Charlie had the coppers in Fort Lee in his pocket. We had to call it a loss. That Fooking Yanowsky!

That cost me, personally. Mary Kate was placated with a mink stole from Saks Fifth. Still, I was steamed up about Yanowsky until Jimmy had the idea of letting the G-men get a call. The Fort Lee coppers had to bend for the G-men. I had Jimmy drive to the London Chemists' Drug Store on 23rd to call the FBI. The call was made from the same phone booth that "Mad Dog" Cole got chopped in years before. I thought that it would be a nice touch.

That didn't get him. It only flushed Yanowsky out of Fort Lee to a Pompton Lakes cabin. We kept at it. The G-men received another anonymous call about Yanowsky's whereabouts. It was too bad that Dick Tracy wasn't on the Yanowsky job because J. Edgar's guys were more like Keystone Kops than Dick Tracey. The FBI missed him at the cabin because Yanowsky was out robbing banks!

We continued to shadow Yanowsky. We had to give the FBI another anonymous tip that finally led the FBI to Charlie standing on a Jersey City street corner. He pulled a heater provoking the G-men to shoot him down in barrage of gunfire. Charlie was taken to St. Mary's Hospital. Unbelievably, he recovered. Charlie Yanowsky survived to end up in Alcatraz. We never found the Russian sables.

I went back to business as usual, including Mary Kate. I told Red MacGregor that I was going marry his sister. He gave me his 'permission' even though I never asked for it. That night at the 21 Club, I had the waiter serve Mary Kate a champagne cocktail with a big diamond engagement ring glittering in the glass. When we went back to her College Point place, we announced our engagement to Red and Elizabeth. Elizabeth was excited. I said that once Mary Kate and I were married I would adopt Elizabeth. She squealed and jumped happily. Everyone was happy for us.

That is except for Mikey.

"Sean, you're just getting over Heidi's murder. You and Heidi were great together. I think that you should wait."

"You don't like Mary Kate. You never liked her when we were kids at St. Joe's either."

"Mary Kate is a self-centered…all she cares about is herself. She doesn't even care about her daughter. Proof, the girl is more devoted to you than her own mother. Are you sure, sure that Mary Kate really loves you?"

"Look here, I'm going to marry her and that's that."

Chapter 33
Madison Square Garden

Sean
19 February 1939

New York Capital Theatre premieres "Stagecoach" with Claire Trevor and John Wayne

"Boss, it's the phone. For you."

"Tell 'em I'm busy. OK Liam, hit me with another card."

Once again, we were killing time playing poker in the Union office. With his hand over the mouthpiece Padric hissed, "Boss, I think that you should take the call. It's somebody who you shouldn't refuse."

"Who is it?"

Padric leaned closer, "It's Meyer Lansky."

"Sure, I'll take the call," I said loudly. "Callaghan here," I said into the phone.

"One moment, please."

Then Meyer Lansky's voice came over the phone, "Sean, my favorite *goyim*, how are ya?" I knew that his favorite *goys* were all Italians, not Irish.

"Fine, Mr. Lansky. How are you?" I always addressed Meyer Lansky politely as I was instructed when I started out in the Bronx. For a long time now, together with Lucky Luciano, he ran the Commission, the National Crime Syndicate primarily for the Mafia. In Florida, the Bahamas and Cuba, Lansky was making good money too. Lansky ran 'carpet joints' or gambling casinos that gave the twits who went there the idea that the odds weren't stacked against them.

Also, I knew that both Lansky and Luciano had contracted Lepke Buchalter's Murder Incorporated to rub out Dutch and his boys back in '35. At that time, Dutch was being relentlessly pursued by Thomas Dewey, then the U.S. Attorney for the Southern District of New York. Dutch wanted to kill Dewey. He even asked permission from the Commission to do it. Luciano and Lansky thought that it would put a spotlight on the rackets, so they put the kibosh on killing Dewey. Dutch left the meeting saying that he wasn't going upriver when Dewey could be in a Chicago overcoat. With that Dutch's signed his own death warrant. Besides, Dutch had some good producing rackets that the Syndicate wanted.

With Dutch no longer on his docket, Dewey turned for bigger headlines. Dutch had been right, Lansky and Luciano should have taken out Dewey. In '36, Dewey trained his prosecutorial sights on Luciano. Thanks to Ian's former classmate at Fordham Law, Eunice Hunton-Carter, Dewey got Luciano. She was Dewey's Assistant District Attorney. Eunice was as good a detective as she was a prosecutor. She figured out that the bail bondsmen and lawyers for prostitutes in the city were Lucky Luciano's people. Eunice's work on Dewey's indictment resulted in conviction of Luciano on forced prostitution. Luciano received a thirty-year sentence.

Meyer Lansky was too shrewd for Dewey. Dewey got absolutely zilch on Lansky. He kept his operations clean and profitable. Lansky is rumored to have a Swiss bank account so that he wouldn't get charged for tax evasion like Al Capone. I knew that Meyer Lansky was a real *mensch* as Mordecai Friedman would say. If Lansky wanted something, then you had better listen or you would end up as fish-bait in the East River.

"Sean, I need a favor, I need you to do something for me."

"For you Mr. Lansky, I am always ready to be of service."

"Do you remember the fun that Benny Siegel and I had with the Friends of the New Germany at their 82nd Street meeting? Well…"

***

Colleen

"Colleen, your Ma is here," said Sally Owens, one of Dottie's original prep cooks. I glanced out at the tables nestled around the bar and there she was. Mom was sitting at the bar adjusting her hat like some uptown prima donna.

"Thanks, Sally."

I pulled out a bar stool next to her and said sarcastically, "What is it this time, Ma? Food money? Rent money? Or do you just need a new hat? The one you are wearing is looking a bit shabby."

"This is how you talk to your mother? Shame on you girl. You have this lovely restaurant, and you treat me with such sarcasm and ugly words. You can't even greet your own mother without being rude."

When I just continued to glare at her, she said, "It so happens that I have a job for you that is worth a good bit of money."

"What kind of job would that be?"

"There is a big event in the Garden next month. And they are looking for a caterer."

"Well, it might surprise you to learn that I am not running a catering business. This is a restaurant," I said smugly.

My dear mother rolled her eyes and ignored my remark. "Listen to me, girl. It's not a big catering affair. It's just coffee and sandwiches for the important people running the event. I'm thinking you can meet the requirement for makin' a few sandwiches and coffee and maybe some good Yorkville German pastry, now, can't you? Am I wrong? Is it too difficult for a restauranteur of Second Avenue to make sandwiches?" she said her voice now dripping with sarcasm.

I thought for a moment and a little extra income would not hurt now.

Not willing to display any level of acquiescence, I said, "For how many people?"

She settled back in her chair and crossed her thick legs. "For about 20-30, I expect."

"When is the event scheduled?"

"In February, on the 20th."

"Who do I contact?"

She smiled a wide grin, "I will have him come round to see you and bring his financial offer. It will be the event manager of the Garden."

I hated to take anything from her but a little more income for my business was always welcomed. My kitchen and table staff could use a few extra dollars too.

I said rather sheepishly, "Thanks, Ma."

Her eyes were shining brightly as she said, "And I expect your gratitude will include a little finder's fee, now right?"

Knowing that I was once more falling into one of her traps I nonetheless said, "Sure a little finder's fee would seem appropriate."

"I was thinking," she said, "that we would go in 50:50."

"And leave all the work and the costs to me? I do not agree, Ma!"

"Ok then 40%…"

"I think 10% would be more likely."

"Make it 15% and we have a deal. I'll talk to the event manager today."

"Since I don't know what they are going to ask for and pay yet, I will agree on the condition that I can still cover my costs plus make at least 15% for myself. If that works, we have a deal."

"Ah Colleen, you drive a hard bargain. Let's shake on our agreement." Feeling that I had been taken advantage of, reluctantly I took her outstretched hand.

Not more than one day later a small bespectacled man named Oscar Steiner came to see me. I had not expected to see anyone about the catering event so soon but I ushered him into my small office and said, "My mother told me you would be coming to see me but I did not expect to see you so soon."

"Your mother?"

He looked questioningly at me. Then in a thick German accent he described the food that he needed and told me that they would pay $100! I was thrilled! They would pay me $50 in advance and the rest upon completion of the job. He also said I must arrive at the Madison Square Garden with the sandwiches and coffee by 10:30 AM precisely.

"We haf much to do to arrange for the meeting unt we vant everything set up in advance."

As Mr. Steiner was leaving Dottie's, I thanked him for the opportunity. This could be a great side business. Madison Square Garden had many special events. If I can handle adding catering to my business, it could be profitable.

I said, "I will be there by 10:15."

He turned to me, "10:30 is what I need Miss Callaghan."

"Mr. Steiner, thank you for listening to my mother and in choosing Dottie's. I won't let you down."

"Your mother? Who's your mother?"

"Her name is Mrs. McBride."

"I don't know a Mrs. McBride, your mother. But the event organizers requested your restaurant. The *Kleine Konditori* could not do the catering. So

Dottie's, also in Yorkville was their first choice. I expect you to do the job and be there at 10:30."

I watched him open his notebook and thought, 'Right-o. My dear old Ma had done it to me again. What a sucker I am! I actually believed that she had recommended me and my restaurant to the officials at the Garden. Then she comes asking for a 50:50 cut. I'll give her a cut alright! I'll cut her out completely for lying to me,' I thought furiously. The little German man was eyeing me curiously.

I cleared my throat and said, "I expect you have some menu requests. Let's go over what you want in detail."

Later that evening, I recounted the whole episode including Ma's treachery to Sean. He just laughed at me, "Mikey, Mikey, Mikey when will you learn? Our dear ole Ma is not to be trusted. She is lookin' out for herself and no one else. And she is always lookin' for more dough. And not the kind you make your pies with!"

He laughed. I rolled my eyes at his last comment.

I said dejectedly, "I actually thought she recommended me! And worst, I thought I did a good job negotiating with her."

Sean said, "Hey kid, with you, I gotta be sure you understand. Mikey, you are just too willing to think good about people. Even our ole Ma, who we both know has a heart that is as black as night."

He asked me about the event itself and I was embarrassed to tell him I didn't know what the event was exactly. "Well, no matter. It will do you good to take on this job. It might open up more business in the future."

Then his face darkened, "There is a lot of talk about coming war in Europe. Looks like Germany is taking over Eastern Europe and heading west toward Denmark."

***

On the morning of February 20, I arrived at Dottie's at 6 AM. My kitchen staff was all there by 7 and work on the catering job commenced. We loaded up our truck with trays of sandwiches and several coffee pots, pitchers of cream and bowls of sugar. We loaded table linens, napkins, plates, cups and saucers, spoons and by 10 AM we were ready to make our way across town to the Garden. I obsessively double checked the inventory as we drove and reminded our three servers to keep track of the china and spoons. I did not have much in the way of spare tableware and I did not want to lose any if possible.

Sally Owens was crammed in the front seat with me, "I love going to the Garden. I saw a fight there last month. It was bloody but very exciting. My boyfriend Freddy gets tickets for all the big events. I asked him about this one, but he said he didn't know anything about it. Besides he's working now. We only go to the nighttime events when I have the night off." She prattled on about the events she had attended in the past.

I was only half listening as I was silently going through the menu requirements. I wanted to be sure I hadn't forgotten anything that Steiner required. As always, Sean had come through with the meat we needed for the sandwiches as well as two dozen loaves of bread. I swear I don't know how he gets all this stuff. But it sure helps; my profit for this will be almost 70%!

We entered through the alley door and was immediately greeted by a big brawny Irish cop who barked at me, "What have we here? Who are you?"

"I'm Colleen Callaghan, from Dottie's Restaurant. We have the food for the event officials," I stammered. He looked from me to Sally who was carrying a huge tray of sandwiches.

Stepping aside, he said, "Well, I guess I should let you go to work then."

I held the door open while two more servers lumbered by carrying trays of food. "Can I prop this door open while we finish unloading?"

"Sure, I'll be right here to keep it open for ya, so you go ahead."

As I passed by him, the cop said, "Callaghan…Callaghan…any relation to Cockeye Callaghan?"

I turned on my heel. "Don't be calling him that, that name. Sean Callaghan is my brother."

"I thought I saw a resemblance, but your blue eyes are at least straight," he chuckled.

I ignored him and went on down the narrow passageway. I asked another cop who was standing at the end of the passageway, "Where is Mr. Steiner's office?"

The cop said, "I dunno. But if yer lookin for the man in charge, he's up on the stage."

"Thanks."

I was glad that he wasn't loaded with remarks about Sean, and I looked toward the stage. There were several people standing at a podium. One of them was probably Mr. Steiner. There were several more cops milling about on the stage and standing in the back while workers were setting up rows of chairs for the audience. Must be some kind of big meeting.

I asked Sally, "Do they always have so many cops here?"

"Not that I've seen. They do have a few coppers here during fight nights. Some of the men get pretty riled up after the fight is over and start brawling with each other. Kind of adds to the excitement," she glanced around, "but I don't know about day time events."

As I mounted the steps to the stage, I saw several eight-foot tables positioned to the left of the stage. I turned to Sally. "'Tis for us to set up, I'm thinking."

Mr. Steiner was talking to two other men at the podium at center stage. "I'll check with Mr. Steiner."

As I approached all three men turned in my direction. 'Must be some sort of club', I thought. All three were wearing the same light tan shirt and brown trousers. They had a belt across their chests and their trousers were tucked inside their boots.

I said, "Good morning, Gentlemen. Mr. Steiner, are those tables for the food service?"

"Yes, Miss Callaghan. Please get the food displayed quickly." He pulled out his vest pocket watch and smiled.

"Of course." I turned to Sally and nodded my head, "That's for us to set up."

Sally took charge of the other two servers and spread one of our white linen tablecloths onto the first table. I wanted to make sure that there was nothing else that Steiner needed from us. The trio at the podium had resumed their conversation. I realized they were not speaking English. Workers wheeled a large trolley with some other equipment onto the stage breaking up their conversation.

Steiner turned to me and said good naturedly, "Let's see what you haf brought for us today, Miss Callaghan."

At that moment, a tall man dressed in the same manner was climbing the steps to the stage.

Steiner said, "Excuse me." He turned abruptly toward the approaching man.

We placed the tray of sandwiches artfully on the tables then set up the tableware, cups and saucers, napkins. Two servers carried the coffee pots into the kitchen so we could get the coffee brewing. I had promised to have the entire set up completed by 11:15 and we were right on time.

As I folded the last linen napkin, I watched the workers climbing ladders apparently getting ready to hang some enormous backdrop. Steiner was nowhere to be seen and I wanted him to approve our set up. So, I stood by the sandwich laden tables waiting for him to return. The tall man I had seen before was escorting someone all in black up the stairs to center stage. Both figures were bent in whispered conversation. I could not see their faces. The tall man placed several pages on the podium. I don't know what made me continue to look in that direction. Perhaps it was instinct or just curiosity. But something made me intent on seeing the face of the mysterious person in black.

The workers on the ladder at the back of the stage fumbled with the backdrop, one of them dropped a tool and it clattered onto the stage floor. Even at this distance, I heard the voice that barked something out at them. The words were lost on me. But the voice made my heart skip a beat. I've heard that voice before. It echoes in my nightmares. As if on cue, the lights were being tested. They illuminated the stage and the black clad figure turned around, no doubt sensing my stare. I shivered, as if someone had just opened the door allowing a gust of cold February wind to blow inside. My mouth was suddenly dry. It was inconceivable. There at the podium was the nun who had caused Sean and me such pain and hardship. She was looking straight at me. It was Hilda Perpetua!

What on earth was she doing here? I saw it, her lips curled in the oh-so familiar cruel smile of hers.

"Come-en-ce here girl!" she ordered.

Despite my abhorrence of her, I found myself falling into the familiar habit of following her commands. The next thing I knew, I am in front of the podium. Rearing up straight, she placed her long bony hands on either side of the podium. Her steel blue eyes went dark. Like the witch in Sleeping Beauty, she lifted her right hand to point an index finger.

"I know you. I know you. *Ja!* You are the same little hussy who stole from my kitchen! Once a wretched sinner, always a wretch…"

I blinked hard. I was not going to let this witch control me or hurt me or Sean ever again. I grasped her bony finger and pushed it roughly away from my face.

"Don't point your *hexen* finger at me!" I hissed. "I've had enough of you to last two lifetimes."

Her cruel smile grew bigger enjoying this moment. She was pleased that I was defying her.

"You made our lives a living hell, I will not put up with you anymore. You have no control over me. You are pure evil. I don't know how you convince people that you are a sister of God. Your soul is black. You will rot in the fires of hell for what you did to me, my brothers and all the children at St. Joseph's."

She threw back her head and laughed. "How high and mighty you have become. You miserable wretch! I am going to have you thrown out into the gutter where your kind belongs!"

At that moment, the enormous banner that the men on the ladders were trying to position finally unrolled into place directly behind the podium. It was red with a large black Swastika.

As Perpetua and I continued glowering at each other, I saw pinned to her black habit a gold swastika pin. Suddenly, it made total sense. She was a member of the Nazi Party too. I looked at her in disgust.

"You are a Nazi! I can't stand those jackboot, goose stomping idiots! And you know, I am not surprised you are one of them. You are a disgrace to religion and to this country."

The tall man and Mr. Steiner having heard our exchange came trotting onto the stage.

Steiner yelled, "Vot is this? Vot is going on"

Understanding dawned on me, they were wearing Nazi Party uniforms.

I said, "You are all Nazis! What is this event?"

It was Perpetua who answered me. "This is a Pro-America Rally on George Washington's Birthday. We are rallying against Roosevelt and his Jewish kind. It is the American Nazi Party!"

Another man in Brown Shirt uniform was at Perpetua's side. He looked familiar, in a bad way.

"I am Bundersfuhrer Kuhn. This rally will make America free from Jewish news and Jewish Hollywood. America will be White, Gentile and patriotic!"

At that, a loud canvas snap turned all eyes to the curtain at center stage.

Another banner fell into position. To my shock and horror, it was a likeness of George Washington. This is a nightmare!

Having heard our loud exchange, Sally rushed onto the stage. She touched my arm. "Colleen, what's going on? Are you OK?"

"Pack it up! Pack it all! Pack it all back up! I will be damned if I have anything to do with Nazis!"

Puzzled, Sally looked at the banner of George Washington. Then seeing the banner with the swastika, she understood. She called for our servers to return to the stage. They began to hastily pack up the food.

"This is a Nazi Party Rally! Not anything I support! Sally look at all the Nazi symbols and flags!"

"Oh, my, god."

Perpetua laughed, more shrilly now. "Go, take your miserable food. You've lied and cheated as a child and now you will default on your promise for this work today. Once a miserable gutter girl, always a miserable gutter girl."

At the table, I took one of the sandwiches, turned and threw it at her. Right in the kisser! Wiping mayonnaise from her chin, she laughed at me.

"Get the coffee! Load it back into the truck!" I shouted orders at my helpers.

The big Irish cop who stopped us at the alley door and made the crude remark about Sean was suddenly at my side. He picked up two trays of sandwiches, "I'm pleased to give you a hand."

We left the Garden the same way we came in, through the side alley. As we walked up the alley toward our truck, the Irish cop said, "I was wondering what you were doing with the likes of these. You may be Sean Callaghan's sister, but you are no Nazi."

I noted he used Sean's name and not the derisive name, Cockeyed.

"I'm proud to be Sean's sister. I will not help Nazis. And I will not help that evil woman."

He smiled at me. He was actually a good looking fella despite his being a cop. There's no cop that I trust. They had it out for Sean. This one had already given himself away when he called Sean, Cockeyed. We loaded the truck and started backing out of the alley when our truck was enveloped by a mob of people.

The mob was carrying Anti-Nazi placards calling for boycott of German made goods. Some had slogans like 'Down with Hitlerism'. The big cop was ordering the crowd to give us room to back up. I told the driver to stop and pulling open my door, I jumped down from the safety of the truck.

The crowd surged toward me but the cop was at my side yelling at me "Get back in the truck!"

I said, "Help us!"

I grabbed his arm and together we pushed our way to the back of the truck. As I opened the back of the truck, people were yelling, "Nazi! Get out of America!"

The cop stood at my side with his nightstick in his hand. I grabbed one of the trays of sandwiches, turned to the crowd and in my loudest voice said, "I refused to give them this food"

I yelled at the top of my lungs. "I am not a Nazi!"

Someone in the crowd rushed forward. With the business end of the nightstick in the man's chest, the cop stopped him in his tracks. "She's tellin' the truth. Once she saw what they were about she packed it all up and left."

The leader of the protestors emerged from the crowd. He raised his right hand and the yelling subsided somewhat.

I said, "I did not know who they were. But now I do. I took the food back from those Nazis. You good people must be hungry. I'll give it to you all. It's a cold day. I've got hot coffee too!"

Before I knew what was happening trash barrels were turned over and my beautiful sandwiches trays were set on top. The mob availed themselves of ham and cheese sandwiches that were originally destined for the American Nazi Party. People sipped coffee from my china cups and thanked us profusely. For all my worry about losing cups and spoons at the Garden event, every cup and spoon was returned to us by the mob of protestors.

The cop said to me, "You are something else, Miss Callaghan."

"You are not so bad yourself," I smiled at him. "What's your name?"

"He bowed slightly, Michael Francis Xavier Malloy, at yer service. And I apologize for using that moniker for your brother."

I shook his hand.

"Come by Dottie's, I'll treat you to a good steak dinner."

Sean

The Same Day, 20 February 1939

As a brutally cold wind off the Hudson greeted us we parked our trucks on West 50th just off Tenth. I had twenty-two longshoremen as well as a half dozen of my union hall leaders. No one was carrying iron just some stick-ball bats, leather wrapped coshes or maybe a cargo hook or two.

Even before we crossed Ninth, the crowd noise and police whistles could be heard. There must have been hundreds in the crowd. In the distance, a horse-mounted copper was backing up some of crowd while foot patrolmen with long nightsticks held others at bay. Angry voices added to the din.

Even this far away, I read the marquee "Pro America Rally". Had Lansky got this all wrong? Well, I was going to find out. I led the boys to the Madison Square Garden workers' entrance. The same door my dear ole mother used for work. She was in charge of the charwomen who cleaned the Garden between shows. This particular show was a real circus but without clowns.

There were thousands surging around the Garden's entrance on 8th Avenue. The horse mounted cops were now swinging batons on some of the crowd. It was nearly a riot. Mayor Fiorello LaGuardia must have ordered a major police presence to prevent just that, a riot. That didn't seem to be working very well.

From behind us, I heard a loud voice, "Company, Forward March, Left, Right, Left." A large group of men being led by an American flag carrying man in doughboy uniform were marching eastward on the sidewalk. They had a banner: 'Jewish-American War Veterans'. Grim determined faces passed us as they marched toward 8th and an inevitable collision with the coppers.

"Let's stay put!" I ordered.

A moment later the Garden side door opened. With her face a vivid red as her hair, Ma, the General strode through. She angrily pushed her way through the longshoremen until she met a group of angry protesters. The protesters must have thought that she was with the rally people since she wasn't in her Garden uniform. She was knocked to the ground.

"Boys!" I shouted, "That's me mother!"

A half-dozen strong backs pushed the protesters off her.

"Ma! Ma! For Cripes sake, what are you doing here?"

Startled, she whirled to face in my direction. Then she rushed over, throwing herself into my arms.

"Save me from these hooligans!"

I ordered two of my biggest union reps to escort the General to her apartment. With a wave of my arm, we continued toward 8th Avenue. We hadn't travelled the distance between home plate and first when I had another surprise.

There on the street, Mikey was handing out sandwiches from a tray perched on an overturned trash can. Her crew from Dottie's was serving sandwiches, coffee and buttered rolls to the Jewish War Veterans. What was happening?

"Mikey!" I yelled over the crowd. "Mikey! What the heck are you doing here?"

"Sean, it's a nightmare, a goddamned nightmare," she replied still handing out sandwiches. "You wouldn't believe it."

"Believe what? What is going on in the Garden?" I asked as if I didn't know.

"Sean, there must be over a thousand Nazis in there and you'll never guess who is among them. That fucking Hilda Perpetua!"

"What?" My head was spinning, "You mean Mother Superior from St. Joe's? What's going on in there?"

One of her staff, Sally handed a coffee filled cup to me.

"Your sister and us were here earlier, inside the Garden but as soon as she realized it was a Nazi rally she pulled out. Pulled out!" Sally said while handing a sandwich to a longshoreman.

I recalled Mikey saying that Ma had gotten her a money-making catering job.

Sally said, "We packed up and then set up the food and coffee out here. You would not believe what it looks like inside." Breathlessly, she continued, "I had to go back inside to make sure we had not left anything behind. They have a big banner with George Washington on it, but everyone is wearing an armband with a swastika. There must be two thousand Nazis in there! There are swastikas all over the stage. I saw children carrying Nazi banners marching up and down the aisles. They are doing that Nazi, Heil Hitler salute! Others were rehearsing their speeches, saying crazy things from the stage like 'make America a white Gentile country again.' In one speech, the speaker called President Roosevelt, 'Rosenfeld' and Dewey, 'Thomas Jewey'! If that wasn't enough there was a Catholic nun wearing a Nazi Party pin!"

I knew from Lansky what was going on here. He sub-contracted roughing up the Nazis to me.

Now with her face flushed with anger, Mikey growled, "Well, Mother probably didn't know who the event was really for! She made it seem legit. I should have known. She even tried to chisel me into paying her a 'finder's fee'. Ha! Ha to that!"

"Let's get you out of here. Weren't there any coppers in the Garden?"

"Sean, there are loads of cops in there. I have to get my staff back to the restaurant."

Mikey buttoned up her coat against the biting wind. There was a roar from the crowd on 8th. Then more cops came into view pushing several protesters.

"Sean, I have to get my staff safely out of here and back to the restaurant."

I looked toward 8th Avenue and the roiling crowd. It seemed that most of the crowd was concentrated at The Garden's entrance between 49th and 50th. The crowd appeared to thin out above 50th street.

"Me and my boys will get your truck safely to 9th avenue and away from all of this."

With the sandwich supplies depleted, Mikey's crew loaded linens, cups and saucers and other stuff on their truck. I had my boys surround the truck as we led it to 9th Avenue. Once the truck was safely rumbling the cobblestones uptown, I got back to the job that Lansky wanted.

We circled the block coming out on 51st and 8th. Milling about were over several hundred protesters on the sidewalks, some even standing in the middle of the avenue unconcerned about traffic. Their signs read. 'Get me a Gas Mask, Nazis Stink', 'Smash Anti-Semitism', 'Act Now! No Concentration Camps Here!'

Using the middle of the avenue, I walked closer to 50th street and the Garden's entrance. That's when I saw Detective O'Boyle use his cosh on someone dressed as a doughboy, one of the Jewish-American war veteran protesters. Uncannily, he turned, seeing me, locked eyes with me with a wolffish grin. Stone faced, I turned walking slowly back up in the middle of 8th Avenue to my boys.

Me and the boys never got inside the Garden as Meyer Lansky wanted. The police presence was thick as flies on a dead horse. They were at every door. I saw several cops push a Negro into a paddy wagon. It was so easy for cops like O'Boyle to pick on colored guys.

I sent several guys to positions at nearby bus stops or subway stations. We cracked skulls of a dozen or so brown shirted Nazis as they left the Garden.

Lansky was pleased when I told him that Mikey's people took care of the anti-Nazi protesters, especially the Jewish-American war veterans.

Later, I heard on the radio that a man rushed the stage during Kuhn's speech. The brown shirts jumped on the man beating him badly. About a dozen cops had to save him. He was beat up pretty bad. I heard that he was taken to nearby Columbus Hospital.

The whole thing was bollocks up.

Sean
24 August 1939
Treaty of Non-aggression between Germany and the Union of Soviet Socialist Republics

Red and I drove over to Sunnyside from my new house on Ithaca Street in Elmhurst. I had married Mary Kate, found a nice four-bedroom house, sold her place in College Point but still kept Elizabeth in Mary Louis Academy. I kept my Bank Street apartment in case I had 'night work' on the docks. Tonight, we were taking in the Golden Gloves at Sunnyside Gardens. The boxing competition had some really good amateur fighters, especially the welterweights.

We picked up Paddy Clarke at his gin mill in Sunnyside then took Queens Boulevard. From the back seat, Paddy was rattling on about a Negro fighter named Sugar Ray Robinson.

"I'm tellin' ya, dis guy is going to go professional and be a major contender."

"So do you have any money on this Robinson guy?"

"Yeah! I have him to KO his opponent on fourth. If you want, I have a bookie who works in the Blarney Stone nearby. You can get in on the action."

We never collected our winnings that night. As a matter of fact, we ended up downtown in the Tombs. It was our bad luck that Detective Robert Emmet O'Boyle and a half dozen blue wool coppers were waiting for us to leave the fights. While O'Boyle grinned, his blues slapped their bracelets on us. That done, O'Boyle was brave enough to give me a gut-punch.

"What's the charge?" Red stormed.

"Consorting with known criminals. You two are on parole."

"Whadda mean? He's my brother-in-law."

"So what! He's a criminal, ain't he?"

We spent a few nights in the Tombs before a judge ordered us upriver to Sing Sing for breaking parole. We were herded to Grand Central for a train to Ossining and Sing Sing Prison. The prison is right on the Hudson River. While the views from my cell was better than the Biltmore, the accommodations were less than luxurious. The room service stunk. This was my second trip to Sing Sing. It always reminded me of St. Joe's.

The first night, a guy tried to shank me as we were being led back to our cells from the dining hall. I broke his jaw and stomped on his knife hand. The next day three guys cornered me out of sight of the screws. They didn't have a shank, thank goodness. They got the better of me. I managed to get a few good shots in but three were two too many. After that Paddy, Red and I traveled like Siamese triplets attached at the hip.

Elizabeth took the New York Central from Grand Central Terminal every Saturday to visit. The girl never missed a visit. Mikey visited every Monday when the restaurant was closed. She'd even call me once a week to see if I needed more Pepsodent or something to eat. Mary Kate would drive two Sundays a month the first year. After that, one Sunday every four to six weeks. It was always something—weather, the car, something. Prison is all about killing time while being sure that you weren't killed. Special attention is required for the screws, some could have their palms greened but some wouldn't. It was good to have some connection with the Italians and Meyer Lansky. Luciano still ran the Mob even from Clinton Prison near the Canadian border. Both Lansky and Luciano got us cigarettes.

Chapter 34
The Drumbeat of War

Sean

December 1941

Sing Sing Prison, Ossining, New York

We heard about Pearl Harbor even behind the walls of Sing Sing. It was followed four days later by Nazi Germany declaring war on the US. I knew that US destroyers had been fighting the U-Boats since the Lend-Lease Act was passed. Hitler wanted unrestricted submarine warfare just like 1917.

A few days before Christmas, Mitch, one of the prison guards or as we prisoners called them the 'screws' said that I had a visitor. Mitch didn't say who it was. Hoping it was Mary Kate I went to the visitation room but instead of my beautiful blonde wife, I saw Mordecai's son Joel sitting there. Mordecai Friedman's kid was all grown up. He graduated from Columbia University's Law School a few years after Ian had graduated. Fordham Law School accepted Negros and Jews not just Irish Catholics.

Funny how I have a hard time not thinking of Joel as a kid. I still think of Joel as a little boy climbing into his daddy's lap on a cold Troy morning. As Joel Friedman unsnapped the brass clasp in his briefcase, he looked serious, all business.

"Joel, thanks for coming. How's your father?"

"You're welcome Mr. Callaghan. We have an offer to discuss." He looked up, let out a pent-up breath, then looking somewhat shaken, said, "As for my dad, he isn't doing well, his lungs are bad. His doctor says it's emphysema. He's coughing all night and day. He had to close the shop. I moved him and Mother to an apartment in Morningside Heights to be near his doctor, the famous Dr. Alvan Barach. You won't believe it, but he has my dad doing abdominal breathing with a bag of buckshot on his stomach. Then he has him breathe out as if he was blowing out candles. He calls it 'pulmonary rehabilitation'."

"Sorry to hear all that. That rehabilitation? Interesting. Does it help?"

"Yes and no, it seems to relive the shortness of breath but Dad has another cigarette and he's blue all over again."

"What brings you here to see me."

"As I said, I have an offer that can do you some good. I have been approached by the Office of Naval Intelligence or ONI to get you released to help them keep the Nazi saboteurs and spies from our westside docks."

"Nazis! What the fook! How soon can you get me outa here? But tell me, what's going on?"

"The Germans have started something they call "Operation Drumbeat". U-boats have been sinking ships up and down the East Coast. Some right outside New York harbor. The Navy has been sucker-punched. Now, Naval Intelligence is desperate to protect New York's shipping. The ONI wants you on the Westside docks while Luciano helps with Brooklyn and the Eastside docks. It's good for Luciano, especially good for Red, and you. They've promised to have your parole violation sentence reduced considerably. You might be freed in a few weeks. The ONI are bargaining with Governor Lehman to free Lucky Luciano also. But Lehman is reluctant to reduce his sentence because Luciano is a political hot potato. However, Governor Lehman is rumored to be going to a State Department job. If that happens then Charles Poletti becomes governor that could be good for Luciano. But I am here about you. The Navy is transforming ocean liners into troop ships for the war effort. The ONI wants you to root out Nazi sympathizers, spies and saboteurs. They want you out and on the docks to keep them safe from the Nazis. Soon, we may be calling you 'Lucky' too."

"Luck has nothing to do with it. I bet Lansky has his hand in this."

"I'm working on your commutation and release. Be patient and keep your nose clean."

"Can do."

Sean
February 1942

10 February 1942, New York Daily News: The Normandie catches on fire and capsizes.

While we were still inside the joint, I learned that a clumsy guy with a welding torch set kapok life jackets afire on the converted luxury liner, *Normandie*. But sabotage was strongly suspected. Radio reports and papers kept up a constant stream of stories of Nazi sabotage on the docks. So, thanks to this burnt and capsized luxury liner that could not be converted to a troop ship, Red and I had our sentences commuted. We also had to promise that there would be no union strikes to hamper the war effort.

Immediately after release, I stayed true to my word, no union trouble. A union agitator from the west coast showed trying to cause trouble. My boys roughed him up enough for him to need a week in St. Vincent's Hospital. He took all his meals by soda straw. After that, union agitators got the message.

The ink wasn't dry on my release form when I reported to the ONI 'Special Activities' Commander Charles Radcliffe Haffenden. I met Haffenden at his Astoria Hotel suite in Times Square. For some reason, I expected the Navy Special Branch to be in Brooklyn, at the Navy Yard not at a hotel for the famous and rich.

When I arrived at the Hotel Astoria, I asked for Commander Haffenden. The front desk clerk tapped a highly polished brass call bell. Magically, a bellhop dressed like he should he a Phillip Morris advertising poster appeared.

"Take this gentleman to room 196."

The bellboy escorted me to the bank of gleaming polished brass elevator doors. Then an elevator ride to the 11th floor suites. Very posh suites.

At number 196, he rapped only once on the door. Before long, a broad in Navy WAVE uniform opened the heavy door to admit me. Her uniform fitted well, accenting a trim waist. She led us to a large sitting room where four naval officers had a big navigational map of New York Harbor and several dossiers spread open on a table.

The one in the fanciest uniform with a black cigarette holder clenched in his teeth, said, "Let me introduce everyone. This is Admiral Andrews who is in command of the 3rd Naval District. I am Commander Haffenden. My team includes Lieutenants Marsloe and Treglia. You must be Mr. Sean Callaghan. Thank you, Miss Rodgers, that will be all. You're dismissed."

"Just call me, Sean"

"Fine, Sean, it is."

"Commander, I must get back to Headquarters. Carry on with this operation," Admiral Andrews said.

Haffenden and his two lieutenants stood to salute, "Aye, aye, sir!"

I took a seat at the table facing Haffenden who was flanked by Treglia and Marsloe.

"I am ready to help you deal with the Nazis on the Westside docks."

"Deal with the Nazis? I will make a deal with the devil himself to stop those U-boats!" Haffenden said with his finger tapping the pile of dossiers. "And you are one of the devils I am dealing with."

He was a smooth talker with that Ivy League flair. I could visualize Haffenden in a raccoon coat with a Yale football pennant and a cloche-hatted flapper on his arm. Dressed impeccably in his navy officer uniform, he had the air of a swashbuckling pirate even with razor creased pressed pants and gold braided sleeves. He offered me a cigarette from a silver case, Lucky Strikes I noticed. He then lit mine with a tallboy lighter. He was already smoking one in a long black holder, a la FDR.

"Lt. Marsloe, brief this gentleman in on the situation on the coast."

Lt. Marsloe stood to attention, "Yes, sir. Since late December U-boats have torpedoed or used their deck guns to sink nearly 100 ships. All right off the East Coast. In radio intercepts, U-boat commanders refer to their cruise as 'happy times.' They are so brazen as to send the messages uncoded, in the clear."

Haffenden interrupted, "Thank you Lieutenant that's all." He turned to me, speaking through teeth clenching that black cigarette holder, he said, "Listen Sean, last night a U-boat sunk a tanker only 60 miles from where we are sitting. How did they know when the tanker was sailing? Also, U-boats operate on diesel. To get to our side of the Atlantic they burn a considerable amount of fuel just to get here. Yet U-boats still raid up the coast and down to the Florida Straits. Now how do you think they got this far across the Atlantic? How can they operate so long on this side of the ocean?"

"I'm no expert on submarines so why don't ya give me a hint."

Treglia said, "Commander Haffenden, may I jump in here?" Haffenden nodded his assent.

"We suspect that Nazi sympathizers, some former bootleggers who ran hooch from Canada are supplying the U-boats with fuel, fresh water and food. Also, German agents work the docks, learn when freighters or tankers sail, getting that information to the U-boats. So, with the shipping news and supplies, these agents rendezvous with the U-boats off Long Island or the

Jersey Shore. Also, there are fifth columnists here on the docks. They are dangerous too. Causing work stoppages, strikes, slowdowns and actually sabotaging shipments for the war effort."

I interrupted, "What's a fifth column."

"Lieutenant Marsloe, enlighten Mr. Callaghan."

"In the military we organize in fours, four columns if you will. The fifth column is the enemy spies, and saboteurs."

"So let me get it straight, I'm going to spy on the spies and sabotage the saboteurs while making sure that the union keeps the docks working, no strikes, right?"

"Right-o sport, that is what we require of you for the duration of the war. However now I have another order for you. You are to go to Brooklyn, the Brownsville area. You will speak with Mr. Albert Anastasia. You are to tell Mr. Anastasia that I order him to get the Brooklyn docks in line with those in Manhattan."

With that I stabbed out my Lucky Strike as I stood. "Mr. Anastasia? Albert Anastasia! Are you fooking kidding?"

"No, I am not joking. Mr. Callaghan sit back down. I asked Mr. Joseph Lanza of the Fulton Fish Market to approach Mr. Anastasia. But he argued that he was busy enough on his fishing boats patrolling for U-boats and their suppliers."

"Joey Socks on a fishing boat?" I laughed. "Joey Socks is so big, he could capsize a fishing boat reaching for a sardine. Joey Socks out on a boat searching for U boats! He's just pissing on your back telling you it's a warm rain. Joey Socks ain't no fool. If he or I went to Anastasia to ask him to work for the government, then we'd be looking for U-boats while wearing cement shoes. Anastasia ain't called the Mad Hatter and Lord High Executioner for nuthin."

"I must have all the New York City docks in on this, not just the Manhattan ones. I need you to talk to Albert Anastasia..."

"Look here, Commander, you don't understand. In '31, Anastasia, Bugsy Siegel, and Joe Adonis shot their old Mafia boss Masseria. Anastasia's old Mafia boss! Together with Lepke Buchalter, Anastasia set up a contract killer racket for the Cosa Nostra. They call themselves, Murder Incorporated. Anastasia runs his racket out of Midnight Rose's Candy Store in Brownsville. Sweet operation out of a candy store, get it? Some shootings they do

274

themselves, some they hire guns. Only a few years ago, Buchalter and Anastasia hired two torpedoes to shoot up Dutch Schultz and three of his key guys in Newark's Palace Chop House."

I paused long enough to see Treglia raise an eyebrow at Commander Haffenden. He looked familiar but I couldn't place him. Frowning, Haffenden tapped his cigarette holder on a crystal ashtray rim as I continued, "Recently on the Brooklyn piers, an ILA troublemaker Peter Pano disappeared. If that ain't enough, when his hitman-supplier Abe Reles looked like he was going to rat out Anastasia, Reles was thrown off the roof of the Coney Island Half Moon Hotel. Anastasia has a hair-trigger. He is mad as a hatter."

Haffenden set his cigarette onto a crystal ashtray. The three Naval officers went silent. Haffenden sat considering everything I said. As I waited, the ash on the cigarette grew. Suddenly, he leaned forward.

"What do you suggest I do about Brooklyn piers, Mr. Callaghan."

"First, you need Joey Socks, Red and me alive. You'd only get me and Joey wacked if you sent us to the candy store. You need us for the Manhattan docks, east and west. Westside especially. That's me. Alive. Second, you need someone that Anastasia fears and respects."

"Who might that be?"

"It's two someones actually, Charles Luciano and Meyer Lansky."

Chapter 35
House on 67th Street

Colleen

February 1942

It was just past midnight. The dining room at Dottie's was empty and cleaned. The kitchen had been scrubbed and the staff were packing up to leave for the night. I missed seeing Sean for his late-night visits as we closed up Dottie's. Since Heidi was killed by the Nazis, he was spending more and more late nights with his boys, Jimmy, Liam and Paddy. But he usually called me. Tonight, he did not call.

I walked over to the bar, catching Harold the bartender's eye, I gestured 'what's up?' Harold shrugged as the lone occupant on the corner stool was lingering over what was now a tepid scotch and soda. Harold was polishing the last few glasses behind the bar as I approached the slow drinker. He was well dressed and not the 'lonely hearts old doffer' type you'd expect lingering at a bar until closing time. He wore a dark suit of nice material though I could readily see it was one of those off the rack suits. He certainly wasn't spending money on fine tailoring.

I leaned on the bar a few stools away from him and smiled, "Sorry, Mister. We are closing. Can we call you a cab?"

"You are Miss Callaghan." It was more of a statement than a question.

I raised an eyebrow, "Yes, I'm Colleen Callaghan."

He placed a badge on the bar in front of me. It was an FBI shield. "Here are my credentials," he said matter-of-factly.

My heart was racing, I thought 'Oh God, this is about Sean. What's happened!'

As if reading my thoughts, he said, "I'm not here about your brother, Sean."

I gave him a puzzled look, "What's this about, Agent...?"

"I'm Special Agent Miller. I am here to talk to you, Miss Callaghan."

"Me! Whatever for?"

"I'm here to ask for your help. Actually, your country needs your help." I stared in disbelief as he continued. "One of your waitresses is a German spy."

With that startling statement, I sat down heavily on the bar stool next to him. "Hey, Harold! Give me an Irish neat." Agent Miller told me that Anna Lange, a lovely blue-eyed blonde who started working at Dottie's about 6 months ago was a Nazi sympathizer. The FBI had been watching her for several weeks. She was using her job to chat up and flirt with some of the City's heavy weights that frequented Dottie's. Some of the Union guys that Sean introduced to Dottie's were also a great source of information on ships leaving New York's docks heading to England with much needed supplies.

"But that hurts England, not America," I said.

Agent Miller narrowed his eyes, "It hurts us because it kills American merchantmen, sinks American ships and wastes our supplies needlessly. The President has made a commitment to Great Britain that he intends to keep. American troops sail out of New York City. We don't want German saboteurs killing our boys in our waters."

Chastised for my thoughtless comment, I remained quiet while he continued. "She got information on supply shipments that FDR was sending to England out of the port of New York. German U-boats are lying in wait a few miles offshore in the Atlantic awaiting these ships ready to take them out. And they have been successful in sinking the last three shipments."

"I haven't seen anything in the papers about our ships being blown up," I said. "That's because we stifled the news. We need to find the group responsible for sending the information to the U-boats and that is where you come in. We want to find out how these spies communicate with each other and where the information leaks come from. But it's important we do this without alerting the U-boat captains. That way, we can track the U-boats before they disappear in the Atlantic."

"How does Anna fit in this?" I asked.

Agent Miller continued, "Anna works with a group, formerly called the Friends of New Germany, also the German American Bund. They claim to be isolationist American but they are National Socialists, thinly disguised Nazis and definitely pro Hitler. Some are naturalized American citizens while others are native-born. All claim to be patriotic Americans of German ancestry. So, by alerting the U-boats about which ships contain the supplies, their dates, routes and other details they effectively keep needed American-made war materials from ever getting to Great Britain."

Then Agent Miller looked me in the eye saying, "Miss Callaghan, you are in the best position to find the information we need without alerting Anna Lange and her associates that we are onto them."

I shifted uncomfortably on the bar stool. "I don't know where to begin," I stammered.

"I know this is asking a lot of you, Miss Callaghan but I will walk you through every step of the way. And I will stay close to make sure you are safe."

I stared at my reflection in the mirror behind the bar. Maybe this is the way I can redeem myself from all the lies, looking the other way when I know perfectly well Sean was stealing and worse and of course clobbering Eucharius without any thought to possibly killing her.

I turned to face Miller, "I guess, I need to befriend Anna Lange in a way that I do not with my other wait staff without making her suspicious. And, if we are going to work together, you better start calling me Colleen."

***

Anna and I were about the same age. So, it was reasonably easy for me to strike up a conversation about the single male diners at Dottie's.

"That man at table seven looks promising! He has dreamy eyes and broad shoulders," Anna said.

I chuckled, "And his wallet is fat. He buys the most expensive champagne cocktails and never has the same girl with him." We compared notes on customers and laughed at their menu choices and companions.

Agent Miller gave me a short course on avoiding detection.

"Keep in mind," he said, "she is the professional. She will be alert to any surveillance. So, you need to keep your distance. Always have an excuse as to why you happen to be in the same area if she discovers you. Use store windows to keep track of her direction. Always wear a hat to cover your hair, you don't want her to recognize you from the distance. If possible, keep a city block between you. If you lose her, you can try again the next day. The most important thing is, she is unaware that you are following her."

***

Across from Anna's house on 67th street was a small French Restaurant called L'Escargot. I planned to use the excuse that I was checking out competing restaurants by reading their posted menus if she discovered me there. I had been following Anna during the daytime before Dotties opened for a couple of weeks. Most days she just went for a walk or did a little shopping. But on two consecutive Mondays she left her brownstone on 67th street precisely at 9 am carrying a small mesh bag. She followed different routes but ended up visiting the same bookstore on 52nd and First Avenue. On the third Monday, I followed her again. As I had done before I made sure my red hair was tucked completely under my dark grey wide brimmed hat. I wore a long dove grey coat that I hoped would allow me to blend into the cloudy February morning.

Once again, she left her apartment at 9 am. She turned on 65th Street and headed straight for Lexington. Anna ambled along on Lex stopping for a coffee and buttered roll at a small coffee shop across from Bloomingdales. I busied myself with window shopping for 30 minutes until she exited the coffee shop. She looked, for any casual observer like she had all the time in the world. At 57th Street, Anna crossed at the corner and made her way to Third Avenue. She stopped in a flower shop and emerged a few minutes later having purchased nothing. She zig-zagged from 2nd Avenue to 3rd then to 1st Avenue as she continued to walk downtown. Finally, she entered Stihl's Rare Books. Keeping my distance was easy as I now knew the bookstore was her destination. Sol's Fountain and Sweets shop was across the street, and it afforded a reasonable view of the bookstore's doorway. I planted myself on one of the stools and ordered an egg cream soda. It wasn't the best choice for a breakfast drink, but I loved the soda. Watching the young man behind the counter mix chocolate syrup, milk and seltzer water into a froth, I mused that egg creams contain absolutely neither eggs nor cream. As I had noted on the two other occasions, Anna was in and out of the bookstore quickly, leaving with a small brown parcel which I could plainly see in her mesh bag.

When she turned the corner at 51St to head across town, I finished my soda, wiped my lips and left the candy store. I stood in the doorway and waited a few more minutes then crossed the street to Stihl's Rare Books. The door had one of those bells attached to the top of the doorframe, so it rang announcing my entrance. An old man with thinning white hair and thick glasses looked up disinterestedly as I entered. I ignored him and browsed around the shop. It was a small store with bookshelves lining every square inch of wall space. An old brass ceiling lamp provided meager light and I noted the front window needed a thorough cleaning. There was an old fashioned cash register on the counter behind him. By the looks of the dust covering every square inch including the cash drawer I figured he was not making many sales. Obviously, Miss Anna Lange had not paid for her purchase this morning either. I picked up a dusty tome from one of the stacks. Its title was in German.

"May I be of assistance, Miss?"

I turned to see the old man standing right behind me. I had not heard the sound of his approach. It unnerved me and I stuttered, "Th…Thank you, yes. Your store is such an unexpected find."

He just stared at me through smudged thick glasses, "What book are you looking for?"

"Oh, I don't have one in mind. I 'er love all sorts of detective and mystery novels."

His stare was absolutely creepy. He replied dismissively in a slightly Germanic accent, "This is a rare bookstore. We have first editions of literary works. We do not carry detective stories." With that he took the book I was holding and returned it to the stack. Obviously, it was time for me to go. He locked the door to Stihl's Rare Books and flipped the open sign to closed as I exited. Apparently, he had no interest in making any sales.

Not wanting to follow Anna's route, I walked to 50th Street before heading across town. I reviewed in my head what I had learned. Anna was meeting that old coot or someone else in the bookstore on a weekly basis. When she left, she had a small brown paper parcel. The significance of which I could not fathom. What was she doing with those books in her house of 67th Street?

I don't know whether it was my encounter with the creepy old guy in the bookstore or just all this sneaking about, but I suddenly felt like I was being watched. Stopping suddenly in front of a leather goods store, I observed in the window's reflection a rough looking guy wearing a black watch cap and leather jacket abruptly stopping a few feet behind me. I pretended to adjust my hat and my follower took his time to light a cigarette and check his watch. Crossing the street in midblock, I stopped again to admire a stationery store's

Valentine's Day display. My follower was still there across the street but now he was tying his shoelace. Right, I've got to lose this guy. I walked up 53rd to Fifth Avenue. On the corner was St. Thomas Church. I always loved this Gothic looking church. It has coffered oak ceilings and the most beautifully ornate altar including a World War I Memorial. Names of parishioners who fought in the war are inscribed there and those who died are etched in gold on the top. Though I was not religious (my time at St. Joe's had insured that) I visited the church on several occasions just to admire its stained glass windows and symbolic artwork. And I knew it had side doors along 53rd street, so I figured I could enter off 5th and leave via a different door if necessary. I ducked inside the Church and slouched down in a pew in one of the shadowy corners of the nave. The church was empty at this hour on a weekday morning. Feeling safe, I turned up the collar of my coat and sat up straight. I figured I could stay there for an hour or so to lose that guy. Suddenly the 5th Avenue doors groaned open and pale grey light from the street shone in. Twisting in the pew but ducking low I observed my follower entering. He turned his head looking left and right for me. I slid off the pew and knelt silently on the floor. I listened to his footfalls in the absolute quiet of the church. He walked further down the center aisle. Then the footfalls stopped. From my position on the floor, I could not see where he was. I held my breath thinking that any moment he would discover me. It seemed like a long time though it was probably only a minute or two, but I had to know what he was doing. I peered over the pew just in time to see him turning into the Chantry Chapel that is used for baptisms and small weddings. This is my chance to leave. Crouching, I crab walked to the side door on 53rd. It never occurred to me that the door might be locked. It wasn't! I opened it as quietly as possible and ran as fast as I could through the door. I ran toward 6th Avenue. I kept running and dared not look back. At 8th Avenue I saw a cab rounding the corner with its rooftop light on indicating it was free for a passenger. I jumped into the street with my arm raised. He skidded to a stop at the curb where I was standing. I bounded into the rear seat and slamming his door I said, "Let's go."

"Sure thing", he said putting the cab in gear. He eyed me suspiciously in his rear-view mirror as I was fully turned in my seat looking out the back window of the taxi. As we drove up 8th he said, "Are you OK?"

"I'm fine."

To my great relief the man who had been following me was nowhere to be seen.

***

The following Monday Anna Lange and I went shopping. When we met at Bloomingdales on 59th street she was carrying that same mesh bag that I had seen many times before when I followed her. I saw a small brown paper package inside of her bag.

"Oh, you've already been shopping without me," I exclaimed.

"It's just a book," she said dismissively.

"Let's grab a cup of coffee before we get going" I suggested.

We stopped at Bloomingdale's cafeteria and ordered a couple of cups. As we finished, Anna excused herself for the Ladies Room. She asked the waitress where it was.

"You've got to take the escalator down one level then go through lingerie. You'll see signs directing you."

"No problem," I said, "I'll pay the bill and meet you at the entrance to the cafeteria."

"I have to powder my nose but let me pay for my coffee." She fumbled with her large handbag for her coin purse putting the mesh bag on the seat next to me.

"My treat!" I insisted.

"Thanks Colleen. Still fumbling with her handbag, she started to take the mesh bag."

I said, "I'll hold your bag for you. No reason to carry that into the toilet with you!" She hesitated for a second then smiled, "Thanks I really have to go and I do hate the Ladies' Room floors. I don't think they clean them enough."

"Go. I'll meet you at the cafeteria entrance."

Anna left for the ladies' room. When she was out of sight, I opened her mesh bag. I carefully slipped the string from around the little package. It was a leather-bound copy of Poetry by Emily Dickinson. I returned the book to the paper and retied the string careful to keep the folds neat just like it had not been opened. Grabbing the mesh bag, I threw down a couple of ones for our bill and quickly exited. At the entrance to the cafeteria was a bank of public telephones. Entering one of the booths, I quickly closed the door. I inserted a nickel and

282

dialed Agent Miller's number. A woman answered. Breathlessly I asked for Miller.

"Who's calling?" she said imperiously.

"Please hurry, tell him it's Colleen Callaghan."

Thankfully, he got on the phone immediately. "Colleen?"

Without preamble, I said, "I've got a small 5 by 3-inch brown leather copy of Poetry by Emily Dickinson. Can you get me a reasonable substitute in a couple of hours today?"

"I'll do my best..." he started to say. I interrupted "Just get it for me. I need it wrapped, in brown paper tied with string use a simple bow. We are in Bloomingdales, near the cafeteria where ladies' handbags are." I hung up and quickly exited the booth. Next to the cafeteria was a display of ladies' handbags. I picked one up to examine it as Anna Lange approached.

"Cute bag," she said as she sidled up to me.

"Hmm, maybe," I uttered as I set it back down on the display table. I wanted to move along so my heart would stop hammering in my chest. "Let's see what spring dresses, Bloomingdales has today," I offered.

We tried on dresses and laughed at some of the patterns and colors. By 1 pm we were ready to leave. Hoping that Agent Miller had come through with a reasonable facsimile to Anna's brown paper parcel I suggested we stop in the cafeteria again for lunch.

"Why don't we try that new little bistro on Madison and 64th?" She suggested.

"I just need a quick bite," I confessed, "but mostly a place to sit down!" Anna Lange laughed, "You are a shopping light weight!"

As I surveyed the menu, to my relief, I noted Agent Miller standing near that same display of ladies' handbags. I asked Anna if she would order for me and excused myself for the Ladies' Room. He followed me to the escalator and rode down with me. He surreptitiously handed me a brown paper package tied with string, then promptly disappeared. It looked the right size so that was something. I'm sure the book inside bore no resemblance to the rare book that Anna was carrying. But she was in and out of that bookstore so quickly I was guessing the book was already wrapped when she got it. I stowed Miller's book inside my handbag.

Leaving Bloomingdales, Anna and I walked uptown for a few more blocks, at 67th Street I set my shopping bags down on the pavement. I complained that

I was suddenly dead on my feet and needed to grab a cab or faint on the spot. Anna rose to the occasion as I hoped she would.

"Colleen, please come with me. I live just blocks from here. You can put up your feet and rest awhile."

"You are a life saver," I smiled.

Once inside her brownstone I did my best to get a feel for the layout. I noted that she went immediately to the second door down a short hallway with her brown paper package, she unlocked the door and returned immediately having left the book inside. I heard her relock the door. When she returned to the sitting room she tossed her keys back into her purse. We sat in her little sitting room that was infused with afternoon sunlight while we reexamined our purchases together.

"I have just the thing to perk you up, Colleen! I make a great Manhattan! I'll mix up a couple for us."

"Sounds great, where is your bathroom?" I inquired.

"Third door on the right," she indicated the small hallway.

When Anna left the room for the kitchen, I retrieved the package from my purse and stashed it in my skirt pocket then I quickly grabbed her handbag. I rummaged around for her keys. Finding her key ring, I silently strode to that locked door. Trying several keys with trembling hands, I finally found the right one.

Turning the lock, I opened the door to find a room dominated by an enormous oak desk with a strange looking typewriter on it. At first glance it looked like any ordinary black Royal typewriter. However, on closer inspection I saw a mess of wires in the back. What kind of typewriter is this? There was also a large wireless radio to one side of the desk. On a small table I saw some type of microscope and lamp. Behind the desk was a window which was closed but curiously I saw a thin wire snaking from the window to the radio on the desk. There were several sheaves of paper on the desk but I was too nervous to examine them. Her brown paper covered package sat unopened next to the typewriter. I grabbed it and substituted mine for it. Shoving Anna's package into my skirt pocket, I closed and locked the door and slipped back into the sitting room. Since Anna had not returned with the cocktails, I took the key for the room and pressed it into the soft clay of my compact. Agent Miller had given the compact to me in case I needed to make an impression of a key. I hid the compact and little book inside my handbag. My heart was beating so fast and loud, it seemed to me that people on the street below could hear every beat. I heard Anna speaking to someone on the phone. Then her heels clacked loudly on the shiny hardwood floor as she quickly approached the sitting room. With a pounding heart I literally threw her key chain back into her handbag. Her bag toppled to the floor and I quickly retrieved it, throwing it back on the chair just as she entered the room. Slipping my right foot out of my pump I staggered hoping that this might cover any sound she might have heard as she entered the room.

"Colleen! What's wrong!"

"I am so dog tired I stepped out of my own shoe and nearly toppled into that chair. Actually, I did trip into it," I said with what I hope sounded like humiliation.

She set down a small silver tray with two Manhattan highballs and said, "Colleen, why are you so tired? Are you pregnant?"

I fell back into my chair and laughed. "Pregnant! No. I am not pregnant. To be pregnant, you have to have sex."

At that she laughed at me and fell into her own chair knocking her handbag to the floor. Her keys tumbled out. "Thought I had beat that habit," she explained, "I trained myself to place my keys in the zipper compartment so that they don't fall out."

Changing the subject, I asked if she was dating anyone and we resumed our gossip about the male diners at Dottie's. I sipped her concoction and gave her my approval.

"You know Anna, you could give Harold a run for the bartender position at Dottie's. But I must admit this is a bit stronger than Harold makes it. I think this has to be the only one I have, I don't want to show up at Dottie's tonight tipsy, you know!"

Later, she walked me to the door and said, "I'm so glad to have a friend. I had a great time today."

I smiled and muttered something or other then exited the brownstone walking briskly to 2nd Avenue to hail a cab. At any moment I expected to be stopped or worse. But miraculously nothing happened.

Sean

1942

Gen. Montgomery presses the El Alamein attack; Rommel is in retreat; British-American forces invade Morocco

Together with Liam and Jimmy, we drove down Broadway past City Hall Park to Fulton Street. We turned on the cobblestones to South Street. I had Jimmy park in front of Sloppy Louie's Fish Restaurant. Socks ran the Seafood Workers Union Local 359. In addition to his union dues, Socks had a bigger racket with the wholesale fish dealers. If the dealers didn't pay up then their fish would rot. They paid. He made millions. Still, he remained loyal to Charles "Lucky" Luciano, his boss. Loyalty meant helping your boss. So, when the Navy contacted Joey Socks, he saw the opportunity for Luciano too.

As Joel Friedman had done for me, Joey Socks sent Luciano's lawyer Moses Polakoff to meet with the Naval Intelligence. Polakoff then met with Luciano in Dannemora Prison way upstate near the Canadian border. This location effectively isolated Luciano from his pals and family. Luciano was not likely to have his 30 year sentence reduced but good things could happen with an arrangement made by the Navy in return. Joey arranged for a "mouthpiece" Polakoff who also worked for Myer Lansky to meet with Commander Haffenden. At that meeting, Joey and Polakoff convinced Haffenden to have Luciano moved to Great Meadows Prison outside Albany, an easy train ride from the City. It would be more convenient for dock bosses and Mafia families to get their instructions regarding the Luciano-Naval Intelligence thing.

Great Meadows was more than just a meeting place for Luciano to give orders and keep his hands on the reins. There, he enjoyed his own large cell if you could call it a 'cell'. It had regular bed, tables, a Morris chair and ottoman. I heard that the accommodations, food and yes, wine were similar to luxury cabins on the Normandie or even the Queen Mary. There were even girls. Luciano delivered for the Navy. He commanded that Anastasia's Brooklyn docks join the war effort.

Around the corner from Sloppy Louie's we climbed the stairs to Local 359 offices. Joey Lanza is a big man, over 200 pounds with head of a bear, a round face that looked like it had taken its share of punches. He could take a punch and he could deliver a hell of a hay marker. His nose was flattened like some prizefighters' were.

Besides, Joey Socks, there were three others in the room. Two were about Joey's size while the third was a skinny fellow in waterproof coveralls and newsboy cap. That guy looked familiar, then it came to me, it was Lt. Treglia from Haffenden's suite. Seeing Treglia dressed like this jogged my memory of rum running. Treglia had run a boat service for me. From the Hudson River piers, we made running giggle-juice from ships out beyond the three-mile limit into New York harbor profitable. In those days, I had paid off more than a few Coast Guard sailors and NYC Harbor Police not to see his boats. He nodded to me, knowingly.

"Wouldja like some cawfee, tea or somethin' stronger?" Joey Socks asked. This was unusual. Joey rarely said more than three words at a time. His presence was all that was needed to accomplish what he wanted.

"I'll have what you're having." There was nothing in front of Socks except his baseball glove sized hands. He smiled, then nodded toward Treglia.

"Mr. Lanza is providing the Navy with union cards so as we can put our men on fishing boats undercover. Certain fishing boats will be equipped with a deck gun with lights to attack any submarine on the surface at night or, if necessary, any Nazi sympathizers' boats running fuel and supplies to the U-boats."

"Okay, I don't see how I can be of help, as much as I'd like to blast the Nazis and their damned U-boats."

"I know that you can handle a boat even outside the harbor," grinned Treglia.

"That's back in my rum-running days."

"It's like riding a bike, only this time you won't have to worry about breakage. We need you to do the same as Mr. Lanza. Provide Navy men with ILA union cards for the Westside. They will help you keep the westside docks free of saboteurs."

"My boys can smell out those Nazi rats without any help."

"True, but the Department of the Army is considering putting armed soldiers on the docks. We need to establish a net for intelligence now before the dogfaces show up and screw this up. Also, recently Mr. Lanza has some legal trouble. The Navy is trying to make it go away but the judge on the case is an ornery old coot. If we cannot persuade the judge to work with us then you become the back up for Mr. Lanza. He tells me that you two have teamed up before."

Joey Lanza raised his huge palms in that gesture that says, "I'm resigned to this harassment."

"Joe, are you fine with this?"

He merely shrugged those broad shoulders, "Wa-can-I-do."

Chapter 36
Breaking the Code

Colleen

As soon as I got home from Anna Lange's, I locked the front door and pulled down the shades. Turning on a lamp, I sat at my desk placing the small brown paper package in front of me. I wasn't sure what to look for, but I felt a nervous excitement at its possibilities. I turned each page carefully looking for a secret note. Nothing. I inspected the binding looking for any slit or opening in the brown leather. Nothing. I worked my fingertips systematically across the leather looking for any bump that might indicate something hidden inside. Nothing. I held each page up to the lamp light. Nothing. Glancing at my wristwatch, I saw that I had about two and half hours before I needed to leave for Dottie's and the dinner service. I made a cup of strong coffee and sat down to read the poems of Emily Dickinson. It had to be in the book, whatever it was, and I was determined to find it. I read the little book cover to cover and found nothing but the poetry of Emily Dickinson. Thinking about Anna's study, there was that strange looking typewriter, the radio connected to a wire threaded out her window and...I couldn't recall the rest of the room. Papers on the desk, the little brown paper package and suddenly I remembered the microscope device in Anna's study. That must be it. How would I get a microscope? If only I had a magnifying glass that might be enough to search the pages. Then I remembered the old man downstairs in my building. He was a stamp collector. Surely, he would have a magnifying glass, wouldn't he?

I knocked on his door desperately trying to remember his name. He opened his door just a crack and seeing me he opened the door completely. His glasses were smudged and thick as he pushed them up on his bird beak nose.

"Colleen! How are you this fine evening?"

"I'm well, but I have a favor to ask of you."

He looked surprised. "Ask away, my dear!"

"I have some, some er silverware that someone donated to me for the restaurant. I want to check the silversmith's markings to see if they have value. I er would like to look at more closely. I wonder do you have a magnifying glass I might borrow?"

"Silver eh, I'll have a look. I can tell you if they are worth anything."

"Oh, I don't want to take up your time, they are probably not worth much. Still, I want to examine them more carefully."

He looked a bit disappointed at my rejection of his offer to help. But he said, "I have two magnifiers. You may borrow one for as long as you like."

Armed like Sherlock Holmes with my new detection device, I re-read through the book. Nothing. Annoyed, I slid the book across the desk knocking my coffee cup off. I stretched out my hand to catch it before if fell to the floor and as a result, the little book slid off the desk as well. As I picked up my now broken coffee cup, I noticed the book fell open to a certain page. That happens when you spend more time on one page causing the binding to relax a bit. With a flurry of excitement, I retrieved the book and read the lines:

The Soul has Bandaged Moments (512)
The Soul has Bandaged moments—
When too appalled to stir—
She feels some ghastly Fright come up
And stop to look at her—

Salute her, with long fingers—
Caress her freezing hair—
Sip, Goblin, from the very lips
The Lover—hovered—o'er—
Unworthy, that a thought so mean
Accost a Theme—so—fair-

The soul has moments of escape—
When bursting all the doors—
She dances like a Bomb, abroad,
And swings upon the Hours,

As do the Bee—delirious borne—
Long Dungeoned from his Rose—
Touch Liberty—then know no more,
But Noon, and Paradise

The Soul's retaken moments—
When Felon led along,
With shackles on plumed feet,
And staples, in the Song.

The Horror welcomes her, again,
These, are not brayed of Tongue

Nothing stood out as I read through the poem. So using the magnifying glass more carefully I restarted my search over the text very slowly. Each of Emily Dickinson's poems were numbered. This one is number 512. I moved the magnifying glass down to the first line of type when my brain kicked into gear. The number looked odd. I placed the magnifier smack on top of the number 512. Then I saw it. The 5 and 1 were in slightly darker typeface than the 2. This had to mean something. I read each line noting any discrepancies in darkness of the typeface on my note pad. Actually, once I tuned into this it was fairly simple to glean the message. I found the letter a in the first line shared the same color discrepancy as did the letter i in line two. So now I had 2, a, i. As I read the remainder of the poem it was startling. The words Bomb, Liberty, Noon, were all slightly paler in tone. OK I thought, 'Bomb,' that's a scary message but what is missing? If I were going to send a message ordering a bombing, I would provide a date and location. Timing is obviously noon. When and where? I looked back at the poem's number 512. Could it be that simple? Pier 51? Liberty could mean one of the freighters bringing supplies to Great Britain. Then I had it. Linking the alphabet to corresponding numbers would give me a=1, i=9.

Anna was scheduled to be off that night, and I was glad for it. I did not want to face her just yet. The evening dinner service went on without a hitch. As the kitchen staff bade me good night, I walked out front searching for Sean. He was not there. I worried that something was amiss. I haven't heard from him in over a week now.

Once again Harold caught my eye by snapping a bar rag. Sure enough, sitting at the far end of the bar nursing a drink was Special Agent Miller of the FBI. I asked Harold for my usual, an Irish neat. After he served us, Harold said, "I'll be back in a few minutes, Colleen. I need to move the beer kegs for tapping tomorrow."

"Take your time, Harold. All is OK here."

Harold walked out to the two steel cellar doors on 2nd Avenue. Through the restaurant window, I watched him unlock the heavy Master lock. Noisily he lifted and secured the doors safely open. Like a slowly sinking ship, Harold cautiously descended the steps down into the cellar.

Miller turned to me. "I thought I would hear from you, Colleen. What going on? Did you switch the books?"

Without answering him, I reached over the bar to an inside shelf. I handed him the little brown paper package. He raised his eyebrows.

"I'm impressed," he said.

I sipped my drink. "Agent Miller, do you know when the next Liberty ship leaves and from which pier?"

He stared at me for a long moment then said yes. I took a folded piece of paper from my pocket. Let me know if this is correct." He unfolded the paper, read it and whistled softly.

"Was this in the book?"

"Not exactly."

I explained, "Emily Dickinson's poems are numbered. A certain one is number 512. There is the slightest difference in the color of the typeface in the number 2 and in some of the letters and words in the poem. So, I was able to figure out that the next shipment leaves from Pier 51 on February 19. By the way, I am very familiar with Pier 51. I know that Liberty Ships bound for England with supplies often leave from Pier 51. I also have a book of Dickinson's poetry myself. I compared the words and layout of poem 512 with Anna's copy. It was exactly the same except for the typeface tone changes. I guess they used this poem because it held the words that completed their message. And quite frankly the typeface discrepancy was not visible to the naked eye without the use of a magnifying glass. But the really disturbing part of the message relates to the words in the paler typeface. Bomb, Liberty, Noon. If my interpretation of this message is correct, you've got some work to do and quickly."

Miller seemed nonplussed at my revelation about a potential bombing of a Liberty ship. Instead, he asked, "How did you figure it was that specific poem?"

I explained about the book falling open. He peppered me with questions, and I gave him a complete picture of the study in Anna's apartment.

He whistled softly, "That wire is her antenna, no doubt. She probably has it wired up onto the roof of the building. That weird looking typewriter is actually a Morse code device. She probably doesn't have a 'good fist' for sending Morse code accurately. The Morse typewriter helps to overcome this and quite frankly looks more innocent to the casual observer, which you apparently are not!"

Miller took the key impression compact from me as well as the little book.

"Thank you, Colleen. Not only did you get us some valuable information, you broke their code as well! If you ever want to leave the restaurant business, I have a place for you in the FBI."

I laughed at that one. Imagine Sean having an FBI agent in the family, oh that was rich. As if on cue, Sean walked through the kitchen door. He smiled that crooked grin of his upon seeing me. But the smile left his lips just as quickly when he got a load of Agent Miller. He needed no introduction, Sean could recognize law enforcement from a mile away. Miller had the good sense to get going.

He said, "Thanks Colleen. You've done your President and your country a great service."

I shook his hand and said, "I hope you and the President keep that in mind if I ever need some help."

He raised an eyebrow at that then turned and quickly walked to the front door. Harold was there with the keys. He let Miller out and relocked the front door. "I'll be goin' home now, Miss Callaghan."

"Night Harold, thank you."

Sean sat on the bar stool next to me and took a long drink from my whiskey. "So, Mikey what's that all about?"

Chapter 37
Nightmare on Pier 51

Sean
February 1943

Rommel attacks the British in Tunisia, situation grim

Haffenden called me to give the bad news that I already knew. He was spitting bullets. In January '43, Joey Socks Lanza was convicted of six counts of extortion. The judge threw the book at him with a sentence of seven to fifteen years.

"I'm flabbergasted! All my work to protect shipping in the Third Naval District is at stake."

"Look, I can keep the docks safe even without Joey."

"Oh yeah!" He growled. "One of my undercover men heard something about a Thompson gun theft. Today, we picked up intelligence of a sabotage or a bombing on the Westside piers. Supplies for the British fighting Rommel in North Africa and bombs for the air raids on Germany must be protected..."

I interrupted, "Tell me what you heard."

"According to an FBI informant, a liberty ship is going to be targeted and possibly bombed on the nineteenth of February at Pier 51. The ship will be transporting bombs and other war materials needed for the war against Germany."

"Commander, I know which ship that is. It's the Ocean Vanguard."

"That's supposed to be top secret!"

"Listen Commander, there nothing going on in these docks that I don't know about. So why don't we make a plan so that nothing happens to the Ocean Vanguard."

The Ocean Vanguard was one of the first 'Liberty' freighters built for the war. It displaced over fourteen hundred tons while having a capacity of almost eleven hundred tons deadweight or at least fifteen hundred pounds of high explosives. That's one hell of a load of bombs. Blowing up the Ocean Vanguard would end shipping from the Westside piers for a long time. Maybe for the duration of the war. The Ocean Vanguard had to be the saboteurs' top target.

I thought that the Walther that I liberated from the Bund asshole at Hunter College would be the right iron for the job. Besides, the 7.65mm round would punch some mean daylight into a Nazi saboteur. Any shells left at the scene would puzzle the coppers into thinking that the Nazis were fighting each other.

Haffenden, Treglia and four Navy sailors joined my boys. All were armed with .45 caliber pistols. Treglia and his sailors were going to be inside the freighter. Me and my boys would stay on West Street to keep the Nazis off the pier. Haffenden would have another team of sailors as backup.

During the loading of the Ocean Vanguard, the Navy sailors were dressed as longshoremen riding the cargo nets into the hold. Also, in those nets were fooking crates filled with 500 pound bombs. I wouldn't ride those cargo nets. The 'longshoremen' secured these crate-loads in the aft holds #4 and #5. Holds #1 and #2 had been loaded with small arms and machine gun ammunition. The day before, Grant tanks had been loaded into the largest hold, #3 just forward of the bridge structure and engine room at midships. At midships, the bridge, accommodations for the crew and the engine room separates the forward three holds from the aft two holds. Treglia and his sailors worked the loading then stayed behind. If someone had counted during the shape-up, they might realize that five "longshoremen" were 'stowaways.' To account for that we adjusted the shape-up roster to account for five less guys.

Meanwhile, we watched the pier from West Street. Liam and I were in a two door Ford Super Deluxe on the cobblestones under the elevated Westside Highway near Horatio Street. I had Jimmy, Paddy and Padric sitting in a Buick a half a block away in front of the Jane Street Hotel.

It was about dusk when the rain started. A typical nasty, raw, cold February rain. Noisy drops shattered on the windshield and hood. Inside the Ford, I was surprisingly comfortable with my waxed boots and merino wool socks. We had a hard time seeing the street with all the rain. Liam was continuously wiping his glasses as though it would help.

Then Liam lit a Lucky Strike with a shaking hand.

I reached behind the bench seat for a thermos.

"Here, drink this. Put out the smoke, we don't need to attract attention."

I offered a thermos cap of coffee to Liam who took it with the cigarette between his fingers. He took a last puff then stabbed it out in the ashtray. He held the cup of coffee with both hands.

"T-thanks."

"Thanks for putting out the smoke."

We sat silently. The rain became heavier, and a wind picked up.

"Can I have another?" Liam asked.

"Here, let's ration the hot coffee. It could be a long night. No more smoking. If we are to surprise the saboteurs, we can't be seen."

If the wind was creating swells in the Hudson, you wouldn't know it. The big freighter hardly strained its hawsers. The Ocean Vanguard was full to its load water-line. With the crew still ashore and with the loading finished, only the Naval Intelligence sailors were on board. On the pier, a poor miserable sailor in a slicker, white Dixie cup cap and a rifle marched to and fro. Poor bastard. The weather was too bad for any saboteur but not bad enough to get the sailor out of guard duty.

The ships' crew would come on board in the morning to get underway by tomorrow evening. The Ocean Vanguard was scheduled to rendezvous with a convoy moving out of Boston. When the crew came on board, about a dozen sailors would be among them to man the freighter's deck guns against a raider or a surfaced sub. I didn't envy them. In February, the North Atlantic can be colder than a polar bear's pajamas.

I must have fallen asleep when a hand on my mouth awoke me. Blinking, I saw Liam with water running from his hat brim.

"They're here," he whispered.

"Where?" My blood was pounding in my ears.

"I had to pee, that's when I saw him," Liam said calmly.

"*Him*; him who?"

Leaning across me, Liam opened the vent window. He pointed to a form on the pier that had a white Dixie cup cap next to it. It was the sailor on guard, only face down on the pier. He wasn't guarding anything now.

"Go tell the others to keep their peepers peeled. I'll meet you at the net-crane on the pier."

I checked the action on the Walther. Liam slipped two buckshot rounds into the side-by-side, then silently closed the action as he vanished into the darkness and rain. I was glad that we switched off the interior light so when we opened the car doors we remained in the dark. Once outside the car, huge drops splashed on my hat brim like dropped cue balls. I closed the Ford's door silently. Thunder rumbled in the distance. The streetlamp on the corner of Horatio Street cast precious little light. Under the elevated highway, it was darker still. So dark that I switched the Walther to my left hand so that my right could feel along like a blind man as I moved. Lightning flashed across the river in New Jersey revealing a support pillar directly in front of me.

Ahead, in the dark, on the pier, someone kicked a can or something noisy. A voice hissed, "*Rhule!*" Silence.

Overhead, thunder rumbled. I stopped and slowly counted to ten before moving even a finger. My left thumb felt for the Walther's hammer then the safety. Cocked and safety off, I was ready. Someone ahead in the dark wasn't. He pulled the slide to chamber a round and cock his pistol. Looking behind I realized that I had been outlined by the corner light. Oh, shite! My right found the cold wet steel of the support pillar. I put it between me and that light on Horatio Street.

In front was only darkness. A sound of boots brushing the cobblestones was close. I wished that I had brought a knife bigger than the little clasp knife in my pocket. I switched the Walther back into my right hand. Downspout water rushing to the cobblestones made listening for movement maddening. I moved quickly to another steel support pillar. Wind blew rain into my eyes. As I tilted my head for my brim to shield me rain poured harder. Then a lighting flash was followed in a second by loud thunder.

He emerged like Max Schrek in *Nosferatu*. Unlike the vampire, this one wore a black fedora and had a heavy automatic in his claw. The barrel was swinging quickly, in my direction.

I fired. Max Schrek fired. His shot ricocheted off the pillar. I fired again. Max sank to his knees then dropped to the cobblestones. I must tell Bram Stoker that Vampires can be stopped with a well-placed 7.65 mm slug.

All hell began.

Muzzle-flash from Liam's shotgun was like a news camera flashbulb, blinding. Bullets and buckshot ricocheted off steel. I saw one man scramble across the pier. I fired. As Liam's gun flashed, I sprinted to the boss loader's shack. The man was now running for the hanging gangway. As I aimed, a bullet snapped past my ear from a different direction. I fired at the guy muscling his way on the hanging gangway. Behind me I heard Liam's shotgun blast. I fired again at the figure on the gangway.

He dropped to the pier like a sack of potatoes.

Hearing running footsteps from behind, I whirled, only to see a shadowy figure disappear. Lightning flashed. I went into to a crouch and edged my way along the shack. A blinding muzzle flash with a deafening roar was so close that I felt heat. Blinded, I fired two rounds in the direction. A black fedora blew past in the rain. How many rounds were left in the Walther? The slide was still forward indicating a live round in the chamber. I had no spare magazine. Now every shot had to count.

"Throw down your guns!" A heavily accented voice yelled from the deck of the Ocean Vanguard. It was immediately followed by a fusillade of gunfire.

"Fook you!"

I heard Liam snap open the action of the shotgun to reload.

Scuffling footsteps, then Liam boomed, "I killed two of them, but one got me." In the darkness, Liam hopped over to the shack. Using the shack wall, he slid down to the pier, then bent to touch his leg wound.

Putting down the Walther, I took a handkerchief from my leather jacket pocket. I balled it up and pressed it hard against his wound.

"Fuck that hurts!"

Jimmy, Paddy and Padric appeared, guns ready.

"Padric, you take Liam to St. Vincent's. Don't say nothing to nobody, just call Commander Haffenden. We need help here. We're outnumbered and outgunned! Go!"

Padric had Liam up and doing a three-legged race to Jane Street where his car was. I turned to Jimmy and Paddy, "We have to get on board the ship."

Before I could say another word, Jimmy said, "I can operate the net-crane to get you on board."

I never felt so exposed, so vulnerable, as I did riding that net to a deck where men were ready to shoot me. Paddy was along for the ride, but I still felt alone. I have a very good idea what paratroopers felt riding their 'shutes into enemy territory.

No one shot at us. No one was on deck. The rain eased up. I could see better. That saved Treglia.

He and his sailors were wearing longshoremen's caps. I hoped that the Nazis on the ship all wore black fedoras like those Nazis on West Street. I held my fire as a capped head emerged from a forward hold. As he climbed to the deck, I recognized Treglia.

Over the wind and rain noise, I told Treglia what happened on West Street under the elevated highway.

"We have a real problem," he said. "The saboteurs are in the aft hold #5 where the aircraft bombs are. If they set them off, it will destroy most of the war effort in New York."

"OK, but how in hell do you think we can get into #5 without getting killed?"

"Come with me."

Paddy and I followed Treglia to the bridge where he opened a door to the bridge deck stairs. He produced a flashlight and a blueprint of the Liberty ship.

Pointing to the blueprint, he said, "We're at midships. According to this, behind the engine is a tunnel for the propeller shaft and we can come up into #5 from below to get the drop on these bastards."

Treglia's face was animatedly flushed. Paddy and I exchanged glances.

"Let's go! Follow me! Okay, watch your head, stay low."

"Oof, Fook!" Paddy exclaimed as he banged his head on the low ceiling.

I said, "Keep low!"

The Seven Dwarves would have a hard time keeping low and moving in the shaft tunnel. Bent over, Paddy and I followed doing our best not to knock our brains out. It seemed that we walked crouched over the length of the Lincoln Tunnel to New Jersey when Treglia suddenly stopped and switched off his light.

Gingerly, he pocketed the light then slowly rotated the large latch counterclockwise. As he raised the hatch door, a distant light flickering gave the darkness a twilight. The three of us climbed silently into the #5.

I heard movement, hushed voices. The distant glow of light was on the port side opposite us. Treglia who was outlined by the glow, motioned for us to follow. Crates of bombs were packed tight so they wouldn't shift in heavy seas. It was tough to move. Like moths to a flame, we inched our way toward the light that became brighter with each step. By now the saboteurs' voices were more distinct along with the sounds of wire cutters and pry bars.

"Horen!" A voice ordered. Listen.

We stopped moving to listen too. Everyone listened to the steady rain on the hold cover. My mouth was sticky dry. My feet were cold. Another roll of thunder clapped. The rain on the hatch became harder.

"Get back to work."

Treglia pulled us close together. The rain-noise gave cover to his whisper. To Paddy, he said. "Climb up to the top of the stack then when you are in position yell for them to stop and put down their guns."

Paddy nodded, wedging his pistol in the small of his back behind his belt. Deftly, he climbed into the darkness above.

"Follow me," Treglia said, as he moved toward the saboteurs' light.

The two of us inched along. The sound of the rain began to lessen. As I looked ahead over Treglia's shoulder, I saw three figures moving. We were as close as thirty feet from them when Paddy yelled, "Drop it or I'll plug ya!"

Their light went out plunging the hold into blackness except for the muzzle flashes. Gunfire drowned out the thunder outside. Suddenly there was the sound of a body crashing to the hold's deck. Out of the corner of my eye there was movement. I pivoted and fired. The Walther's slide stayed back. I was in a gun fight with no ammunition. Cripes.

We moved forward. Treglia leading. Then a pistol barrel pressed into my temple. The hot breath against my ear wasn't a chorus girl's. "Drop your weapon, mischling."

Calling me a 'half-breed'. I let the useless Walther clatter to the deck. "You vill throw down your weapon or I vill kill your man." Then a light pinned Treglia like a butterfly. Slowly, he lowered his .45 pistol to the deck, then stood while raising his hands. Out of the darkness a man wearing a black fedora suddenly pistol-whipped Treglia to the deck.

The gun poking my temple pushed me forward until I was standing over Treglia's limp form.

"Ver did you get this?" A voice from behind said as my Walther with its slide still open was thrust in front of my face. The empty Walther was just that, a gun without ammunition. The voice however sent chills through me.

"Haupsturmfuhrer, what would you like me to do?" This voice sounded familiar as well. I searched my memory instead of letting my life pass in front of my eyes. But my eyes were blinded by a flashlight beam. My mind raced.

Then it came to me. I was shocked! Hans Rupp! Of all the people on earth to be a Nazi, it couldn't be. Who was the other voice, the voice of the

'Haupsturmfuhrer', the Nazi captain? Before my mind could work it out, a man dressed in a black jacket, trousers and fedora walked into the beam of Rupp's flashlight. Even dressed as the figure was, I immediately I recognized her. In every one of my nightmares, she was the star tormentor. Now she was here in a wide – awake-nightmare.

"Remember me?" Mother Superior asked peering into my face. "Tsk, tsk, you are still the little fool. Are you surprised, mischling?"

"Not really, I knew that you were a bitch at St. Joe's, now you are just a Nazi bitch." That smart comment earned me the Walther slammed across my face. Light exploded in my head and I was out for the count.

Sometime later, hearing came back first, vision was a little slower. Shadows and light danced in my brain. Slowly, I could see as well as hear. Outlined by their flashlight's glow, Rupp and Hilda Perpetua were working against the bulkhead speaking softly in German. My vision was still clouded but the pain was not. Treglia was tied up next to me. He flopped to his side and whispered, "Do you have a knife?"

My tongue was thicker than a side of liver, "In my pocket but I can't reach it. My hands are tied."

"Maybe I can."

Treglia wiggled closer.

Treglia's hand found my pocketknife. At that moment, Rupp and Mother Superior stood, turning their light on us. Treglia became as motionless as I was.

"Make it look like they shot each other. No matter, there vont be enough left of either after this goes off. Shoot them and meet me on deck."

I could hear her climb the ladder to the top of the hold and main deck. Rupp dragged two bodies closer to us. One was Paddy Clarke's the other was a saboteur with blood still oozing from his chest. He raised his pistol first at me. I closed my eyes and braced for the bullet. Hans fired twice.

I heard *two* gunshots. I didn't feel them. Breathing. I was still breathing. I smelled the burnt cordite. I was in no more pain than before. The saboteur's forehead had two neat holes but I didn't. Treglia seemed alive as well.

Producing his wire cutter, Hans quickly sniped my ropes.

"You have twenty minutes. Be very, very careful."

"Hans, how could you be working with these Nazis!" I said. His eyes spoke volumes.

Then he whispered, "I'm undercover. I'm going to bring the whole Nazi spy ring down. I can't let her escape. I got to get topside. You take care of the bomb. Meanwhile, Treglia' eyes were wide and roving from Hans' face to mine. Hans left me the wire cutter, turned wordlessly, ran to the ladder and climbed.

"Who the hell was that? What was all that?" Treglia asked.

"It's a long story. Turn on your side. I'll cut your ropes Hans is anti-Nazi, always has been. We still have to stop the bomb. I have the wire cutter."

Treglia trained his flashlight beam over the crates. My head was roaring in pain. It was as if I went ten rounds with Jake LaMotta or Sugar Ray Robinson. Above us, the rain was still thumping on the hold cover. That's when I heard a clock ticking. I crawled in the direction of the sound.

The bomb crate lid had been pried and carelessly put back. I didn't have to move the lid, to see inside. Attached to a dozen sticks of dynamite was one of those Bulova clocks, a bedside windup with the two bells on top. The time shown was 11:40. At the 12 o'clock position was a small screw with a thin black wire. Another wire was attached to the base of the minute hand. Once the minute hand touched the screw at 12 o'clock this thing would wake people on the Westside and New Jersey across the Hudson River.

Treglia was at my side as I reached with the cutter to snip the wires. He put a hand on the cutter.

"Hold it. I think I see a booby trap."

Taking the cutter, he gently nudged me aside. "You are blocking my light, move more to the right but whatever you do, don't touch or lift the lid."

There was another wire running from the crate lid through several screws with open loops to a piece of wood held by the jaws of a clothespin. The clothespin had two wires running to a piece of metal at the end of the clothespin jaws. At the other end of the wires were two sets of batteries.

"This was their back up detonator. If the clock timer failed and even if the ship made it to England, then this little devil could still do some serious harm. When some poor Lymie lifted the crate, the wood between the clothespin would be pulled, the wired metal on the clothespin jaws would close completing the circuit and boom. It was a good thing that you only peeked inside, or we'd be blown to kingdom-come already."

"I was told to be very, very careful."

After a dozen careful snips, Treglia gingerly lifted the damned thing out.

"Well, that was exciting," he said.

We climbed up to the ship's deck. It was still dark but at least the rain had been replaced by a cold fog. Even so, we heard activity on the pier and the glow of lights. Looking down, the pier was crawling with sailors. Commander Haffenden with his cigarette holder jauntily clenched in his teeth was looking straight at us. He took the holder out of his mouth and in his best Ivy Leaguer voice shouted, "Glad to see that you sports are alive. Did you find the bomb? I've got an EOD team here. They will be on deck in a minute."

As Haffenden spoke, I looked at the activity on the pier. The headlamps of several Navy trucks illuminated the draped body of the guard along with several stretchers awaiting their loads. One truck had a Red Cross painted on its canvas. Four or five sailors were already walking up the steep gangway to the Ocean Vanguard's deck.

As the sailors stepped on deck they saluted saying, "Permission to come on board."

"Permission granted." Lt. Treglia returned each salute. "Follow me."

He led them to the hatch and down the ladder. I, on the other hand, walked down the steep gangway. My head was still going ding-dong. Haffenden had his foot up on the bumper of a Navy staff car with that damned cigarette holder held so that he had to pretentiously speak through clenched teeth without opening his mouth.

"Tell me old sport, what happened? I understand that we have a number of bodies to remove."

"Yes, we have a few good Nazis for you. They won't be talking but the last two, a man and a woman still can. Treglia and I were too busy with the bombs to give chase. Did you catch the two? A man and a woman."

"Why old sport, you are the first person to leave the good ship. I threw up a cordon around the pier then my boys set up the gangplank just as you and the lieutenant appeared on deck. No one else has left the ship. My sailors would have noticed a woman. You are the only one so far. Perhaps the two are still aboard the ship."

"Cripes! They could still be on board!"

Haffenden did not reply. He turned produced a whistle and gave it two sharp blasts. A blue coated young officer ran up, saluted, saying, "Sir!"

"Lieutenant put together five two-man teams. Search every inch of this ship. There are two armed Nazis on board. I'd like to take them alive if possible. Now be quick about it!"

"AYE, AYE, SIR!"

In a matter of a minute, heavily armed sailors thundered up the gangplank.

Chapter 38
A Loss and a Gain

Sean

They didn't find anyone. Hilda Perpetua and Hans slipped through. After that, we cleared the pier before the first of the Ocean Vanguard crew arrived. Rain returned to help rinse blood from the pier, not that anyone would notice. We took Paddy Clarke's body to a funeral parlor on Northern Boulevard in Jackson Heights. The parlor's director was somewhat taken aback that Paddy's death certificate was signed by a U.S. Navy doctor.

"I see the cause of death is listed as stroke. What's with the bullet holes?" the funeral director asked.

"It says stroke, don't it! Don't make me lose my temper!"

The funeral director took a step back swallowing hard before saying, "We can patch him up. Make him presentable for the viewing."

"Get on it!" I ordered.

I muttered as I left the funeral parlor, "I guess that a bullet can cause a stroke."

In the weeks that followed, I learned that Haffenden was a prophet. The military took over the docks. The Army cut us off from our shape-up money and loading donations. I couldn't complain. I was out of prison. My wife on the other hand complained. She needed money for shoes, a dress or a hat. She insisted on going to posh supper clubs. Her favorite nightclub spot was the Copa on East 60th Street. I had to find another way to make more cash. What was coming in from union dues, sharking and the numbers was not nearly enough to keep Mary Kate happy.

In the meantime, I had Ian petition Family Court to legally adopt Elizabeth. On March 4th, the four of us went to Court to finalize Elizabeth's adoption. Ian impressed the judge by wearing his Navy Lieutenant Commander's uniform.

He was the executive officer on an escort destroyer, or as he referred to it 'a tin can.' We all dressed to the nines. Mary Kate wore a stunning black and red silk number. Her little black veiled hat gave her a look just like Carole Lombard. Meantime, Elizabeth wore her blue taffeta dress and her favorite Easter bonnet. Me, I wore my gray double-breasted wool suit from Best & Company, white shirt with a cranberry tie.

Ian moved the proceedings along quickly. Then both Mary Kate and I signed the paperwork. Elizabeth's face was flushed with excitement.

Afterward, we celebrated by taking in a picture show, *Mrs. Miniver.* The newsreel at intermission showed that we had given the Japs a beating in the Bismarck Sea with the Nips losing 22 ships, 102 aircraft and thousands of soldiers. Even in the theater darkness, I saw Ian leaning in to capture every detail of the naval battle.

I decided to top off the day with a steak dinner at Peter Luger's in Great Neck but Mary Kate said that she was fatigued. We put Mary Kate in a taxi for home then Elizabeth, Ian and I continued to Peter Luger's.

"Now, I can really call you Daddy!" Elizabeth gushed. "Elizabeth Callaghan has a nice ring to it too!"

We had skillfully charred yet medium rare porterhouse steaks, baked potatoes with all the trimmings. Now we were awaiting dessert, chocolate mousse for Elizabeth and apple strudel for me. Ian just had coffee.

I lit up a Lucky Strike and asked, "Elizabeth, you'll be a senior at Mary Louis next year, what are you thinking of doing after high school?"

"Yes, Elizabeth have you given any thought to college?" Ian asked.

Holding up a finger for time, she touched her napkin to her lips.

"I hadn't thought much about it."

"I understand that you are doing very well in school. Why don't you investigate Fordham or NYU? I may be able to get you an interview with Fordham's Dean of Admissions."

"Thank you...Uncle Ian. Holy smokes, I have another uncle now!"

"Yes, in Ian's Law School there were women. As a matter of fact, one was even a Negro. Smart dame too. What was her name?"

"Eunice Hunton-Carter! Yes, she is an excellent assistant district attorney. Eunice was the editor of the Law Review at Fordham. You could be as good as Eunice."

"I'm not sure what I want to do," Elizabeth said.

"You could start with a major of history, sociology or even English literature while you learn what interests you."

"Listen to Ian, he's not just bumping his gums."

"I'll think about it," Elizabeth said. "Let's finish dessert first."

Chapter 39
Working Vacation

Sean
March 1943
Miami, Florida

Red and I took the train to Miami for a working vacation. There wasn't a lot to do on the docks now that the Army and the Naval Intelligence had taken over. Neither of our wives were happy about our limited income. Neither were they happy to be left in cold, icy, snowy New York while we were off in the Florida sunshine. Red said that we would be looking into the Florida casino racket, not a clip joint but something classy. I told Mary Kate that I am getting into the jukebox racket in Florida just like Meyer Lansky does in New York. This could supplement our money nicely.

Mary Kate wasn't having any of it.

"You have your crust thinking that I'm going to be sitting here breathlessly awaiting on you while you go gallivanting in the Florida sunshine!"

"Whassamatta? It's your brother's idea not mine."

"Then let him go."

"Hey, Red and I are partners Dollface. How would it look if I wasn't with him? Huh?"

"First you claim that you are getting me a Russian sable coat and all I get is a cheesy mink stole. You treat me like some sweet potato you found in some gin mill instead of your wife."

"I explained that. We got highjacked. Cripes. What do you want from me?"

"I want to go to Miami."

"Dollface this is business…"

"Business, my keister. I know you! You'll start out being a big shot union boss, but it won't be long before you're with some tomato on your lap."

"Mary Kate!"

"If you chisel me out of Miami, you'll be sorry!"

With her mouth tight, she suddenly stood up. The kitchen chair clattered over as she stormed out to our bedroom slamming the door behind her.

I packed my summer seersucker suit, a few shirts, ties, a .38 revolver, and the Walther with extra magazines. Outside, Red was already in the Pontiac. Liam stood beside the open trunk. Big wet flakes were starting to come down as I carried my valise to the Pontiac's trunk. Liam put it in, then closed the trunk lid. I climbed in beside Red. Liam slid in behind the wheel.

"Squint, you know how to get to Penn Station on West 32nd? It's opposite the Pennsylvania Hotel."

It bothered me when Red called Liam, Squint. I never heard Liam complain, but I'm sure that he didn't like it.

"Liam, take the 59th Street Bridge then cut across Central Park South past the Plaza. That'll be the faster way to the West side."

"Sure."

"Squint, don't forget to collect from the Doyle Trucking. They've welched on their payments again."

"Sure, Red. Will do. It's top of my list, just like when you two were up river."

Liam had his own way of putting Red in his place.

We took the Silver Meteor sleeper train from Penn Station shaking snow off our topcoats as we boarded. In 36 hours, we were sweating and fanning ourselves with our fedoras in Miami. On the platform waiting for the boy to pull our bags, it was hot, steam bath hot. Red's face matched his hair. Sweat was rolling down my spine. I might be sweating right through my suit jacket. Briefly, I thought of taking my suit jacket off, but I didn't want some cinder-bull railroad copper to see the .38 in my waistband.

The Silver Meteor was huffing like a racehorse chomping at the bit in the stable after the first race bugle. Most of the passengers who disembarked with us were already heading toward the street and cabs.

"What's taking the Pullman boy so long?"

"I dunno. It's fucking hot," Red replied.

"I have to use the toilet," I said.

"Go to the one in the waiting room. I'll meet you outside on the street side. I already wired for a car to pick us up when the Meteor stopped in Atlanta.

This fucking train is heating up the whole platform. Can't wait to get out of here."

"I see my big Oshkosh grip on the cart the Pullman boy is pushing this way. Look."

"Christ on the cross, it better be ours."

"You handle the luggage and I'll see you out by the curb."

As I walked into the Miami Station's men's room, I could feel my hair plastered to my skull. Before anything else, I went to the line of sinks. I splashed cold water on my face, soaked my handkerchief to chill my neck. In the mirror, the face that stared back was pale and moist. Then I saw them. Two grease balls in dirty shirts had stepped out of bathroom stalls behind and were taking fast steps toward me.

The two made sure that I saw the long stilettos gleaming for my blood. In this tight space, knives are killers. There's no way of getting out of a knife fight without a serious cut. They slowed to a stop several steps away. The one to my right grinned showing a big gap between his front teeth. But it was his eyes, they shone with that crazed look that only "Mad Dog" Cole or Lepke Buchalter had. I saw that his left forearm was shaved. A lot of these knife guys like to test the sharpness of their blades by shaving their forearm. The other guy tossed his knife from hand to hand as if he was deciding what hand should gut me. His eyes were so dark. His pupils were huge black holes to his soul. That soul must be black too. Then with his right forearm he wiped his runny nose, a cocaine user.

Each took a half step toward me. I didn't back up. Now they were close enough for me to smell their rancid body odor.

Even if I could pull my .38 fast, at best I would only stop one, not both. If I could. I stared between them to see which one would lunge first. To get to the revolver, I pulled my shoulders back to unplaster my suit jacket from my back. Subtly, I turned my right side toward the crazy one to make it a little harder to stab me in the gut. My left had the wet handkerchief.

Almost whispering, I said, "Let's get this done."

As Mr. Cocaine's knife was tossed to the other hand, I moved. First whipping off my suit jacket covering the crazy one like a matador's cape on a bull. My left went for the knife still in the air between hands. It clattered to the porcelain tiles. He bent to pick it up but my left brogue caught him square in the face.

310

The crazy one fought my jacket like a cat in a bag. Blindly stabbing, he still was able to stab my right arm. He stabbed hard. The blade went through my arm muscle to my ribs on the other side but stopped there. With a left roundhouse, I hit his ear snapping his head sharply. He went down. Using my left, I had the .38 backward so I clubbed him hard with the grip. Many times.

My eye caught movement on the tile floor. Mr. Cocaine was up like a punch-drunk palooka. Head down, looking through his eyebrows like a maddened bull, he charged at me. Again, like a matador, I stepped to the side as his stiletto slammed into the sink next to me. The blade snapped. I grabbed his neck and bashed his forehead repeatedly into the sink until he folded up like a cardboard suitcase in the rain.

With the immediate threat down, I ripped off the remainder of my right sleeve, which I used to staunch the blood as I pulled the knife from my arm. Then, I used the knife to make it look as if they fought each other. Quickly, I checked my side. It was a superficial cut, but it bled. I put my .38 in my left trouser pocket draped the suit jacket over my right shoulder to cover both the arm and side bleeds.

I walked out to the curb where Red stood. He found the cab. The Negro driver was loading our bags into the trunk.

"What the fuck took you so long?"

"Let's get in and get to the hotel, huh!"

"You look like shite, Well, what are ya? Constipated? Your suit is a wreck. You better have another in your grip."

"Let's just say that some guys tried to sell me some Everglades property."

"You said no right? Christ, how do people live down here in this heat?"

"I don't know how they live here, but I know what kills them."

The cab taking Red and me to the hotel moved smoothly down NW 37 Street. I asked the cabbie, "No traffic, eh? Ain't Hialeah Racetrack nearby?"

I saw the driver's eyes in the rear view as he said, "Rationing has stopped pleasure driving as it's called, sir. Gasoline and rubber tires are rationed for the war effort. Only on race day do we have traffic on Northwest 79th and that be buses."

"Oh, how long will it take to get to hotel?"

"'Bout ten minutes. Say mister, you don't look so good. Is you going to be sick in my cab?"

"No, no I am getting over some surgery. That's all."

"I can stop by the Hialeah Hospital, if you like."

"No, that's not needed. But hey, is there a hospital supply shop near the hospital?"

"Yassir, there be one on corner of East 8th. Want me to go there?"

"Sure."

Red had been eyeballing me and now leaned into my left ear, "What the fuck is wrong?" he whispered. "What fuckin' surgery are you talking about."

"I was stabbed in the men's. Stabbed in my arm," I whispered back.

"Fuck."

"I'll be OK. Just go into the supply shop and pick up some hospital gauze bandages, tape and painkillers."

"You gonna be good for the meeting? They say that they have a job for us that'll pay good."

"Thanks for your concern. Don't you worry. Just get some things so I can stop bleeding, put on a new shirt and suit and get to the meeting."

Red hopped out and the driver turned off the cab's engine. "Gotta save gas," he explained. Good thing because Red was at least five minutes in the hospital store and another five in the package store across the street.

"I figured that we could use some medicinal vodka and celebrate with rum."

"I like your thinking."

We tipped the driver an extra sawbuck and asked if he could pick us up at 5. I asked his name. Leroy. I suppose that they were allowing Negros to drive at night in Miami now that the war was on. Even so, I saw a street sign on the corner proclaiming that Negros needed a police pass to be on 'the beach' at all times. Most of the beach hotels were housing Army Air Force soldiers, somehow Red wrangled us a room at the Carlyle on Ocean Drive.

In the room, I went directly into the bath. The sharp stiletto missed arteries and veins. The shirtsleeve had stopped the bleeding, but it throbbed. It hurt like a son-of-a-bitch. Of course, I took a long pull on the bottle before I poured the vodka on the stab wound. Wow! I almost bit my tongue to avoid screaming. Red came into the bathroom to help with the bandages.

As he put a plaster bandage on my rib wound, he said, "I have to get rid of your bloody clothes before some house maid or house dick sees 'em. Then have a local flatfoot start asking questions. Christ, did you have to get into a knife fight?"

"Well it was the dirt bags idea not mine. I used their own blades to end it. If I shot them, the cinder-dicks would have got me at the station and this whole trip would be for squat."

"Who the hell were those guys?"

"Probably just cocaine hopheads looking to score from a well-dressed traveler. Now help me into a shirt. Forget a tie. I'll need help with my seersucker jacket later. You can be the dandy as usual."

"I think the hotel has an incinerator. I'll be right back."

Red picked up the remains of my shirt and my blood-stained suit jacket. I poured myself a rum and Coke as he left. Even with the ceiling fan going like a dive-bomber's propeller, it was stifling in the room. I took a good pull on the rum and Coca-Cola then laid on the bed. I was out for the count.

As promised, Leroy was waiting outside the Carlyle with the car engine off, of course. I let Red get in first so I wouldn't have to move too much. As he started the cab's engine, Leroy asked, "Where to gents?"

"A place called Hallendale, 612 Hibiscus."

"Sit back gents, enjoy the ride up the 1 A 1."

As the cab travelled the coastal road, the beaches gleamed in the golden light of an early twilight. On the pavement, the walkers were all in tan Army Air Force summer uniforms. Some had a dame on their arms, but more were in groups of twos and threes. I wondered how many would survive the war to return here for a vacation. My thoughts were interrupted by the powerful roar of a squadron of aptly named Thunderbolts overhead.

"They are fucking noisy! They better not fly at night. I need my beauty sleep," Red said loud enough to be heard over the Thunderbolts' Pratt & Whitney engines.

As the P-47s squadron continued on into the cerulean sky to the east, Leroy spoke, "Those be the really good flyboys, else they wouldn't be flying in the night. Be looking for U-Boats, like B-25 bombers an' flying boats. Trainers fly in daytime only. You'll get used to it. After a while you'll don' even look up."

"Leroy, how long before we get to Hallendale?"

"Mebe, another dirty minute, mebe less."

It was less. The cab pulled into a semicircle drive outside a modest single-story house abutting a canal. Actually, a series of canals between islands with low roofed homes. Leaving Leroy with the Racing Form, we rang the bell next to the door. I knew enough to ring once and wait. Maybe two minutes later, I heard shuffling feet on the other side of the door.

"HOO!" Cough. "Who's there?"

"It's Callaghan and MacGregor, Mr. Lansky" I recognized the voice.

You don't expect a big shot like Meyer Lansky to be answering his own door but there he was. When the door opened there was Lansky dressed in a white embroidered Cuban light gray guayabera shirt, linen trousers that were pearly white over feet in brown sandals. Lansky looked like every short Jewish grandfather from Delancey Street on a visit to the Florida sun. But there was no mistaking the brilliance that his eyes revealed.

"Come in boys. Make yourself at home."

Lansky's home was spacious with the vestibule leading to a large room with a long window admitting the reds and oranges of sunset. From a hall of the vestibule, a tall rail-thin man emerged.

"This is my associate Izzy, Izzy Redman," Lansky said. "You may have met him at Ratner's"

"Good to see you," I said. Redman had the grip of a gorilla and the eyes of a snake.

"Izzy, get our guests some rum runners."

I smiled at the name of the cocktail having a sudden memory of bounding through the city's harbor in a fast boat with a load of Scotch, Seagram's hooch and cognac during Prohibition. Those were good days.

"Let me introduce you or reintroduce you to the others." As we walked behind Lansky. "My brother, Jake here. And, you remember my associate, Benny? Benny, this is Sean Callaghan and John MacGregor. Benny is visiting from Hollywood. Hollywood, California. He's been working with Mickey Cohen on some offshore casinos. My brother Jake also lives in Hollywood." Lansky smiled. "Hollywood, Florida that is."

"Pleased to meet you."

"Pleased to meetchew."

"Pleasure."

Handshakes all around.

Using his whole hand to point, Lansky said, "Sit. Please."

Framed by the picture window behind, I saw for the first time that Lansky was bowlegged, short and bowlegged. I mean much shorter than I am. At least I'm not bowlegged. It must have been rickets when Lansky was a kid. Very little sunshine made it down through the narrow streets on the lower East Side south of Delancey where Lansky grew up.

Red used 'John' instead of his real name. We called him 'Red' not Hamish as Mary Kate did. He didn't mind.

Now it was different for Benjamin "Benny" Siegel, only the papers called him "Bugsy". If you did, it would be the last time you spoke. Nodding to us over his lowball glass, and seated on an ottoman, Benny was dressed in a natty hounds-tooth checkered sport coat, and jet-black linen trousers. Siegel had that movie star kind of good looks that all the dames went for. No surprise that he ended up in Hollywood.

There was a distinct bulge of a shoulder holstered revolver in his left armpit. With Siegel in the house, Lansky had no need for more protection.

"Mr. Siegel, do you mind me calling you, Benny."

"Naw! If Meyer calls me anything, he calls me late for dinner." Siegel smiled in the way Vincent Coll did, no real warmth.

Izzy appeared handing Red and me tall highball glasses. Rumrunners. I took a sip. Tasty, I could get used to it. I set the glass on a metal coaster on the coffee table, sat back.

"Hollywood." Interjecting, Red said, "You must be getting a lot of starlets to keep you warm?"

"I have a real tomato. She's smart too. My Ginny has a good memory, buttons her lips when needed but can fool you by her chatterbox talk."

Siegel had taken up with Virginia Hill, who was once a sweet patootie for Capone's bodyguard in the Chicago Outfit some time ago. I heard that she was in New York and keeping Luciano's capo, Joe Adonis, real happy until she met Siegel. She knows which side her bread is buttered. One smart dame.

"Hollywood" I mused. "Say, do you see anything of my old buddy from Hell's Kitchen, George Raft. He's doing swell in the pictures now."

"Yeah, wasn't he your wheelman or was it for Owney Madden?" Red asked.

Ignoring the question, Siegel said, "George and I are good friends. He vouched for me when I had a little trouble with the law in LA."

"Let's get down to business, shall we?" Lansky picked up a frosted tall glass of iced tea then sat on the large sofa with a window behind him. He became a dark silhouette as the sun began to set.

"We have nothing to fear from the FBI here. We are on an island of sorts with a large open lot behind and another to the south. We have a commanding view in all directions. Even extraordinary surveillance is ineffective here."

"I was wondering about that myself," I said. I felt the rum runner. I also felt Lansky's eyes on me.

"You don't look so well, Mr. Callaghan. Can I get you anything?"

"I had a run-on with a pair of guys from a welcome wagon at the train station. It's nothing that a pint of blood, some sulfa and a scotch can't cure."

"Izzy!" Lansky shouted.

A squeak of a chair pushed on linoleum preceded Izzy's entering the room.

"Izzy, call Dr. Moccia to make a house call here as soon as he can." Turning to me, Lansky asked, "What did these guys look like?"

"Two greaseballs. One with a crazy look in his eye the other high on coke."

"What kind of shape did you leave them in?"

"Oh, I gave them as taste of their own medicine. One is decorating the men's room with his brains and the other guy must have fell on his knife. They won't be bothering anybody anymore."

"Let me look into it."

As Izzy left, Lansky cleared his throat. "Get down to brass tacks," Lansky said, "I need you two to move my money from my carpet joints, the It Club, the Aristocrat and the Hollywood Yacht Club. The FBI eyeballs here don't know you, so they'll tail my goombas not you. You didn't register under your real names, did you?"

"No sir, Mr. Lansky, we registered as two real estate brokers looking for investments. I'm Mr. John Pepper and Red here is Mr. Hugh Potter."

"Good."

"How's business in your casinos?"

"I don't run clip joints either here or in Havana. I insist that all the games aren't rigged. Still, the 'house' always wins."

"Aces!"

"Not aces-and-eights as with the cowboy Wild Bill Hickok. By the way, can either of you drive a boat?"

"I can," I said. "When I was rum running, I drove a large boat out of New York Harbor to pick up hooch from a Canadian freighter beyond the three-mile limit. Some nights it was tricky if a storm or fog set in, I but I always made the run without breaking a bottle of Johnny Walker or Seagram's."

316

"Good," Lansky said. "You two need to understand that when the war ends you can run your docks as before. Well…" he trailed off shrugging his shoulders. "Well, with one difference, when we get the military off the piers you two will have to show some respect to Vincent Mangano, Albert's underboss. We are thinking of ten percent. A token of respect, you understand."

"Of course, respect, we capisce, Mr. Lansky. We would still be up-river if it wasn't for you and Mr. Anastasia," I replied not even glancing at Red.

"It's settled then." Lansky smiled like some wise old grandfather.

The doorbell chimed. "That must be Dr. Moccia. We'll talk more after Dr. Moccia fixes you up."

Lansky stood. Red and I stood. Once again, I was struck at just how short Lansky was. Big in reputation and influence but short in stature.

"Sir, Sorry to interrupt. Doctor Moccia is here," Izzy said poking his head into the room.

"Go get treated and come back, we have more matters to discuss."

Lansky nodded in the direction of the front room. As I rose, I smiled to myself, a 'discussion' with Lansky is one-sided. It was always best to listen carefully and talk as little as possible. I heard that recently a fellow who 'talked too much' took a one-way ride into the Everglades. We each shook Lansky's hand.

In the front room, a tall man with head of curly jet black hair and a meticulously trimmed mustache was arranging the contents of his doctor's bag on the table. Already, he had his suit jacket off and shirtsleeves rolled up above his elbows. There were several wicked-looking needles with syringes and two vials of medication. The silvery medical instruments arranged on a blue cloth suggested a medieval dungeon.

Without looking up, he asked. "Have you had a tetanus vaccination in the last five years?"

"Are you Dr. Moccia?"

"Yes," he said extending his hand. "Now sit in this chair, take off your jacket and shirt so that I can clean, suture and treat your, your…accident. Have you had a tetanus shot recently?"

"No."

"Fine, I will inoculate you against tetanus then I will inject you with something to prevent *Clostridium perfringes*."

"Inoculate me for 'closet prefer-in-gist?'"

"You can thank Mr. Lansky for my supply of benzathine penicillin. The war effort makes it difficult to obtain this miracle drug." Dr. Moccia wiped the top of one vial then turning it upside down advancing a long needle into the milky liquid within it. "I have seen too many die of gangrenous wounds. Now stand and drop your pants. This won't hurt much."

I stood unbuckled and unbuttoned my trousers. Without a word, Dr. Moccia pulled down my briefs, swabbed my right ass-cheek with something cold then immediately stabbed my ass with the long needle. I could feel the injecting milky liquid as he pressed the syringe plunger.

"You aren't going to get 'the vapors' as some dame would, are you?"

I swallowed hard as it felt as though he was injecting my ass-cheek with a quart of Esso motor oil. "No, and I ain't no nelly either. I can take it. I took the knife, didn't I?"

"I have had some big, rough, tough patients that could go several rounds with Sugar Ray Robinson pass out and fall looking a needle."

***

It seemed that Red and I hadn't been back at the Carlyle but ten minutes when there was a heavy fist on our door. After my encounter at the train station, I was taking no chances. We had our irons in our hands and flattened against the wall on either side of the door.

"Who's there?"

"S'me Izzy."

Red nodded to me, open-the-door. With my .38 trained on the door, I reached the knob with my left and threw it open.

"Whoa! Put them bean shooters down. Let's go collect money."

Izzy walked in shutting the door behind him. I tucked my .38 in my waistband then I picked up my fedora and Lucky Strikes. Red opened door. We both froze. There were two uniformed coppers and one obvious detective.

We didn't move a muscle until Izzy's voice said, "Don't be putzes, they are our protection. This is Deputy Bob Clark of the Broward County Sheriff Office. He provides special policing for us."

Clark extended a big meaty hand to me. He was nattily dressed, bow-tied, with wire-rimmed glasses. Bob Clark looked more like some country doctor than a county deputy. When he spoke, it was obvious that he was a Southern wheat or whatever they call backwoods country boys here.

"Y'all gonna be mighty pleased to work with us'in. Pleased to meetcha."

I shook Deputy Clark's mitt; it was sweaty and sticky like he just finished a fried chicken dinner. Red was threading his arm into a brown double breasted. I started sweating just looking at him.

"Are you gonna be warm enough in that?"

"Fuck you, Callaghan."

"Let's shake a leg," Izzy said. "We got bidness to conduct."

We had plenty of 'bidness' to do. With us three in Izzy's Buick and Deputy Clark leading in a Sheriff's car, we began our pick-ups at Lansky's clubs. Izzy, Clark, Red and I would go in to collect the moola while Clark's deputies would cover us. First stop was the It Club on US 1. From there we convoyed to the next three casinos, the Club Bohemia, the Aristocrat, and the Greenacres. With each stop Izzy's oilskin grip became wider and heavier. He produced a second valise for the big collection at the next casino. With a pump shotgun at the ready, a deputy guarded the Buick and the grip full of cash as we made the final pick up, the Hollywood Yacht Club. I felt like a target with so much moola. I became more nervous when upon leaving the Yacht Club, Deputy Clark left us. I watched the red taillights on his Broward County Sheriff's car fade from view. We were loaded with a lot of Meyer Lansky's money.

I started to relax as we climbed in Izzy's big Buick. With Izzy behind the wheel, we continued north on 1 A 1 until it became a sandy road, North Coast Drive.

The sedan rattled over a rickety bridge as Izzy said, "Dis'is Whiskey Creek. Back in Prohibition we would bring in our gigglejuice from de ocean here. We had an understandin'. De Coast Guard is nearby, so's de Navy Coastal Defense station. Down dere's our boat."

In the dark below, men using flashlights illuminated the boat. Clark's men. I knew the boat as a '36 Chris-Craft nineteen foot 'barrelback'. This was a fine machine to cut through waves.

Izzy pulled the Buick alongside the Sheriff's car. Hauling the oilskin valises of cash, we walked across the moonlit sand to the Chris-Craft.

"Dis got a flathead V-8 with 150 horsepower. We can be in Nassau or Freeport in 6 hours if the weather don' blow up," Izzy said.

"What are Clark's men doing?" I asked, watching the sheriff's men carry three long bags to the dock where the Chris-Craft bobbed.

"In-surance. Nebber be too careful."

One of Deputy Clark's men arrived at the dock with a big Browning water-cooled machine gun on his shoulder. It was clear that we would have good insurance coverage. The other copper started screwing the feet of the Browning's tripod to the barrel back cover on the stern. Deputy Clark, himself, stepped aboard with a long heavy bag.

Clark opened up the bag. He lifted a long wicked looking gun amid a clatter of boxy magazines.

"Y'all evah use a Johnny-gun?"

"No, only a Thompson. What's up with the heavy iron? Didn't I hear that killing was bad for business?"

"On shore it's one thin', out whare y'all goin', 'nuther." Deputy Clark grinned. "Thompsons fine but y'all gonna love this Johnny, she's a peach. Just slam the twenty-round magazine in oner' left side of the receiver, yank the bolt an' she's good to go. Don't fire her standing. Makes her harder to hold than a three-leg pig. Use the bipod an' y'all ken put out a possum's eye a field away."

"I don't expect to shoot any possum where we're going," Red said.

"It's a welterweight," I said hefting the Johnson M1941 while looking at the two coppers struggling with the heavyweight Browning on the stern of the rocking boat. The two were having a devil of a time mounting the water-cooled Browning on the tripod. What the heck did they expect us to encounter out on the salt? The Bismarck?

"Last year, U-boats were settin' ships afire within sight of Miami. So's the Coasties don't care whatcha toting," Izzy said as he dropped two metal boxes of ribboned ammo next to the two men struggling with the Browning.

"Yous guys really don' have any boat shoes? It's gonna ruin those nice two-tones."

It was making me breathe easier that the Lansky crew of local coppers were loading guns and bullets not cement. I wouldn't be keen on trading my two-tones for cement shoes to be fish-bait.

With the Browning mounted on the tripod, Deputy Clark, and his two coppers left the boat, were up on the dock and walking to their car without as much as a goodbye.

"Where are we going?" Red asked as the boat thumped gently against the dock bumpers.

"Freeport."

"Where the fuck is Freeport?"

"Don't' blow your wig," I said. "It's in the Bahamas, Red."

Then turning to Izzy, "Just how far is Freeport from here?"

"It's 94 miles east northeast but we'll head due east lettin' the stream carry us far enough northeast. This time o'year the stream runs two knots. We'll run at a steady 20 knots east. If we headed southeast fighting the stream, it would reduce our speed. I wanna make Freeport well 'fore the bank closes."

"I was going to ask 'why we were taking a boat' with all the cash from the casinos. I thought you were being a real smart-ass, like a real Abercrombie," Red said.

"Meyer deposits his cash in a Swiss bank. The Bahamas have Swiss Banks. The Swiss don' report to the Feds. Don' wanna end up like Al Capone on tax evasion."

"Don't that beat all!" "When are we going?"

"Go'in soon as I check the boat," Izzy replied.

Izzy set about with his flashlight poking around the boat. I looked over the Browning while Red sat in the captain's seat starting to light up a Chesterfield. Out of nowhere Izzy slapped the lighter from Red's mitt. Even in the dark Red's face turned a shade darker as he grabbed Izzy by the buttons.

"What kind o' schmuck are yo'? I'm checking fuel, you schmuck!" Izzy said.

"You do that again and I'll plug ya, pally."

"Red, don't be a twit! You could have set us on fire like the Normandie. Why don't you and I give Izzy a hand getting the boat ready?"

Working with Izzy, Red checked the V-8. He knew big Olds and Chevy motors. Meanwhile, I checked the two fuel tanks. I was about to close the fuel cabinet when I saw a sparkle of reflected light on the reserve line. I ran my hand along the line. Wet. I smelled it.

"Izzy! Red! Come here!"

Izzy and Red were at my shoulder in two shakes of a lamb's tail. Izzy nudged Red aside as I held up my wet fingers to his large nose. "Fakackda!" Shit!

Izzy moved fast. Faster than I thought he could. He had a hose from somewhere on the dock. Like a fireman putting out a blaze, Izzy methodically flushed the bilges. Periodically, he turned to glare at Red. I could easily see his thoughts in those eyes.

I used a manual bilge-pump to dump the water-fuel mix into the bay. It was dawn before we finished. A morning mist drifted along the bay. Our shirtsleeves were wet and stained. Forget about our hands.

Only after Izzy checked all the lines and bilges did he turn on the fans to vent any remaining fumes. With one arm draped on the wheel, he rubbed his whiskers.

"Izzy is it safe? We ought to go. Whoever did this will come to see if they need to finish the job," I asked.

"I'm thinking that they don't expect to get the cash, just send a message to Lansky," Red said.

"We've been 'messaged' since we got here."

"We can still make the bank." Izzy turned the key. I was ready to jump if the Chris-Craft blew but it didn't. Red's strained face showed the relief I must have on mine.

"Cast off!"

As we motored past the Coast Guard station, Izzy reached into a compartment then handed a pair of sunglasses to Red then another to me. He was wearing one already.

"Traded moonshine for these. Army Air Force fighter pilots' glasses for squinting into the sun. We head east but the sunrise is southeast. Hold on to your fedoras, we have to make a wake."

Izzy let me take the wheel after traveling south along the coast. He was looking at the console compass then lining up the swivel compass sight with a water tower on the Miami side.

"Bring 'er 'round due east," Izzy said.

"Aye, aye," I replied.

"I want you run south, line up with the Bimini drop then on a heading 90 degrees 'lettin' the Gulf Stream carry us northward to Freeport. At noon, I'll use a sextant for latitude adjustment."

"Can you show me how to use a sextant?" I said.

"Vy not."

In an hour, Florida coast disappeared, and the morning mist was burning off. Behind the barrel boat's wheel, I held it on course through increasing swells. I scanned the skies for a squall. That's when I saw them.

"Izzy get your binoculars! What's that to our starboard?"

Izzy stood to look over the spray-screen. He had the binoculars to his eyes when he said, "Oy. Oy. You, Red get the Johnies!"

Izzy went aft to the barrel back. Red had been asleep on the bench seat. Now as he stood his hat flew off, bounced once on the Izzy's back then into our wake.

"Where's my fuckin' aviator's?" Red yelled.

"Never mind them! Get the Johnson! Izzy! Get ready! We have trouble closing fast!"

"Turn hard to port, mebbe we can use the Stream to outrun them," Izzy said as he slapped a belt of .30 caliber ammo into the Browning and pulled the bolt. He fired a short burst.

"Mebbe that will tell 'em ve ain't easy pickins."

The fast boat behind leaped over a two-foot swell like a lion charging a gazelle. Even at full speed with the Gulf Stream helping the Chris-Craft, the fast boat was closing the distance.

"I'm going to zig-zag," I shouted over the roaring V-8.

"No! Don't!" Izzy shouted back. "Lose too much forward speed."

But looking over the stern, it was apparent that the Chris-Craft was no match for the pursuit boat. Izzy was at the Browning with Red on his left with the Johnson. I had the Chris-Craft two degrees north and wide-open throttle as bullets stitched the swell we were cresting. The Browning shook our boat in reply as our pursuers disappeared behind a swell.

I heard another engine above the roar of the Chris-Craft, the Browning, Red's Johnson and the banging of Chris-Craft breaking through swells. A shadow passed overhead. I glanced up to see a large twin-engine airplane pass through a cloud on our bearing.

Did these bastards have airplanes too? Not a minute later the sea erupted several hundred or more yards off our bow. My feet on the deck and hands on the wheel felt the concussion. Shite! They have bombs too! I swing the wheel hard to port. More bullets stitched the sea where we had just been. We would meet our pursuers head-on. The Chris-Craft compass was bobbing south.

I brought my Johnson up over the spray screen as the pursuit boat roared toward us. I emptied the whole magazine. One man toppled overboard as the speed boat passed on our port side. Red's Johnson fired, stitching the side of the speeder to its stern. The Browning thundered.

Again, I swung the wheel now to pursue our pursuers. We were heading north-northeast again. Another series of explosions erupted a nautical mile or less off our bow. Now we were closing with the speeder. Izzy was on the stern barrel-back loading another belt. Red handed me another magazine as he pulled his bolt back to fire.

As we came up on the slowing speeder, it exploded. Fragments flew all over the sea. Another explosion hit what remained of the speeder. I turned to see not two hundred yards away a U-Boat! A Nazi U-boat! There was a binocular glint from the conning tower. Three men were on deck loading an 88mm gun similar to the gun on a Liberty ship.

All three of us fired at once. Sparks flew off the U-Boat's deck and conning tower. One of the gun crew fell. The remaining two swung the gun around toward us. The three of us fired at the U-boat. With my Johnny gun empty, I turned the Chris-Craft toward the U-boat's bow hoping to put the conning tower between us and the deck gun. On the U-boat a heavy machine gun stitched a line of tracers skyward. Not at us.

The sea around the U-boat erupted in shuddering blasts. The twin-engine airplane passed overhead. Smoke poured from the conning tower. Through the smoke I saw that the 88mm was out of action. A moment later there was an explosion inside the U-boat. Then two more.

We watched as it disappeared stern first.

"That U-Boat was 86ed!" I said, thinking about Chumley's prohibition raids.

"That's a B-25 submarine hunter," Izzy said as the aircraft passed overhead waggling its wings. "It was dropping depth charges that brought the U-boat to the surface. Our pursuers pushed us into crossfire between the B-25 and the U-boat."

"Damn good thing the U-boat took them out not us," I said.

"Meyer hoid dat dere was a U-boat wolfpack and it's Milch-cow or tanker U-boat spotted five hundred miles east of Bermuda. Don' think dey would attack a pleasure boat."

"Pleasure boat? You fucking think that this is pleasure?" Red said, the cigarette shaking in his hand. "Dis ain't no pleasure cruise." Then, he vomited over the side, just for emphasis.

Despite increasing swells Izzy had us in Freeport in five hours. But five hours of plowing into rough seas was no trip to a sweetshop. Red was green. Turning into the harbor seemed to calm the ocean into a gentle chop. With Izzy at the helm, the boat reduced speed to no-wake as we slowly motored into the Dundee Channel. The water was as placid as a bath. Going this slow, no breeze, the sun felt really hot, tropical heat.

Once at the Dundee channel dock, we had stored the Johnny-guns and canvas covered the Chris-Craft from stem to stern. A barefoot Negro with a ragged shirt spoke to Izzy. The Negro was handed a few dollars, a crowbar and a fresh pack of Lucky Strikes, my Lucky Strikes. We left him to guard the boat with his crowbar as we walked from the dock. Walking felt as if the land under my feet was pitching like the Chris-Craft out in the Gulf Stream.

With the large oilskin bags, Izzy led us past the dock's ship's chandler to a gravel street. Izzy hailed a cab. A rusty old Model T rattled to a stop. I climbed in next to the Negro driver as Red and Izzy sat in the back.

"BIS bank on East Mall." Izzy leaned over the driver's seat.

Under the ragged top of the T, we were out of the sun. Out of blazing sun tropical heat. Actually, it felt cool. The driver had the T moving, creating a little breeze. As the T entered a round-about, Red whipped off his aviator sunglasses.

"Hey, you're driving on the wrong side of the road!" Red yelled as the driver turned on to Pinta Avenue. Izzy pulled Red back into his seat.

"Hey! Goy! Dey drive like the Brits here. Now sit back and enjoy the ride."

Off to the southeast, clouds gathered, towering up and looking like the anvil of some ancient world's god. A good squall was approaching.

Fat rain drops exploded small dust clouds in the dirt street as the T stopped at the BIS bank's ornate door. The wind picked up. We were inside the bank as the first large raindrops struck the bank windows. Izzy walked up to a desk where a pretty Negro secretary in a long sleeve black dress with a white ruffle collar sat behind a large Royal typewriter. Her fingers were so quick on the keys that it sounded like a long burst from a Thompson. Seeing Izzy, she stopped typing. She pressed a button on the desk intercom that lit a small red light below a grill. She spoke into it, *"Monsieur Redman sont ici, Monsieur Lambeur."*

She turned to Izzy, *"Un moment, s'il vous plait Monsieur Redman."*

From somewhere in the back of the bank a black suited man with a high-collar shirt appeared. He walked with a stiffness that only a broken back could have provided. As he shook Izzy's hand he bent slightly. They said something that I could not catch. Izzy turned to us, "Youse relax here."

Izzy carried his large oilskin bags as he accompanied the stiff-backed banker to his office. Red and I waited for Izzy while the rain smashed against the windows as if it was trying to break into the bank.

"Glad to be in here, not out on the Gulf."

"You ain't just bumping your gums."

In no time at all, Izzy emerged from the office clipping his bags closed. Rain continued to smash against the windows. It blurred the street into a watery blue-green as though we were looking through a shower curtain. The future was a blue-green blur as well.

***

Two days later, I picked up the telephone in the hotel to call Leroy to pick us up. We were going back to New York City on today's Silver Meteor. Red was in the bathroom shaving.

A woman answered. I asked for Leroy to drive us back to Miami to catch the Meteor, she replied. "So nuf', I be pickin' y'all up in hour."

Before I could reply, she hung up. As I hung up the phone, Red said, "You're looking like somethin' strange."

"We'll be picked up in an hour."

"So?"

"So it was a broad that answered, not Leroy."

"So what?"

Leroy's yellow DeSoto slid smoothly to a stop in front of the Carlyle's canopy. A Negro woman wearing a cap stepped out.

"You Mista Potter? Mista Pepper?"

"Yes, that's us."

"These be y'all bags?"

"Yes, mam."

She opened the door for us then loaded our bags into the DeSoto's trunk. Before getting in, she leaned on the door asking, "Y'all goin to Miami train nattrilly."

"Yes, we are taking the 2:10 Silver Meteor."

"All righty then."

She had the DeSoto away in a flash. As we drove, Red and I exchanged glances.

"Mam, excuse me, but we thought that Leroy would be driving…"

She cut me off, "Leroy a black man. Black man can't be near Deputy Dog."

"Deputy Dog? Who's that?"

"Deputy Clark ain't nothin' but a lynchin' racist. He kilt po' Reuben Stacy, strangled-hung and shot 'im. No way I be lettin' my boy be 'round Clark an' his like. I had Leroy join up with the Tuskegee Army Air Cor'. We seen y'all drivin' 'round with Clark in tow."

"That was business."

"Business, piss-ness. That mo-fo would kill a Negro fo' fun."

"We didn't know."

"You Yankee white folk don kno' nuttin 'bout the South and how us Negroes live. Y'all just thin' that we be happy as pigs in shit. In shit is what we be in. Mo-fo Jim Crow gotta' croak."

She went silent after that.

By 2:11, Red and I were on the Silver Meteor to Penn Station New York. We had made a pile of money.

Chapter 40
No Peace on the Docks

Sean

15 August 1945

A great day for democracy. – President Harry Truman

Germany had surrendered to the Allies on May 7th. We were ready for the military to turn our docks back now that the war was over. But the Mafia was in control of New York City now. We were free to operate as long as we paid them ten percent of our gross.

For weeks after the Kraut surrender, there had been a gloom that we would have to invade Japan. We had read the reports about Iwo Jima and Okinawa's fanatical Japanese defense. Our losses were 12,281 killed. Meanwhile, the Japanese lost over 110,000 soldiers and about 100,000 Japanese civilians. An invasion of the Japanese main islands was estimated to cause over 225,000 Americans killed and ten times that in Japanese deaths. All that was made unnecessary by the bombings of Hiroshima and Nagasaki.

It was a great feeling to stride the piers, glad-hand longshoremen and be in charge once again. As the song went, happy days are here again. I wore my Panama hat, blue seersucker suit with a crisp white shirt and a bright red tie for the occasion. As Liam and I met with the longshoremen on Pier 51, everyone was giddy as a schoolgirl at her first dance. More than a few men broke into a spontaneous jig. Others passed around hip flasks and slapped one another on the back. The end of the War was joyous.

I sensed an undercurrent that wasn't happy both on the pier and at home in Queens.

It was only a few days later that I learned of the unrest of the dock workers on the Westside. We were playing cards in the back of the Pier 51 union office.

As Liam shuffled the deck, he said, "The dues, vig, protection and sharking collections are all going fine. We've had no problem installing Lansky's jukeboxes in Westside ginmills. But the Army's way of running the docks means that it's gonna be hard to go back to doing shape ups."

"Why do you say that?"

"Some of the older guys remembered that you had scheduled crews for a short time before the War. Then you went back to shapeups. During the war we got no shapeup donations, so's shoremen had a few more silver dollars in their pockets. Dere'our troublemaker," Liam said tilting his head toward the window as a longshoreman walked past.

"Who's that?"

"Dengler, Peter Dengler. He lives just off Sheridan Square. Been trying to organize a union of his own, like the ones on the West Coast."

"He's one guy, so what?"

"So, so," Liam almost choked. "So, between Dengler and the stuff your lovely bridie was pulling, we got problems."

"Wait, first Dengler and now Mary Kate?"

"Yup, you know I told ja, youse wasn't in Florida a day before she shows up at the Varick office askin' 'bout collections. When you an' Red were in Florida, your bride was nosin' around, she even collected some vig."

"You never told me that!"

"Well, I'm tellin' ya now," Liam said.

"I'll put the kibosh on that. Tell me more about this guy Dengler."

Chapter 41
Suicide or Murder

Colleen

After my run-in with the Nazi Sympathizers at the Garden, Michael Francis Xavier Malloy became a regular at Dottie's. It didn't take an Einstein to figure it out. Malloy wasn't coming to Dottie's for the food, though he could pack away a steak with the best of them. Mike Malloy was sweet on me. So, even though he didn't want to have anything to do with Sean, he made my restaurant his favorite dinner spot. On most nights, I'd find him hanging out on one of the corner bar stools having a steak with mashed potatoes and a tall glass of Guinness.

My youth taught me to trust my own instincts and not to accept authority figures at face value. Cops in general were to be avoided. Usually, any coppers hanging around Dottie's meant they were looking for Sean to try to pin some crime on him. But Mike Malloy was different. Not only was he interested in me, he was most definitely not interested in Sean. Anytime Sean showed up, Malloy made a quick exit.

Michael Francis Xavier Malloy is a big guy. Standing over six feet tall he towers over me. When he arrives at Dottie's, he waits at the corner of the bar but doesn't sit until he sees me. He leans against the bar with big arms folded across his chest, one ankle causally crossed over the other. Once he sees me his face turns into a wide grin.

As I approach, he bows his head ever so slightly, "Good evening, Miss Callaghan."

Then he picks up his cap which has been resting on the bar stool next to him and he pulls out the stool for me to sit. It's become a ritual between us. I take the seat even if for just a few minutes. His blue eyes twinkle with amusement like he is thinking of some really funny joke. Tonight, he is wearing a white shirt and dark trousers. His leather jacket is draped over the back of his stool. While jamming his cap inside his jacket sleeve, a lock of sandy blonde hair falls onto his broad forehead. He has a nice face, a friendly face.

"Good evening, Michael, how are you this fine evening?"

We talk for a few minutes then I go back to work. As the evening progresses, I glance intermittently over to the corner of the bar. Most of the time I find him looking back at me smiling. It is disconcerting and comforting at the same time. I kind of like that he is there because I know he is there for me.

As Dottie's was closing down for the night, I took the bar stool next to him while I had my nightcap and awaited Sean's nightly visit. Michael told me about growing up in Woodside a suburb of Queens in a tiny tenement apartment. He had seven brothers and sisters who somehow all shared two bedrooms and one bathroom while his parents slept on a pull-out couch in the living room.

"I learned to eat fast. Otherwise, one of my darling brothers or sisters would steal the meat right off your plate," he laughed. "Actually, we all get along if you leave out fights over chocolate cake and baseball."

"You still are close even now?"

"Sure. We're family." He paused for a few seconds then said, "I guess that's why I know you love and support Sean. He's family."

"Yes, for a long time it was just me and Sean against the world. Then he helped me get this place. Well, I had help from a friend and her husband too." I looked away suddenly as my eyes filled with tears.

Mike Malloy didn't notice as he said, "Oh are they regulars here too? I'd like to meet them sometime."

Fleetingly, I wondered if he thought that my investors, Dotty and Alistair might be criminals. But I just said, "No. They don't come here. They died."

"How? I mean how did they die?"

"The police said it was suicide, but I don't buy it."

At that Mike Malloy raised an eyebrow. "Why don't you think the police were right?"

"Well, for one thing, my friend was supposed to meet me for lunch the next day. She was clearly happy about something and said she was excited to tell me, but we had to meet in person. Her husband was a Wall St. broker who lost a bundle of money in the crash, but his family was very wealthy. They were OK financially. So, I don't believe he was suicidal either. The police said he shot Dotty first then himself. I don't buy it. He adored her! No matter what he would never have killed her."

"It's hard to know what in a person's heart," he said wisely. "Her name was Dotty? I presume you named this place for her?"

"Yes, I did. We did. Sean and me."

We both turned toward the back of the restaurant as we could distinctly hear Sean's voice as he chatted with one of the staff in the kitchen. Mike Malloy stood, picking up his cap and jacket he said, "What was Dotty's last name?"

"MacMillian. He husband was Alistair MacMillian."

"I'm gonna look into this."

"Oh, Michael! Would you really?"

"Yeah. No promises. You might not like the outcome anyway. But I'll let you know what I find out."

Over the next couple of weeks, I had to bite my tongue to keep from asking him repeatedly if he had any news about Dotty and Alistair. His answer was always the same.

"You've got to be patient."

"That not my strong suit. I've never been good about waiting. It just makes me think things are hopeless."

"Hopeless? This is a cold case investigation. I reserve the word hopeless for a situation more dire!"

"Yes, but I've faced situations where I had to wait without knowing when or what would happen. My feelings at those times were just that. I'd try to hope for the best but believed in my heart it would be disaster. Hopelessness creeps in. It's just how my life has gone."

"This place, what you've accomplished here has been terrific! Hopelessness is for the defeated. You, Miss Colleen Callaghan are not a defeatist. I knew that the day I met you at that Nazi rally in the Garden."

I smiled at him. He really is a good guy even if he is a cop. He did not know my story. He did not know about Sean's and my childhood.

I said, "I don't know what you have to do to look into a cold case, but if I can help, I would like to. I am very good at figuring out puzzles. Really, I am!"

"You just might be able to help me. I have to do this research on my own time before or after my shift, so having another set of eyes working on this could make it go much quicker. I've been able to get a hold of all the necessary files concerning the MacMillians. As well as some other cases that looked similar. I'm thinking there may be a connection. My Sargent thinks I'm nuts doing this. But he also thinks I'm bucking for a Detective shield, so he let me sign out the files. Only thing is I can't let 'em out of my sight. So, if you're going to help, you have do it at my place."

We arranged to meet at ten in the morning at his Greenwich Village apartment. He lived over Marionetta's Italian restaurant on Greenwich Avenue. As I climbed the three flights of stairs to his apartment the aroma of simmering tomato sauce filled the air. He answered the door wearing his dark trousers and a white undershirt that displayed strong biceps and a trim waist.

"How do you live here and not be eating pasta every day! My stomach started rumbling as soon as I opened the downstairs door. And it's gotten louder every flight."

I entered the tiny apartment which is surprisingly neat and clean for a guy. It was a studio style place, all one room. Kitchen, living and bedroom all in one contiguous space. On a small kitchen table was a stack of files. A percolator was bubbling on a two-burner stovetop. Malloy took my coat and hat and placed them over the well-worn sofa.

"Did you have any trouble finding my place?"

When I shook my head no, he continued, "Let's get started then. I've made some coffee. It's kinda cop regulation. Going through files is boring as all hell so you gotta have lots of black coffee."

I laughed. "Can I have mine with milk and sugar?"

"You can have whatever you want."

Feeling the heat of a blush blooming on my cheeks, I said, "Right, let's get started."

"First, you need to read the actual police report and notes on the MacMillians. When we suspect murder, we write down everything we can, sketch the scene and include it in a file we call the Murder Book. Since the MacMillians was considered murder-suicide the notes are not as complete as they might have been for a straight up murder."

He pointed to a towering pile of papers on the floor. "However, all notes from those first on the scene are contained in a daily reports file which is in that mess of documents for the month and year that corresponds with their date of death."

We worked for several hours. I made my own set of notes in a school composition notebook. It was amazing, after spending just few hours in his apartment, I could no longer discern the smell of the Italian cooking downstairs. But my stomach was not as immune as my nose.

Mike Malloy, stood, stretched and said, "I'll be right back."

A few minutes later, he pushed open the apartment door with his foot carrying a steaming plate of spaghetti and meatballs. It smelled delicious! He handed me a napkin and fork and without a word we both dived in. I struggled trying to scoop up the long strands of spaghetti, but I noticed that Mike had a system for it. He would separate several strands and swirl them around his fork. I raised an eyebrow at this as he munched on the pasta.

Wiping his lips, he said, "Benefits of living above an Italian family restaurant. They have invited me in several times and taught me how to eat spaghetti without wearing it."

He placed his hand over mine and said, "Just grab a small bit to start."

Then leaning closer over me, he deftly twirled my hand holding the fork until I had a neat package of spaghetti contained on the tines. Still holding my hand he raised the fork to my lips. I took a bite. It was definitely better not wearing tomato sauce all over my face. Though I was acutely aware of how close he was to me. He returned to his seat and we resumed eating in silence. I needed a lot more practice to perform this twirling operation as expertly as he did, but I got a lot more food into my mouth and a lot less of it on my chin.

At three pm, he rose from the table. "I'm working evening shift for a pal of mine tonight, so we have to stop now. I gotta get into uniform and get going."

"I've got another hour and half before I need to get uptown to Dottie's. Can't I stay here and keep going through these files?"

He looked at me for a long moment thinking.

"I'm gonna change now."

He opened the closet extracted his uniform and took it to the small bathroom to change.

When he emerged dressed as a policeman, I recalled that day at the Garden when he helped me hand out coffee and sandwiches to the anti-Nazi protestors.

He put a key on the top of the paper I was reading. "Lock up when you leave. I'll get my key back at Dottie's tonight. I should be there about 12:30."

I worked on the files until quarter to 5 which meant that I needed to get uptown fast. I locked up and pocketed Mike's key. Dashing out onto Greenwich Avenue, I figured my best bet to get a cab was going to be on 7th Avenue. I was right, I waited only a minute or so before an open cab swung to the curb for me. I made it uptown by 5:20 not too late. My staff was all there well into the preparation for tonight's dinner service. There was still a lot to do so I had little time to think about the files we had gone through at Mike's apartment.

Around 11 pm, we started closing up. I grabbed my handbag and retrieved the composition notebook from within. Sipping an Irish Whiskey, I reviewed my notes.

1. Alistair and Dotty were found in a pool of blood by their driver.
2. Dotty had been shot in the right temple. Alistair was also shot in the right temple.
3. Bullet: 7.65mm caliber.
4. Weapon: Walther PP pistol.
5. Other cases where a Walther PP or a weapon with the same 7.65 caliber bullet had been used:
    a. 1929 shooting in Yorkville. Bund sympathizer Bruno Kruger shot and killed Ira Abramovich, the owner of Ira's Jewish Delicatessen. Tried, convicted, sent to Sing Sing prison for life. Weapon was submitted into evidence. Question: what happened to the weapon?
    b. 1930 shooting with a 7.65 caliber in the alley behind Billy's Castle a speakeasy in Jersey City. Victim was the owner of the gin joint. He was seriously wounded but survived, stating he did not know his shooter. No weapon recovered.
    c. Date questionable – notes are difficult to read. Probably around 1929-1930. Murdered victim's name illegible. 7.65 caliber bullet retrieved from the wound in his right temple. No weapon recovered.

I sipped my drink, that feeling of hopelessness was descending again. All those hours and I only found three cases that had the same caliber bullet. For all I know, that could have come from any number of guns other than a Walther PP. One case, I could hardly read the notes. The scribbling was horrendous, and it had been written in pencil. The pencil lead was badly faded. But at least I could read the caliber and that the wound was similar, in the right temple.

I glanced at my watch; it was almost midnight. Sean wasn't here yet. Harold the bartender freshened my drink. There was something my brain was trying to remember, there was something I was missing. I'd have to go through those files again before starting a new pile of documents. The right temple. The right temple.

Then all at once I had it. The right temple was the wrong temple! I clearly remember Alistair going through the list of things I needed to prepare to open a restaurant. We were sitting at the MacMillians' dining room table. Alistair was at the head of the table. Dotty on his right. Me on his left.

He held his fountain pen aloft as he said, "It's most important to have the right location. Location, location, location! You can renovate, you can change the look of a place. You can cook the best food. But you cannot change the location. You must find one that is surrounded by a community that can afford to eat out even in tough economic times."

As he said all this, he was writing on the notepad in that beautiful handwriting of his, *Location, location, location* using his left hand. Alistair was left-handed! I remember because the nuns at St. Joseph's used to hit the kids' hands that were lefties. "They'd say use your right hand you devil! The left hand is made to do the work of Satan!"

I'm no expert. But it seems to me that if you are a lefty, shooting yourself in the right temple would be pretty darn awkward.

When Mike Malloy arrived, I excitedly said, "I was right! It wasn't suicide. I have proof. Alistair' MacMillian was left-handed. He couldn't have shot himself in the right temple!"

"That is good. But it is not definitive. He could have been ambidextrous; you know capable of using both hands."

"I guess, but as I think about it, I never saw Alistair use his right hand for much of anything. So, I don't think he was ambidextrous."

"Mike Malloy looked over my notes. Tomorrow, let start with these cases. I have more in-depth files that might yield some more answers. Looks like you are pretty darn good at puzzles!"

At that moment Sean stepped through the kitchen's swinging door.

"Still here, Mikey?"

Mike Malloy obviously thought Sean was addressing him. He started to push back his bar stool to stand and confront Sean. I put a hand on his arm to stop him.

"He means me not you." Turning to Sean, I said, "Yes, it was a long night here Sean."

Mike Malloy looked at me quizzically, he whispered, "Mikey?"

"That's Sean's nickname for me," I replied. I turned then remembered Mike Malloy's key so pulling it from my trouser pocket, I handed it to him. "See you tomorrow."

"Good night, Colleen," he said as he pulled on his jacket. He placed his cap on his head and tipping it ever so slightly at Sean, Mike Malloy made a quick exit.

Sean took possession of Malloy's vacant bar stool. "What's that all about? I don't like you seeing that guy."

"It's not like that."

"OK, I'll bite. What's it like, Mikey?"

"He's a friend and he is looking into Dotty and Alistair's murder."

"Murder? I thought it was suicide. And believe me, that cop wants to be more than a pal."

Sean was concerned with me investigating Dotty's death. He didn't explain why but I knew it was more than keeping me from fraternizing with the enemy wearing a policeman's uniform. But I was not going to be deterred.

The rest of the files at Mike Malloy's place yielded nothing more than lots of questions. But going through all these documents that recounted murder after murder it got me thinking. Each case report had a different reason for the violence. Sometimes it was just plain avarice. The shooter wanted the victims' money. In several cases, jealousy was the precipitating factor. Just like so many detective stories, *cherchez la femme*. Find the woman. She cheats and he kills her. He suspects she cheats, and he kills her and her presumed paramour. He cheats and she kills the other woman. He cheats and she shoots him. Then of course there was the gang killings. It was mind boggling. But it occurred to me if we were going to move off the dime, we needed to start looking in another direction. We needed to understand the motive. Why would anyone want to kill Alistair and Dotty MacMillian?

Mike Malloy agreed that we should concentrate on finding a motive. We began going through files that had similar head wounds despite the caliber bullet used. Quite by accident, I was reading through an arresting officer's notes on arrest of a man suspected of murdering an Irish guy in Brooklyn in 1932.

"Mike, listen to these notes, this cop took considerable notes during his interview of the suspect."

Thanks for the cup of joe. Yeah so, it's like we're sittin' here like a couple of Wall Street swells. "Course, most of em blew their brains out when the market crashed. And your questioning me? Those Wall Streeters steal more in a day than any boyo gets in a year." Cop noted his own question, "Are you confessing to robbery too?"

"Whatsamatter with ya? We just having coffee. But I'm right ya know. Those bigshots got what's coming to 'em. Shootin their brains out." The cop noted that his suspect gestured with his hand like a gun to the temple. "Would have been easy to snuff a few of em out by blowing their brains out for em. So many did it themselves you know. Yeah, it was real easy in those days."

The suspect's name was Jimmy Byrne. He was released for lack of evidence.

The next afternoon, I went to the New York Public Library to see if I could find Jimmy Byrne in any news articles.

Mike Malloy was back on day shift so we could only do research at his apartment on his days off. Malloy was adamant. He would not permit me to go through the files without him anymore and I could not take any of them home with me. So, progress had slowed down drastically.

Apparently, his Sargent warned him that keeping the files at his place was risky, someone might gain access to them there. If he only knew! He wanted him to bring the files back and soon.

I entered one of the reading rooms and asked for copies of the New York Times from 1930-1938.

"That's a long time frame," the librarian remarked. "All of those files are on microfiche."

Once she gave me access, I settled down for a long read. I went through page after page looking for a reference to Jimmy Byrne. I got pretty quick at scanning the pages. If the headlines of any articles screamed about violence or robbery I focused in. It took three consecutive days of searching the microfiche files. Finally, I saw a name that jumped out at me. It was an article on 18 December 1931 about Legs Diamond. I recalled Sean telling me he had a few run-ins with Jack "Legs" Diamond. So, I scanned the text. The name, Johnny Byrne jumped out at me. He was a known associate of Diamonds who died during a bootleg heist in Vermont. Could be a coincidence, but if Johnny had a brother named Jimmy, I could be onto something.

As I took a cab uptown to Dottie's that afternoon I was struck by a memory. Sean had come to see me at closing time after a trip up north. I remembered that he was limping. He told me he got a little frostbite but that it was treated, and he was totally OK. He said he met a great gal; I think Debbie was her name. "But it won't work out," he said. "She lives in the country and I'm a city boy. In fact, that's what she called me. City Boy." Typical of Sean, he gave me just enough information to see he was a bit heart-broken but refused to dwell on it. Even so, I connected the timing of Sean's frost bite and the girl in the country with the news article about Johnny Byrne, pal of Diamond, killed in Vermont.

When Sean arrived at Dottie's that night, I asked him if he knew Johnny Byrne.

"What's this about, Mikey?"

I explained about the cop's interview and my research at the library. Sean sipped his drink then turned to face me.

"I did have a run in with Diamond a while back. I recall he had a boyo named Johnny. But I never knew his last name."

I was excited. I was on to something I could feel it.

"Listen Mikey. Diamond is dead but there is a lot of bad blood out there between rival gangs. I don't want you lookin' into this anymore. It's too dangerous."

"But Sean, what if this Jimmy Byrne is Johnny's brother? What if he killed Alistair and Dotty? Don't you want to know? Don't you want to know for sure it wasn't suicide?"

"I do! But I also don't want you nosing into something that could get you hurt." Sean took a big swallow of his scotch. "But I'll look into this for you."

I put my arms around his neck and kissed his cheek. "Oh Sean, thank you!"

In typical Sean fashion, he got answers a whole lot faster than the New York City Police Department. When Sean asked, he was very persuasive.

Three nights later, I was sitting at the bar talking with Mike Malloy when Sean strode through the kitchen door.

He walked straight over to Mike and said, "We've never been properly introduced."

He extended his hand and the two men shook.

"You and my sister have been looking into our friends' deaths. I've got some info that will end this." He looked at me, "Mikey I told you I want you to stay out of this poking around. It's dangerous." Turning to Mike Malloy he said, "I expect the cops can do their own investigating without the help of my Sis."

"Her safety is my concern too. I've made sure no one knew about Colleen's involvement in this case review."

"I appreciate that, but I think once I tell you two the info I've got, well I think you'll both be done with this."

Sean proceeded to tell us that Jimmy Byrne was indeed Johnny's brother. He erroneously though that Sean had something to do with Johnny Byrne's death.

"Which I did not. I never touched the guy."

Apparently, Jimmy Byrne followed Sean and Alistair when they pulled the permits for construction of Dottie's.

"This boyo thought that Dottie's was gonna to be a speakeasy that I was gonna run and he wanted to exact revenge. But it took this goon a long time to get his courage up. He saw me meet with Alistair after Dottie's took off. This son of a bitch followed us again and saw me hand Alistair an envelope of cash. I was paying Alistair back most of the money he lent us to get started. Somehow, he figured that I was paying Alistair to do some 'work' for me and that by bumping off Alistair it would screw me up. Dotty was just collateral damage. He confessed this all to me about an hour ago." Sean took my hand. "I'm sorry Mikey. Even though I didn't do any of this it happened because of me. I'm so sorry."

Tears flooded my eyes and I pulled Sean into a tight embrace. "I'm sorry too. It's not your fault, Sean. You didn't know. You couldn't have done anything to stop this."

Mike Malloy stood, "I think I need to go make an arrest."

"Sorry, Mike. That's not gonna happen. See, this guy took off. We lost him. I don't know where he is now."

Michael Malloy and Sean stared at each other for a long moment.

Pursing his lips, Michael Malloy said softly, "Hmm. I see."

A few seconds passed then, he said, "Alright we put out an APB on him and see if we can locate him. Bring him to justice."

Turning to me, Malloy said, "'Night Colleen."

After Malloy left us, Sean went around the bar and poured us some Irish Whiskey. He sat down next to me and touched my arm.

"There more I've got to tell ya."

"Sean, did you, did you hurt that Jimmy Byrne?"

Brushing my question aside, Sean said, "It's not that. I found out more information. This guy wanted to hurt you and your husband Jim Baker too. Because of me."

"What? My Jim?"

"Byrne found that one of Jim's poker pals was behind on his payments to a Mob loan shark. Byrne paid off the loan shark for him in return for him beating your Jim to death."

"Oh my God!"

"He was gonna come after you too. But his gang boss got wind of this. And he was told in no uncertain terms to lay off me and my family or he'd end up in a war with me that he couldn't win." Sean touched my cheek. "I'm sorry, Mikey all this pain. It's because of me."

"No Sean. It because evil men do evil things. You did not kill Jim. You did not kill Dotty and Alistair. You are not evil."

I cried on his shoulder for my Jim. I cried for Dotty and Alistair. And I cried for Sean. Since Dotty and Alistair and my Jim died all within months of each other I should have drawn a connection. But I had my loss of Jim locked away in a compartment of my heart and that was that.

Later that night as I got into bed, I remembered a passage from Robert Louis Stevenson:

In each of us, two natures are at war-the good and the evil. All our lives the fight goes on between them, and one of them must conquer. But in our own hands lies the power to choose – what we want to be, we are.

Sean and I have had to make tough choices all our lives. People think Sean is bad because they see him in only one light, the tough Westside dock boss. But I know the truth about him. I know his heart. Sean is good. We are what we are.

Chapter 42
Dengler

Sean
1946

"Some guys only need their knuckles rapped, some needed their ears boxed but one or two required a little extra to bring them back in line. Of course, there were some who just would not learn. I expected no trouble getting the piers back to the way it was before the War," I said.

"Yeah, it wasn't as if we had let things go," Liam replied. "Even when youse was up river or in Florida, you gave orders through me. You could trust that they were carried out."

"So now guys are shedding their uniforms for canvas pants, flannels and picking up cargo hooks again, it should be back to the old ways. It's the clowns who got some ideas from the west coast docks union organizers that make trouble."

Red said, "Now, we are 'showing respect' to the Italians like we said in Florida. It's a fucking business expense for Christ's sake. Joe Ryan, the national president of the International Longshoremen Union don't want no trouble with the Mob."

"We can't afford smart alecks taking up the ideas of the west coast dockworkers. So, we break a few heads. But I'm tellin' ya Sean, one guy is a real problem, this guy Dengler. He started on the docks after getting injured at Great Lakes Naval Training Center. A Section 8 declared him unfit for further military service. He gets a job on the docks. He goes along with the military scheduling longshoremen, no shape-up. Longshoremen didn't have to show respect to the dock boss. Without shape-ups there was plenty of overtime so guys like Dengler made some extra folding green. Plenty of work, the War had ships loading day and night."

"It's not so now. Fewer ships," Red said. "Fewer cargos to load or unload. We re-started the shape up. That don't sit well with guys like Dengler."

In the 14th Street union office, we were counting the day's shape up money as Liam continued, "Dengler is a real wisenheimer. I hoid the somabitch has been talking up a new union, not ILA but a union that teams up the west coast union under the American Federation of Labor. An AFL organizer is nosing around. The AFL wants union seniority so they can schedule dock workers, not shape-ups. It's the AFL against our ILA. Right?"

I said, "Oh yeah, I remember reading about a strike when I was in the slammer. The strike went from Seattle, Portland, Oakland, San Francisco to every other west coast port. The four-day strike in San Francisco was called 'Bloody Thursday' when a bunch of strikers were shot gunned by the cops."

"Yeah, but the west coast union guy, Harry Bridges stopped doing shape-ups hiring longshoremen based on union seniority. Then he was made the West Coast Director for the Congress of Industrial Organizations, you know the CIO."

"But Bridges is a Red. The CIO don't like commies, neither does the government. So, now he covers just the California ports," I pointed out.

"How do you like that! Harry Bridges gets re-elected the West Coast Director tho' he a commie," Red said.

"Hey! There's an ace idea!" I chortled. "Let's talk up Dengler as a communist agitator. Look, this hiring hall bullshit of his has to stop now. It's cuttin' our money and control."

"Mabee we should see if we can do like Lansky. Talk to Dengler. Then if he don't listen…" Liam smiled.

Liam arranged a meet with Dengler at Marie's Crisis Café, a boy-bar just a few steps from Dengler's third floor apartment off Sheridan Square. I wanted Dengler to know that we knew where he lived. I didn't care if he lived or took a long walk on a short pier. What he said tonight would decide.

Marie's Crisis Café was a dimly lit smoky piano bar favored by cabaret types and homosexuals who were theatrical. The Italians ran several gay bars around the city. The dagos paid the cops not to revoke the liquor license of joints. The Club 82 on East 4th Street was the Copacabana for homosexuals. With Wedgewood white and blue walls and tuxedoed waiters, the shows were fantastic. The Hollywood famous like Greta Garbo and Judy Garland were frequently seen at Club 82 shows. A classy joint. In the West Village, the

Stonewall was the opposite, a gay dive bar. Still, the Mob paid the NYPD 6th Precinct about a grand a month to keep the gay bars open despite raids.

We sat well back from the piano, in a banquette with Red in the middle and me on the right. That would free up my right hand. Liam sat on a chair, leaving room next to Red for Dengler. The boy on the piano was hitting a rag-time tune. I nursed my whiskey.

Liam squirmed uncomfortably in this joint. Red was unconcerned by the clientele. He was more concerned about ghosts that haunt the joint. Me, I was watching the door with my cocked .45 resting on my thigh. The safety was off. Ghosts weren't the problem.

"You know that Thomas Paine, the guy who wrote the pamphlets 'The American Crisis' died upstairs? You remember, *these are the times that try men's souls.* The guy wrote stuff that fired up the American Revolution. He haunts this joint," Red said stabbing out his cigarette into an ashtray.

"Queers and ghosts, maybe queer-ghosts! I'm leavin'!" Liam said pushing his chair back.

"Relax," I said tugging his sleeve and trying not to smile.

"Did you know that Paine's ghost is looking for his bones?" Red continued undeterred. "He was buried in New Rochelle but a guy dug him up for reburial in England. Except, then Paine's bones disappeared."

"Will you stop with all the fookin' ghost shite."

Liam was already on his feet. Again, I tugged him back.

"Ghosts can't harm us. They're like cigarette smoke. Liam, the ghost is probably just looking for his final resting place, not for you."

Slowly, Liam settled back into his chair to light up another Lucky Strike. His thick glasses obscured his eyes but I knew they were darting around the smoky room.

"Let's stay focused. Maybe the ghost of Thomas Paine can scare Dengler. In any case, let's not let a ghost gum up the works."

Liam nodded, then pointing with his chin, said one word, "Dengler."

I turned. I never met Dengler, so I didn't know which of the two men walking to our booth was him. One was taking off his brown fedora uncovering pomaded brown hair. He was of medium height with a well-fed belly. His suit was as cheap as a cardboard suitcase. The other guy was dressed in a brown double-breasted topcoat. He kept his hat on even when he doffed his topcoat and draped it over his right arm. He was slimmer and taller with a suit that was a reject from Rodgers Pete. Which was Dengler?

Dengler didn't have my problem. He looked straight at me.

"You must be Callaghan." The well fed Dengler said without offering his hand.

He didn't call me 'Mr. Callaghan', just Callaghan. Not a good start. His suit jacket looked like its buttons were about to pop off. As if he knew what I was thinking, he unbuttoned the jacket to relieve the pressure. Since he didn't reach for a rod under the suit jacket, I thumbed the .45s safety on. Casually, I eased the pistol under my suit jacket back into my waistband.

Politely, I stood. With my .45 pressing into the small of my back, my left waved the two into the banquette next to Red. A waiter appeared as the two sat, I asked, "What are you two gents havin'?"

Hat man said, "Beer."

Dengler without taking his eyes off me, said, "Scotch and soda." The waiter left.

They sat. We sat. I used the joint's matchbook to light up my Camel cigarette. The kid on the piano tried crooning like Crosby while his fingers danced on the keys. He did a good job. Except, we weren't here for the song or music.

"I guess that going upriver can make you appreciate a gay bar," Dengler said. Red stiffened but I put my hand on his arm.

"Funny, you're a funny guy Mister Dengler." I didn't take his sucker punch. "But we are serious people. We are here to discuss serious things." I had paid the maître d' a sawbuck to keep the nearby tables free. You never know who could be listening or just curious.

The five of us sat in silence until drinks were placed on the table. Neither Dengler nor his friend touched a glass. Stabbing out the Camel for emphasis, I said over the piano music, "Let's get this started, I asked you and your, your friend…"

"Lou Foppiano…" the man in the hat said.

"You and Mr. Foppiano here to iron out some misunderstandings."

"What misunderstandings?" Dengler said nonplussed.

"Some of the boys don't like the way you've been calling meetings. Making the boys unhappy…" Liam said.

"Some like my meetings. Some like what I have to say."

"Mebee, you talk too much."

I interrupted, "Listen Mr. Dengler, I said that you're a good fellow. You shouldn't be harmed."

With that Dengler turned from Liam to me. "Don't threaten me, Callaghan. I don't scare."

"Look Mr. Dengler," I continued. "Look at it this way, you can make some dough, buy yourself a decent suit, get your wife nice things but only if you cooperate."

"Either the hiring of workers is democratic or it's not. The west coast uses union seniority for hiring and open public elections. The ILA here doesn't have hiring halls or open elections. You use shape-ups and the devil only knows how you became the local's president."

"Sorry you think that way." I stood, dropped a sawbuck on the table. Liam, Red and I walked out.

A night later, somebody broke Foppiano's knees with an iron bar as he walked down Commerce Street toward Bedford. The next day it was Dengler's turn. Someone in a passing car shot Dengler in the thigh. Word on the docks was that his wife drove him to New Jersey where she knew a doctor who wouldn't talk to the coppers because he performed abortions. If he had gone to St. Vincent's Hospital on West 11th, the coppers would have made the doc wait to remove the bullet until they grilled him. O'Boyle at the 6th Precinct would let him bleed until he was dizzy enough to get a charge on me.

It was no surprise that Detective O'Boyle barged into the 14th Street ILU Local without knocking. Liam and the boys had finished with the morning's collections, I had just spun the safe's dial as the door opened. O'Boyle had two blue-woolen uniforms at each shoulder.

"Callaghan where were you last night around 7 pm?"

"Good mornin' detective, and to what do we owe the pleasure of your visit?"

"Tell me where you were last night Callaghan." Still keeping his baby-blues on me, he said to the uniforms, "Toss the place. Search these sons-of-bitches too."

O'Boyle had walked within inches from my face. Looking into that big fat face and his icy cold steel eyes, I was suddenly reminded of Mother Superior.

"I was in the Homestead Steakhouse having one of their well-marbled tee-bones."

"Yeah? When ja' leave?"

"Mebbe 10 or 11. Do you have a reason to come here to interrupt union business?"

In reply, he hawked up some phlegm and spat. Padric's trouser leg was the beneficiary. Padric leapt to his feet, his face on fire, his fists ready. One of the uniforms sunk his right deep into Padric's breadbasket. Padric collapsed retching.

"Take a look around, boys, let's find the pistol."

"Do you have a search warrant, Detective?"

"I don' need no fucking warrant, Callaghan. I got a gold badge that says I can do whatever I need to, to send you and your scum upriver. Hopefully for a long stay or better yet, the hot seat. You know 'Old Sparky'. Old Sparky took care for Lepke Buchalter. I'd like to see it fry your ass good."

They tossed the joint, made a mess, found squat.

We had our irons in the drop ceiling. Available if we needed them but not available for the coppers to haul us in on a Sullivan Law rap.

To make things clear, Liam and I walked each pier, 40 to 51. As we walked each pier, guys would put down their cargo hooks and line up. At each pier, the old timers doffed their caps and came to shake hands. By the end of the day, I needed to get off my feet, my dogs were barking. Rather than the office on 14th and 8 Ave, the Viaduct Bar was closer, a great joint to put your feet up and have a few. We had made our point with the rank and file. It was a good day.

Things went back to the old ways. Pier bosses made money and kicked back to us. The haulers paid to make sure that loads didn't 'fall off' their trucks. Union dues rolled in. Trucking owners paid to have their tailgates closed on a full load. We made loans to longshoremen who hadn't made the shapeup and sold numbers to the chumps.

I kept up jukebox collections for Meyer Lansky then made personal deliveries to the 385 Local office at Fulton Fish Market. Even with Joey Socks upriver everything was smooth on the lower East Side docks. One of Joey's fishing boats would deliver the cash to wherever Lansky wanted. I wanted the West Side docks as quiet as the East Side but a few nights later trouble started again.

With the War over, Ian was discharged from the Navy but not without making some good Wall Street connections. In no time, he was with a big law firm located on Moore Street between Pearl and Water Streets. He and Mikey invited me to a hoity-toity party at Dottie's. I was glad that I wore my $300 suit. That was chump-change compared to what I spent on Mary Kate's Bonwit Teller chic cocktail dress. Naturally, the dress required some baubles from Harry Winston to glitter from her neck, ears, wrist and fingers. She was the reincarnation of Carole Lombard but without the ditz.

The sign on the door read, 'Sorry, Dottie's is closed tonight for a private party/ Reopen tomorrow at 6 pm'. Mary Kate and I weren't ten steps from the coat check before she attracted a half dozen men eager to light her cigarette or get her champagne. I let her dangle her bait as I picked up my scotch. As I approached Mary Kate, her new-found beaus made themselves scarce. I had her take my arm for the evening.

Mary Kate and I were introduced to Ian's fellow lawyers before a pair of Navy admirals moved in on us like Halsey did on Manila. Judging by the aim of their eyes, they decided that they needed to get some cleavage as an appetizer.

"Mr. Callaghan, you must introduce me to this beautiful creature."

"Admiral Andrews, may I present my wife, Mary Kate Callaghan."

That raised an eyebrow, a conspirator's grin and an elbow in my ribs from Rear Admiral Andrews. He had been Haffenden and Treglia's boss when we swept the docks free of the Nazis. I bet that he thought that I had some dumbbell blonde showgirl on my arm.

"I am so pleased to meet you Mrs. Callaghan." He beamed with his eyes on the powdered hills of Mary Kate's bosom. "So, pleased indeed." Then turning to me. "May I borrow your lovey wife to introduce her to my staff of the 3rd District? They must learn to mingle."

Before I could reply, he had Mary Kate's hand on his arm. She gave me a butterfly's kiss on the cheek, turned and strode off like a harbor tugboat guiding a battleship. The crowd closed behind Mary Kate and Admiral Andrews just as Ian appeared at my elbow.

"Do you know the Admiral?"

"I may have met him once, you know, after the Normandie fire on the West Side. I did a few favors for him. Anyway, I am happy that you survived the North Atlantic to use your Fordham Law education."

Mary Kate's laugh could be heard over the cacophonous din. Her laugh was followed by a roar from the Navy boys. She had them enthralled. She was probably telling a story that only a sailor would like, peppered with some salty words. The Admiral guffawed with both hands on his thighs. What was she telling them?

"Mary Kate has her own fraternity going over there," Ian said.

"Apparently so," I replied then switched the topic. "How are you fixed Ian? Need any cash? Anything?"

"Sean Callaghan where have you been?"

I was startled by Mikey's voice at my side. I think I jumped.

"Cripes Mikey one day I'll have a heart attack with you sneaking up on me."

"I should find a *pied a terre* for you, like the great apartment I found for Ian on 63rd off Lex. Maybe I'd see you more often."

"63rd and Lex is a great address."

"You should see it," Ian said. "Colleen helped decorate. After living like a monk on a destroyer, it's luxurious."

"Sure, first chance I get."

"Sean, you have circles around your eyes and you look on edge. Are you okay?" Mikey said, as I replied with a shrug. "You really can relax here, you're safe. I mean, I have half of the mayor's office here, the Navy and even some police that I trust. As a matter of fact, there's Mary Stanley, the best NYPD detective."

"Cripes, what's this world coming to? A broad who's a detective!"

"Get with the times Sean, the times are changing. Soon there'll be women who will be mayors, governors, doctors and someday, President. Why I remember that Heidi Rupp would talk about women curing polio or at least stopping polio…"

Mikey must have seen my face. I didn't have a poker face when it came to Heidi. I caught myself tearing up. I changed the subject.

"Ian, here had a broad in his law class that became a DA. She even got Charlie Luciano sent upriver to that 'Siberia', Dannamora."

"That 'broad' was Eunice Carter, she's no 'broad.' Eunice Carter found the crucial evidence that gave Dewey his conviction of Luciano." Ian took a breath. "I cannot believe that now Dewey is the New York governor, and he is going to free Luciano. That may come back to haunt him if he ever decides to run for President." He took a sip of his scotch. "Luciano is rumored to have helped Patton destroy the Krauts in Sicily. Still, the government doesn't like

Luciano. As a matter of fact, my law firm heard that Luciano is to be deported to Sicily soon."

"Ain't that a kick in the head," I said. Then seeing and hearing the raucous sailors around Mary Kate, I excused myself, "I have to save my wife from all those sharks in blue."

"Once they're on dry land, sailors of any rank only want two things, one is booze," Ian said, as Mikey smiled.

"You round up your blonde bombshell, I'll find Liam he wants to see my new apartment," Ian said.

I was able to get Mary Kate home by one. She was absolutely thrilled at being the object of attention by so many men. I was tying the knot on my silk pajama bottoms when I heard a sexy husky voice.

"Hey sailor. Looking for a date?"

There she was outlined by the bathroom light one arm high on the doorframe and the other on her hip. Her negligee barely made it to her knees. Still wearing her stilettos, the negligee outlined her hourglass shape. Sinuously, she slowly cat walked. With each step, the strap of her negligee slipped, revealing more and more until she was only an inch away. She pulled on the cord of my silk bottoms undoing my knot. Her warm hand found me.

"Well, well, sailor, you ARE happy to see me."

She pushed me back until I met the bed. Then with a firm push, I was on my back. She slowly let the negligee slip completely from her shoulders. With her right holding me she straddled my hips easing me inside. She started slowly but soon lost control. She was a jungle cat with her prey. She leaned back, both hands on my knees bracing her undulating hips. Her eyes were closed, her head back. Suddenly, she was over me whipping her hair across my face. Her breathing was ragged.

"Fuck me harder!"

"Harder! I need that cock deep!"

With both hands on her hips I met her every thrust as she screamed to a crescendo.

"Yes! Yes! YES!"

We went at it a second time with me on top, then a third with her on her knees. We were sweating, spent and exhausted. I was done for the night. The night wasn't over for me. The bedside phone rang.

"Hello," Mary Kate answered. "Unha. Unha, OK, I'll put him on."

She dropped the phone on my chest as she rolled over. "It's for you."

"Mr. Callaghan, this is New York Hospital calling." The voice on the phone said. "There's been an accident that injured your brother."

"My brother?" I struggled to clear my head of sex, scotch and fatigue. "What happened? Is he alive?"

"Somebody shot a man he was with." The voice on the phone said. "He's a little banged up a bit. He'll be alright."

"I'll be right there. It's New York Hospital on York Avenue, right? OK. Thanks."

Chapter 43
Dorian's Red Hand

Sean

A small fleet of NYPD black-and-whites jammed the Emergency Room entrance. Inside, I found Ian fully dressed, his shirt front bloody, his right arm in a sling. His suit jacket was draped over his shoulders. His lower lip was red, swollen, it looked like he took one on the kisser from Sugar Ray. Across from him, there was a number of uniform police and two obvious detectives milling around a stretcher. I could only see the bottom of the injured man's shoes.

"Who's that?" I asked.

"Liam. He got shot but he'll live. Grazed in the head and his side. Nothing serious. It wasn't a German 88 mm or a Messerschmitt machine gun that can tear a guy apart. I tell you, the guy who shot us is a lousy shot."

"Yeah, now tell me what the hell happened?"

"After the party, Liam and I went to Dorian's Red Hand for a nightcap. When we left Dorian's, we walking to Liam's car when this guy pops out of an alley shooting."

"Liam pushed me to the pavement. Liam and the guy exchanged a few shots. I don't think Liam hit him even once. But he made the guy take off. Liam saved me by pushing me to the pavement. According to the ER physician, I fractured my forearm breaking my fall. I don't know how I split my lip."

"What did the guy look like?"

"Brown suit and hat, about 5 foot 8 with a good sized gut. He ran with a limp. I didn't get a good look at his face. All I could see was the revolver barrel."

"What did Liam do with his gun?"

"He had me throw it down a storm drain on the corner."

"Don't say nothin' to the cops. Nothing."

"You mean 'don't say anything'." Ian smiled causing his lip began to bleed again. "I am a lawyer, if you remember."

"I remember," I said.

Ian's tongue licked at the blood on his lip.

"I'll have someone else bleed real soon," I muttered to myself.

The doctor at the New York Hospital ER patched Liam up, released him only to be taken to 19th Precinct on East 67th Street. I called Joel Friedman, my lawyer who had one of his associates go to the 19th. The associate learned that the cops had nothing to hold Liam on, so he was released. I sent Padric and Eddie Hammer one of the Westside crew to pick him up. Evidently, Liam didn't wait at the 19th. But Padric knew where to look for him. Liam was having a liquid breakfast at the Subway Inn Bar & Grill across the street from Bloomingdales.

At my house, Elizabeth was still fussing over Ian, playing nurse. I was pouring some scotch into my black coffee when Liam and Padric knocked on the door. Eddie stayed in the car to keep an eye on the street. Elizabeth immediately homed in on her new 'patient'. Evidently, according to her, Liam had other wounds that the ER docs missed. As Elizabeth went to find mercurome and Band-Aids, I called Liam and Padric into the sitting room for a private talk.

"Liam, you and Padric follow Dengler around. Day and night. I want to know where he is and what he's doing at all times. I want to know if he buys Chiclets or Bazooka gum at the corner newsstand."

"Boss who's gonna collect the vig an' the shape up money?" Padric asked.

"Don't worry, I'll get it covered."

"Sean, I could use a few winks," Liam said.

"Sure, why don't you take forty right here on the couch."

Elizabeth appeared in the door to the sitting room looking for her new patient. She had this serious look on her face.

"I put Uncle Ian to rest in the guest bedroom," she announced.

"Elizabeth, get a blanket and a pillow for Uncle Liam, would ja? He'll get some sleep here on the couch."

"Sure thing, Dad. Right after I take care of these scrapes and scratches before they become infected," Elizabeth said her ponytail bobbing as she trotted off.

With Elizabeth out of the room, I said, "In the meantime, Padric track down Dengler. Let him see ya, make him nervous. Got it?"

"Sure, thing Boss, right away."

Chapter 44
The Shepherd's Pie

Sean
6 January 1947

President Harry S. Truman makes the first State of the Union speech on television

A war is bad for business. Dengler was making noise on the pier that had to stop. Cripes, if the ILU heard about him hiring longshoremen by union seniority instead of the shapeup then my position could be in jeopardy too.

Dengler was a smart fox. He enlisted the Catholic Workers Union and a loudmouth priest from Holy Cross Church on 42nd Street. Dengler held "union" meetings in the church basement. Padric and a few boys tracked some of the attendees down to remind them whose union local they belong to. That settled things for a week or two until Dengler or the priest found a newspaper reporter. The reporter listened to Dengler and his fellow rats using their bullshit to pad his stories. That set the docks afire and woke up the sleeping bears at the DA's office. Now, because of the sensational news stories, the Manhattan DA's office began to look to the Westside and the docks. This had to stop.

Then, I thought we had caught a break.

Liam called me at the office from a street phone booth in Hell's Kitchen. Dengler had just entered the Landmark Tavern on 11th Avenue. He had been meeting with the crew on pier 86. Cripes, this rebellion was spreading. In less than a minute, I was in my Studebaker with Padric at the wheel.

We entered the Landmark by the West 46th Street side door. The place was jumping. That was both good and bad. The three of us found Dengler alone in

357

a booth wolfing down a shepherd's pie. He must have been pretty confident, a real wisenheimer.

Taking a spoon out of his mouth, he said, "Sit."

"Naw, we'll stand. This won't take long."

Dengler eyed me. He must have made some signal as two lugs in long black coats and porkpie hats slid up to the booth at Dengler's shoulder. He took a shovel-full of shepherd's before sitting back with his left hand draped on the booth's plush side.

He wiped his mouth.

"I've been expecting you, you cockeyed bastard."

I let it slide.

"You're as subtle as a fart in submarine."

"Dengler, you have to stop this shite. It's causing problems up and down the Westside."

"That's your problem Callaghan, you can't see that times are changing, you're old hat. The rank and file want a living wage, regular hours, fair hiring practices..."

"Yeah, yeah, what if I said that I'd cut you in. Say 30% of the shapeup and whatever falls off a truck?"

"I'd say, you're pissing into the wind. Now fuck off!"

I moved so fast that the two strong arms didn't have time to dig into their coats for their irons. I smashed the pie bowl into Dengler's face. Hard. The bar had grown quiet as we talked. Now you could hear a pin drop.

"You'd better consider my offer. You won't get a second one."

We backed away, only turning as we found the side door. Outside Padric took the Ithaca pump shotgun from under his topcoat before opening the Studebaker door and getting in the back. As I climbed in behind the wheel, Liam still faced the Landmark's door.

"Get in," I said leaning over to push the door open.

As I started the Studebaker, I said to no one in particular, "That went well."

Chapter 45
A Dusting of Flour

Colleen
Two Days Later

As soon as my head hit my pillow, I was sound asleep. It had been a long day and several patrons lingered way too long over after dinner cocktails. Sean had not stopped by for his usual whiskey but since he took up with that skank, Mary Kate, his late night visits to Dottie's were not as consistent as he once had been. I missed those talks. He was always checking in on me. And I could end my day knowing he was alright. Anyway, it felt like I had just fallen asleep when I heard knocking on my bedroom door. *What the heck?*

"Mikey! Mikey, it's me." I stumbled out of bed pulling on my robe. I opened the door to see Sean standing there. "Sean, what's happened? Are you alright?"

"I'm fine. I need you to do something for me, Mikey."

He looked alright. He was clean shaven and was wearing a white shirt and his favorite brown leather jacket. He looked good.

"Sean, can't it wait, I'm beat! Had some customers last night who just didn't want to leave. What time is it anyway?"

"Mikey, you have to do this now."

He pushed a paper sack in my hands. It was heavy. "Keep this for me but Mikey don't tell anyone and hide it. Hide it good."

Without waiting for an answer, he kissed my cheek and let himself out of my apartment. I heard him turn his key re-locking my front door.

I padded back into the bedroom and sat on the edge of my bed. The room was dark and my shades were pulled down so I could sleep. I turned on the bedside lamp filling the room with soft yellow light. I opened the paper bag. Inside the sack was a stained cloth wrapping a heavy object. I slowly unfolded the oily rag with trembling hands. As I did, my heart began to race because the shape of the item in that dirty rag gave the contents away even before I unfolded the last crease of the cloth. Not wanting to think why it was so important for Sean to bring this to me I heard his words echo in my head, "hide it and hide it good."

I looked around my room. Where could I hide Sean's gun? I opened my lingerie drawer and nestled the sack in the bottom scattering silky underwear on top. No, not good. I ran to my closet and standing on a chair I placed the sack behind a hatbox on the top shelf. OK, OK, I thought. Then what if I reach for the hatbox and dislodge the gun from its hiding place? I don't even know if it's loaded. Yeah, it's probably loaded. If cops came around to search my place the drawer or the closet would be the first places they'd look. I retrieved the sack and sat back on the bed. I had to hide this and insure no one would find it. And I needed to do it quickly. Sean's done something and the cops may be on to him. They could be on their way to my apartment now. I had to protect Sean no matter what's happened.

Over the years Sean was always handing me rumpled paper bags that usually contained wads of cash. Or he would waltz into Dottie carrying boxes of booze smiling that devilish grin of his.

"Here you go Mikey. Keep them customers happy!"

I remembered how he got the ham and loaves of bread when I stupidly tried to start catering for the Garden. Too bad it was a Nazi rally. But at least I got to give the food away to the protestors outside the Garden. OK, think. And there it was. Suddenly, I was filled with memory of the first time Sean had asked me to hide something for him. No, it was for us. He handed me a sweaty palmful of coins, dimes and nickels and pennies. "Hide this Mikey, we need it to get out of here." I had wrapped it up in toilet paper so the coins would not clink in my skirt pocket. Then when I could I made my way to the kitchen and hid it. On the top shelf so that even tall, skinny Jimmy, Mr. Abernathy's boy assistant, would not be able to see.

I dumped out half of a big sack of flour into two mixing bowls and placed the oily rag and its deadly contents inside the sack. Then I poured most of the flour back into the sack. So once again, I hid Sean's secret package in the kitchen inside a ten pound sack of flour just as I had done so many years ago at the Orphanage. I placed it on the top shelf with sacks of brown and white sugar in front.

Then I went back to bed. Of course, sleep totally eluded me. I tossed and turned for another hour or so, then I gave into my insomnia. I took a hot shower and dressed hurriedly. Something was going on and I needed to be ready. The mixing bowls were still on the counter with enough flour in them to make a pancake breakfast for all of my Yorkville neighbors. I made some coffee and turned on the radio. Art Linkletter was telling stories about the funny things kids say and I smiled at one of his jokes. But my nerves were on edge. I wanted to call Sean. But I knew better. He would call me or come back for his package when it was safe. He would come back at the right time. I sipped my coffee and briefly considered making pancakes.

The news came on the radio and the announcer excitedly reported that a union organizer had been found slumped on the stairs of his apartment. He had been shot on his way to work earlier this morning. The report did not mention who was shot or exactly where and I worried that Sean had been the victim. No, not Sean! He can't be hurt or worse dead. My eyes strayed to the cabinet door that was closed housing sacks of sugar and the flour sack.

Oh, my God! Had Sean shot someone…I stopped the thought right there and then. I would not even think it. I had to do something. I had to get rid of the gun. Just then, my doorbell rang. The sound startled me, and I dropped my coffee cup. It clattered to the floor spilling a puddle of black coffee at my feet. The doorbell rang again followed by insistent knocking.

A man's voice called out, "Colleen! Are you there?"

I rushed to the door skidding in the spilt coffee as I went. Pulling open my door, my heart almost stopped.

It was the police!

"Hey Colleen, are you okay?" Michael Malloy was standing on my doorstep in his blue policeman's uniform. He eyed me with concern.

"Yes. I'm fine."

"Can I come in?" As I hesitated, Mike said, "We need to talk. It's important."

Spying the coffee on the floor, he bent down and picked up the pieces of china. "It's cracked," he said.

"Huh? What? Oh, the cup. No matter. I had a long night at the restaurant. The doorbell startled me and I dropped it. That's all."

I grabbed a kitchen towel but he took it from me and began to wipe up the mess.

"Thanks Mike but you needn't bother with that—"

"'Tis no trouble. Got anymore coffee or did you dump it all on the floor?"

I waved him in the direction of the percolator on the stove top then immediately regretted it as the cabinet with the flour sack was next to the stove.

"Cups?" he inquired.

"I'll get them. Please sit down, Mike."

He eyed me curiously, "You seem rather jumpy this morning."

I poured a cup for both of us and sat down at the small kitchen table.

"I'm just tired. It was a really late night. We had some customers who were thinking of spending the night at Dottie's. We finally booted them out at 2 am!" I smiled. "What brings you here so early in the morning?"

"Hmm, I must inform you it's almost lunchtime." I looked around the kitchen as if somehow it would confirm the time.

"But I am here to tell ya, well you need to tell Sean. The cops think he is the doer. You heard about Dengler, I presume?"

"Dengler? No. What?" Then it dawned on me. I just heard it on the radio, but they did not say who was shot.

"Do they think Sean is responsible for this?"

"Yeah they do. Apparently, several fellas saw a bit of an altercation between your brother and Dengler at a pub a few days ago. It's no secret they hate each other. Do you know where Sean is? Can you get word to him?"

"Word, what do you mean?"

"Look Colleen, you know how I feel about you. I don't care much for your brother, but I don't think he is really a bad guy. I'm thinking if he gets out of town for a few weeks, maybe a month they will pin this shooting on someone else."

He continued, "The detectives on this case, especially O'Boyle are really hard asses and frankly they are after headlines. A union shooting is just the ticket."

I reached for his hand, "Thank you, Michael Malloy for coming here to tell me this. But Sean is innocent I know it."

"Innocent, or not, these detectives are out for him." He stood then and as he straightened his uniform jacket, I saw on the side of his pants a light dusting of flour. He apparently chose the chair I had used to reach the shelf to hide the sack of flour. With a clean dish cloth, I slapped the white on his trousers leg. Now he looked startled.

"Sorry," I muttered. "I was going to make pancakes."

I pointed to the mixing bowls on the counter.

"Oh, well, don't let me hold up your breakfast. I hope you can get Sean to take my advice." He opened the door and smiling that big Irish grin of his. "I'll see you later."

It was almost a question.

"Yes," I said. "Come to Dottie's when you get off shift. And thanks, Michael."

I waited until I heard his footsteps retreating on the stairs then I raced to the phone. I needed to call Sean. Michael Francis Xavier Malloy was right. Sean needed to disappear and quickly.

I didn't reach Sean. As it turned out the warning came too late. The cops had already marched into the union office and were arresting him while I was still on the phone.

Sean
The Same Day
8 January 1947

President Truman names General George Marshall to be Secretary of State

It was a clear cold January morning. Driving west across town, the late morning sun reflected in my rear view, it was blinding. I was glad to turn downtown on 7th Avenue to get the sun out of my eyes. It was so cold that the Studebaker's heater barely kept my feet warm.

I found a parking spot around the corner from the 14th Street office. Locking the car door, I braced myself for the walk into the teeth of a bone chilling wind. It was a brisk walk. Closing the building's door behind me may have kept the wind at bay but not the freezing cold. The stairwell radiator steaming, hissing and rattling gave little respite from the cold outside.

It wasn't until I opened the door to the local's office that I could feel the heat. Through the cigarette haze the boys looked up as if I surprised them. I had barely closed the office door behind me when someone said, "Hey Boss didja hear? Somebody put the kibosh on that rat."

"What?" I said as I hung my good brown leather jacket on the hall tree.

"Yeah, somebody put some daylight into Dengler."

I poured myself a coffee from the hot plate pot. Turning back to the boys, I took a sip of the strong black coffee before asking, "When did this happen?"

"I hoid about two maybe three hours ago."

"So, Dengler's dead?"

"Naw, they took 'im to St. Vinny's to patch up the leaks."

"He ain't dead?"

"Not yet." Someone sniggered.

Looking around I asked, "Where's Liam and Padric?"

"Ain't here. Don'cha remember that Liam took his wife and kid to Florida. Padric went out o'town on some ILA businesses."

"Oh," I said and took another sip. "How was the take on this morning's shapeup?"

"Good, even picked up somethin' extra from one of the truckers too."

"Nice. How's this afternoon shapeup look?"

Sirens and screeching tires interrupted the reply. Eddie was at the window. The cold light streaming through the window bleached out his face as he said, "Shit! Coppers! Fooking bunch o' 'em!"

"Quick put the cash in the safe and look busy. I have to pee."

Even in the small toilet, I heard heavy, stamping feet thundering up the stairs. I buttoned up. Outside the toilet, I stood with my back to the window facing the door, my shadow reached to the office door. Hammering on the office door began. The boy closed the safe door then spun the dial. Someone tried the door. Of course, it was locked.

"Open up!" A voice shouted. "Police!"

I nodded to Eddie. He barely turned the doorknob when, like a breaking Johnstown dam the blue woolen cops flooded the office. Within a minute each of us had at least one arm held by a copper. I had one on each arm. As we complained, they said nothing. Slow deliberate steps were coming up the stairs.

Detective Robert Emmett O'Boyle walked slowly through the open door taking off his gloves, one finger at a time. His hat brim sat low on his forehead putting his face in shadow.

"You've been a busy bee this morning Callaghan."

"What are you talking about?"

O'Boyle looked me straight in the eyes. The sun was in his eyes yet they were unblinking as a gun barrel.

He said. "I've got you good this time, Callaghan. You and 'Old Sparky' are going to meet and I'm going to see you fry."

He turned to the copper holding my right. "Cuff 'im."

"Hold on! What's the charge?"

O'Boyle walked up within inches of my face, "Attempted murder."

"Attempted murder! Of whom?"

"We'll take a quick trip to St. Vincent's. He'll put the finger on you."

"What? I ain't done nothin'."

"Ain't done nothin', eh?" he said. "After St. Vincent's then we'll book ya at the 6th."

"Call Mr. Joel Friedman," I said to Eddie. "He'll have me out before lunch."

"Not this time Callaghan. You're done. Done. Done." O'Boyle draped my leather jacket across my shoulders almost gently. How did he know that was my coat?

As they marched me out of the office, the phone jangled.

Chapter 46
Mike Malloy Was Right

Colleen

I poured myself a whiskey and called Ian. We needed a lawyer. It didn't take the reporters very long to begin blasting the story about Sean's arrest. Headlines in the evening editions, screamed: 'Union Boss Shot!' or 'Crime on the Waterfront'.

Mike Malloy had been right about the arresting detectives. They were interviewed by the Times, Post and Daily News. On radio, O'Boyle was interviewed by Walter Winchell. I laughed at Winchell calling Dengler a Communist. Still, together they embellished a history of Sean's supposed crimes over the past several years. O'Boyle described, in lurid detail how Dengler, whom O'Boyle made out to be saintly, was gunned down in his stairway. He bragged that he was the first at the scene. How he found Dengler, bleeding in his distraught wife's arms. I turned off the radio. I could not take another minute of this crap.

Not waiting for Ian, I went down to the 6th precinct, but they would not let me see Sean. I pleaded with the desk sergeant to at least tell him I was there, and that we were getting a lawyer to represent him. I was stonewalled.

Not knowing what else I could do, I caught a cab to the restaurant. I had to keep an appearance of normalcy. Many of my customers knew that Sean is my brother. My presence at the restaurant would be a message. By my behavior, they would know he was innocent and that I had nothing to hide. Besides, we needed to keep the business going, we were going to need money for lawyers!

In the middle of the dinner service, the news reporters stared buzzing around the restaurant's door. Over the years, Dottie's has had the famous and infamous at its tables. To respect some of Dottie's clientele, I shielded them from these reporters and photographers. So, I had experience handling the press. Some can be extremely pushy.

Around 7:30, one reporter with his photographer marched up to the hostess podium demanding loudly to speak to me. Even though I was in the noisy kitchen, I heard the commotion outside.

"Yeah, like I said, I need to speak with Miss Callaghan and now!" One of my waiters was vainly trying to push the two back out the front door. "Where is she? Is she hiding out?"

I opened the kitchen door and walked directly to confront them.

"Miss Callaghan! What do you know? Did Sean tell you he was gonner bump off Dengler? Was this a Westies' mob hit? Miss Callaghan!"

Seeing this, four more reporters began pushing their way into Dottie's. Light bulbs were flashing. I raised my hand.

"Gentlemen. Stop shouting. My guests are trying to enjoy their dinner. I will step outside."

My bartender, Harold, grabbed my arm, "Colleen, don't do this. Ya can't trust what they will print. It could hurt your brother more than it could help."

"I know what I am doing." I pushed his arm aside gently. "Please make sure the rest of the staff take care of our guests. I will be right back."

I went through the front door and was immediately encircled by reporters. With flash bulbs stinging my eyes, I endeavored to appear calm. "Gentlemen, the only thing I know is that my brother is innocent. He was arrested on false charges this afternoon."

I was interrupted by, "Callaghan hated Dengler!"

Another shout demanded "Did Callaghan shoot Dengler because he wouldn't do his bidding?"

"Was this a mob hit?"

Another reporter shouted at me, "If Dengler dies, it will be murder!"

With one hand, I shielded my eyes from the explosive glare of the flash bulbs. "I am trying to run my business here. I cannot answer any more of your questions. Please respect my restaurant and my patrons and do not come here again."

Harold appeared at my side, he put an arm around my shoulders, and we retreated back inside Dottie's. I guess they got what they wanted. The reporters left then, having harassed me enough at that point.

But the next morning, headlines screamed, *Callaghan sister runs mob-owned restaurant. What does Colleen Callaghan know about Cockeyed?*

When I left my apartment the following morning, a throng of reporters were waiting for me. I tried to go for a walk, but it was useless. Neighbors who used to bid me 'good morning' or 'good afternoon' cast their eyes down at the sight of me. I was a social pariah.

Ironically, business at Dottie's boomed. It seemed New Yorkers had quite an appetite for sensation. They filled my tables hoping to glimpse a mobster. Some guests let their food go cold and the ice in their drinks melt hoping to catch a view of George Raft, who did visit fairly regularly. Well, when he wasn't in Hollywood.

One night, Meyer Lansky came for dinner with his little daughter! Customers didn't recognize Lansky. He was in plain sight. It was the way it always had been. From the day we first opened Dottie's, we had an eclectic mix of mobsters, politicians, Wall Street types, neighborhood working people, and even Broadway show folks. The mob had come to dine at Dottie's too. During the Depression, they were the only ones with money, so they filled half my tables. For regular folks, once again, it was chic to hang out with the dangerous. Fashionable Park Avenue types sipped martinis, old fashions and Manhattans as they whispered about mobsters, cops or politicians who they hoped were dining at the table near theirs. But that wasn't the best.

The best was Mike. Michael Malloy had not only taken me up on a free dinner at Dottie's, but he started to come by at the end of his shift every day. He sat at the bar. Sat on the same stool that Sean always chose and sipped a beer. I sent him a plate of dinner in an attempt to thank him for looking out for me and Dottie's. When reporters showed up, he would, like a good guard dog, make them scatter like pigeons in Central Park.

Fewer reporters congregated outside the restaurant, while the majority, the most insistent of them posted themselves in front of my apartment house. They harried my neighbors, the mailman, even the milkman. Just as I thought it could not get worse, Sean's trial began.

Every day of the trial as I left the courthouse, the gauntlet of reporter and their photographers seemed to multiply, becoming louder and more strident. Every phrase of testimony was shouted at me for comment. They were at my apartment house stoop morning and night. The trial brought reporters back outside of Dottie's nightly.

My regulars were kind though, always concerned about me. During the first days of the trial, I hid out in the kitchen until 'last call.' It was with Mike's support to 'brass it out' as he referred to hiding in plain sight that I resumed my restaurateur role. My customers wanted to see me. I wanted to thank them for running the gauntlet of reporters. But nerves started fraying. One of my regulars, became tangled in a tussle that could have had him arrested but for Mike's intervention.

Chapter 47
.38 Caliber

Sean

When O'Boyle dragged me to St. Vincent's, he had a police stenographer recording everything Dengler said. He said that he hadn't recognized any of the guys who shot him. Then he was taken off to surgery. O'Boyle threw me into a black-and-white. At the 6th, he held me as a 'material witness.'

Meanwhile, Sylvia Cornelia Dengler went to see ADA Kerry. She told the ADA that her husband told her that me and two of my boys were the shooters. In the slammer, I stayed.

Mary Kate had come down to Court Street with a bail bonds for $25,000 to get me freed from the lockup. But the DA convinced the judge that I was a flight risk, so the judge denied bail.

For weeks after being shot five times, including one in the face, Dengler hung on. Then, Dengler died. The charge against me went to 'Murder in the First Degree.'

Since then, I saw less of Mary Kate. During the week, I talked on the jail telephone with either her or Elizabeth. Before I ended a call, I scheduled my next one. Many times, when I telephoned, it was only Elizabeth who was there. No matter what, it felt good to be out of the cell even if I was still in jail.

The jailhouse screw jangled keys as he unlocked my cell door. He stepped back saying, "Callaghan your lawyer is here to see you."

While I was glad to meet with Joel about the upcoming trial, but I would have preferred a Mary Kate visit. The screw led me to the 'mouthpiece room'. When he opened the door, I was surprised to see Ian sitting next to Joel. He grinned. I must have grinned too. He came around the table to give me a bear-hug.

"How are you?"

"Good, could be better. This place ain't got no room service."

"Had to see you. Joel brought me in saying that I was another lawyer in his firm. The moron at the front desk didn't connect my name with yours. I bet he can't count higher than ten without taking off his shoes and socks."

"Can we get down to business?" Joel interjected.

"Colleen sends her love." Ian continued, "She'll visit on Monday. Elizabeth will be with her. Mary Kate has some kind of appointment, but she'll be by later."

Joel said, "Ian was insistent on getting in to see you, but he'll have to leave before we discuss the case against you, otherwise it could muddy-up lawyer-client privilege."

"Red has been working on things too. He is also keeping up the cash for the trial expenses and your house in your absence."

"How's Mary Kate doing? She's been saying that she hasn't been feeling good."

"She can't go anywhere without some flashbulbs popping in her face. Speaking of wives, Dengler's has gone missing."

"Don't get excited," said Joel while he sorted some papers on the table. "Ian, I have work here with your brother and you can't stay."

"Sure counselor," Ian said, then gave me another hug. "If you need anything just tell me."

"A one-way boat ticket to Rio would be nice." I laughed.

As soon as the door clicked behind Ian, Joel started.

"You are big news in the papers and that isn't good. The papers are howling for blood, yours. Judge Eddington is a real curmudgeon who is in contention for a seat on the State Supreme Court. He wants to appear tough on crime. That's only the beginning. The papers keep asking the DA for a trial date. But the DA has a problem. Sylvia Dengler, the crucial witness if you will, has vanished. If Sylvia Dengler stays missing, then we won't have to contend with the 'deathbed' pronouncement. If she reappears, testifies and holds up under my cross-examination THEN we'll have a problem. Still, I have an ace up my sleeve. While Dengler was still in St. Vincent's, a stenographer took down Dengler's statement. He stated that he could not be sure who shot him, but it was three guys he had never seen before. We have witnesses who can testify that Dengler knew you. Even waiters from Marie's Crisis bar or the Landmark Tavern can attest to that."

"Good news. Doesn't that blow the DA's case against me?"

"Not quite, here's the bad news, the jury. The jury is a Blue Ribbon jury of twelve politically connected businessmen. At Columbia Law, we referred to the Blue Ribbon jury as "hangmen". Anyone who is not one of them is guilty before proven guilty. They are a hard bunch. Still, if the Assistant DA Kerry cannot produce witnesses, the murder weapon or establish opportunity we can get the case dismissed before it could go to the jury to decide. I am working to avoid that jury."

"That would be very good if you can get it dismissed," I said. "Joel, I have to ask you a question. The word in here is that Padric has been picked up and is being extradited back to the city. Has the ADA found Liam yet?"

"Oh, yes more bad news. Liam McGee was staying in a hotel in Hollywood Florida with his wife, Marybeth, his daughter and her girlfriend. Looked like he had an airtight alibi."

"Cripes, what happened?"

"For reasons I cannot fathom, Marybeth McGee sent the little girl friend back to New York on Monday's Silver Meteor. Well, the ADA learned about the girl. She was picked up at Grand Central Terminal. She said that Mr. McGee had been in Florida with the girls since New Year's."

"Well, that's good. So why the face? You look like you are sucking on lemons and eating prunes."

"Then the girl told ADA Kerry that 'Mr. McGee had made a business trip to New York on January 5th and only returned on January 7th'."

"Well, that put the kibosh on his alibi," I said.

"Your best defense is for me to defend you separately from Liam and Padric."

"What's the charge?"

"Murder, in the first degree. It carries a death sentence."

***

Two months later, I was sitting in Superior Court looking at the jury. There was one guy who looked familiar, but I couldn't place him. Maybe I saw him at the Cotton Club, Dottie's, the 21Club or who knows, maybe a gin mill on the Westside. Those Wall Street swells were known to slum with us.

The first to testify was Dengler's driver who had been waiting on Grove Street. Then, it would be O'Boyle and Sylvia Dengler. Yes, Sylvia Dengler had called the ADA's office, came back to the city and was rumored to be in a Gramercy Park apartment on the Eastside.

Dengler's driver was a scrawny dago named Artie Carmano. ADA Kerry skillfully led him through his testimony.

"I honked my horn and watched Dengler's third floor window from the car. I saw Mr. Dengler's face in the window. He waved, meaning that he'd be right down."

"Then what happened Mr. Carmano?"

"Meebe, five minutes goes by when I hear a car back-fire, bang, bang, bang, a pause and another bang. But I realized that it wasn't a car on the street, it was coming from the apartment house."

"By that you mean 61 Grove Street where Mr. and Mrs. Dengler lived?"

"Yeah, like I was sayin', I was parked right in front of the stoop of the apartment house. Like I do every morning."

"Then what happened?"

"I seen dese guys come down the stoop stairs. Den run around the corner to Sheridan Square."

"Are these men present in this court, Mr. Carmano?"

"Yeah it's dat guy over dere." Carmano pointed at Padric.

"For the record, the witness indicated one of the defendants, Mr. Padric Pierce."

"N de other guy in glasses!"

"Let the record show that the witness indicated the defendant, Liam McGee."

On cross-examination, the attorney for Liam and Padric did his best to shake the dago's testimony. I had to hand it to the scrawny dago, he stuck to his guns. The judge recessed the court until Monday.

On Monday, NYPD Detective Robert Emmett O'Boyle took the stand. He didn't have the guts to look at me after they swore him in. ADA Kerry let O'Boyle ramble on until Joel started objecting. Both the ADA and O'Boyle became flustered and angry. When Joel started his cross of O'Boyle, Joel's voice became honey and sugar. Now O'Boyle came off as a hot head.

"I see, I see Detective. You are just doing your job. Only following orders, just like the Nazis did when they tortured and gassed Jews, Gypsies and other 'sub-humans' as they called these human beings. You think that longshoremen are sub-human, don't you?"

"There are a few bad apples. A lot of good people like Mr. Dengler, a good apple."

"Did you know that Mr. Dengler was a communist, a red?"

"Objection!" shouted ADA Kerry. "Mr. Dengler is not on trial here."

Joel looked at the jury and said, "I withdraw the question." He knew that he planted the seed of a Red Scare in the jury box. That's all he wanted. Those Wall Street types fear and hatred of communists was well known.

"Detective please tell the court what Dengler said when you brought Mr. Callaghan to St. Vincent's Hospital after he had been shot."

"Mr. Dengler became very agitated. He started to pull at his Johnny-coat and the bed sheets."

"What did Mr. Dengler say?" Joel asked.

"Like I said, he was very agitated, He pulled off some of the bandages, saying, "See! See! See whatcho done."

"But did Dengler identify Mr. Callaghan as the shooter?"

"Well, he was agitated like I said."

"Did Dengler say that he recognized the shooter?"

"Well, he said that he didn't know the gunman for sure but...'

"Just answer the question. Did he recognize the Shooter?"

"He said he wasn't sure."

"He did not recognize his shooter, right? Answer the question, yes or no."

"Well, no."

Joel consulted his notes.

"Did Mr. Callaghan say anything?"

"Yes."

"What did Mr. Callaghan say?"

O'Boyle paused, swallowed as if he had a lousy taste in his mouth. "He said, 'I hope you get better, Mr. Dengler. Let the good doctors and nurses at St. Vincent's help you get better.'"

"In your experience, Detective has anyone accused of a violent crime ever wished their victim a speedy recovery?"

"No. Usually they send flowers to the funeral."

Trying to keep O'Boyle off balance, Joel asked, "Detective have you recovered the murder weapon?"

"Not as yet, we are sure that it will turn up."

"What kind of weapon was used to injure Mr. Dengler?"

"There were no shell casings found in the stairwell. Ballistic test of the bullets taken from Mr. Dengler's body showed .38 caliber. So, the weapon was a .38 caliber revolver."

"Paraffins are used by police to find gunpowder residue on shooter's hands. Did you do a paraffin test on the defendants' hands?"

"Yes, only Mr. Callaghan was tested. The other two defendants were booked several weeks after the shooting, so they weren't tested."

"What was the results of the test on Mr. Callaghan's hands?"

O'Boyle made a face, "The tests were negative. I think that Callaghan urinated on his hands to screw up the test."

"Did you see Mr. Callaghan urinate on his hands, Detective?"

"No, I did not."

"So, the tests are negative, thank you Detective." Joel paused then he asked, "Who suggested moving Mr. Dengler from St. Vincent's Hospital?"

"I did."

"Wasn't Mr. Dengler recovering quite well at St. Vincent's? In fact, didn't Mr. Dengler's surgeon at St. Vincent's object to the transfer?"

O'Boyle swallowed but said nothing.

Joel continued, "Wasn't moving Mr. Dengler in his condition highly dangerous?"

"I didn't hear any doctor's objection."

"Isn't it a fact, that transferring Mr. Dengler in his precarious condition resulted in his death."

"Objection! Counselor has made medical assumptions that he has no knowledge or experience."

"Objection sustained."

"If Mr. Dengler died then you could raise the charge to Murder One. That would be your ticket to a big promotion, wouldn't it?"

"Objection!" ADA Kerry roared.

"Objection sustained. Mr. Friedman, if you persist in this line of questioning, I will hold you in contempt."

"I withdraw the question." Speaking to the jury men, Joel said, "So let me summarize your testimony. Detective O'Boyle, you do not have a murder weapon. Do you? No need to answer. The paraffin tests on Mr. Callaghan were negative. What DO you have Detective? Hearsay, nonsense and rumors." Joel waved the papers in his hand as if he was swatting flies away. "I have no further questions at this time; however, I reserve the right to recall this witness at a later time."

Joel Friedman's cross on Sylvia Dengler brought her to tears. The ADA asked for a recess to give her some time to recover. Her testimony was dangerous. As the court reconvened, Joel with his best stone face, honey gentle voice continued.

"Mrs. Dengler, the court is having difficulty with your testimony. At one time you claimed that your husband said to you that he saw only one gunman. Later, you said there were two. Were you lying when you said it was one or when it was two? Now you say that he 'saw three gunmen'. What's the truth? Which is it? Remember you are under oath."

"Objection, badgering the witness!" ADA Kerry said.

"Sustained."

"There were three killers, three," Sylvia blurted.

"Yet your husband told Detective O'Boyle that he didn't recognize the gunman. He said 'gunMAN' to Detective O'Boyle, not gunMEN."

"My husband told me that they'd come for me next. He said to me, 'that rat Callaghan shot me' right before the cops and the ambulance arrived. He said it as he lay bleeding in my arms."

In exasperation, Joel interrupted Sylvia's testimony. He turned to the jury, "Oh, I see we are back to ONE shooter again."

"As my dear husband lay bleeding in my arms, he said that it was Callaghan, McGee and Pierce who done it"

"Oh my, we are back to three! "Joel walked to the defense table. "It seems that you, Mrs. Dengler are the only one who knows who the shooters are. Even your husband said that he did not know the man or men who shot him. So, were you in the stairwell when the shooting occurred?"

"No, I was NOT in the stairwell. It's the unwritten law on the waterfront. You don't say nothin' to nobody, 'specially the cops. When he was taken to St. Vincent's, the doctors said that despite his wounds, he'd make it. We thought that he'd survive. We had to be smart."

"So, to be clear, you thought that your husband would survive his wounds?"

"Yes" Sylvia Dengler said dabbing her eyes and blowing her nose loudly.

Sylvia Dengler's shoulders shook and again she blew her nose into her handkerchief.

Joel Friedman turned away from the witness box looked straight at the jury and said, "If St. Vincent's was taking such good care of Mr. Dengler, I mean your husband was improving. Why did you move him across town to the East Side? Post-Graduate Hospital is on 20th and 2nd."

"Detective O'Boyle wanted him as far away from the Westside and the Westside Callaghan Gang. He said that they might come to finish killing my dear husband."

"Mr. Dengler died just a few days after being transferred. The chief of surgery at St. Vincent's was not in favor of Mr. Dengler's transfer. The trauma of the transfer killed him."

"Objection!" ADA Kerry shouted. "I don't hear a question. My esteemed counselor is testifying, not the witness."

"Sustained. Mr. Friedman, I've already warned you that I would hold you in contempt of court!" Judge Eddington ruled.

"Let me rephrase: Mrs. Dengler, why did you agree to transfer your husband from a hospital where he received life-saving care only for him to die at another hospital?"

"The police said it would be better if he was at a hospital closer to a police precinct only a half block away. Post Graduate Hospital is close to the 13th Precinct."

"I can see your reason for not trusting the 6th Precinct and Detective O'Boyle but..." ADA Kerry was pushing back his chair to object when Joel said, "OK, I withdraw the question."

He paused, then asked, "$10,000 is a lot of money, isn't it, Mrs. Dengler? Isn't $10,000 more than two years' earnings for your husband?"

"Yes, it is quite a lot of money. My husband made only $4,000 a year."

"When did you learn that Mr. Dengler had a $10,000 life insurance policy?"

Sylvia Dengler's jaw dropped. She stammered, "I, I, I found out when I got the death certificate."

"How? Who informed you?"

"I, I don't recall."

"Isn't it true that you called New York Life the day your husband died?"

Sylvia Dengler in shocked silence licked her lips.

"Really, Mrs. Dengler, really?" Joel said waiving a piece of paper. "I have an affidavit that you contacted New York Life the same day your husband died in order for you to get your hands on the life insurance money." Joel made a disgusted face walking back to the table. With his hands on the defense table, Joel said, "No further questions your honor."

Joel sat as ADA Kerry rose to ask, "Your Honor with your permission I would like to ask a re-direct."

"You may proceed counselor."

ADA Kerry walked slowly to the witness box, turned and while facing the jury asked, "Mrs. Dengler did your husband serve in the Navy during the War?"

Between sobs and eye dabs for dramatic impact, Sylvia Dengler replied, "Yes, he was."

"Was your husband honorably discharged?"

"Yes, after he was seriously injured in a training accident. He was medically discharged from the Navy."

"Did your husband have Servicemen's Life Insurance?"

"Yes."

"Did he transfer his policy to the New York Life Insurance after discharge?"

"Yes, he did."

"I have no further questions your Honor."

"The witness is dismissed" Judge Eddington said.

Joel Friedman was on his feet, "Your Honor, may I re-cross the witness?"

"You may re-cross the witness."

"Mrs. Dengler let's get this straight. You just told the court that you did not know that your husband had a policy with New York Life. Is it NOW your testimony that you did, in fact know about the $10,000?"

"Yes."

"No further questions you Honor."

Several of the jurors sat back and folded their arms.

"Your Honor, the Prosecution rests."

"We'll recess for the day. We'll hear arguments from the Defense when court re-convenes at 10 a.m. tomorrow." Judge Eddington banged his gavel.

Chapter 48
Witness for the Defense

Sean

The next morning, Joel Friedman called his first witness.

"The Defense calls Miss Elizabeth Callaghan to the stand."

"Elizabeth Callaghan, do you swear to tell the truth, the whole truth and nothing but the truth, so help you God?"

"I do."

"State your full name for the court."

"Elizabeth Bridget Callaghan."

Elizabeth was dressed in her best Catholic school girls' uniform. When she entered the courtroom, she appeared nervous but as she sat in the witness chair, she looked poised and composed.

"Miss Callaghan, how old are you?" Joel asked.

"I'm sixteen."

"Where do you go to school?"

"I'm in my junior year at Mary Louis Academy," she replied, her hands clasped on her lap.

"Miss Callaghan, please recall the morning of January 6th for the court," Joel asked.

"It was a school day. I was nervous. I had a math examination."

"How did you did you do on the test?"

"I got an A."

"Yes, good job. Please continue, Miss Callaghan."

"I awoke about 8 am, dressed and went downstairs. Dad was preparing scrambled eggs and bacon."

"About what time was this?"

"As I recall it was 8:30."

"How can you be so sure?"

"I remember that I looked at my new watch that I received for Christmas. It was 8:30 as I sat at the table for breakfast."

"And your father was home making breakfast of scrambled eggs and bacon?"

"Yes."

"Was it usual for your father to make breakfast?"

"Oh yes, every morning."

"So, Miss Callaghan we can safely assume that your father was home cooking breakfast between 8 and 8:30 a.m. that morning?"

"Yes."

"Therefore, it would be impossible for your father to be in Mr. Dengler's Greenwich Village stairwell at the time of the shooting, 7:45 a.m. then be in Elmhurst, Queens a mere 15 minutes later cooking breakfast at 8:00 am in your kitchen. I have no further questions your Honor."

ADA Kerry tried to discredit Elizabeth and her timing of the events of that morning. Tough little gal. She withstood a withering barrage of questions by ADA Kerry. She was unshakable.

Both Colleen and Ian Callaghan presented credible character witness testimony. ADA Kerry passed on cross of both of them.

Then Joel Friedman called his last witness, Mary Kate Callaghan.

I watched Mary Kate glided to the witness stand. My god she looked good. From the perfect hat to the long white kidskin gloves draped across her left forearm, she still had that Carole Lombard look, elegant, beautiful and seductive. Every man in the jury box had eyes on her.

Joel Friedman took advantage of her looks positioning himself so that the jury men had an unobstructed view.

"Mrs. Callaghan can you recall for the court the events of the morning of January 6th 1947 at your home?"

"Well," Mary Kate paused dramatically. "I am a little unclear."

Obviously surprised, Joel looked at me before asking Mary Kate, "Why is that?"

"Because I took a sleeping pill the night before."

Unsettled, Joel took quick steps to the Defense table. He consulted his legal pad. We had discussed Mary Kate's testimony. This 'sleeping pill' hadn't been brought up before by Mary Kate.

"Mrs. Callaghan," Joel resumed. "Please tell the court, to the best of your memory, the events of January 6th."

"I slept in and came down to the kitchen about 8:45 or even 8:55. I was concerned that Elizabeth would be late for school."

"Was Mr. Callaghan making scrambled eggs and bacon?"

She laughed, "No! He has a hard time making toast. As I recall, all he was making was toast."

Trying to salvage her testimony, Joel said, "You've testified that you overslept that morning after taking sleeping pills the night before. Is that correct, Mrs. Callaghan?"

"Yes, I often take sleeping pills when my husband is out late doing…"

Joel interrupted, "Please just answer my questions with a yes or no unless I ask you to clarify."

Mary Kate shifted in her seat and re-crossed her long legs. "Sure."

"Since you arrived in the kitchen at…" Joel consulted his notes, "…8:45 or 8:55 you were not in a position to know if Mr. Callaghan had already cooked breakfast, were you?"

Smiling at the jury, she said, "Like I said. Sean had trouble making toast…"

"Please just answer the question, I'll repeat it a different way. You arrived in the kitchen at 8:45 or 8:55, so you did not know what was happening in the kitchen earlier. Isn't that true?"

Fixing her big blue eyes squarely on Joel, she said, "Yeah." Her voice was dripping with sarcasm.

ADA Kerry smiled. It was a wolfish grin. He made sure that I saw it.

When ADA Kerry made his cross-examination, he went in for the kill.

"Mrs. Callaghan was there any evidence that your husband or anyone else for that matter made breakfast? I mean was there an odor of freshly cooked bacon? Were there dirty pans or dishes?"

"No, my kitchen was clean as a whistle."

"Mrs. Callaghan, let's clarify this for the jury. Your testimony is that your husband WASN'T making breakfast that morning?"

"Yeah," Mary Kate jeered. "I don't even recall seeing him in the house at all that morning."

Chapter 49
It Stinks

Colleen

Elizabeth and I were sitting together as we watched and listened to the testimony, or should I say the lies told by Mary Kate. I always knew this blonde was trouble. Sean, Sean how did you fall for her! It was incredible! Even, Sylvia Dengler tried to make herself sound credible when all she really cared about was the life insurance payout. But at least she really suffered loss. Mary Kate is only concerned with herself. She does not care about anyone else. Not even this lovely young girl sitting next to me.

When Mary Kate uttered her lies, I heard Elizabeth draw a deep breath in. Still gasping, she struggled to not look frightened lest the jury see her. I, on the other hand, used the face that served me so well. The face that did not betray my fear when Perpetua barked at me. The face that I resolutely kept when I heard that the nuns at St. Joseph's hurt Sean, again and again. The face I wore when I saw his eye damaged by that Puss-faced sister. I squeezed Elizabeth's hand hoping to reassure her.

I could not concentrate on the words being uttered by the judge and the attorneys. All at once, it seemed, the judge stood and left the bench. Behind, the murmuring crowd in the gallery stood and began milling on their way out of the courtroom.

Sean turned, looking at me. We locked eyes. Once again it was Sean and me. As if we were back at the fence in the playground of that awful orphanage. It was Sean looking into my eyes and holding my hand when I awoke from the horrible influenza that nearly killed me. It was Sean and me rushing Dotty out of the orphanage's big wooden door to freedom. It was Sean and me aboard the ferry bound for Manhattan with a woman who said she was our mother, a woman we did not know. It was Sean and me opening Dottie's. It was Sean and me at the kitchen table talking about getting funds together to help Ian go to college. My eyes flooded with tears, I gulped them back although Elizabeth saw. She pulled me to my feet and ushered me to the ladies' room. Once inside, we stood locked in a tight embrace each of us crying because we understood the damage that Mary Kate had done.

Elizabeth pulled back from me and wiping tears from her eyes, she said, "They won't believe her. The jury won't believe her. They see her for what she is."

I touched this beautiful young girl's cheek and whispered, "I hope. I pray you are right."

I straighten my skirt and sighed. I thought 'ours is a sad story without a happy ending'. For Sean and me, it's never a 'happy ever after ending.' I turned and walked into the nearby stall closing and locking the door behind me.

From the stall, I heard Elizabeth washing her hands with such vigor you'd think she had an infectious disease on them. I visualized her staring into her red-rimmed eyes in the mirror over the sink. Under her breath, I heard a not so silent prayer for an outcome that she knew in her heart was not forthcoming. Visualizing her, she probably reaches to fasten a stray wisp of hair behind her ear. The door of the ladies' room opened with a bang. It was followed by the distinct reports of stiletto heels.

I recognized the cadence of that walk. It was Mary Kate. As the door hissed closed behind her, the sound stopped. Mary Kate must be standing there, probably surveying the scene. Then with high heels loud on the tile floor, she strode into the room. At the sinks and mirrors, Mary Kate stopped.

"You really should try fixing your hair, Elizabeth. You look awful."

Elizabeth did not answer.

I imagined Mary Kate shrugging, turning to take herself in at the mirrors. In my mind's eye, Mary Kate tilted her head this way and that, admiring her reflection as I've seen her do so many times before.

"Suit yourself. But you really do look terrible." She paused. "Want to borrow my rouge and lipstick?"

No reply.

Then I heard the snap of her purse clasp. In the pregnant silence of the room, the soft sound of her compact opening so Mary Kate could touch up her rouged cheeks seemed loud. This was immediately followed by the pop of a lipstick cap. The cap of the lipstick carelessly clattered into the sink like the sound of a roulette ball being dropped in a casino. I imagined her leaning into the mirror, applying the fire engine red lip tint, then pouting her lips checking that her lipstick was in place.

"Last offer, rouge or lipstick?"

Silence.

"No? Well, you'll probably start bawling again anyway, ruining your make up. So, it doesn't matter."

"Why are you looking at me that way?"

I heard the hiss of taffeta as she patted down her dress, all the while, I'm sure, trying to ignore the burning outraged stare of her daughter a few steps away.

She was standing at the sink directly across from the stall I was in. I peered through the narrow slit of the doorframe. Mary Kate pivoted around to confront Elizabeth.

"So, what? You think I was unfair to dear old step-dad?"

"He is my dad. He adopted me, or don't you remember?"

"You've got a lot to learn Missy. I am done with this loser! He can't give us what we need. I found a fella who will get us an apartment on Park Avenue. Park Avenue! Not some row house walk up in Elmhurst, Queens! I mean, really? Queens! He actually thought we would live with him in Queens!"

Elizabeth growled at Mary Kate, "WE? Us? You mean YOU, don't you, Mother? It's always about you. And YOU don't care who you hurt in the bargain. Even if it means a good man loses his life."

Mary Kate just laughed. "What do you know? You think you know everything. What I could tell you about that man would make your hair stand on end!"

At that moment, I had had enough. I flushed the toilet and pulled open the stall. Mary Kate whirled around, surprised, shocked to see me. I strode right up to her, my face just inches from hers. She tried to back away, but I grabbed her shoulders, I would not permit her to retreat.

"You have no idea who Sean is or what makes him tick. You think you know everything. But I have news for you. You are a useless woman who is interested only in what expensive clothes you wear and how your hair looks as you feign modesty. Modesty is something you know nothing about. Dare I say for most of your miserable life. From St. Joseph's to this very day you have been a ruthless, egotistical, and mercenary bitch! My only regret is that I did not tell Sean just how treacherous you are!"

She laughed at me. Though her laugh was shrill, nervous and sounding a bit shaky.

"Your Sean is going to the death chamber for what he did!"

I looked into the pitiless eyes of this cold beauty who stole Sean's heart. NO, she stole his life not his heart. Anyway, I was suddenly filed with the same fury, I felt so many years ago when I belted Eucharius with a cast iron skillet. I hauled off and punched her so hard she staggered backward to the wall. A good sucker-punch. She slid down the tiled wall opposite Elizabeth and me. Her taffeta dress had ridden up, so she sat garter belt exposed on the tile. Stunned, she just stared at me furiously blinking her right eye where I socked her. She was going to sport a really good shiner. Oh yes, out of a really bad day, I got some measure of satisfaction by ruining her beautiful face, even if just temporarily.

Elizabeth grabbed my hand and said, "Colleen, let's get out of here."

"Yeah, this ladies' room stinks," I said, slamming the door behind us.

Chapter 50
Blue Ribbon Jury

Sean

Joel slammed his leather briefcase on the Tomb's lawyer-defendants' room table. His face was pinched and red.

"We need the original stenographer's record of Dengler saying that he saw the shooter and that he did not recognize or know him. The one that was admitted in evidence was missing the last page with that statement."

"What?"

"ADA Kerry said that the complete transcript had been given to the District Attorney's Office by Detective O'Boyle. This transcript had been admitted into evidence. Kerry argued that it was the complete and true transcript. Judge Eddington concurred. I said that the complete and true transcript had not been presented to me during Discovery. He denied my request for more time to locate the original and complete transcript. Also, he refused my motion to take the jury to an early morning visit to the scene. I wanted the jury to see that in the bright winter light, Dengler would see and easily recognize the shooter in stairwell. Judge Eddington said that we have heard enough evidence in the courtroom. Motion denied."

I said, "I clearly heard Dengler saying that he didn't know the shooter. I saw the police stenographer take it all down."

"Sean, we have the ADA, the "Blue Wall" and Judge Eddington standing between us and the original."

"Now what?"

"Tomorrow, we give summations. The judge will instruct the jury then they will begin deliberation."

"Cripes, it's like they already have found me guilty! And worse yet they are not listening to all the evidence. The day after tomorrow is New Year's Eve, I could be convicted. This time O'Boyle is right. He really got me."

In his summation to the jury, ADA Kerry used Mary Kate's testimony to say that it was no problem for me to drive from the murder scene to my home in Queens by 8:45. He dismissed Elizabeth's testimony as that of teenager who only wanted to please her adopted father. He went on that I had a beef with Dengler. I was known to have threatened Dengler. I had motive and opportunity. As for means, he brought up my arrests for bootlegging, gun possession and assaults. I was a 'career criminal'. It was in my genes. I was no good.

For his summation, Joel Friedman did his best to counter each and every point that Kerry made. There was no murder weapon. My paraffin test for gunpowder residue was negative. The principal witness, Sylvia Dengler was caught in multiple lies. She was not credible. That all the evidence against me was purely circumstantial.

I watched the jury as Joel spoke. I can read faces. I didn't think that they were buying Joel's arguments. No wonder, Columbia Law called any Blue Ribbon Jury, 'Hangmen'.

Chapter 51
Snows of New York

Colleen
31 December 1947

*NYC digging out of record snow; Ship the Exodus with War Refugees
driven off Palestine shore (New York Mirror)*

Last night we had a record snowfall which shut Dottie's early. The elevated
subways stopped running. New York was a winter wonderland with white
frosted tree limbs and mountains of snow in the streets. It always amazed me
how this noisy city became silent under a blanket of snow. Windswept
sidewalks had snowdrifts almost six feet high. The few people who ventured
out had to walk down the middle of the street with snow up to their knees to
gain any kind of sure footing.

It was the next afternoon, New Year's Eve, when my phone jangled. Joel
Friedman, Sean's lawyer was on the line. "The jury has reached a verdict. You
have an hour to get here, Colleen."

***

Sean

With my best poker face, I sat silent at the Defense Table. Joel Friedman did
not unpack his briefcase, he sat to my right tapping his fingers on the scarred
leather.

"All Rise!" The bailiff announced as Judge Everett Eddington solemnly
ascended the bench.

He waited for the court to quiet before addressing the jury, "Gentlemen of the Jury have you a reached a verdict?"

"Yes, we have your Honor." The foreman, the guy who looked familiar handed the envelope to the bailiff for the judge. The judge opened the envelope to extract it contents.

After reading, Judge Eddington asked. "Is your decision unanimous?"

"Yes, Your Honor."

"You may read your verdict for the court."

"We, the jury find the defendant guilty of murder in the first degree."

***

Colleen

My heart sank. Guilty. Murder in the First. A capital crime punishable by the electric chair. That "Blue Ribbon Jury" was indeed a hangman's jury.

Thankfully, the blizzard kept reporters off me that evening, Ian and I sat around the kitchen table in my apartment working on our options. Ian knew that the District Attorney was a real political animal who would use Sean's dead body to win the race to be mayor next November. He had been one of Governor Dewey's Assistant District Attorneys when Dewey was DA. He intended to follow Dewey's example. Dewey got Lucky Luciano convicted and sentenced to thirty years for prostitution. What office could be won with a Murder One conviction? Mayor? Governor? Senator? Or, President of the USA?

Joel Friedman arrived at my apartment to work with Ian and I on new scenarios for an appeal. We divided responsibilities. Joel and Ian looked into case history for deathbed attestations and mine was to do some politicking. Dewey had been a good customer, a Dottie's regular when he was the DA of the Southern District of New York. Recently, he freed Luciano. Not truly 'freed'. Dewey deported Luciano back to an Italy still digging out from under the rubble of the War.

Chapter 52
Calling in the Markers

2nd of July 1949—*United Nations officially recognizes the state of Vietnam in the southern portion of the country with Bao Dai as head of state of South Vietnam*

Sean
Sing Sing Prison, Ossining, New York
July 1949

Within hours of the verdict, Joel Friedman had submitted an appeal. That failed. Over the last eighteen months, he persisted with appeal after appeal. They all failed.

Liam and Padric's trials went just like mine. Convicted of Murder in the First Degree. Now we were bunk mates again, this time in Sing Sing's Death House.

Then, out of nowhere, Liam tried to get me and Padric freed.

His attorney contacted the DA to say that Liam had signed an affidavit stating he was fully responsible for the murder of Dengler! In the affidavit Liam admitted shooting Dengler with two other guys, John the 'Russki' Gochenko and Vincent 'the Bull' Mastrobuoni. I was shocked. Liam claimed that Gochenko and Mastrobuoni had done some shooting for Charlie Yanowsky on the Hoboken and Jersey City docks. Yanowsky had provided the trio with guns for the killing of Dengler.

Liam attested that he was the Dock Boss, not me. He was afraid of Dengler's challenge to his leadership of the ILA Local. Also, Liam wanted revenge for Dengler's shooting him the year before outside of Dorian's Red Hand.

The DA investigated Liam's story. He was the only one alive of the hit team. Gochenko had been killed, stabbed at a Hoboken Ferry landing one night in January '48. Mastrobuoni had had been pushed under the wheels of a Jersey City trolley in February. Charlie Yanowsky had been trying to muscle in on a Mafia gambling operation. He shouldn't have done that. He was found dead in Clifton, New Jersey with multiple icepick wounds in around his heart. Clifton police wrote it off as a robbery since Yanowsky's wallet was not found. Although, his big expensive ring and diamond-studded belt was still on his body when it was found.

Liam was good. At the motion for a new trial, ADA Kerry questioned him extensively. Liam said that we were innocent of the murder. When asked why he came forward with his admission at this time. Liam said that the parish priest from St. Joan of Arc came to see him and had awakened his conscience to repent and make things right.

ADA Kerry failed to shake Liam. He told his story without a mistake, omission or wrong word. I'm sure that ADA Kerry thought that Liam was an uneducated half-wit who would be easy pickins'. Liam shook up Kerry instead.

When Kerry asked Liam if he found killing Dengler easy, Liam testified, "It was easy as ordering a cup of coffee."

The prosecution table looked nervous as the judge returned with his decision. They were relieved when the judge denied the motion for a new trial. Liam was declared a non-believable witness, except for his confession of shooting Dengler.

The judge said in his ruling, "It is a well-known trick of gangsters substituting guilty participants for dead men whose lips are sealed."

Relentless, Joel Friedman didn't stop. He followed up in June of this year with the Court of Appeals. He went over the shortcomings and omissions of my trial but the court upheld the murder conviction. The execution date was set for 13 July 1949. It was days away.

Meanwhile, the DA leaned on me to go state's evidence on the ILA and Joe Ryan. There was no love lost between me and Ryan. Immediately after our convictions, the American Federation of Labor (AFL) stripped me of the Presidency of the Local. The DA's office had us on the ropes. They offered commuting my sentence to life if I testified against Ryan. They were on a crusade. The papers and the Catholic Workers' priest who had worked side-by-side with Dengler joined the crusade to 'clean up the waterfront'. Now this alliance was taking on Joe Ryan.

Earlier, Ryan had skillfully orchestrated a dock strike threat then with a "last minute contract" he recommended longshoremen ratify. The contract with the United States Shipping became public. The *Sun* published that it was the same contract that the US Shipping had offered before the strike threat. The papers had a field day with Ryan.

The Sun headlines screamed, "Mobsters, Linked to Vast Underworld Crime Syndicate, Rule New York Piers by Terror; Reaping Untold Millions."

I offered to rat on Ryan for clemency. I detailed ADA Kerry on Ryan's involvement with cargo theft, loading kickbacks, payroll padding and outright theft of union dues.

Then I asked, "When are you going to commute my sentence of death?"

ADA Kerry capped his fountain pen, collected his notes, and stood, "Your execution date is already set Callaghan."

With that he left the room.

The fooking bastard never intended to honor his word.

Now, I was really afraid. They were going to fry me in the electric chair. I lost all hope.

Not Mikey. Not Joel Friedman.

"If only we could get the original police stenographer's report that she took at Dengler's bedside in St. Vincent's. From Dengler's own lips, he exonerated you Sean!" Mikey banged her fists on the table. "He said that he did not recognize or know his shooters! He said it wasn't you!"

"Well, the coppers at the 6th have it. I don't see them handing it over. Besides, Judge Eddington wouldn't allow it to be admitted as evidence at my trial."

Joel Friedman calmly interjected, "Sean, Colleen and I talked about this. If we could get the original document, take it to the Governor. We might be able to get a stay and a new trial."

"Hold on a minute! Hold on, I have an idea. There's this guy I know in Florida."

Using Mikey as a messenger, I had her call Red who was staying low in Florida. "Have him contact Giuseppe Doto otherwise known as Joe Adonis. During Prohibition, Doto had become a 'gentleman bootlegger' to the Manhattan theatre crowd. One of the Ziegfeld Follies showgirls called him 'Adonis', the Greek god of male beauty. It was true that Joe Adonis was something of a narcissist, especially about his looks."

I explained further to Mikey and Joel, "Joe Adonis has many high ranking cops and politicians on his payroll."

"So, we need Joe Adonis to help us get our hands on that police stenographer's record of the Dengler death bed statement," replied Joel.

Then a few days later, I learned that Joel mysteriously received an envelope with no return address. It contained the actual transcript. Along with Mikey, Joel was on the first express train out of Penn Station heading to Albany the next morning. Governor Thomas Dewey was our last hope. Mikey knew Dewey personally. They could act like a hammer and anvil to blacksmith Dewey into a stay of execution and new trial.

Colleen

Governor Dewey was cordial to Joel and I when we met with him to discuss Sean's stay of execution. Friedman produced the original transcript from the police stenographer that detailed Dengler's death bed statement. "Dengler said he did not recognize or know his assailant. We tried to have this admitted into evidence, but the judge ruled against it stating that the transcript provided by NYPD did not include this death bed statement. But it clearly exonerates Sean Callaghan from Dengler's murder."

Dewey looked over the transcript, placing back on his desk as if it were a poison pen letter, he said, "Mr. Friedman, how did you obtain this transcript?"

"It was sent to me anonymously, Governor."

"Then how can you be sure of its veracity?"

"Hold the paper up to the light Governor Dewey. See that watermark? It's the actual original transcript. That watermark is exclusive to the NYPD."

"But you've not obtained this in a proper legal process, so I do not believe it is admissible. Weeks v. United States in 1914 established the 'exclusionary rule'. Evidence gathered illegally cannot be used as evidence. A watermark only proves it was written on police stationery not that it is a true record of the actual event. And besides there are conflicting accounts of Dengler's death bed statement. I'm afraid you've made the trip here for nothing."

It wasn't a total loss. Dewey promised to call the investigator he worked with when he was Manhattan DA. "If he can find some evidence using proper legal channels that corroborates this transcript, I may be able to take some action. But…" he held his hand up, "Colleen, I said *if and maybe*. This is not a promise." So, we returned to the City feeling dejected but with a glimmer of hope.

The guilty verdict was disastrous to hear but when the DA called for the death penalty, my heart broke into a thousand little pieces. After so many failed attempts at getting a retrial and stay of execution I was at the end of my rope.

So on Monday morning, July 11th, with fraying nerves, I made calls to Special Agent Miller of the FBI, Rear Admiral Andrews and Commander Haffenden of Naval Intelligence to remind them of what Sean and I had done for America during the War.

"We kept Nazi saboteurs out of New York Harbor and protected the port of New York. Without our efforts, military supplies would have never reached Great Britain or our troops overseas. We rose to the occasion when you needed us. Now we need you."

"That's not the way it works, Colleen," began Miller. "You and your brother did perform an invaluable service not for just me but for your country. As a patriot, I know you understand this. I would do anything in my power to help." He hesitated a moment, then said, "But this charge and conviction is, well Colleen, it's for Murder One. I'm afraid there is nothing I can do."

To my horror, Rear Admiral Andrews deferred to Haffenden. Commander Haffenden said pretty much the same thing to me as Agent Miller had. He prattled on about our patriotic duty in that insipid tone of his. I wondered how Sean was able to work for a man who clearly saw himself so superior. In the end, I was able to prevail on both men to call the Governor directly to tell him about Sean's help during the War though according to them the official secrets act would prevent them from describing any real details of Sean's or my efforts for that matter.

I knew I had to continue to press Governor Dewey myself. It was time for him to pay me back for looking the other way and keeping my mouth shut when he dined with lovely ladies who were not his wife at Dottie's. Morals aside, this was about Sean's life. I hoped that with Sean's war record and my leaning on Dewey it would be enough to get a stay of execution. If we could overturn the death penalty, we could then start to figure out how to get Sean out. The DA's case was circumstantial, and it was only the media hype and politics that really put the noose around Sean's neck. Dewey was kind even when I alluded about his dinner companions. He promised to give commutation of Sean's death sentence full deliberation but that was as much as he was willing to say.

Finally, I called Joel Friedman for a telephone number of one of Sean's former pals, Meyer Lansky. Mr. Lansky listened solemnly as I explained how the case was built on flimsy evidence and nonetheless Sean was convicted and facing the electric chair. He told me to expect a phone call from a Moses Polakoff. Then Lansky hung up the phone. Within an hour, Polakoff called. He told me that Sean would have a few final visitors, one of which would be a priest. "Sean's not the religious sort," I said. "We spent too much of our youth being beaten down by Sisters and less than godly priests. Any priest going to see Sean better be ready for rejection, oh, and he better not be German."

"You just make sure he accepts the priest's visit and don't worry he won't be German." The whole conversation lasted about three minutes and while his message was quite obscure, I dared to hope.

Hope and hopelessness are two sides of the same coin.

Chapter 53
Too Late for Regrets

11 July 1949

*King George 6th gave British Government Emergency Powers to deal
with London Dock Workers Strike*

Sean
Death House, Sing Sing Prison, Ossining, New York
Two Days Before Execution

"Mikey, do you remember me saying that a guy on the jury looked familiar?"

"I think so."

We sat across from one another in the Death House visitors' room that we in death row called the 'mouthpiece room'. She looked terrific in her blue silk 'business' dress, white cotton gloves and hat. She had her composed yet determined face that belied her worry. I thought that I'd talk about something other than the obvious.

"What is it, Sean?" she said, reaching over to place her hand on mine.

"It came to me the other night. After our first wonderful night in Hell's Kitchen stairwell, I looked for a job downtown. Do you remember?"

"Yes, I do. I got a job as a page. But for some reason, you didn't."

"I didn't because of that guy on the Blue Ribbon Jury. He is the one at J.P. Morgan who wouldn't hire Irish. He was that s.o.b.!"

"Oh, Sean, you never told me."

"After St. Joe's, we were so desperate to have a life. That day, J.P. Morgan advertised for good paying positions. It would have been my real opportunity, but that crumb snatched it away from me. I don't know if you remember

Colleen, but we were starving. After I got turned away from J. P Morgan, I returned to Hell's Kitchen. I was famished. So, I stole some food from Briamonte's. I almost got away with it but I got collared by Patrolman O'Boyle."

"What! O'Boyle! Even then!"

"Yeah, that s.o.b. he had it out for me from the beginning."

"Oh Sean! You never, ever got a fair shake."

"I really wanted to do good. Instead, I was stymied by that guy. If I started at J.P. Morgan, I would have had a life. I would have shown them that I was no bum, no Irish donkey but a hard-working American. Things could have been different."

"Sean, don't dwell on it."

"Cripes, Mikey, in here, all I can do is dwell on the past. I think of what could have been. Who knows? I could have been a Wall Street tycoon."

"That would have been until the Crash. You might have ended up like some Wall Street tycoons who used their stock certificates to line the holes in their shoes."

"Yeah, but I could have made money without a gun."

At that point, one of the screws rattled his keys.

"Visiting hour is over Callaghan."

"Sean, I have another iron in the fire. I'm not giving up. Neither should you. Someone is coming to see you…"

The screw interrupted us rapping his baton on the mouthpiece room door.

He said, "There's a priest to see you. I'll bring him around."

"I didn't ask for no priest."

"Well, he's a new chaplain and here for you anyway. Let's get you back in your cell, Callaghan."

Colleen kissed me on my cheek and whispered insistently in my ear, "Sean, you must see this priest. It's important."

"Fine. It's not like I have somewhere else to be."

An hour later, a black robed priest was standing on the other side of the cell door. "I'm Father Scarcinni. May I hear your confession?"

Looking at the screw, I asked sarcastically, "Can the good Father be permitted in my cell. Permitted in with a convicted murderer?"

The screw smiled at me, "Sure Callaghan for your confession," as he unlocked the door then stepped back to let the priest enter. "I will be right down the hall Father Scarcinni."

"Father Scarcinni are you from a local church here in Ossining?" I asked leaning against the cell wall while proffering the more comfortable cell bed as a place to sit. Usually, I wouldn't give a priest the time of day, but the way things are now, I put the lid on my feelings about the Catholic Church. Besides, it gave me someone to talk to and Mikey was insistent.

"No, I have my ministry here. Prisoners are my flock."

"Well, your flock is about to be reduced soon."

"I attend my flock."

I detected an accent.

"Father Scarcinni are you from around here? I presume that you are Italian."

"How astute of you." Scarcinni sat back on the cell bed and crossed his legs. "I am a displaced person. In the American vernacular a 'D.P'. I refer to myself as a displaced priest." He smiled at his joke. "I grew up in Trieste before the War. I lived in Vichy France during the War then immigrated to the US last year."

"Your English is very good, only a slight accent."

"The good sisters in France conducted all classes both in English and French."

"Oh," I said. Father Scarcinni's eyes darted around my cell. My instincts smelled a rat. I have no use for priests anyway.

"I spent my youth in a Catholic orphanage. Since then, the only time I go to church is for weddings and funerals only. Even my own."

"Would you like to confess your sins, my son?"

"Son? Son? I'm no one's son."

"You are a son of God…"

"No, Father, I'm a son of a bitch!"

"There is no need for profanity."

"When I go to the chair, there will be no one to protect my sister Mikey. That's my confession. So, forgive me Father, that is my sin. Making her an orphan again."

The screw appeared at the cell door, "You gotta another visitor, Callaghan. You can stay Father, if you like. This visitor can be in the cell with a murderer."

Behind the screw, I saw Liam being escorted by another screw toward the mouthpiece room. A tall man in a gray flannel suit stood nearby. As the screw unlocked the cell door, I stared at the man in the gray flannel suit. It was Hans Rupp!

Father Scarcinni stood, blessed me with the sign of the cross as Hans Rupp stepped aside to let him pass out of the cell. Rupp looked Father Scarcinni straight in the eyes.

"Take as much time as you want, Special Agent," the screw said.

Rupp merely nodded.

"We gotta stop meeting like this," I said, as he sat on the cot, taking out a pack of Lucky Strikes then proffering me a cigarette.

Rupp smiled, "I've just come south from Albany, speaking with the governor. As you know, I have been sworn under the Official Secrets Act therefore I cannot talk about the War work we did on the waterfront. I did say to the governor that Naval Intelligence and the FBI are extremely grateful for the assistance that you provided during the War."

"Thanks for putting in a good word for me with the Governor." Changing the subject I said, "Hans, your work rounded up the biggest Nazi spy ring. What was it, thirty or so Nazi spies?"

"Yes, I made it crusade to avenge Heidi. I was glad to hear that Heydrich had been killed but that was ruined when we learned about the Nazi slaughter of the entire town of Lidice in Czechoslovakia in reprisal."

"I hate the Nazis too. But did you say that you spoke directly with the governor?"

"I asked the governor directly to commute your sentence. He didn't say 'yes'. Then again, it wasn't a 'no' either. So, let me ask if you need anything?"

"Hans, I could use a way out of here like the way that you and Mother Superior escaped from the Ocean Vanguard that night." I laughed. "But I suppose that you cannot tell me."

No reply.

"Let's talk about more pleasant things. How's your parents."

"They are fine. Still living in Yorkville and are regulars at the Kleine Konditori restaurant on 82nd. My father did get a professorship at NYU. A lot of returning veterans are taking advantage of the GI Bill by attending college. So, NYU needed more professors. He is so grateful to America, first sheltering us seeking asylum, defeating Hitler and now his American Dream is fulfilled."

"If only Heidi was still alive. Then it would be perfect."

"Yes, my father has a little shrine to her in the apartment. He lights a candle nightly. Do you remember Professor Mildred Harnack?"

"Harnack? Oh, yes, she was the lecturer at Hunter College that inspired Heidi."

"Well, Harnack continued to resist Hitler. It was her White Rose resistance group that spirited me out of Berlin. They believed they could overthrow Hitler and his thugs from within. They believed that until the war started. Harnack spied for the Soviets in what the Gestapo called 'the Red Orchestra' while still teaching in the Foreign Studies Department of the University of Berlin. The Gestapo and the RSHD, a Nazi Counter-Intelligence service, labeled the Morse code radio operators 'pianists', and the cell leaders 'conductors'. Hence the 'orchestra'. By late 1942, Gestapo radio intercepts gave them enough. They moved swiftly to shut down the orchestra. Her husband and others were given a military trial and quickly executed. As an American citizen, she was initially given a six-year prison sentence. Then suddenly, on Hitler's direct orders, Mildred Harnack was guillotined on 16 February 1943."

"So, she was a commie?"

"What we have about both Mildred and her husband is that they were anti-fascist patriotic Germans. The Harnacks visited the US Embassy in Berlin several times before December 7th. Oddly enough, that's where she and her husband were recruited by a Soviet spy who was having an affair with the American ambassador's daughter." Hans laughed at the irony. "The Harnack cell was provided with a Soviet radio that sent intelligence to the Brits as well as the Russkies. In 1942, we needed the Russian allies to keep those divisions of Nazi troops away from France and Italy. Imagine what could have happened if all those German divisions were not on the Eastern Front but were at Anzio or Normandy?"

"How long have you been a G-Man?"

"After I returned from Germany, I went to Washington to see if the State Department could do something, at least get Heidi's body returned. While I was there, a fellow at the State Department asked if I would be willing to purchase European clothing from immigrants at Ellis Island in New York. I did not know the reason, but I learned the clothing was to dress OSS and Jedburgh agents for the partisan war in Occupied Europe. It wasn't long after that the FBI came calling. My first assignment after finishing training was to be a double agent with a Nazi cell in the City. Mother Superior, as you call her, was the cell's SS Haupsturmfuhrer Hildebrandt, captain if you will. Hildebrandt was her real name. She was devious, sly, cunning and ruthless. Unfortunately, she managed to slip out of the country as we closed in on her. At least we terminated her spy ring. Hildebrandt was the only one we missed. The Bureau believes that she could be in Paraguay, Brazil or Argentina."

I said, "She always was a mean bitch. At the orphanage, she beat us or had us beaten, starved us and even stole what little we had. It's too bad that she isn't in here with me, Padric and Liam. We'd save the taxpayers some money."

Hans stood smoothing down his trousers. Highly polished wingtips glistened from under the trouser cuffs.

"Sean, I must get back to Manhattan, but I want you to know that I will call Gov. Dewey again on your behalf as soon as I hang up my hat at the office."

"Thanks Hans."

After Hans left, all I could think about was Heidi Rupp. What if I had married her and she didn't go to Germany to be killed? What would my life had been? But before Heidi, there was Debbie Sabotski. She taught me many things. I was her 'city-boy' and she my Vermont milkmaid. Back then life was just beginning. After St. Joe's, all things were possible. I actually thought about becoming a Vermont farmer or something. But then Joe was killed and that ended that. As Red's Scottish poet Robert Burns wrote: 'the saddest words of mice and men are the words, it might have been.' Too late for regrets. Way too late for might-have-been.

Just then Liam returned from his visit with his wife and daughter. He was in the neighboring Death Row cell. In the Death House, everybody hears everything from a fart to a whimper. So, I easily heard what Liam said to the screw.

"No more visitors. Tell my wife no more visits. I left them smiling. I was smiling. That's the way it should be."

"I'll do that," the screw replied.

I heard Liam settle on his cot. I could picture him lying there with his hands behind his head staring at the ceiling. I wondered about his might-have-been.

Colleen
12 July 1949

Earlier today, I had Governor Dewey on the phone. I considered him a friend.

"Colleen, I have some political and public opinion problems with your brother's case. We have this Catholic Workers Union's priest who thinks of himself as Abraham Lincoln freeing the longshoremen from slavery, an Assistant District Attorney who plans to run against me in the Fall and a crusading newspaper reporter who is making his reputation on reporting New York waterfront crime. They are all after your brother's head."

"Come on Tom, you were a prosecutor. You know that this is all circumstantial evidence. They cannot even produce the murder weapon. The paraffin gunshot residue test on Sean's hands was negative! Why won't anyone listen?"

"Colleen, I need some time."

"Tom! Time is something that Sean does not have. For God's sake, he is scheduled for execution tomorrow!"

"Alright, I'll call the warden in the morning if I can find a way to make your last appeal stick. I will try, Coll."

"Do not 'try', Tom, do it!"

"Alright, alright, I will try."

13 July 1949
Execution Day

The drive from Manhattan to Sing Sing Prison in Ossining was interminable. In the Bronx, it seemed that I caught every stoplight under the Broadway elevated subway right to where it ended at Van Cortlandt Park. Broadway became Route 9 in Yonkers, but it was not much better. I had considered taking the train from Grand Central to Ossining, but I might need the car for a trip to Albany to see the Governor. Conflicted, I wanted to get to the prison though I can't stand the very sight of that horrible place. It even smells of death and despair. As I drove through the picturesquely quaint towns of Dobbs Ferry, Irvington and Tarrytown my mind raced back-and-forth from hope to despair.

I passed the Old Dutch Church of Sleepy Hollow and briefly I was transported to the Washington Irving story, *The Legend of Sleepy Hollow*. I half-expected to see a dark horse with a headless Hessian cavalryman holding a flaming jack-o-lantern. The road ran uphill. Tall, stately oaks that separated the road from the cemetery made the morning sun flash like news reporters' flashbulbs.

As my DeSoto crested the hill the sign, "Welcome to Ossining" brought my thoughts back to brutal reality. The DeSoto descended into the hell that awaited me. Hope for a stay of execution and re-trial faded. Even Meyer Lansky and Moses Polakoff failed me. Their chaplain was worthless. I felt despair that all of my efforts would end in failure and the loss of my Sean.

The next thing I knew I was turning at the First Baptist Church in Ossining then left on Main toward the prison. After a slight left, I was on Hunter Street with the walls of Sing Sing looming in the brilliant sunlight.

My last visit with Sean was brief. He took me into a tight embrace.

"Take care of Elizabeth for me, Mikey."

"You know I will," I sobbed. I looked at my brother through my tears which were flowing fully now. His slightly closed eyelid did not give him that devil may care look any longer. He looked sad, resigned and lost.

"Mikey, I don't want you to be there…"

"Sean you look at me. No one else. I will be the last person you see. We will always have each other right to the end," I croaked.

"Mikey, Mikey," he said in a strangled voice.

We hugged knowing it was the last time.

The prison guards told me I had to leave. Sean needed to be readied for the electric chair. He needed to see the chaplain. I had to smile in spite of everything at that comment. The very last person Sean would want to see was a priest after our childhood at St. Joseph's.

Chapter 54
Gold Double Cross

Sean
13 July 1949
Execution Day

Brooklyn Eagle: House Group Votes Hawaii Strike Investigation Washington Post, The House Committee on Un-American Activities voted to investigate the 68-day Hawaiian dock strike to determine whether it was Communist-inspired.

It's another hot, humid day in Sing Sing on Hudson. I wear only a tee shirt, pants, and prison socks. The tee shirt is wet with sweat. I hardly touched my last meal—ham, beans, and eggs. The coffee is stale and bitter as the heat in my cell.

I pass my tray to the screw from the Death House kitchen. He is pushing a cart of the collected meal trays from us prisoners. He stops waiting for the screw to open the hallway door that must lead to the prison kitchen.

I hear them talk.

"Didja hear about what was clogging the drains?"

"Naw, I hear nutin' in this fucking ward."

"It was a body."

"No shit."

"No shit."

"Whose?"

"Dunno, but the guy was stabbed with a stiletto."

"How the fuck do you know the guy wasn't stabbed with a fucking kitchen knife?"

"'Cause a stiletto doesn't cause much bleedin'. A stiletto plugged up the wound with the guy's guts when it was pulled out. Guy musta bled out inside."

"No shit!"

"No shit. I wouldn't shit you, you're my favorite turd."

A friendly punch.

"When dis happen?"

"Coulda be only a couple a days ago when the drains started to back up."

"Who's the dead guy?"

"No one knows. Not one of us. No prisoner neither."

"Holy shit. Well, lemme know when ya know."

"Will do."

The tray's cart wheels rattle. Door slams.

The silence begins again. Time is warped on Execution Day. Time seems to stall, yet race faster. Stall that is, until a group of screws, the warden with Father Scarcinni entered Death Row. Father Scarcinni wears a purple scarf around his neck and a large golden crucifix dangling on a chain to his chest. Purple and gold, the only color others than black. Well, besides his white collar.

At 11 am sharp, Liam is taken out of his cell. He stands outside his cell door as they locked it behind him. He will not be returning. I can't see his face. With the jingling of keys, I see the screw take Liam by the arm. Together, they walk like they are leading a parade. Liam moves like Marley's ghost with his chains.

Liam pulled up sharply in front of my cell.

"Give me a minute, for Christ's sake?"

"Liam, you have always been a good friend. THANK YOU!" I said.

"Sean, I'll be seein' ya."

With that, he turns his face to the door at the end of the cell block where 'Old Sparky' awaits him and me. With his leg shackles, he is shuffling toward the door.

As the door opens, I shout, "I'll be seeing you too!"

They enter. The door closes behind the group leading Liam. The quiet is deafening. Those of us on Death Row are listening to the screams in our heads. Our turn is coming. For me, I am next. Time stalls.

The cellblock lights flicker.

Time is distorted in prison. Time bends in different ways, backward yet forward in exorbitantly vivid shapes. Maybe it is that I had seen my life pass through my mind these past days. All I think about is what lies behind the door at the end of the cell-block. I stare at the door, my mind blank. Like a leaf in a river eddy, time is circling, whirling. Outside my cell window a seagull flew by.

Rattle and CLICK!

I jump. The sudden sound of the cell door being unlocked is pistol shot startling. My mouth is dry, my feet freezing. In comes the warden, the same screw, and Father Scarcinni.

"It's time, Callaghan," says the warden.

"Warden, can I have a moment with Mr. Callaghan, just a moment. I will give him Extreme Unction and hear Confession."

"Only a minute or two."

"There's no need. I have nothing to say and I don't think rubbing oil on me with get me to a better place."

"As you will."

Father Scarcinni blesses me with the sign of the cross as I stand. Shackles are placed on me. Outside my cell, we turned toward the yawning door at the end of the hallway. It is an open grave, a casket. I swallow the metallic taste in my mouth as best as I can. There it is. 'Old Sparky'. We stand there as behind me, my cell door is slammed shut, the finality of a dropped casket lid. I ain't comin' back. As I take one shuffling step, my vision narrows to a dark tunnel. All I can see is the open door to the electric chair. My heart is pounding in my chest. My blood thundering in my ears.

Then a wall-phone's bells clatters, ringing like an echo in a crypt. I hear a voice. It seems far away. Everybody freezes in place. I blink, open my mouth to speak but nothing comes out.

A voice is saying, "Yes, Governor, I understand. I will get the warden."

What? What's going on? Let's get this over!

The warden picks up the earpiece, then speaks into the horn, "Yes, Governor Dewey. Uh huh, uh huh, I understand. Yes, sir. I will."

Father Scarcinni stands at my right with his hand clutching the crucifix hanging on his neck. He looks calm, resolved. The warden walks back to us. He looks me in the eye.

"Well, Callaghan, aren't you the lucky one. It seems that some new evidence has come to the Governor's attention. He is granting a stay and a new trial." I am stunned. Could this be happening? My vision is blurred with tears.

"Return the prisoner to his cell."

In my cell, the guards unshackle me then leave, surprisingly without closing the cell door. Only Father Scarcinni remains. I stand trembling in a state of shock. What just happened? Father Scarcinni stands in front of me, his hand on my shoulder. It does nothing to stop my shaking.

Father Scarcinni steps closer, leans in, whispering, "O'Boyle sent me here to make sure you get what's coming."

Then there is a quick movement. A flash of silver in the yellow light of my cell. Father Scarcinni has pulled a long-bladed stiletto from the crucifix!

Quick as a snake, he thrusts it under my ribs. He pulls the blade from my ribs. Breathing in pain, I grab his wrist to parry the blade. Somehow, he still manages again to get the stiletto in under my breastbone. Looking down, I expect to see my blood. Instead, I see the blade disappearing into the crucifix. He pushes me down to the cot.

As I fall back, sudden pain becomes my whole world. Scarcinni calmly walks out of the cell. Fighting through the pain, I sit up. I cough bright red blood. Scarcinni has disappeared from my sight. I press on the wound with both hands. It erases the pain but not the shortness of breath. I am breathing rapidly and shallowly. As I try to lay back, the pain becomes massively excruciating.

Suddenly, a stained white radiance is in front of me.

Colleen-Execution Viewing Room

My head is pounding. Every breath I take is shallower than the last one. I'm the only woman in the room. Newspaper reporters from the Sun, Herald-Tribune, Daily News and others that I never heard of are there, of course. O'Boyle is sitting first row center staring at the viewing window.

This is the last place on Earth I ever wanted to be, the Viewing Room for Sean's execution. A black curtain covers the window. It wouldn't be pulled back until Sean was strapped into the electric chair.

I wanted to see him one last time. I would be the last person that he would see. Sean and I made a pact that we would close our eyes at the same time. His eyes would be closed forever. I would have to reopen mine but part of my heart will die here with Sean.

Despite hot tears streaming down my face, I look up at the clock over the window. Its second hand moves with excruciating deliberateness. The minute hand clicks inexorably toward the Roman number for twelve, XII. The hour has come. The last time that I will ever see Sean has come. The room was deathly quiet.

The black curtain remained closed. Reporters began to fidget.

"What's the delay?"

"I'm gonna miss my deadline!"

All the reporters were talking. A guard walked to the front of the room followed by the warden. Shouts of questions filled the air. All the yelling added to the cacophony. The warden raised his hand for silence. It took some time before the warden spoke.

"Gentlemen, there will no execution of Sean Callaghan."

What?

With that, the room erupted into a barrage of questions shouted at the warden. I leaped to my feet to hear better.

"What happened, warden?"

"Did the governor call?"

Raising both hands as though he was pushing the questions back, the warden tried desperately to control the room.

"Did Dewey call?"

"What happened?"

The warden spoke over the shouts, "Yes, Governor Dewey called. There's a stay of execution. There will be a retrial."

I collapse into my seat, sobbing uncontrollably with relief. The reporters swarm around the warden like bees in a hive. But one reporter pencil poised over a notepad appears suddenly in front of my chair.

"Colleen Callaghan, how do you feel about this?"

"How the fuck do you think I feel!"

I pushed him aside and strode over to the warden and with a strong voice louder than the shouts, "Warden, I want to see my brother. I want to see him NOW!"

Reporters parted opening a path for me to the warden. Just as I reach him, he takes me by the arm, saying, "No more questions at this time." To me *sotto voce*, he says to me, "Let's get you away from these reporters."

He led me down a corridor to a small room. After I entered, he closed the door behind us.

"There's been an accident."

"Accident! What accident? To Sean? Where's Sean?"

"Well, at this time he is on the way to Ossining Community Hospital."

"Hospital! What?"

"I can arrange to have you driven there."

"Just tell me where it is. I'll get there on my own."

***

Ossining Community Hospital did not look like any hospital in the City. It was a one-story building that had maybe ten beds. It looked like a place where people paid the doctor in livestock. I was not reassured.

A doctor in a white lab coat approached me.

"I'm Colleen Callaghan. I'm Sean Callaghan's sister. How's my brother?"

"I'm Dr. Dobbins, I examined his knife wounds. It appears that it punctured his left lower lobe of his lung."

"Knife wound!" I interrupted.

"The lung has collapsed," Dr. Dobbins continued. "There is a lot of internal bleeding. I have to stabilize him. That's all I can tell you right now. I have to prepare to treat his wounds."

"Can I see him?"

"Yes, of course."

Dr. Dobbins led me to a curtained part of the room.

"Miss Callaghan, make it short. I have to start treatment as soon as possible," Dr. Dobbins said as he drew back the curtain.

"Sean! Sean!"

Sean's eyelids fluttered open. He was so pale lying there on a stretcher. A prison guard stood by cradling a shotgun. Sean's right wrist was handcuffed to the stretcher.

"Hey, Mikey, looks like I escaped the chair only to find a knife."

409

I kissed his cool damp forehead. His eyes closed as he drifted back into unconsciousness.

A nurse appeared at my elbow. She escorted me to a chair in a small waiting room.

"You can wait here."

About two hours later, Dr. Dobbins pulled a chair next to mine.

"I've re-inflated his lung. The knife punctured the lung causing it to collapse. I inserted a chest tube to re-inflate the lung and remove the blood so your brother can breathe. I started an IV for fluids, gave penicillin and some morphine for pain. He is resting comfortably. You should go home, my dear."

At that moment, the warden and two men appeared. Dr. Dobbins stood and reiterated to the warden the same information. As I listened, I realized that I had to get Sean back to the City. Get him away from whomever stabbed him. Besides, in the City, he'd get more advanced care.

In the last two hours, I have been careening in a crazy swing of emotions. I went from desperate hope to elation to shock to horror and panic back to desperation. I'm a wreck but I'm not out of the fight.

As soon as Dr. Dobbins left, I stood. I walked to within inches of the warden.

"Can you explain how my brother got stabbed in your prison?"

One of the two with the warden said, "I'm Homicide Detective Wilson. So far, what we know is that a body was found a day ago. It was the brand-new prison chaplain. No one had ever met him. So, it looks like the fake chaplain killed him and took his place. He was most likely a hired assassin."

"Assassin! Sean was going to the electric chair!"

"True, but whoever hired him knew that Governor Dewey was reconsidering the Sean Callaghan case. This was their way of insuring that your brother would die today."

"I'll have my best men guarding your brother," the warden said.

"Your best men!" I laughed. "Your men could not protect my brother in the Death House. What kind of fool do you take me for? That assassin is still at large! I want my brother transferred to Bellevue Hospital as soon as possible!"

"Now be reasonable, Miss Callaghan," the Warden said.

"Reasonable! Reasonable is moving my brother back to New York City!"

Detective Wilson pulled the Warden away whispering but I still heard what he said, "Let's get this mess out of our jurisdiction. Send Callaghan back. Make it the NYPD's problem."

Chapter 55
Telltale Heart

Colleen

New York City

With Sean safely transported to Bellevue Hospital's Prison Ward, I was somewhat less apprehensive. But his assassin was still on the loose. He was obviously resourceful, ruthless and determined. I worried that the assassin would try to finish the job that he started in the Death House. I didn't trust Bellevue's prison guards any more than the ones in Sing Sing.

All of Sean's crew was gone. In desperation, I called the only person who could help, Hans Rupp.

He took my call at his office immediately.

"Special Agent Rupp, how can I help you?"

"Hans, this is Colleen Callaghan, let me tell you what happened."

Hans interrupted, "I already know."

"Sean has been moved to Bellevue, but I fear that the assassin will come back to kill him."

"I can protect him, Colleen. Leave this to me."

As I hung up the phone, I thought, we just might get through this. The emotional drain of the last hours weighed me down. Fatigue swept over me. With my shoes still on, I fell back on my bed fully dressed.

When I awoke it was the next afternoon. I checked in with Hans. Sean was resting comfortably but still unconscious. To keep me occupied, I got ready to go to work at Dottie's.

Still nagging my dreams and my days, like Edgar Allen Poe's *Telltale Heart*, the flour sack in my kitchen was threatening to reveal its contents.

Even now, a reporter or two still stalk my street. Despite the fact that there are fewer reporters circling, I am paranoid. I have a real dilemma to consider.

The flour sack is still on my cabinet shelf. A new trial brings new hope but what if O'Boyle obtained a search warrant? If the thing in the flour was the murder weapon, I would become an accessory to murder and Sean would be facing execution once again. I have to ditch all of the reporters and get rid of the damned thing once and for all. Also, I need that my new bodyguard in the form of Mike Malloy to be none the wiser.

It was an unseasonably cool rainy day for July, heavy storm clouds were brewing in the Atlantic. I set out for work at Dottie's wearing my Burberry raincoat and a soft wide-brimmed fedora. The hat brim would be useful to conceal my face from view. With the damned thing weighing a ton in my handbag, I lock the apartment door.

At the restaurant, there are two reporters clustered near the door. Dinner service is normal. At 9 pm, I tell Harold that I have a supplier meeting. I am going to slip out the back to avoid the press.

At that, he arched an eyebrow, "A supplier meeting tonight? Zat all you avoidin'?" Then he nodded toward Mike Malloy's place at the bar. Right now, it's an empty barstool. Harold lifts the service bar bridge to assist me with the Burberry.

I said, "Best if he doesn't know. Tell him that I went home early."

As I pass my cooks and dishwashing crew, they give me quizzical looks as if saying, 'leaving early?' In the alley, I surprise a feral cat that quickly scampers out of sight. There, I turn toward Third Avenue. Hat pulled low, I walk to the Lexington Avenue subway while pulling my Burberry collar up against the damp coolness of the evening. I was pretty sure someone could be following me. It was just a feeling. I'm probably just being paranoid. But when you are planning to do something illegal, it isn't paranoid, it's prudent to be observant.

By the time, I reached the stairs down to the Lexington Avenue line, I was cold to the bone. Was it the weather or my nerves? The Lexington Avenue subway train warmed me some as it took me down to 59th Street station.

At 59th Street station I go through the turnstile for the stair adjacent to Bloomingdale's and its canopy over the Lexington Avenue sidewalk. The sky rumbles with thunder. There, as if on cue, is a yellow cab with its roof light lit. It is heading in my direction, downtown. I wave to catch the driver's eye as the cab stops for a red light. I raise my arm again as the light turned green. The cab pulls up right in front of me. I jump in the rear seat.

"Where to, Miss?"

"South Street. The Whitehall Terminal for the ferry."

"Ah, wife's family lives in Staten Island." When I did not respond, he shrugged, moved the meter flag clockwise to start the cab fare meter. Maddeningly, he starts whistling the tune of Perry Como's *Some Enchanted Evening* all the way downtown to Whitehall.

A cool rain starts to fall as I pay the cabbie. I take shelter under the overhang near Gate 2. I pull my hat brim lower on my forehead. Not only did I want to avoid the rain, but I did not want anyone to see my face. I'm pretty sure that if anyone is actually shadowing me he would have had no time to hail another cab to follow me downtown. When the ferry was just about finished boarding, I drop my nickel in the slot then sprint across the gangway as the last cars loading clatter onto the ferry below the passenger deck.

Other passengers move inside the ferry cabin as I try to melt into the darkness on the stern deck. There I was surprised to find a few passengers standing under the upper deck overhang. Leaning against the rail, a young man and woman are kissing, oblivious to everyone else. As the ferry moves out of the slip, the wind and rain pick up. The bitter wind-driven rain drives all to retreat inside the ferry, even the lovers. I am alone.

As I step to the rail, my thoughts flooded back to the trip so long ago. Sean, Ian and I on the Staten Island Ferry for the first time. The trip with our mother, a woman we did not know, going to a place we did not know. The unknown was almost as frightening as that miserable orphanage we left. I was frightened then but it was nothing compared to the fear I feel now. In the inky blackness of New York Bay, only the torch of the Statue of Liberty glows in the distance. The night, the rain, the water all merged into black. Looking in the direction the ferry was heading, I couldn't see Staten Island. In the ferry's wake, the lights of the City were blurring fast, fading into the darkness and the rain. Only the wake of the ferry churning white relieved the oppressing darkness.

I fumble with my handbag. My icy fingers grasp the gun still wrapped in the same oily rag. I pull it free, clutching it close to my chest as I snap my handbag closed. I sense something. All at once, I know someone is right behind me. I half turn, trying to keep the gun hidden against my chest.

"Colleen."

Oh God, it's Mike Malloy!

"I, I…"

414

"Give it to me, Colleen."

Fear strangles me. I swallow though my mouth is cotton dry. He is going to take the gun away from me. It could end all the appeals to clear Sean's name. The gun could doom Sean. I try to free it from the rag still tightly wrapped around it. If necessary, I will aim it at him. If I have to shoot him, I will. He will not hurt Sean.

He says nothing. Looking me straight in the eyes, he looks as if he is reading my thoughts. Gently, Mike takes the gun from my shaking hands. He takes it as gently as you would take a dead infant from a grief-stricken mother's arms. He opens the rag and looks at the gun. The rain funneling from his hat brim splashes on the gunmetal. Then he looks at me. A tear is forming at the edge of his right eye. He rewraps the gun tightly. Then with a sudden burst of movement, he hurls it into the black water.

He pulls me close. "Let's go inside, it's colder than an ice box out here."

Sobbing, as I fall into step with him, Mike pulls me even closer as we walk to the passenger compartment doors.

The brightly lit interior compartment of the ferry warms me. It is sparsely filled with passengers, probably due to the late hour. Nonetheless, Michael Malloy finds seats for us far away from the other passengers.

Dabbing my eyes, I say, "You must think I am a horrible person."

"That is the last thing I would ever think about you, Colleen." He shifts slightly to look into my eyes. "I think you love your brother and are willing to do anything to save him. I wish someone would love me half as much."

"I do. I do love Sean. I know him to be innocent. But…why did you help me?"

"I think you know the answer to that one," he says, his voice sounding a bit choked up.

Now it is my turn to shift uncomfortably in my seat. We sit in silence for a few moments listening to the sound of the ferry's engine and the sound of the rain beating fiercely against the window panes surrounding the compartment.

"We spent many years on Staten Island, in an orphanage. We, Sean and I, were dumped into an orphanage there by our own mother. You see, she didn't care about us. We were just a bother to her. She left us there for years and didn't come for us until we were of an age that we could get jobs and pay our way."

"That's so sad. I lament that my family was and still is pretty damn dirt poor, but my Ma would never have done that to me, my brothers and sisters. I am sorry for you and for Sean that must have been an ordeal."

"Oh, you have no idea," I say matter-of-factly. "The orphanage was a place of hunger, pain, and even terror. It was a place where frustrated and angry nuns beat us for the least infractions. In Sean's case, for just breathing! The head nun was a miserable wretch but really, they all tortured us and took pleasure in it. Oh, there were a few bright spots. A few friends that were kind but mostly, we suffered tremendously. It was a miserable experience. Sean never gave up. He took care of me every day and every way that he could."

I look straight at Michael Malloy. "Once, you asked me why Sean calls me Mikey. I told you it was a form of endearment between us. What I never told you, never told anyone was that name saved me from starving. The miserable nuns of the St. Joseph's Orphanage decided that I deserved punishment for some small bit of disobedience. For punishment, I could exist for days on a cup of water and a piece of stale bread. Sean wouldn't have it. He snuck me food then dug a hole under the fence separating the girls from the boys. He dressed me like a boy and got me into the boys' dorm for meal service. He told the other boys that I was a new arrival, named Mikey."

A big fat tear rolled down my cheek. "I owe my life to Sean. He stayed by my side when I had the Spanish influenza and almost died. I know my brother better than anyone. He is a good man. I know he has done things on the other side of the law. But he was and is just trying to live, to make a living. Yeah, I know what you are going to say. But he tried to get legit jobs. No one gave him a chance. So, he took his own chances. He helped me open Dottie's. He signed for the lease when I was considered too young to sign myself. Then he turned it over to me when I was old enough. Sean would do anything to help me. I will do whatever it takes to help him. Period."

Mike puts a muscled arm around my shoulders. He is quiet for several minutes while I collect myself. I dig a white handkerchief from my purse then I blow my nose, noisily.

With a tight smile, he says, "I guess this means you won't want to go sightseeing in Staten Island then." I turn fully, stare at him, and punch his arm, then we both laugh. I blow my nose again, loudly.

"It's a damn good thing there ain't any ducks this time of night. The way you blew your nose, they'd think it was one of their brethren dying in here!" Mike laughs.

"Very funny!" I smile at him. He really does have great-looking blue eyes.

CPSIA information can be obtained
at www.ICGtesting.com
Printed in the USA
LVHW011348230723
753197LV00014B/1023